Dedalus Ireland

Dara Kavanagh is a writer, academic, translator and poet. A native of Dublin, he spent more than a decade working in Africa, Australia and Latin America before returning to settle in Ireland. He has written several books and poetry collections.

He is the author of two novels published by Dedalus: *Prague 1938* (2021) and *Jabberwock* (2023).

Dara Kavanagh

JABBERWOCK

Dedalus

Published in the UK by Dedalus Limited
24-26, St Judith's Lane, Sawtry, Cambs, PE28 5XE
info@dedalusbooks.com
www.dedalusbooks.com

ISBN printed book 978 1 915568 41 0
ISBN ebook 978 1 915568 45 8

Dedalus is distributed in the USA & Canada by SCB Distributors
15608 South New Century Drive, Gardena, CA 90248
info@scbdistributors.com www.scbdistributors.com

Dedalus is distributed in Australia by Peribo Pty Ltd.
58, Beaumont Road, Mount Kuring-gai, N.S.W. 2080
info@peribo.com.au www.peribo.com.au

First published by Dedalus in 2023

Printed and bound in the UK by Clays Elcograf S.p.A.
Typeset by Marie Lane

KEY TO THE CHARACTERS

Bletchley, Æthelred 2nd Lord — Home Secretary (1935-38), son of Æthelred 1st Lord Bletchley who founded the Semantics branch of CID.
Bracken, Brendan — Wartime Minister of Information and First Lord of the Admiralty.
Chandler, Charlie — Hackett's 'Handler' in the Eirish Department of Foreign Affairs.
Chapman, Seumas — Eirish Cultural Attaché to the Court of St James.
Clarke, William — Member of the notorious 'G' Division of the Dubilin Metropolitan Police. One of the 'Four Horsemen of the Apocryphal'.
Doolittle, Seymour — Professor of Applied Linguistics at Keys College Oxenford who oversaw the publication of the *Oxenford Engelish Dictionary*.
Fleming, Aloysius — Army veteran, inmate of Swift's Institution for the Insane at the same time as Ignatius Hackett. Another of the 'Four Horsemen of the Apocryphal'.
Fraiser, Duncan — Deputy Chief Inspector of the Semantics branch of the CID.
Hastings, Harold — The Royal Academy of Letters' Decommissioner of the Otiose.

KEY TO THE CHARACTERS

McCann, Malachi, Mc — Student at University College Dubilin at the same time as Ignatius Hackett, member of both the Dubilin Cervantes Society and Ouroboros Society.

McTurcaill, Turlough — Royal Academy of Letters' Commissioner of Words.

Mulcahy, Edmond — Printer, Gaelgóir and member of both the Eirish Citizen Army and the Ouroboros Brotherhood. One of the 'Four Horsemen of the Apocryphal'.

O'Brien — Hereditary Title of the Director of the Royal Academy of Letters.

Quibble, Cecil — Chief Inspector of the Semantics branch of the CID.

Sangster, Agatha — Double agent. One of the 'Four Horsemen of the Apocryphal'.

Smyllie, Robert Maire — RM or "Bertie", legendary editor of *The Eirish Times*.

Von Beruf, Graf Ernst — Prussian Count instrumental in the programmes to develop both the **Übersetzungschreiber** and its feared successor, the **Unsinnschreiber**.

PREFACE

In the darkest hour of the Emergency,[1] at a time when U-boats moved like predatory fish beneath the grey Atlantic and the skies over Dover's chalk cliffs were daily scored with the vapour trails of dogfights, a trawler was bobbling some twenty nautical miles off Penzaunce. She was gaily decked-out; her provenance, the port of Waterfjord in the Eirish Free State. A huge tricolour painted on either flank proclaimed her neutrality. All the same, were a periscope to draw close enough, and there's more than a suggestion that one did, it might have picked out a flippant Jolly Roger frabbling above the cabin.

If a clandestine rendezvous did occur it was short-lived. Already, from North-Northeast and East-Southeast, two of His Majesty's corvettes were bearing down on her. For the **JABBERWOCK** was no innocent fishing-boat. What happened next has been a matter of debate ever since, but this much

---

1 A period of shortages and travel restrictions occasioned by Neville Chamberlain's infamous declaration of war on Germany on the morning of September 3rd 1939.

is beyond dispute. Had her nefarious cargo been landed and distributed as planned, the **JABBERWOCK** might have proved every bit as fromulous to His Majesty's Empire as all the bombs of all the Dorniers and Heinkels then being mustered throughout Occupied Europe. That she wasn't, and that her story is so little known, shall be the subject of these pages.

VOLUME ONE

THE GATHERING STORM

CHAPTER THE FIRST

in which our hero endeavours to evade his landlord, fails in this, and is handed an official summons

To begin with, Hackett may not have been Hackett. He may have been Rooney. But that's another story. Our story begins in the year of the Abdication Crisis.[2] It is a pivotal year in the history of the European continent, and one moreover that finds our hero at a low ebb, shundling out of a dive off Lower Dorset St in order to give the landlord, Needles Nugent, the slip. A native of Cavan, Manus Nugent was scant of height, scanter of breath, and scantest of all of respect for his tenants — oh, a nice collection of scapegraces and ne'er-do-wells. That one of them had once enjoyed a reputation as a newspaper columnist was a matter of the utmost indifference to his calculus. Mr Ignatius Hackett was thirteen pounds ten and six behind in his rent, so he was, and pounds, shillings and pence were the Holy Trinity of the Nugent creed.

2 From the Latin *ab-dicare*, to 'declare with a parting gesture'. In December 1936 Edward VIII abdicated the throne in favour of his brother Albert, Duke of Yorvik, so as to marry an American heiress. There is considerable debate as to why he did so. Sikorski's proposition that Bishop Blunt of Bradford may have threatened to expose his identity as a German mole has been generally discredited.

Hackett shundled out the door, gazed myopically up and down the street, then gravitated down a side-alley in the general direction of the river Liffey. From his shambling gait, which like his politics was left-leaning, it was apparent that he had no particular destination in mind, or if he had, no particular hour at which he was appointed to arrive there. He was as short of prospects as he was long in the tooth, that was the long and the short of it. The one concession to directing his perambulation was to periodically correct the innate tendency to drift to the left occasioned by having, since birth, a slightly shorter left leg, or slightly longer right one, depending on how you looked at it. The effect of this effort was to impart onto the rhythm of his movement a secondary motion comparable to the epicycles with which Charles Boyle, 4th Earl of Orrery, had modified the circular motion of the planets.

That morning, Hackett had nothing on his mind. It is a phrase that needs to be clarified. Now as is well documented, during an idle patch in the Thirty Years War, a notorious cardsharp named René "des Cartes" had tried to demonstrate the correlation between being and thinking by plotting modes of being ('être') on a horizontal axis and of thinking ('penser') on a vertical axis — as for instance 'je pense que je suis fatigué' vs 'je suis vraiment fatigué', and then joining the dots. By extrapolating backwards, he came to the startling conclusion that it was impossible to think of nothing. Although the corresponding graph has arguably had a more far-reaching effect on coordinate geometry than on either philosophy or psychology, in the field of affective psychotherapy the maxim 'je le pense, donc je le suis' is to this day referred to as the Cartesian Proposition. Be that as it may, what Ignatius Hackett was engaged upon was not thinking *of* nothing, but rather thinking *about* nothing.

In particular, he was considering whether the nothing that poetry makes happen is the same nothing as the nothing that philosophy makes happen. For each had its own claims. He was distracted momentarily by the old story of the bishop in the brothel who, when asked whether he'd like his 'lady companion' to appear in lace lingerie, replied 'Nothing would please me better.' Now, was that an example of a poetic nothing, or a philosophical? Or both? Or neither? Were there other kinds of nothing? Were there, in fact, as many categories of nothing as there were categories of thing? Hackett was getting nowhere, but if he was, at least he was getting nowhere fast. By the time he'd reached the *Ne Plus Ultra* of Parnell's monument,[3] nothing could have been farther from his mind.

From his earliest childhood, Ignatius Hackett was possessed of what is termed a Pangúr bán mentality:[4] one that, rather than sticking to the task or text in hand, is perpetually racing down a labyrinth of bye-ways and footnotes in pursuit of imaginary mice. If it wasn't the problem of nothing that his thoughts were stalking, it was the old chestnut of the chicken and the egg; and if not that, the conundrum of the tortoise and the hare; or of the polygamist from St Ives; or of the Copenhagen Interpretation; or of Zeno's Paradox; or that of the Cretan Liars; or the poser of the Prussian philosopher's attempt to navigate the bridges of Königsburg. This last was a

3 The Latin legend is a reminder the obelisk was originally intended as a traffic bollard to mark the apex of Sackville St., which it was said would thereby become Europe's widest cul de sac.

4 Named for a fabled white cat who stalked the marginalia of Eirish medieval manuscripts.

childhood favourite his father, Walter, had framed thus: "*Can you cross all seven bridges without crossing any bridge twice? — I Kant*." Before his breakdown words themselves had been the favourite quarry of his errant thoughts. But these days he was nervous of words.

Like many a man of letters — and in his heyday Hackett could've walked into the office of any editor in the country and commanded nine column inches — the parlous proximity to words had been his downfall. Some seven years before, around the time when panic shook the financial world, the intrepid columnist began to display many of the symptoms of early-onset dysphasia. When he first heard the diagnosis, he was at a loss for words. A psychoanalyst specialising in the condition warned him, 'If the condition develops into anacoulothon… well, you see what I mean.' He did, and it didn't. Not immediately. But before another year was out, the dysphasia was complicated by secondary aporia, side by side with peritaxis. One morning, a colleague was dumbfounded to discover Hackett sitting at his desk entirely unable to speak or type. Not long after that, our hero spent an unspecified number of undignified months in the incomparable care of Swift's Institution for the Insane.[5]

---

5 The madhouse was a legacy to the Eirish people from the author of *Gulliver's Travels*. A dedicatory plaque above the main entrance reads: 'He gave the little Wealth he had / To build a House for Fools and Mad. / And shew'd by one Satyric Touch, / No Nation needed it so much.' Though no Hibernophile, Swift won lasting renown in his native land for his contention that held the Engelish "to be the most pernicious Race of little odious Vermin that Nature ever suffered to crawl upon the Surface of the Earth". So distraught was the Dean to have been posted to Eirland that, to take his mind off the exile, he designed a mechanical device for dressing the bishop. It was a coping mechanism.

Long months had passed since that dark time. Still, no more did the journalist risk inventing anagrams or constructing etymologies, no more did he assay the maze of the cryptic crossword, and if he invariably scanned the headlines of the newspaper vendors as he passed them by, it was merely to stay abreast of current affairs in this most fromulous of times. The one verbal weakness to which he was still prone was involuntary inappropriate wordplay. For Hackett had inherited from his beloved father that debilitating condition known as Witzelsucht,[6] a verbal manifestation of the gag-reflex. However, these days he generally succeeded in internalising the incessant procession of puns that cavorted before his eyes.

By this juncture, Hackett was in the shadow of the monument to the Admirable Nelson known to generations of Dubiliners as 'the Pillar'. His father had oft remarked how all along O'Connell St, every one of the statues gazes wistfully toward the Southside, and it was to the Southside that the former columnist was, as though by one of Mr Newton's universal laws, gravitating. The point was, Nugent was too tight-fisted a tyke to venture much onto the more salubrious bank of the Liffey for fear of spending a farthing more on any item than could be got for less in the vicinity of Dorset St, Lower. With Needles Nugent, no quarter was asked and none given.

For a while Hackett dawdled, listening to the clang and

---

6 A condition first identified by the Austrian neurosurgeon Otfried Förster, who coined the term in a dig at his colleague Franz Witzel. Förster had suggested for one of Witzel's patients that trepanation might relieve the pressure on her frontal lobes contributory to the pathological condition, to which Witzel had replied: 'so ein Unsinn, *she needs trepanation like she needs a hole in ze head*!'

clamour, the music of cow-bell and slow glissando of the electric trams as they glided their heft through the heart of the Hibernian Metropolis. He gazed myopically at the portico of the General Post Office and, as is natural, he thought briefly of his glory days. For it was at this very spot that, two decades since, his journalistic career had had its unlikely baptism. If there was one thing that Hackett had been celebrated for down the years, it was for his uncanny knack of being in the right place at the right time. As though prompted by muscle-memory, his fingers remembered fondly the keys of his *Underwood* typewriter, and it was not unnatural that from there his reverie moved to the three brass balls hanging over the pawnshop on nearby Marlboro St.[7] *In hock signo.*

It was too painful to think of the typewriter gathering dust on a pawnshop shelf, and futile to think of the shop itself as a possible palliative to his present penury. For pretty much the entirety of Hackett's earthly estate was residing in one pawnshop or another. This inventory extended as far as his spectacles, which explained the myopia blurring the august pillars of the GPO. Could he chance redeeming them so he could spend the day in the reading room of the National Library on Kildare St? His fingers made an inventory of his pockets. He had, by this blind reckoning, seven pence ha'penny, scarcely the wherewithal to keep body and soul together for that day much less redeem his glasses.

As was his wont in passing the newspaper vendors that adorn the capital's busy thoroughfare, Hackett pushed index fingers and thumbs together to fashion a pinhole, and through

7 Named for the Duke of Marlboro (1650-1722), the illustrious ancestor of Winston Churchill (q.v.) who made his vast fortune importing tobacco.

this tremulous lens of air he perused the headlines. Swimming into focus were the words "MAYHEM IN MEDWAY" and "ANOTHER VERBAL OUTRAGE ROCKS UK ESTABLISHMENT." Though he'd been avoiding the living room where, of an evening, Needles Nugent would treat his paying tenants to a quarter-hour of the Marconi wireless, he was aware of the rash of counterfeit terms that were lately being passed off in the Home Counties — so-called, he mused, because these were the counties identified in the Tudor Walters report as suitable for the building of homes.

As his thoughts wandered, his perception became aware that a figure had been watching him. Or *not* watching him. For it was a casualty of the Great War, dark glasses and white cane, a tray of sundry items dangling from the neck. Beret and greatcoat, and across his chest the rainbow ribbons of campaign medals, a language beyond Hackett's ken, even if his myopia could bring them to focus. Now, there was nothing at all unusual in seeing a war cripple begging. Mustard gas alone had resulted in a veritable legion of seasoned veterans. What made Hackett uneasy was that the previous day but one, he'd bumped into one outside the doss-house off Dorset St., upsetting the tray of lucifers. That was unlucky. And as Hackett was of a superstitious bent, a bad feeling had dogged him all that day. He shivered at the memory. Nothing for it, then. Hackett resumed his slow perambulation southward.

He was rounding the railings of Trinity College when a felicitous thought struck him. The last time he'd spent the day in the National Library's reading room, hadn't the Chief Librarian told him that Trinity College had plans out to tender to build a Berkeley Library. Which is to say, a class of library named for Bishop Berkeley of Cloyne, who posited the principle 'esse est percipi', viz., to be is to be perceived.[8] It made perfect sense. The college was surrounded on all sides by a teeming capital. Space was at a premium. To conceive and construct a library which only took up space when it was being perceived was a capital idea. The word from America was they'd gone for broke and constructed an entire University on the Berkeley principle. The problem of course was how to measure the amount of space that one had saved. Because it was plain as the nose on your face that any attempt to measure the absence of the library would ipso facto cancel out that absence. Hadn't the old song about the arrival of a mere nightingale re-conjuring Berkeley Square suggested as much? The Bursar of Trinity College had offered a reward of a hundred guineas to anyone who could crack that particular chestnut.

Hackett would have been gripped by the conundrum had the Bursar offered the meanest reward. That said, the prospect of recovering his goods and chattels, not least the precious *Underwood*, from out of hock and of being shot of Needles Nugent for time eternal had his thoughts chasing in a dozen directions at once. For hours, he'd discussed the problem with the Chief Librarian of the National Library, a Mr Best whom everyone referred to as Second Best to distinguish him from his younger brother, the Mr Best who'd 'walked in' during the celebrated debate on whether Hamlet was the ghost of his own father at a time when Lyster was Chief Librarian. Now,

8 Walter Hackett had told young Ignatius that, when asked by a sceptical Dr Johnson if he could thereby explain his own existence, the Bishop replied 'As God is my witness.'

Second Best was celebrated for his dry sense of humour, as evidenced in his retort, 'I can tell you one thing, we already have some class of a Berkeley Library operating here, for if any of your University College students are in, the minute you take your eye off of a book, it's gone'. The felicitous comment came back to Hackett now as he dawdled by the main gate at College Green.

Like many a precocious child, Hackett had been fascinated by Bishop Berkeley's proposition. In those long gone days, the most direct way to test the hypothesis seemed to the boy to be to turn around really fast to see if he could momentarily catch the absence of what would almost instantaneously be there. *Almost* instantaneously, the child considered, since light had a finite speed. He'd never succeeded, but then absence of evidence is not evidence of absence, that too was an axiom. Perhaps it was worth a go now? Hackett pivorted in the general direction of Grafton St, clamped his eyes shut by way of preparation, then spun round and snapped them open. There was the city before his eyes, there the great half-round of the old Parliament, and there, under the portico and bobbling toward him, the unmistakable bowler atop the figure of Needles Nugent.

Seeing the bowler bobbing through the meagre crowd and bearing down on him with determination, Hackett's instinct was to make a bolt — in the figurative rather than metallurgic sense. He had neither the desire nor the wherewithal to deal with Needles Nugent. But where to make a bolt for? Hackett was tall enough of stature to look to the four points of the compass without his view being obstructed, but short enough of sight that the game was scarcely worth the candle. However, it did yield an immediate solution. The porter's gate to Trinity College stood ajar, and so he darted through the passageway and out onto the cobbled quadrangle just as the first falsetto cry of 'Hackett! Hackett!' overtook him. Without looking rearwards he made for the campanile where he veered right (as you look at it, left from its perspective) and shundled down along the side of the Long Room.

Here, he was surprised to find a small crowd had gathered in a semi-circle about the great wooden doors of the ancient library. Taking advantage of his height to peer over the heads as he passed, he found the centre of interest was a garmungling carpenter in a cloth cap, elbows poking from ill-fitting overalls. Sundry tools lay idle on the cobbles before him: awl, saw, plane, riddle, but without a clew. The tools of the trade, then, though the riddle was a puzzle. He was whistling a lively tune while marking off yard-lengths by eye on a wimbling plank with a flat blue pencil he kept betimes behind one protuberant ear, betimes behind the other. A dusting of sawdust over the cobbles suggested he had at an earlier time been engaged in more strumulous work. Hackett listened. '♪♫♪, ♪♫♪,' chirped the chippy.

Recognising the tune to be *Lilliburlero*, a jingle popular with both sides during the Williamite War, Hackett started and stopped. That a tradesman should be whistling *Lilliburlero* was not in itself surprising. It had become a signature tune with Alexandra Palace, always provided you could find the World Service on your wireless. The jingle intrigued Hackett as it seemed to simultaneously invite and evade interpretation: *There was an old prophecy found in a bog / Lilliburlero bullen a la / The country'd be ruled by an ass and a dog /*

Lilliburlero bullen a la... though why it fascinated the British Broadcasting Corporation was anyone's guess. What arrested him now was that *Lilliburlero*, a great favourite of his sometime acquaintance Malachi McCann who would whistle it between a gap in his incisors, was inexorably associated in his mind with that red-letter day at the GPO when his journalistic career had unexpectedly taken wing.

Distracted by the tune and the memory, Hackett forgot what it was that had impelled him to enter the interior quads of the Protestant bastion, and was rudely reminded when he felt his elbow peremptorily clamped. 'Hackett,' rasped a voice, sharp as a needle, 'I've been searching high and low for you so I have.'

'Do you tell me so,' said Hackett, attempting vainly to extract his elbow from the vicelike grip.

'Aye. I do,' Nugent wheezed. Hackett's swallow was dry as the sawdust sprinkled over the cobbles. Never mind the magnitude of the sum he was in arrears, the more immediate prospect of losing the meagre pile of coppers in his pocket, and with it any chance of slaking his thirst, had quite dried his saliva.

'I do tell you so. All morning I've been trying to find you, sir.' Nugent's 'you, sir' had the knack of negating such respect as the appellation should have occasioned. It did not bode well for what was to follow. 'And do you know *why* I've wasted my morning thus, sir? Will I tell you?'

'I feel sure, Mr Nugent, you're about to.'

'Is that so? Is it now? Well, I'll tell you, Masther Hackett. It's because a summons arrived for you, sir, so it did. By messenger boy. And I had to give that wee gasoon 3^{d}, so I did. A sum I may add to what you already owe.' At these words, the addressee felt an envelope thrust into his hand. 'I've served it now so I have,' continued the little man, 'there's no-one can accuse Manus Nugent of shirking his duty.' And with that he marched peremptorily onward, his now contented bowler bobbing across the bowling green until it had swum out of the blurred field of Hackett's vision.

Alone once more, Hackett chanced a glance in the direction of the item that had been thrust into his fist. At once his heart sank. The manila envelope was stamped with the official blazon of the Eirish Free State. Even through his myopia, he could see it was the backward harp of officialdom and not the fabled Guinness harp of which, following a protracted copyright lawsuit which Hackett himself as a young journalist had covered, it is the mirror image. For one in Hackett's straightened circumstances, the reversed harp was ever the harbinger of bad news.

From the figurative sawdust he'd swallowed, Hackett's throat had acquired the parched consistency of sandpaper. The one consolation to which he clung was that the meagre coppers in his pocket remained untouched. Following the promptings of Casey, the people's poet, for there could be little doubt that this was a time of trouble and lousy strife, he ran quickly through the picture-book of his imagination the colourful signage of some half-dozen public houses that were within emergency walking distance of where he now stood. By old habit, without, as it were, making any conscious decision either way, he made for **THE PALACE**.[9]

---

9 A bar on Dubilin's Fleet St perennially popular among journalists, poets and delusionals. In the Roque map (1777) the bar's title is placed in inverted commas, suggesting an ironic appellation.

The choice of bar was a curious one, and is a good indication of the state of consternation into which the summons had cast our hero. Ever since his breakdown, which is to say over a period of seven years, he had been giving any establishment frequented by the demimonde of journalists and literati — **THE OVAL, McDAID'S, THE PALACE** — a wide berth. To imagine this was a matter of hurt pride, for the former columnist was evidently not half the figure he'd once cut, is to misunderstand the man. Put simply, words and their parlous proximity had been the root cause of his illness. Formerly, he'd been addicted to words. And so, like any recovering addict, hard though it was, Hackett avoided any company and locale that would be the occasion of tickling his addiction. Why then, was he an occasional visitor to the National Library? Partly, this was to stay warm, to have an interior seat that cost not a farthing; partly in order to have congress with the knowledgeable Second Best; partly to play out with said Best the chess-games of the incontestable Capablanca, who had been unexpectedly beaten by the unassailable Alekhine, who in turn had been surprisingly outplayed by the matchless Euwe; and partly to consult such publications as dealt with conundrums of a mathematical nature. He made an allowance for articles on Physics which, with Rutherford, he considered the king of the sciences; Rutherford, whose observation upon receiving the Nobel Prize that "all science is either physics or stamp collecting" endeared him neither to chemists nor philatelists.

Hackett soon found himself in the mahogulous interior of the **PALACE BAR**, and as the fella said, no-one as surprised as himself to find himself there. Instinctively, he made for the stool that had once been synonymous with the columnist of yore. But for the fact that the curate was a young gasún of scarcely one-and-twenty, he'd surely have remarked upon the remarkable return.

Hackett was in such a somnambulistic state that he failed entirely to clock the round glasses on the round face that was broadly beaming in his direction until the words boomed out, with just a trace of Glaswegian colouring the Sligo accent.

'Cometh the hour and cometh the man!'

At that instant Hackett was startled out of a seven year trance. He looked myopically at the Cheshire grin floating atop a poncho and said, simply, 'Smyllie.'

CHAPTER THE SECOND

pertaining to a famous parley in the PALACE BAR, *and a most curious chess-game*

The round man in the poncho presiding over the inner parlour of the PALACE was, of course, R. M. Smyllie, a figure who, as he needs no introduction, shall receive none. Asked for a job description, the legendary editor liked to reply "To cut a long story short." Hackett's attention was called back to the young curate, who had set a pint of plain porter before him and was waiting for something to happen in consequence of the action. With a start, three things came to him: that he had absentmindedly ordered the beverage; that a pint of plain cost 10ᵈ; and that his portable goods came to the derisory sum of seven pence ha'penny. It was not the first time his absentmindedness had landed him in a pickle. While his thoughts scattered in chase of imaginary mice to find a phrase adequate to the situation, his fingers counted and recounted the grubby coppers in his pocket. The problem was, even had he recognised the former journalist, the curate could scarcely have allowed him the missing tuppence ha'penny on tick, his credit was so shot by this juncture.

The hiatus at the counter had begun to attract the

attention of the sundry customers scattered about the bar at the periphery of Hackett's myopia. With a magisterial nod toward the curate, R. M. Smyllie dispelled any possibility of monetary embarrassment. He allowed the impecunious customer to nod his gratitude and take the edge off his thirst, then, 'I take it, Mr Hackett,' his voice boomed out, and it was unclear whether it was the once celebrated name that had captured the attention of the bar or the decibel volume, 'that you're abreast of the spate of lexical crimes currently assailing the hereditary foe?'

Now, as Hackett's old college friend McCann would have put it, he was and he wasn't. In the course of his daily peregrinations about the capital, one eye, albeit blurred by myopia, always alighted hungrily upon the headlines hawked by the newspaper vendors. There were also the bulletins gleaned, albeit muffled through the floorboards of his room, from the Marconi wireless in the living room of the doss-house, though Needles Nugent was too tight-fisted to allow the set to be switched on for more than a paltry quarter hour of an evening. So that Hackett was only dimly aware of the series of verbal outrages that had begun to discombobulate the Home Counties. So he made an equivocal gesture to intimate the degree to which he was and he wasn't.

'I see,' nodded the editor, 'I see.' So seeing and so saying, he drew from a stack of newspapers beside him the nethermost and, frabbling it in such a way that a single article was foremost, he passed it along the counter to Hackett. The latter, who had as the attentive reader knows pawned his glasses, made a show of pattling the full array of his pockets before, irrigating the sentence with a watery smile, he declared, 'I appear to have left my digs without my spectacles.'

'No matter,' said the Sligo Scotsman, 'no matter.' He proffered his hand to a bespectacled acolyte sitting nearby. 'Mr Wood. If you would?' Mr Wood would, and his glasses were passed along to the down-at-heel columnist. They were not of perfect focal length, nevertheless, as Hackett held them before his eyes, the typeface, the article, indeed the entire counter swam into view. So too the barman and the mirror behind him. And that was crucial for what was to follow.

Hackett unfrabbled the newspaper — it was a copy of the *Logdon Gravitas* already two days old — and perused the article that had been circumscribed in red ink. 'BEDLAM IN BOTOLPH'S' ran the headline. A cursory glance told him it dealt with another of the spate of lexical outrages then afflicting the south-eastern corner of the neighbouring isle. Such snippets as he'd gleaned from the communal Marconi had tended to be anecdotal, not to say comical, and gave no intimation there may have been a manxome counterfeit cell at work bent on the disarticulation of the United Kingdom. But if no lesser a figure than R. M. Smyllie was taking an interest…

Now, it chanced that in a corner of the **PALACE BAR** there was a chess-game proceeding, and Hackett being an aficionado of the game and ever afflicted with a **Pangur bán** mentality, his concentration flitted between the article in his hands, the chess-game in the mirror, the commentary of the Sligo Scotsman to his side and the unopened summons in his pocket. This wasn't merely whimsy. The fact was, ever since his time as an asylum inmate, Hackett had become more than circumspect when it came to printed matter. However, for convenience, the article is presented in its entirety, without diversion, distraction or interpolation, herewith:

BEDLAM IN BOTOLPH'S

The congregation of St Botolph's in Chat'em was in for something of a surprise last Sunday when Dr Martin Coyne, Bisharp of Rockchester, took to the pulpit. No sooner had his Grace begun to deliver a sermon on the evils of calumny than heads began to turn, one to another, in bemusement. For the learned Bisharp kept returning to the notion of 'segnum'. What could he mean? Was it perhaps a Latin tag? It was only when he stressed the difference between 'segnumi of omission' and 'segnumi of commission' that the more alert began to suspect the Doctor was spraking of good old-fashioned sin. In much the same fashion, 'grodlum' was after some time understood to refer to original guilt, for are we not all born 'grodlumous'? But what 'lali perpengi' might be remains anybody's guess!

As if that wasn't bad enough, the misfortunate Dr Coyne, who is celebrated in Lambert Palace for his eloquence, consistently tripped over the very calumny he was there to preach against, giving the word an extra syllable, not by virtue of a stutter, but, as it were, in full consciousness of the addition. It is with regret that we must tell the reader that his Grace's repeated references to 'cacalumny' occasioned a coconsiderable degree of merriment among the more uncocouth elements in the cocongregation.

All the time, however, the Bisharp remained oblivious to the cause of this gaiety. Worse was to come, for to round off the ordeal, a general sniggering was to be heard when 'bgrrgl' found

> its way unexpectedly into the final paragraphs of the sermon! Following on the farce of the Major of Gillingham's sprake last Wednesday, and the brace of near incomprehensible pamphlets put out by the Rockchester Hysterical (sic) Society the previous month, one wonders if there isn't something contagious in the Medway region that is reducing its public figures to mere stammerers and malapropists!

While one train of Hackett's thoughts was assimilating the gist of the printed matter and a second was ferrying away the ominous image of the reversed harp, a third was distracted by the matter of the chess-game tendered in the virtual bar, itself tendered within the mirror behind the curate. And that runaway train ran loosely as follows.

To the rear of the looking-glass bar, which he supposed corresponded to the front of the pub, there was a game of chess taking place. Now, the player of the black pieces had his back to the bar, and to the mirror. But Hackett was more interested in the white player. He was of similar build, and was wearing an identical beret to his opponent. Indeed, they could almost have been reflections one of the other. Perhaps they were brothers. But what was far more curious was the white stick that was folded up on the white player's lap, and the dark glasses which obscured his eyes. Indeed, but for the absence of a greatcoat and campaign medals, this could have been the very veteran he'd encountered at the GPO. But then, did all the blind not resemble one another? After all, what import could appearance hold in their dark world. And his companion? Hackett wondered if the black player, whose back was to the mirror and therefore, he supposed, to the counter, might be just as blind.

The game was in the early stages, at least insofar as the capture of pieces was concerned. It was difficult to tell who had the advantage from the opening, the asymmetry of which Hackett recognised as the dragon variation of the Sicilian defence. And yet there was something altogether curious about the set-up, altogether not *comme il faut*. It took Hackett several minutes to nail it. There was an incorrect quality about black's fianchettoed bishop, even taking into account that in the looking-glass world the kingside had become the queenside and the queenside the kingside. He knucked his fingers. The black piece was white! Which is to say, its colour was black, as you might expect. But it stood on a white square. Now, Hackett could have sworn that black's king's bishop should be black. It was the black queen's bishop that was white, and the white queen's bishop, black. He ribbled his chin. Unless it was another effect of watching the game in the mirror?

But of course that made not the blindest bit of sense. You might just as well say that the double clocks which sat beside the players ran counter-clockwise. Though now he thought about it, they might, depending on whether the Coriolis effect was reversed in mirrors. But in the looking-glass world, that would still correspond to time moving forwards. Non-plussed, he watched a couple of moves, and noticed that while the black player used the arm on the kingside to move his queen's knight and tap the black clock, the white player, he of the white stick, used the queenside hand to capture the black piece and tap the white clock. Now, normally, that would make the white player left-handed. But then the black player too would have to be a south-paw, since he was facing him. Perhaps if they were brothers it wasn't so unlikely. But in a mirror? It took all of Hackett's willpower not to pivort around and sneak a look.

Wait just a minute. Wait now. Even in a mirror, black's king's knight's second square should be black. That was only common sense. Now, in the looking-glass game, it was white. Small wonder the king's castle was so oddly defended. And yet it appeared to be correctly positioned, viz., to the black player's left, and the white player's right, as they looked at it. Hackett closed his eyes, placed a finger on either side of the bridge of his nose, and squeezed. Mentally, he conjured a board. His eye ran along its front rank. Black white black white black. His eyes opened and checked the reflected board. White black white black white. Was that because the looking-glass board had been laterally reversed, an example of the inverse-square law?

Not at all man, he considered on reflection! Because a mirror fools us with its backwards alphabets and universe of lefties precisely because we *expect* it to laterally invert, and it obdurately refuses. That being the case, they had the damned thing set up arse-ways from the start! It was side-on! Even taking into account the reversals of the looking-glass pub, the damned thing was set up wrong from the outset. There's lateral thinking for you! But, he mentally asked his reflection, would that make the blindest bit of difference, if both players were blind? And if they were both blind, retorted the reflection, how would they know how much time remained on their counter-clockwise clocks?

'So you'll agree, the time is propitious.'

Hackett met the RM's glasses first in the mirror then in

the real world. During his sojourn at the Christian Brothers, he'd cultivated the happy knack, on being snapped out of a daydream, of being able to accurately repeat the final few words of whichever Brother was lifting him out of reverie and desk by the ear. Is there a term for that knack, he now wondered. There certainly should be. Autoretort, say. Autoretort [ˌɔːtərɪ'tort] *v., intr., to echo back the final clause or phrase to an interlocutor without having paid it or him the least heed.* Would the verb also serve for a noun, the way retort itself did? He'd half a mind to submit the word and its definition to that PO Box in Ealing Broadleaf (was it?) to see if he could earn a few bob from it.

In the bar and in the mirror, the Scot and his reflection were looking at him minutely.

'Propitious,' nodded Hackett. 'I see that.'

He didn't. In fact, all the time that he'd been watching the looking-glass game, he'd been employing the camouflage of autoretort. Which is not to say that a fourth train of thought had not been heeding the Sligo Scotsman's interventions, for Hackett had a multitrack mind. Only the fearful summons, and the concomitant possibility of eviction from the doss-house, had by this juncture been sidelined. Because, if Hackett had been famous among his colleagues for his prodigious memory, his capacity to forget was equally astonishing, as though the one facility were the necessary corollary of the other.

'You accept the challenge, then?'

Hackett was on his guard. What this fourth train had gleaned was that the great R. M. Smyllie was making him some class of an offer. Autoretort now dragged from immediate memory the suggestion that his once popular 'Aplestos Pithus' column be revived. What precisely this offer consisted in was less clear, because as soon as a cash advance was mentioned, the Pangur Bán in his head set off in chase of imaginary mice whose fantastic attractions involved the redeeming of his name, his reputation, his glasses, and above all, his beloved *Underwood.* A thirty quid advance — wasn't that the sum the man had intimated? — would go a long way toward such redemption. He owed Needles Nugent thirteen quid or thereabouts, the same again would redeem both typewriter and specs, even his grandfather's fobwatch was all but within reach. It was as though Smyllie had fathomed the precise depth of his pecuniary embarrassment. Suppose he pressed for guineas — an additional thirty pieces of silver? The door to a garden of possibility would be unlocked.

Why then was he so circumspect in his reply? Why had his parallel trains not at once dropped their respective cargos to accept the editor's generosity? The answer may be it was precisely the tantalising aspect, and the unlikelihood of it all, that held him, like the black player in the mirror, in check. More than this, it was that the former inmate of Swift's Institution was vitiated by doubt. Where the younger man might have leapt at the offer to resuscitate the corpse of a career, the present Hackett had been through the figurative wringer. Thirty pounds down plus three per article. It was more than generous. But was he up to it? Could he dare re-engage with words on a daily basis, and on a professional level? Would it not trigger a relapse? A dark figure out of Swift's Asylum swam before his eyes, a hare-eyed demobbed soldier with a mortal fear of being bowdlerised, what's this his name was…?

'Why me?' he asked, eyes narrowing.

'It's the old dog for the hard road.'

'That's as may be,' said Hackett, fighting down a flush equal parts pleasure and terror. 'But even in my heyday, I may have worn many different hats: a correspondent's hat; a columnist's; a writer of opinion pieces. But I was never any class of investigative journalist. And it seems to me that an investigative journalist would be the man for this particular assignment.'

'With respect, Mr Hackett, you'll allow me to be the best judge of what class of beast it is I'm after for this particular assignment.'

Hackett demurred. Briefly. 'Ok. But we both know, as often as not the 'Aplestos Pithus' column was tossed off on a Friday in the reading room of Kildare St. Why send me overseas?'

'I imagined you'd be raring to go,' said the Scot, 'the minute you laid eyes on that wee article.' Now, in truth the article itself had merely wobbled in Wood's spectacles before his eyes, but by a process akin to autoretort, he pulled a word from his perusal of it. 'Bisharp?' offered Hackett.

'Indeed.'

'It's not a typesetter's error?'

Supercilious eyebrows suggested it was not. A silence followed. 'What I mean, Mr Hackett, did you mind who *penned* that article?'

Hackett had not minded, and so, without much thought, he unfrabbled the *Logdon Gravitas* and examined the attribution. Three lines, vertical, scored by a line across their middle, horizontal. Vertigo seized him. It was his own monograph!

Momentarily his vision clouded, and he teetered at the edge

of that abyss klept, in the decorative language of heraldry, mise-en-abyme.[10] It was a debilitating form of vertigo from which he'd suffered ever since, on his seventh birthday, his father Walter had presented him with his first *Oxenford Engelish Dictionary.* That night in bed, when he had exhausted the customary scatological fare that has forever been the delight of schoolboys, it took young Hackett's fancy to look up the word 'word'. Instantaneously, even before he had got as far as the letter W, the book crashed to the floor. It was as if the bed had collapsed beneath him. If words could only be defined in terms of other words, which in turn depended upon more words, or worse again, upon the original word you were looking up in the first place, then the whole ghost of language could float off into thin air! Any time he came across a picture-book which contained a plate with a picture of the picture-book, he teetered at the brink of mise-en-abyme. When, in the *Quixote*, the characters were said to have read the *Quixote*, the world of La Mancha span crazily. And now, seeing his own monograph at the foot of the article he was reading, he was seized by a comparable vertigo. Hackett attempted to stand. The real bar began to reel about. Too many contradictions were cavorting about the floor. 'You'll have to give me leave to think about it,' he managed, as he finally regained the upright and staggered in the direction of the door.

'By all means,' smiled Smyllie. 'By all means think about it.' Hackett was by now pushing on the door, which was refusing to give. 'One other thing,' the voice boomed magniloquently, 'you've not had a wee look at that summons

10 In heraldry, mise-en-abyme occurs when the top sinister quarter of a shield itself contains a mise-en-abyme[10].

in your pocket?'

This was too much. Double vertigo all but floored the journalist. At that moment muscle-memory kicked in and pulled the door, which was inward opening, and by an application of Newton's Third Law of Motion, Hackett was propelled by the door outward into the weak sunshine, bearing away on his nose the spectacles of the unfortunate Mr Wood.

CHAPTER THE THIRD

in which an account is given of Hackett's birth and upbringing

While our hero is teetering dizzily in the watery sunshine, the time has come to give an account of the illustrious career that had brought him to the attention of so great a figure as R. M. Smyllie. In order to do that, it will first be necessary to give an account of his upbringing, for as the popular saw has it, the child is father of the man. In Hackett's case this was doubly the case, for as his mother Henrietta Gowing wryly pronounced, what was Walter Hackett but a child in the guise of an adult?

Walter had been a posthumous child. His father, a train-driver, perished in the infamous 1867 Bray Head Rail Disaster, fully six months before the son saw light of day. Much as his own son would be, Walter was an only child, the only child of one Maisy Hackett. Maisy was a timid seamstress who nevertheless single-handedly raised the boy against the greatest of odds. For the woman suffered from aichmophobia, a dread of all things sharp, and lived in mortal fear of shears and scissors, so that to make ends meet as a seamstress she had her work cut out for her. But as Walter, who from the very first was of a philosophical bent would tell his son, you cut your cloth.

The only two remembrances that came down to young Walter from his late father were a half-hunter fob-watch with escapement, and a daguerreotype of the engineer, William Dargan. Despite this paucity, the boy grew up with a fascination for clocks and for steam-engines, and to his mother's dismay was determined to follow in his missing father's footsteps. Despite tears and injunctions, he took a position as a fireman on the Atmospheric Railway that ran from Amiens St Station out to Kingstown. Daily, the widow lived in mortal fear that her only son would go the way of his father. For the unfortunate seamstress, for whom an innocent tailor's shears was a source of dread, those roaring engines that hurtled along rails and rattled over bridges in dreadful haste were insatiable mechanical monsters bent on havoc.

Her one hope was to enlist the Widow Gowing, whose husband was late of **GOWING, GOWING & GONNE, AUCTIONEERS** of Burgh Quay, as an ally. Now Mrs Gowing was her oldest customer, a huckster who ran a notions shop in Benburb St,[11] and she had a daughter of marriageable age named Henrietta, a perky, headstrong little thing for whom Walter had a soft spot. She also had a roving eye, which was a matter of growing concern to the Widow Gowing. It was clear to both mothers who'd wear the trousers in any future household. Despite her many suitors, the girl tolerated Walter's shy and clumsy advances. But marry a stoker? Miss Henrietta wasn't the type

11 Named for Ben Burb, eponymous hero of the Battle of Benburb (1646), an indecisive action during the War of the Three Kingdoms. The Hackett household was in nearby Prussia St., which helps explain why young Hackett took a personal interest in the conundrum of the seven bridges of Königsburg.

to brook a husband whose aspirations were so low and so dirty.

So the Stoneybatter widows put their heads together and a plot was hatched. Appearances were everything. Before Walter pressed his suit, the seamstress pressed his suit. And the result was that the ledger of St Joseph's Church of the Discalced Carmelites on Berkeley Rd records the marriage of Walter Hackett to Henrietta Gowing on September 1st, 1895. She had no intention, she declared from the outset, of altering her name, and when within a bare twelvemonth she flew the Hackett family home on Prussia St, she bore away her original surname. As Walter would say to his son in years to come, 'your mother was always Gowing.' In fact, the flighty woman's flight had a visibly greater impact on her mother-in-law. Her scheme to wean her son off the railway in tatters, and having broken irreparably with Mrs Gowing — a huckster with notions — the unfortunate seamstress took to her bed.

Thus it was that Ignatius grew up with no actual memory of his mother. There was one bogus memory. All his life, Walter kept on his bedroom dresser a bottle of *Lily of the Valley* toilet water which had been a Christmas gift from Maisy Hackett to her daughter-in-law. It had been opened, sniffed at. Evidently, Henrietta had not cared for the scent, for it was the one toiletry she'd conspicuously neglected to take with her. There were hundreds of aromas the flighty creature might have favoured, *Lily of the Valley* was the only one of which one might say with certainty it had not been. Yet for the boy, who would sneak into Walter Hackett's room when his father was working to sniff the bottle, this very scent became indelibly his mother's. Her absence lent the kind of poignancy to the fragrance that perfumers could only dream of.

It has been noted previously that Ignatius Hackett had a slight limp. The cause of this impediment was not, as most assumed, childhood polio, but was down to the fact that Walter Hackett was an inveterate autodidact and self-improver. Having apprised himself during his wife's pregnancy of the very latest medical journals on the science of parturition, the stoker decided that his primogenitor's arrival in the world should be a home-birth, with himself assuming the role of mid-wife. Contractions began on a blusterly evening at the tail end of a blusterly March. For a man given to the scientific outlook, Walter Hackett was remarkably superstitious. It was a desire to have his first-born born *before* April the first that led to his rather enthusiastic yanking of the child, just as the house burst into midnight chime. Unfortunately, in the course of the delivery, which in no time at all became a botched breech-birth, Hackett Sr managed to disarticulate the ankle and hip of the infant's left leg, with the result that it remained always about five per cent shorter than the right.

In the course of the extraction he also managed to disarticulate his wife's enthusiasm for her conjugal rights, with the result that Hackett grew up an only child. 'Our subsequent efforts,' quoth Hackett Sr, at a time when he was attempting to impart to the boy the facts of life, 'bred only disappointment.' Fancying himself a connoisseur of languages, Walter named his son Ignatius, which he held to derive from the Spanish 'Ignacio' ("he was badly born"). The ledger of St Joseph's Church of the Discalced Carmelites on Berkeley Rd records the baptism on April 6th, 1896.

It has been noted from the very opening sentence that Hackett may not have been Hackett. Although it was not what was intended by the observation, the numerate reader will have noted that Hackett's birth occurred a mere seven months after the marriage ceremony. Following the admirable Austrian precept Wovon man nicht sprechen kann, darüber muss man schweigen, all that will be recorded here is that, in answer to Ignatius's query as to his birthday being on April 1st, which is to say long before the customary term of gestation following the wedding, Walter replied 'your mother was quick with child.'

Despite a flair for invention, improvement and improvisation, Walter Hackett never rose beyond the position of fireman on the Kingstown line. This was due to the emulation of the Chief Engineer, a dour Presbyterian by the name of Caleb Crawley. Time and again, Hackett would propose some improvement, time and again Crawley would put the brakes on the proposal. In June 1904, for instance, long before spotter balloons became a feature of the trench warfare paralysing the Western Front, the lowly stoker proposed hoisting a lookout above the railway whose bird's eye view, telegraphed by semaphore, would be a great aid to the signalmen. The proposal was shot down. For a man of Crawley's envious stamp, Hackett was getting ideas above his station.

Undeterred, Walter took his flair for innovation home to Prussia St. From an early age, Hackett Jr was infected with Hackett Sr's enthusiasm for self-improvement. While the grandmother rested her nerves in a bed to the rear of the bungalow, son and grandson would periodically take paper and glue and paste labels on household objects in whatever language it was that had taken Walter's fancy. It was not rare for a pot, plate or doorknob to have accumulated two or even three labels before her tears and agitation would have the repentant scholars de-label the guilty object. But despite their best efforts, a residue of paste always adhered, and for most of his life Hackett associated mealtimes with a faint taste of resin. Nevertheless, by the time he parted company with the Christian Brothers, young Hackett was already something of a polyglot, bilingual, as the fella said, in umpteen languages.

To the despair of the widow, the two spent long hours together on field-trips made possible by Walter's position on the railway. Inevitably, the fireman would tell anyone who asked that he was "taking the sun and air with his son and heir". From the callumphing engine father and son would point to bird, beast or geographical feature and compare how well the various appellations fitted. capall, they agreed, was superior to *horse* or Pferd, particularly when the going was firm; even as, on a winter's evening, scornach was to be preferred to *throat,* though Rachen was satisfactory with its suggestion of smoker's cough. *Nuage* captured nebulosity far better than *cloud* or scamall; *uccello* was more intrinsically musical than an entire flock of *birds,* ορνιθοι, *pájaros* or Vögel, though oiseaux did suggest a gossamer quality, and птица, flightiness. There was little to choose between *butterfly,* feileacán, Schmetterling, *mariposa,* papillon, ψυχή, *farfalla* and бабочка, each might be pinned with equal validity into a display case. But when it came to encapsulating canine character, you could forget your chien, your madra, your *perro* or Hund. The old reliable, *dog,* was not to be surpassed.

It followed that certain tongues lent themselves more readily than others to particular human pursuits. If law was best expressed in Latin, haute couture in French, metaphysics in Greek, circumlocution in Eirish and music in Italian, then German reigned supreme in the sciences. One of Hackett Jr's declared motives for taking the last as an elective subject while at Newman House was so that he could keep pace with that nation's remarkable advances in the fields of chemistry, psychoanalysis, and above all, physics, which the railway fireman held, with de Selby, to be king of the sciences. For Walter Hackett, the Germans were the supreme physicists, in comparison to whom Thomas Edison was a mere humbug.[12] Gottfried Leibniz alone had discovered the integral calculus; anything Sir Isaac Newton may have added was merely derivative.

Beyond the comparative biology at which he dabbled, Hackett Sr was an amateur of each of the natural sciences, and from the outset father and son carried out every conceivable experiment on anything from beetles and frogs carried home from Booterstown Saltmarsh to the half-inch to the yard scale replica train set, in the livery of the Dubilin & Kingstown line, that ran clockwise around the floor by a clockwork mechanism they tried, with mixed results, to improve. This network of miniature rails, which in order not to try the nerves of Maisy Hackett had been banished to the otherwise unused drawing-room, gradually sprawled over the entire floor-space, after which that space was turned back in on itself with the result that, by the time of Walter Hackett's wake, its elaborate convolutions, involutions and reversals had come to resemble

12 American inventor chiefly remembered for *Edison's Law*, which states that genius is 1% inspiration and 99% perspiration. As Walter Hackett pointed out, this assumes that ambient conditions remain constant. In fact, studies have shown that an increase in either temperature or, especially, pressure gives rise to a concomitant increase in the ratio of perspiration to inspiration.

a fantasy out of the Book of Kells.

History, on the other hand, Walter had little time for, and this may help to explain some of the surprising lacunae in Ignatius' grasp that will become apparent as the story progresses. In particular, the fireman had nothing but scorn for ancient history, or the veneration with which the Archaeological Society displayed their endless shards of broken pottery. The ancient civilisations seemed to have a queer compulsion altogether to throw pottery. But then, he supposed, was it any wonder when so much of their thrown pottery ended up in fragments?

Besides a fascination with railways, foreign languages, clocks (see next paragraph) and the natural sciences, together with a limp, a **Pangúr bán** mentality and a lifelong antipathy to cats, Ignatius Hackett also inherited from his father the congenital weakness for inappropriate wordplay known as **Witzelsucht**.[13] While they were replicating on their 1:36 scale set the infamous 1867 Bray Head Rail Disaster which had put paid to his grandfather, the young Hackett gave his express opinion that the signal failure had been a signal failure.

Clocks, too, were something of a passion with Walter Hackett, and the long association in Hackett's mind between railways and the conundrum of time may well have its origins in the drawing-room on Prussia St. At its zenith the house was home to more than two score of them, largely confined to the same drawing-room in deference to the delicate nerves of the retired seamstress. Although father and son took apart

---

13 Not all his colleagues agreed with Dr Förster that such a condition existed. The French physician Georges Tourette (1857-1904) famously told him where he could shove his theory.

and reassembled the intricate mechanisms with the most meticulous care — only the prized half-hunter fob-watch with escapement escaped these experiments — it was a rare thing for any two of the faces to agree for more than a few hours at a time, and whether any of them ever corresponded to GMT was anyone's guess.

Clocks, with trains, were one of Walter Hackett's preferred resources when instructing his son. That they should run exclusively clockwise as the weights descended vertically, and not vice versa, was an illustration both of the Second Law of Thermodynamics and of the Coriolis effect. The man was better at suggesting then explaining, however. His contention that by timing the periodic motion of a pendulum, you could conclude that the fall due to gravity would be at a rate of thirty-two feet per second per second intrigued the boy not so much because it should be true *per se* as because his eight year old mind could not conceive how you could have any more than one 'second per second'.

Curiously, and this may relate to Walter Hackett's superstitious bent, these clocks were exclusively tickers. Tock, he held to be the past tense of tick, a constant reproach to what to his ear was interrogative. Tick? asked the clock. Tock! it replied, with the finality of a judge's gavel. They chimed magnificently though, and on the hour the house was filled with a cascade of musicality; two dozen twangling bells all told all tolled. Why the chimes should have rung out in concert when the hands so rarely agreed was ever a source of puzzlement to young Ignatius. Interspersed with the clocks was a range of unschooled metronomes, a word which, as they were working on the model of the Bray to Greystones tunnel, the young Hackett misunderstood to be metro gnomes. After his grandmother's departure,[14] the boy would take solace in the drawing-room, closing door, curtains and eyes, lying on the table above the Bray Head rail tunnel, and he'd imagine the cacophony of tocklessly clicking metronomes was the sound of a thousand tiny dwarves chipping away with their picks at the darkness.

---

14 There has been some debate as to what is meant by 'departure' here. While it may well be that Maisy Hackett 'passed' at this time, the lack of a corresponding entry into the parish records has given rise to another view, viz, that her fraught nerves and unshakable phobia had finally led to her committal to Swift's Hospital. Records do show that, about this time, a Daisy Hackett (sic) was admitted 'for being mentally sic (sic)'.

CHAPTER THE FOURTH

in which an account is given of Hackett's meteoric rise as a man of letters

Ignatius Hackett's journalistic career owes its inception to a most unlikely coincidence, viz., that the inimitable Shakespeare and the incomparable Cervantes exited the world's great stage upon the same day.

The year is 1916. All Europe is at war, and Hackett, a lad just turned twenty-one, is a student in his final year at Newman House.[15] The Bachelor's Degree in the Arts was made possible, from a financial point of view, by an exhibition he'd won three years earlier, for as a schoolboy Ignatius Hackett was nothing if not precocious. That date should have been one of unbounded joy and celebration, a red letter day. But it was a date that, for the teenager, would ever be circumscribed by a black border. It was the occasion of his beloved father's untimely death, though it might not have been but for Walter Hackett's superstitious bent.

On the very morrow after he won his exhibition, young

15 Original premises of Dubilin's new Catholic University, built, opined Mahaffey, Provost of Trinity College, "for the cornerboys who spit into the Liffey". There is no evidence that Cardinal Newman ever lived there.

Hackett was whiling away an evening awaiting his father's return to Prussia St when a black cat crossed his path, rippled up a wall, and sat atop to watch him from the imperturbable spirit-levels that served for pupils. Hackett was of an age when boys are still tempted to throw stones and, when he was sure that none but the cat was watching, the boy gave in to the temptation. The cat disappeared, but in its flight it crossed the path of a somewhat tipsy Walter Hackett, who'd been regaling his railway colleagues with news of his son and heir's remarkable good fortune. The black cat darted across the footpath, Hackett *père* stepped out onto the street so that his path might not be crossed, and in doing so he stepped under a van in the livery of Brittain's recently founded Swastika Laundry. From that time, Hackett *fils* could see neither cat nor swastika without recalling that doleful day, and he developed a lifelong antipathy to both.[16]

It was a comfort to the newly orphaned Ignatius that the end was mercifully instantaneous. Notwithstanding the suddenness of the death, he complied with his father's oft expressed wish to have for his epitaph the rhetorical:

Who does not long for this world
who is not long for this world?

---

16 A celebrated lawsuit taken in 1926 to prevent the German National Socialist Party from infringing international copyright on their trademark red and white livery with black Aryan device proved unsuccessful. Although a precedent had been set four years earlier when the Eirish Free State was compelled to reverse the Guinness logo on its stationery, Dr Goebbels argued that as Eirish was Case Law and German Civil Law, the jurisdiction of the former was not recognised. Brittain had the last laugh, however. Decades after the Third Reich lay in ruins, his trademark fleet of electric vans continues to bear their *Hakenkreutz* through the streets of Dubilin.

Out of piety to the late Walter, young Ignatius never again wound the household clocks, and hour by hour over the next several days, the house on Prussia St descended into unregulated silence. It might have been one final illustration by the old man's ghost of the Second Law of Thermodynamics.

We find him an orphan, to all intents and purposes, since his mother Henrietta "had always been Gowing". He has since had to leave the ancestral home on Prussia St, which has been reclaimed by the city council. Three years on, such inheritance as probate allowed the student is scarcely sufficient to keep body and soul together. But if he is down-at-heel his spirits are up, buoyed by a richer inheritance: a childlike capacity for fascination which is, of all gifts bestowed by the gods, the choicest.

Misery, it is said, makes strange bedfellows. Curiosity also, for in Malachi McCann, with whom he shared digs if not precisely a bed together with membership of the Philological Society, Hackett had found a singular temperament every bit as restless as his own. If his faculties were perhaps less mathematically given, they gave themselves more readily to languages. At a time when European civilisation was fracturing due to the movement of Teutonic plates, McCann was engaged on any number of projects to repair the fractures by translating the key texts between the major languages. But if there was one project that McCann was putting his whole heart into that tricentennial year, it was a translation of the *Quixote* back into the original Arabic. Eventually, the project got suspended without having advanced beyond the notorious chapter VIII.

All his life, Hackett would recall the Shandyesque squiggle[17] with which McCann signed off each leaf of the manuscript: ناكم اي ناك , while whistling that tune so beloved of Toby Shandy, *Lilliburlero.* Hackett's translations, by contrast, never proceeded beyond a few scraps and orts. A project to render A. A. Milne's immortal classic into the Eirish, for instance, never advanced beyond naming the hapless ass '**mi-adh**'.

For the time being, McCann's infectious enthusiasm had led to our two bedfellows enlisting in the Dubilin Cervantes Society. There, they fell in with Teddy Mulcahy, only son of ***MULCAHY & SON, TYPESETTERS AND PRINTERS, 33, 34, 35 ABBEY ST MIDDLE*** who had inherited the thinning hair and thinner smile of the Mulcahy dynasty. On a visit to the family business, Hackett was astonished to attest the facility with which printers and typesetters, the young Mulcahy among them, could scan the looking-glass letters with their right-to-left sentences as though it was the most natural thing in the world. He was intrigued by the range of font, symbol and punctuation of the most exotic stamp; delighted to find that upper case letters were kept in an upper case, lower case in a lower one.

There was an element of glamour attaching to this melancholic character. Everyone knew that ***MULCAHY & SON***

17 Laurence Sterne had been a favourite author of Walter Hackett. Following the usage of the Restoration stage, the majority of Anglo-Irish writers from Swift and Steele through Sterne to Wilde, Lever, Stoker, Synge and Bernard Pshaw tended to adopt aptronyms. Edinburgh's Walter Scott and Graham Bell, the Catholic satirist Alexander Pope and Engelish poet laureate Wordsworth were perhaps a little too obvious in their choices. In adopting aptronyms, the Anglo-Irish were following the lead of Waterfjord-born natural scientist Robert 'Boyle', Earl of Lismore (1627-91), whose eponymous law relates the pressure and volume of steam at boiling-point.

had been locked up inside Kilmainham Gaol for the duration of the Dubilin Lock-in.[18] A malevolent dwarf attached to the DMP by the name of Willy Clarke had seen to it that the Abbey St premises and presses were broken up with sledge-hammers. After his release from Kilmainham, it was Teddy Mulcahy, or Eamon Maolcathach as he'd begun to style himself, who, unbeknownst to his father, cast the Cló Gaedhealach, the uncial typeface required for Mr Pearse's nationalist newspaper, An Claidheamh Soluis. He was, though, unable to help McCann with any of his Shandyesque squiggles.

Now, Mulcahy was not himself a member of the Philological Society, but did share with McCann membership of the clandestine Ouroboros Brotherhood, a shadowy international organisation of which Hackett was not a member. On the other hand, both Mulcahy and Hackett, unlike McCann, attended fortnightly Irish language classes hosted by Conradh na Gaedhilge. It is a situation which, if space but allowed, might be usefully illustrated by a Venn diagram. For a while, the three were as inseparable as Dumas' eponymous musketeers.

Now, at that time, the Dubilin Cervantes Society, under the aegis of a barber named Patterson, was gearing up to mark the tercentenary of the death of the incomparable Miguel de Cervantes Saavedra, soldier, poet and only begetter of Don

---

18 A dark period during 1913 when Dublin's Public Houses went on strike. When unionised workers throughout the city went out in sympathy, they congregated in secret behind the closed doors of the said Public Houses, giving rise to the phenomenon of the eponymous "Dubilin lock-in". The lock-in was finally broken when the much-maligned William Martin Murphy mobilised allies within the Catholic Church to institute a retaliatory 'holy hour'.

Quijote de la Mancha, the freelance *par excellence*. Plans had been laid for a cavalcade of doleful knights and portly squires to pass down Sackville St, and the secretary, a Mr E. O'Neill, had even gone so far as to source some dozen suitable nags and almost as many asses for the great occasion. It would be a parade the like of which Dubilin had not seen in many a long day.

There was only one black cloud on the horizon. And that dark cloud was in the shape of the Royal Dubilin Shakespeare Society, which was under the leadership of a publican named Maguire, an incendiary figure with a high colour and a temper to match. Now it happened that they, too, were planning a tercentennial procession up the capital's main thoroughfare, and if it didn't involve the Knight of the Doleful Countenance, it did centre on Sir John Falstaff and his rag-tag recruits, for Maguire had the very complexion and figure to embody the fat knight. The problem, of course, was that the incomparable Cervantes and the inimitable Shakespeare had both settled on April 23rd 1616 to shuffle off their mortal coils.

Now, it so fell out that in 1916, April 23rd coincided with Easter Sunday. Neither chairman was particularly devout, but it was obvious that a concession to the sensibilities of both Catholic and Protestant propriety would have to be made. And both chairmen hit on the like concession of holding off their procession until the following day. The date fast approached, and a fracas appeared inevitable. Neither party was prepared to back down, for in Patterson, Maguire had truly met his match. That Easter Monday, all Dubilin that was not at the Fairyhouse Races was braced for a monumental dust-up.

There were interventions, from the Lord Mayor, from

the Chief Constable of the DMP, from so venerable a figure as William Martin Murphy. And at the eleventh hour, as is so often the way in such cases, a compromise was found by which both parties might save face. On Easter Saturday, E O'Neill duly posted an advertisement in the national papers announcing the cancellation of manoeuvres. So much can be verified in the archives held in the National Library on Kildare St. What is less certain is, why did Malachi McCann, who was evidently apprised of the postponement, neglect to inform his bedfellow before himself heading off to the Fairyhouse Races that storied Easter Monday morn?

Hackett was in the habit of carrying his glasses about in his breast pocket, and some time that weekend, it so fell out that they fell out. Was McCann blissfully unaware that Hackett could not read the paper that lay open on the table since Saturday? Was it neglect that had him set off for the races without clarifying the issue? Either way, it struck Hackett as very odd his companion in arms risked missing the festivities. He set off from their digs in good time, and when he arrived in Sackville St, was put out at how empty the thoroughfare appeared. The races were doubtless to blame, for in Eirland the sport of kings has long been the king of sports. Of greater concern, there was neither hide nor hair of Patterson and Co at the appointed place of assembly, nor of the equipage of nags and asses that O'Neill had promised.

Hackett was on the point of leaving when he heard two things. One was a distant '♪♫♪, ♪♫♪,' a tune he recognised to be *Lilliburlero*; the other, the unmistakable clatter of horses' hooves on cobbles. Squinting against the limits of his myopia he made out, not the distant whistler, if such there was, but the cavalcade, and his heart soared to descry the lances that they bore aloft. As rapidly as his mismatched stride and shortness of sight would allow, he made down on them — they were by now within a plumstone's throw of the Admirable Nelson — but just as he drew level two things occurred simultaneously: he lost his footing, just as a ferocious volley was unleashed from the GPO. Notwithstanding, Hackett survived that volley. While fighting raged over the next several days, he penned an eyewitness account of the impromptu insurrection. And that was the makings of him.

Could the canny M[c]Cann have been in the know? Could his sin of omission in not informing his colleague have been a sin of commission? Could it be that, as he might have put it himself, 'he did and he didn't'? All we shall say is, with the Austrian, Wovon man nicht sprechen kann, darüber muss man schweigen. But one thing is certain. Over the following decade of what was a truly meteoric journalistic career, Hackett had the uncanny knack of being in the right place at the right time.

One other early article should be mentioned before we return to the PALACE BAR, for it seems to have given rise to the outlandish if persistent rumour that Hackett may actually have been Rooney. Several months after the fracas that came to be known as the Easter Rising, the trial and execution took place of Sir Roger Casement, Companion of the Order of St Michael and St George, who being handed the sentence, observed he was to be 'hanged on a comma'. Although the comma upon which Casement was figuratively hanged either occurs or doesn't along a fold in the parchment of the original of the Treason Act of 1351, this was just the sort of gnomic utterance to seize the attention of the budding journalist.

Now, it so happened that Malachi M^c^Cann's grandmother had a shebeen near the seaside town of Ballyhaigue, and in order to celebrate the passing of their final year exams, immediately after the conferring ceremony, the confirmed Bachelors set off on a merry jaunt to the Kingdom of Kerry. It was while they were there that news of the infamous trial, and the escapade that led up to it, reached them. So it was that, in order to consolidate his claim to be a political correspondent, it was suggested by M^c^Cann that they visit nearby Banna Strand, where another of the great might-have-beens of Eirish History had so recently taken place. Hackett might record, as it were *in situ*, his impressions of the heroic fiasco. Mulcahy was due to head back to the capital the following day, and would be pleased to carry the fair copy with him.

The bare facts of the fiasco were as follows. On a moonlit night in the early hours of April 21st, some three days before the GPO volley that all but put paid to our hero, **Seiner Majestät** U-19[19] rose out of the steely waves and dispatched to shore either the war's greatest traitor or the war's greatest patriot, depending upon one's interpretation of said comma. Hackett drew up a precis broadly sympathetic to the enterprise, in which he described in detail the arraignment of Sir Roger and his accomplices in nearby Ardfert Fort. It had been arranged that a jarvey should pick up Casement at the fort, but in a cunning stratagem, the REC secretly untied the pony's harness, upon

19 Originally dreamt up by Eirishman J. P. Holland (1840-1914) to smuggle whiskey out of his native Clare, the *U*- or **Unterschlüpfenboot** formed a key part of German strategic thinking in both world wars. Their tendency towards unrestricted warfare led some to dub them **Unterscheidslosboot**.

which, as Hackett's report put it: 'the trap went off without a hitch.'

The piece was hastily put together, rushed to Dubilin, even more hastily proofed, and printed. Hackett was particularly vexed to read that each time he'd written Banna Strand, all subsequent published versions had inserted an 'a' between the 'n's. It was the first of many typos that would dog his career, so much so that he began to suspect a sinister hand at work. A second typographical error, this time in the attribution, led to the I being placed directly on top of the H so that it resembled nothing so much as the overlapping IHS on a headstone, but without the S that lends to the latter a suggestion of the dollar sign. Hackett was evidently better pleased with this fortuitous error, if fortuitous it was, and from this time adopted it as his lucky glyph. He had little inkling as to the host of misunderstandings that were to attend this whim. Three days later in their pirated version, the populist *Liffey Current* replicated the glyph, and the journalist's celebrity was assured.

The point is that, along with Casement, SM U-19 was also sneaking home the infamous republican spy Ж.[20] At the behest of that German arch-strategist Arthur 'Telegraph' Zimmerman, Ж, along with the benighted Casement, had been drumming up discontent among the thousands of Eirish malcontents then being held in Staligs at the pleasure of the Kaiser. What subsequently became of him is anyone's guess. It may be that, as was reported locally, he slipped and was 'drownded' that

20 Thought to be Ciarán Óg Ua Runai, eldest son of the Fenian firebrand Michael Kieran Rooney, who was himself rumoured to belong to the clandestine Ouroboros Brotherhood. Before he was deported to Van Diemen's Land following the abortive 1867 rebellion, the latter had founded a secret society of spies each of whom later adopted the alias ciaróg.

night while trying to get ashore, or indeed, slipped back onto the boat before it slipped beneath the freijous waves. REC records do record that a badly decomposed body wearing Connemara tweeds but Münster hosiery was washed up at the seaside town of Sneem some weeks later, which is to say, on the very doorstep of the Empire's enigmatic Chief Spymaster, the fabled '**M**' — though as the man's surname was Melville, '**M**' was hardly the last word in cyphers.

Now, Rooney had been lamed in adolescence following an accident involving a bull, though in his case it was his right leg that was a half inch shorter than his left. He was also short-sighted, an affliction common amongst revolutionaries. One way or another, from this time, there developed a rumour, no less persistent for being far-fetched, that the man who penned the Casement article was none other than Rooney himself. How else explain the six-footed I on H glyph, which resembled nothing so much as a geometric form of Ж — the agent's secret cypher? How else explain what appeared to be a first-hand, eyewitness account of the failed subterfuge? How else, the *parvenu* journalist's astonishing rise to a position of trust among the revolutionary brotherhood, even, it was whispered, into the innermost circle of the Big Fellow[21] himself? All that can be added is that, if Hackett was aware of the rumour, as how could he not have been, he never went out of his way to debunk it.

21 Not to be confused with the Long Fellow, who some believe ordered the Big Fellow's assassination.

CHAPTER THE FIFTH

in which Ignatius Hackett takes up the challenge

We left the erstwhile journalist teetering in the utmost confusion outside of the **PALACE BAR**, unaccustomed fantasies together with intimations of failure whirling about his head, an unopened letter sitting in his pocket, and unfamiliar glasses perched upon his nose. The last of these would at least afford him the opportunity to dispel any mystery attending on the penultimate, but whether that clarification would help to calm the antepenultimate remained to be seen.

It was worth a try. A summons, Nugent had klept it. From where he stood, propped at an angle of 30° to an orthogonal lamp post on d'Olier St and 60° to the horizontal, the nearest station of the Garda Síochána was a bare stone's throw away. He was briefly minded of Malachi McCann's quip, how following the founding of the Free State the new police force was divided into two branches: the Garda Síochána, who went out on the beat, and the Garda Suíochána, who didn't. He'd as soon get the business over with. With mutinous fingers Hackett pulled the manila envelope from his pocket, examined with dismay the harp ominously tipping to the right, noted with wryness the governmental absence of a postage stamp.

But though his name had been typed, there was no address. How had the messenger located him?

An Roinn Gnóthaí Eachtracha, ran a legend across the top. Department of Foreign Affairs. He had to read it three times. What the devil had he to do with foreign affairs? He hadn't been out of the country this seven years. Not since… the former journalist hesitated to finish the sentence, even mentally. Something in the interview with Smyllie had revivified the old Hackett, which is to say the young Hackett. It wasn't simply the calculus of how far a thirty pound advance would go toward clearing up his present situation. It was the fact that so revered a figure as R. M. Smyllie wanted him. *Solicited* him. Greeted him with the blazon 'cometh the hour and cometh the man'. But words had once before led to his committal in Swift's Mad House — might they not do so again? He must be circumspect.

But the very second his eye had lighted upon that glyph, three lines vertical crossed by one horizontal — to all intents and purposes the decision made itself. That an article on counterfeit words should have been penned by a counterfeit Hackett was unconscionable. How many more bogus articles were already in circulation? It was outrageous! No-one, but no-one, would be allowed to usurp his literary identity.

A steadier index finger ripped open the envelope. Inside was a card. Identical legend, identical backward harp, though the card was zinc white rather than manila and the writing cursive:

Mr Ignatius Hackett is requested to present at Iveagh House
at 12:30 on Friday 13th inst.
Please present this card upon arrival.

Ok. That didn't sound so bad. He pushed his fingers through his elflocks. No chance of a haircut. The other hand ribbled his chin and encountered there the rebarbative stubble he'd always been prone to. Should he chance a shave in the kip off Lower Dorset St? Had he time?

A thought struck him with the force of a clapper. What time of day *was* it? The half-hunter with escapement he'd inherited had long since gone to the pawnshop. Then a second thought trumped the first. What day of the week was it? He'd neglected to take the newspaper from the bar. Then a third, hot on the heels of the other two. Where was Iveagh House? Beyond in the Phoenix Park, was it? Or by the Iveagh Gardens, maybe?

Had he a chance in hell of making the blessed appointment?

His heart a flighty lark, he strode resolutely to the Garda Station where he promptly discovered the three answers, viz.: that it was already twenty-five minutes to one, that Iveagh House was about ten minutes away by foot, at 70-80 St Stephen's Green; that today was Thursday, which is to say, the twelfth *inst*.

Little is known with certainty about the interview that was held the next day, for such minutes as were taken are protected under the Official Secrets Act and not due to enter the public domain until a period of fifty years has elapsed, which is to say, not before 1986. But this much can be said. By the time Hackett entered the elegant St Stephen's Green establishment that Friday 13th *inst.*, he'd already accepted the challenge thrown down by R. M. Smyllie. Indeed, he'd marched by return to the **PALACE BAR** to tell him so.

No time was lost. He was accompanied to the newspaper

office by Mr Wood, who was mightily relieved to relieve him of his, Wood's, spectacles. There he, Hackett, signed for an advance of five five pound notes with the balance in coin, that he might the more readily discharge his debt at one go to the odious Nugent. With the balance, he redeemed his own spectacles and *Underwood* typewriter, in that order, and also a small, battered travelling case he'd had since his college days. It was a matter of considerable sadness that funds would not, for the present, extend to redeeming the heirloom fob-watch with escapement that was his only tangible memory, as it were, of Walter Hackett.

It is worth pausing to consider this typewriter.

With the payment received for his eyewitness account of the Easter Monday ambuscade, the young student had at once decided to invest in a machine that was, to his mind, the very tool of the journalistic trade, as the trowel is the tool of a builder and the saw the tool of the carpenter. It was wartime, a time of inflation and privation, and he soon found that the money he'd been advanced would extend no further than a secondhand dactylograph that dated from the 1890s. True, it boasted the innovative keyboard that had been designed by Prof. Qwerty for the Remington Mark 2. What it lacked were the safety features introduced with the outbreak of the Great War — the mechanical rotary spellcheck, the autocorrect, the rudimentary bogus term detector — instituted in order to forestall the linguistic mayhem that Count Zimmerman, the German Foreign Secretary, had been threatening to unleash along with bundles of counterfeit money and misleading bulletins: falsche Worte, falscher Sterling und eine Flut triviale Tatsachen, a war-cry recently taken up by Dr Goebbels.

The third member of this triad was greatly to be feared. Counterfeit words, like counterfeit money, were quantifiable annoyances. But counterfeit sentences, generating counterfeit facts? It was scarcely to be countenanced. There was a precedent for Zimmerman's threat. During the reign of Frederick the Great, an eccentric follower of Bishop Berkeley immortalised for setting down the problem of the seven bridges of Königsburg filed a patent for a steam-powered press that was intended to manufacture synthetic *a priori* statements. In the wrong hands the effect such an infernal machine would have had on comprehensibility can only be described as dastardly. However, due to persistent category errors, it only ever produced what came to be called, in ironic tribute to its inventor, cant. But the dream had never died. Nor was experimentation confined to Imperial Germany. In 1884, Sir Hiram Stevens lodged a patent for a semi-automated 'maxim' gun aimed at distributing rapid-fire bulletins throughout the British Empire. It, too, failed. Fearing that Teutonic ingenuity had at last overcome the difficulties, in 1915 a raft of safety measures was rushed in by Lord Beaverbrook, soon to be appointed Minister of Information. All typewriters from this time should at the least incorporate the rotary mechanical autocorrect function.

It might be asked, why did the journalist not now invest in a model that incorporated these rudimentary features, as the vast majority of models did? It might be answered that, even had he the funds, Hackett had inherited from his father a superstitious bent. The ancient machine had brought him luck. Besides, as Smyllie himself had affirmed, it's the old dog for the hard road. Having redeemed this trusty *Underwood*,

Hackett marched directly to the National Library on Kildare St, where he spent the balance of the day and all of the following morning apprising himself of "the spate of lexical crimes currently assailing the hereditary foe."

Second Best was celebrated for the encyclopaedic cast of his mind, and when he wasn't poring over the archives, Hackett spent a most profitable hour in commerce with the Chief Librarian. It was from him that he learned that the carpenter he'd witnessed in Trinity College was repairing the aftermath of a break in. Someone had breached the door leading to the celebrated Long Room where they'd made off, not with the Book of Kells, which would have been an outrage of international note, not with the Leabhar Gabhálaighe, the renowned Book of Invasions which was on temporary loan from the Royal Eirish Academy, but its lesser known sequel, the apocryphal Leabhar Gabh Abhaile. Why anyone would have desired, commissioned or suborned such a theft was anyone's guess, and yet it excited Hackett's attention. The theft put Mr Best in mind of a notorious break in at the Ashmoleon Library several years before the Great War. 'A break in?' Hackett ribbled his chin. 'I never heard tell of a break in.' He considered for a moment. 'I remember a fire.'

'Indeed,' said Mr Best. 'A most devastating fire. It was the night of April the 13th 1912. A fire swept through the entire Russell Wing. Arson was suspected, but never proved. Many museum items were saved. Naturally there was smoke damage. And worse again there was water damage, on account of the Fire Brigade was a little too enthusiastic.' At this point Best paused, to call to mind the doleful litany. Gravely he recited, 'Lost forever was the only extant copy of a 12th century Confessions of St Botolph, apocryphal. Lost, three Mystery plays, incomplete, forming an invaluable part of the Christminster Cycle. Lost, the 9th Century Mayan Xlotopl Codex, with its puzzling depiction of the bearded figure with tonsure rowing a currough. Lost forever, extinct, as you might say, an entire Saxon bestiary. Lost, a fragment of rhinoceros said to be from the inkhorn of Bede. Lost too his rosary, the vaunted venerable beads. And, most grievously, *most* grievously,' he paused for effect, 'lost forever was the Wooton-Hey word-hoard. In its entirety.'

'Remind me,' prompted Hackett.

'Lost, the Wooton-Hey word-hoard, in its entirety. And with it, its wealth of Old Engelish compound-words in the full array of grammatical cases; lost, its smattering of Old Norse and Celtic loanwords not found in other hoards. Lost, the two strong variations on the weak declension genitive that never made it into *Sweet's Anglo-Saxon Primer* and very controversially, lost forever, the future tense of the verbs *ridan*, *lufian* and *beon*.'

'Do you tell me so! Is it any wonder,' Hackett shook his head, 'Old Engelish never had a future?' If he wasn't appalled at the memory of this irremediable loss, he was making a damn good fist of appearing so. 'But you intimated that fire was a smokescreen. I'm not with you.'

'*May* have been a smokescreen,' pronounced the Chief Librarian, for he was a firm adherent of the commendable principle Wovon man nicht sprechen kann, darüber muss man schweigen, 'All I'll say on the subject is that there have been occasional sightings of objects thought lost. Not all genuine, I needn't tell you. A rhino horn and set of venerable beads that surfaced last year in Rome were an obvious forgery. In Zürich during the war, on the other hand, it was reported on better authority that a smattering of lost terms from the Wooton-Hey was for sale on the black market.'

'Do you tell me so,' said Hackett. All this was grist to the windmill of his imagination. At the same time, an imaginary mouse was chasing off in another direction. 'But in the name of all that's sacred, what has any of this to do with the passing off of counterfeit terms in the Home Counties?'

'That I can't say.'

'And tell me, is it really as fromulous as they say it is?'

'Well now,' said Best, scratching his pate, 'that is difficult to say. If there is a concerted attack on the language underway, it might well prove every bit as fromulous as the Δ affair.'

'Δ?'

'Surely you remember. The botched attack on Greenwitch Observatory?'

'The Greenwitch Observatory. I remember a tagline,' said Hackett, and he recited, as though seeing it before his eyes, '*An impenetrable mystery seems destined to hang for ever over this act of madness and despair*.'

'You wrote a piece on it yourself, on the occasion of the thirtieth anniversary.'[22]

A spark lit Hackett's eye and he knucked his fingers. 'You mean, Δ alias Virag?'

'Δ alias Verloc.'

'Not Vidocq?'

22 Best is, of course, referencing the notorious attempt by the French anarchist Martial Bourdin to blow up the First Meridian which took place on February 15th 1894. Curiously, T.S. Eliot's 1928 poem 'Animula' asks us to pray 'for Boudin, blown to pieces', *boudin* suggesting, here, black pudding.

'Not at all, man. Vidocq was alias Vautrin.'

'Oh. Then who was Virag?'

'Virag was nobody.'[23]

Hackett considered. 'I seem to remember,' he continued, 'the Δ plan was to destroy the First Meridian itself.'

'And you, alias Ж, made an interesting comparison to the shock to the calendar that resulted from the Copernican revolution. With your permission?' The worthy librarian here unfrabbled a facsimile of an old newspaper article on the desk.

> 'In 1543, Polish astronomer Nicholas Copernicus proposed that, since the sun's mass was many times that of the earth, it would be more efficient mechanically for the earth to go around the sun in so-called Copernican revolutions rather than vice versa. Such a cosmic shift was initially opposed by the geocentric lobby championed by Pope Gregory, who feared that if the axis of rotation was suddenly removed to the sun, the jolt would lead to a need to recalibrate calendars by a factor of eleven days. His bold prediction was in fact borne out, and the new dating system was named in Gregory's honour. It was a kneejerk reaction to 'all things Roman' which led to Britain and her colonies retaining the old style calendar until 1752. Despite this belated change, in Ulster, the Orange Lodges persist to this day to celebrate the rout of James by Billy at the Boyne on July 1st 1690 as the 'Glorious 12th'.

23 Best is possibly confusing the bomber with the anarchist Verloc (Oscar Homolka) of Hitchcock's *Sabotage* which was showing in cinemas at that time. Who Virag might be is anybody's guess.

> All this is well documented. What is far from clear is what chaos would have ensued had Monsieur Bourdin succeeded in his reprehensible plan to blow up the First Meridian. Train timetables, one assumes, would be the first casualty. After all, it was the need for reliable train timetables that gave impetus to the standardisation that led to Greenwich Mean Time. And the second casualty? Surely the hard-won standardisation of clocks across the maritime world upon which the Royal and Merchant navies rely…'

Hackett smiled, something he hadn't done in seven years. 'I remember penning that chap in this very room. Those were the days, eh?'

Mr Best concurred.

'An outrage to discombobulate time!' he shuddered. 'And an attack on the language?'

'Every bit as fromulous.'

It was food for thought. And when, an hour later, Hackett sat across the desk from a Mr Chandler in a back office in Iveagh House, 70-80 St Stephen's Green, it meant that his attention was very much divided. He scarcely noticed that the letters of introduction and travel documents with which the official was furnishing him were consequent upon his having taken up Smyllie's challenge. And yet it was the summons itself which had impelled Hackett to seek refuge in a public house where Smyllie's offer was awaiting him. And that would be putting the cart before the horse, since until that chance meeting, there was no occasion whatsoever for Hackett to be sitting across the desk from this Chandler character, who together with a ticket for the mail-boat, was passing him letters of introduction all bearing the logo of the backward harp. So which was the cause, and which the effect? It was a problem the match of Baron Munchausen's, the time he pulled himself up out of the swamp by his own pigtail.[24] As Hackett's thought pursued that particular conundrum, his errant attention was snatched by a name. 'Sorry, did you say Seumas Chapman?' he enquired.

Chandler observed him. 'Seumas Chapman, yes.'

'Good old Chippy. I was in school with the man.'

'Mr Chapman is Cultural Attaché at the Court of St James in Logdon. You'll be, nominally, his Private Secretary.'

'Will I, 'faith!' Now, Hackett's first thought was to recall the chubby character with the snub-nose and strubbly fingers from his childhood. His second was, Cultural Attaché, *him*? Sure Chippy Chapman had about as much culture in him as one of Alexander Fleming's Petri dishes! And he must have given voice to the latter thought, for he found the officious Chandler frundling at him. 'Before you go over, you might dig out a dossier to forward to the Cultural Attaché.'

'A dossier. On what?'

Chandler shook his head. 'On some aspect of language.'

'Anything in particular?' inquired Hackett, who was beginning to suspect that the whole enterprise might be some elaborate practical joke. But to what end?

---

24 Based on this remarkable feat, any situation of self-illustration Walter Hackett had dubbed the Munchausen Principle. Like his father, Hackett Jr found something innately satisfying in things that obeyed the Munchausen Principle. It was satisfying that the term desuetude had fallen into desuetude. The word polysyllabic, for being polysyllabic, afforded pleasure to the tongue. Contrariwise, that hyphenated was non-hyphenated and non-hyphenated hyphenated he took as an affront.

‘Might I suggest Geneva with their new Science of Signs?’ the official went on, rising from the desk as though to intimate the interview was ending. ‘In any case, something which will be beyond the Cultural Attaché’s ken.’

Find something to bamboozle Chippy Chapman? It was hardly a Herculean task. Still, he was thrown by the idea. ‘But why would I do that?’

‘It is envisaged he will then pass this dossier back to you for clarification. In this way two birds will be killed with the one stone. You yourself will have gained an overview of Geneva and what they’re up to over there, and you will have gained Mr Chapman’s confidence. Do you follow?’

‘I do,’ said Hackett. He did not. He followed, instead, the official out of the office.

It would be a mistake to imagine that all our hero’s misgivings in regard to reengaging with language had been put to bed. Seven years before, a form of aphasia had petrified his thoughts. It’s a common misapprehension that the condition implies a paucity of words; it may equally indicate a plethora. Hackett was congenitally prone to just such superabundance in which meanings proliferate. Two nights before he sailed, it so happened that a troupe of travelling players was mounting *Hamlet* at Dubilin’s notorious Gate Theatre, the Dane to be played by a celebrated cross-dresser. Hackett had long been an aficionado of the Bard, and as he had no great wish to dawdle in the Dorset St doss, he betook himself to the show. All preceded apace until the famous soliloquy. No sooner had the Prince pronounced the phrase ‘the pale cast of thought’ than Hackett’s irrepressible pangúr bán set off in pursuit of a half-dozen mice. Pale, he mused, signifies etiolated. But also a bucket, though in the early modern period, a defensive stockade. It was invitation enough to think beyond the pale. The crux, the mice taunted, is in the syntax. Was pale noun or adjective? And what to make of cast — noun or verb? And if verb, was thought doer or done to? One might cast a bronze, or a bucket, or aspersions, or a cold eye, or a shadow, or a net, or doubt, or indeed a play. Did not the arrival of the players at Elsinore suggest this last, making the other actors the pale cast of the Dane's thoughts? By the time Hackett's thoughts came to consider whether it was the native colour, cut or clamour of resolution that said pale cast was sicklying over, Polonius had been stabbed in the arras and the Prince, dispatched to Engeland.

CHAPTER THE SIXTH

in which Ignatius Hackett bamboozles his superior with a Socratic dialogue on the value of a 10/- note

On a blusterly Sunday some fortnight later, a Bentley with diplomatic plates was muttling along Oxenford Street in the direction of Mobled Arch, that landmark marble monument named for the eponymous mobled queen. The newly appointed secretary to the Eirish Cultural Attaché, a man by the name of Hackett, was momentarily distracted by its white splendour. Without glancing at his superior, whose nose had been stuck in a dossier from the minute they'd set out, he opined: "faith, they seem to do things on a grand scale altogether over this side of the water.'

'What's that?' frundled Chapman, pressing a strubbly finger to a word midway through a particularly difficult paragraph.

'Whatever else you might say about them, Chippy, and there's a great deal you could say mind, they do think…' his hands forming a wreath, Hackett searched for the adjective adequate to his admiration, '…big.' He nodded, satisfied. 'You'd have to give them that.'

Chapman glanced up from the page and twitched as

though bothered by a midge. Hackett waited to see if the finger would be lifted from the page. It remained fast, as though glued to flypaper. 'The **SASSNAIS** man!' he exclaimed. 'Could you imagine plonking a monument the size of that bloody great wedding-cake into the middle of Dame St? Bad enough they left their Admirable Nelson behind them to keep a blind eye on us.'

'Look it, Hackett,' growled Chapman, 'you're new to this game. Let me give you my candid and considered opinion. There's things you can say, and there's things you can't say. D'you follow me?' The difficult paragraph flopping over onto his lap, the Cultural Attaché peered above his reading glasses to examine the individual who, on his recommendation (it would seem), had been drafted post-haste into the Diplomatic Corps. Hackett was many things: a former schoolmate, the class jester in point of fact; a consummate mimic; a public-house orator; an amateur of natural philosophy more given to speculation than experiment; an incorrigible debtor; an insufferable braggart; a scurril, and a sometime journalist of considerable renown. A man, as the wag said, with a great future behind him. For by all accounts he'd latterly developed into a bit of a scapegrace. He drew his strubbly fingers three times through the thin ribs of his ginger hair. 'There's places you can say things,' he resumed, to quell an uneasy feeling that in some way he was being set up for a patsy, 'and there's places you can't say things. If you want my candid and considered opinion, when we get to where we're going we've to walk on eggshells. D'you follow me?'

All the while that Chapman had been considering the dossier, his secretary had been examining the side-squint with which he was being eyed. It was curiously eloquent, even nuanced, given how poor was its owner in either quality. It was a squint redolent of that incongruous cocktail of emotions with which the doltish superior must needs contemplate the more intelligent subordinate whom happenstance has set beneath him. A *tanner* to a *make* the Germans had a word for it.[25] Three parts satisfaction that service had at last o'ertopped gifted indolence; but undermined by one part existential insecurity based upon their relative merits. Add in a soupçon of guilt, a generous dash of told-you-so, decorate with a smarmy cherry and leave to stand for fear of upsetting the hierarchy. **Smugsguilt** [smʌg'zgɪlt] *n., the uneasy feeling occasioned by finding that one is at last in charge of one's better...* Now, if Hackett, who had just then coined it, could patent the word, could he make a few bob out of it? 'Sorry did you say something?' his reflex queried aloud.

'I mean it now,' resumed the Cultural Attaché. 'By all accounts we'll have to walk on eggshells with these Academy folk. They're not at all used to letting foreigners in on their machinations.'

'Is that what we are now?' exclaimed Hackett. 'Foreigners, is it? If that's the case, would you mind explaining to me just what precisely Britannia thinks she's been at for the last seven centuries over where she was never invited?'[26] But even as

25 Hackett is offering notional odds of 12/1 here, based on the respective Dublin slang terms for 6^{d} and ½ ^{d}.

26 Hackett is being disingenuous. In 1169, Dermot McMurrough, King of Leinster, did in fact invite the Welsh mercenary and cider-brewer Richard Fitz Gilbert de Clare (aka 'Strongbow') to Drogheda to attend his daughter Aoife's wedding breakfast. A notorious mistranslation into the Cambro-Norman led Strongbow to believe that he was to be the groom. Having married, Strongbow was nothing if not acquisitive. This was so much the case that within the year Henry II followed him to Eirland, disturbed by the man's propensity to begin each speech: 'I de Clare..'

he was saying this his mind was elsewhere, distracted by the chauffeur's protruding ears upon which sat his chauffeur's hat. And he could see in the rearview mirror the man had protruding lips that could near whistle into his own ear. Bedamned but Hackett was sure he'd encountered this character somewhere before. But where?

As Hackett pondered, Chapman flicked the difficult paragraph back to the upright. But if his eyes could focus on the words, his thoughts could not. It'd been donkey's since they'd laid eyes on each other, but this much was common knowledge. Ignatius Hackett was a man who, in his day, could've walked into the office of any editor in the country and commanded three columns. Hackett, who twenty years since had been in the eye of the maelstrom with pen to hand on that much-sung Easter Monday. Hackett who'd somehow got the mole's eye view of Frongoch, and Hackett who, it was whispered with something approaching awe, had scooped an interview with that Free State Radical himself, the Big Fellow. His journalistic interventions were admired alike by friend and foe. What was he saying, admired? They were studied, man! They were collected with scissors and paste, and pinned to the notice boards of editorial offices the length and breadth of the country for the edification of the apprentice hacks!

And he was damnably lucky. All his career, it was as though some God of Chance had been looking out for him, giving him the tip-off as to where and when the next big story was about to break. It so fell out that, just prior to his arrival at the Court of St James, the Grimaldi Affair had erupted into full swing. It's hardly necessary to recount the furore that gripped

Covenant Garden[27] when the Italian Foreign Minister Count Giuseppe Grimaldi, a man known for his sense of punctilio, with that characteristic Latin mixture of braggadocio and sprezzatura made his infamous threat at the League of Nations to repatriate all Italian loanwords *senza dire nulla* if the *Duce's* armies weren't given a freer hand in Abyssinia. Characteristically the affair turned out a fiasco. But it was a sight to behold over the next several days the undignified scramble among the tuxedoed classes to find synonyms for the likes of *andante cantabile* and *sotto voce, pianoforte* and *viola da gamba*, and then, how utterly sheepish everyone looked after the imbroglio subsided.

And then Hackett, with his damnable knack of being in the right place at the right time, had arrived just as the threat was withdrawn and the panic waned. '*Finita la commedia,*' he'd written for the *Munchester Warden*. 'To anyone who witnessed the farrago at first hand it was *opera buffa* from start to finish.' In no time at all he'd a piece tossed off that would run to a half-dozen column inches entitled 'Settling Old Scores.' It was enough to vex a more temperate man. Throwing the journalist a squinny, Chapman skipped a couple of pages and resumed his perusal.

For a while they muttled on in fulmering silence in the direction of Ealing Broadleaf, Chapman struggling to come to terms with the arcane vocabulary of the dossier, Hackett struggling to come to terms with the urge to take it off the

27 A fashionable square designed by Indigo Jones for the fourth Earl of Bedford, so named because his great grandfather had received the lands in 1552 by a deed of covenant. It has a long-standing association with fruits, tarts, and opera.

man and spell it out for him. Chippy Chapman had never been the shiniest shilling in the purse. And hadn't the plan all along been to win his supposed superior's confidence by explaining the blessed dossier to him? Hadn't Chandler the handler urged as much? Thrice, he'd suggested he might help with a recherché phrase. Thrice his offer had been haughtily refused. Stubbornness, pure and simple. Hackett would share his erudition if Chapman would share his incomprehension. Chapman, as was his wont, wouldn't.

But if he was impatient to watch the dullard push his strubbly finger from paragraph to paragraph while blowing like a grampus, he was distracted by thoughts of their destination. Like everyone else, Hackett had never heard of a Royal Academy of Letters. Oh to be sure he'd heard rumours. There were always rumours. A secret cartel keeping an eye on matters orthographic and syntactical from behind the stage-curtain. But if he'd heard stage-whispers, they'd remained just that. So much hearsay and so much heresy. He'd remained as convinced as the next man that no Royal Academy of Letters existed. That no Academy of Letters *could* exist. It all seemed too un-Engelish, the way that Catholicism is un-Engelish; or streets that are named for dates; or decimal coinage; or driving on the wrong side of the road. He shuffled in his seat, as though engaging in dialogue. Well might you expect the French to have their precious Académie Française and to do precious little to conceal the fact. Their Académie was a fait accompli; a national monument to francophone hubris was de rigueur. Or the Spaniard, how inordinately orgulous he was of how his *Real Academia* kept a sober eye on their concordance of nouns and adjectives. That was the European way. The continental system. But His Majesty's government? Wayward Edward or George the Stutterer? *Man dear*, it was too far-fetched!

Oh, to be sure there'd always been the Royal Academy. But for the Sciences, mind. British Empiricism. Imperial measure and the statute mile and half a hundred weight the ha'pence. Sir Isaac Newton had been a founding member. And Boyle's Law, wasn't he involved?[28] And then, when that creature was such a roaring success, a twin sister was found and founded for the Arts. But you could equally understand a Royal Academy of the Arts. The academic style, that was by way of the natural order of things. The Arts are run on patronage, on the principle that the aristocracy patronise the artist so that the artist can patronise the aristocracy. But an Academy for the Engelish Language, keeping a weather eye on dangling participles? It was too fanciful by half!

Furtively, he cast a glance at Chapman. The whole idea behind the blessed dossier had been to win the man's confidence. But if his old schoolmate was a dullard, he was an obdurate one. That was the factor that Chandler the handler had left out of the equation. 'How are you making out with our Swiss friend?'

'Hunh! All so much mumbo-jumbo, if you ask me.'

'Might I…' tried Hackett, but Chapman petulantly flicked

---

28 Hackett presumably intends Robert Boyle, Earl of Lismore, who should not be confused with Charles Boyle, Earl of Orrery (q.v.). In 1649, Boyle patented the pressure cooker. In referring to him as Boyle's Law, Hackett is perhaps conflating the Eirish genius with Bonar Law, though their dates scarcely match. While Boyle's Law is an example of a law where the *product* remains constant ($PV=k$), the Earl's cook Cole's Law is summative, so that for a given volume of the eponymous produce, it is the *sum* of the shredded cabbage, C, carrot, K, and onion, O which remains constant ($C+K+O=k$).

the paper away from his impudent Secretary. He bit into the quick of his thumb and stared again at the diagram. Finally, he relented. 'The Sign, mar dhea,[29] Bedamned if I can make head or tail of it.' And he allowed the paper to fall onto his knee in such a manner that Hackett might, if he leaned, peruse it. It was invitation enough. 'The latest from Geneva. It's their new Science of Signs'

The Cultural Attaché squinted. 'What have the Swiss to tell anyone about signs?'

'They rallied four langages to their flag, which is a big plus. Simply put, the Geneva Contention is that there's no necessary relationship between what they term the Signifier and the Signified.' As Chapman's thumb was pitilessly gnawed, Hackett's followed the arrow on the chart back from the figure S to the figure S*.

'What's that arrow, if it's not a relationship?'

'No *necessary* relationship,' Hackett reiterated, as though the qualifier were essential.

'The Signifier?'

'In a word, a word.'

'So the Signified is the thing. Big deal.'

'The *notional* thing.' The glower suggested what Hackett could do with his *notional*. 'An example, perhaps. Take a rose. Then the Signifier is the *name* of the rose.'

'The name of the rose.'

'Which, as the Bard reminds us, bears no necessary relation to its smell. The theory runs that signifiers — words — are held in place only by differences. A rose is a rose by

29 An Eirish interjection which is the verbal equivalent of raising supercilious eyebrows and indicating parentheses with one's fingers.

virtue of not being a nose.'

Chapman smelled a rat. 'Humph! So S is the actual rose.'

'You misunderstand. S is the notional rose.'

'And the real rose?' gruffed Chapman, as his complexion rose.

'Language doesn't require a real rose. A real rose is either red or white, d'you get me? But not your notional rose.'

'Aha! I've got you there! What about the War of the Roses, eh?' A strubbly finger poked his Secretary's chest. 'The Yorvik rose is white, Hackett, and the Lanaster rose is red! So much for your notional rose not being red or white!'

'Not so fast,' retorted the Secretary, before whose imagination appeared a hand of worried playing cards painting white roses red. 'The Yorvik rose may be white as snow. But the Yorvik rose is a *symbolic* rose.' A frundle suggested what Hackett could do with his *symbolic*. 'Whereas the notional rose is at once both red and white.'

The Cultural Secretary whiffed victory and readied his five of trumps.[30] 'Then it's the Tudor rose! That's at once both red and white. I've got you there, Hackett.'

30 Presumably the metaphorical game is 'twenty-five', a simple trick-taking game popular among Eirish children in which, in trumps, the Five beats the Jack, the Jack the Ace; in which the Ace of Hearts is permanently the third highest trump, the Ace of trumps being the fourth highest unless Hearts are trumps; but which has the compensatory merit of allowing the holder of the Ace to rob the turned trump, the dealer naturally enough having the right to rob the same in the event of its being an Ace; in which one must follow a trump lead with a trump but may renege with the Five or Jack, unless the lead has been the Five; and must likewise follow suit in non-trumps, unless playing a trump; and in which the non-court cards follow a sequence from Ace down to Ten in the black suits and Ten down to Ace in the red suits, always excepting the Ace of Hearts, the Ace of Diamonds thus being the worst of Diamonds, unless of course Diamonds have been turned up trumps.

'A notional rose is also pink,' resumed the Secretary, unperturbed. 'And yellow. And damask. In fact, the notional rose covers every possible shape and colour that a real rose might assume. Clear?'

In proportion as the Cultural Attaché sank into his seat, his colour rose along with his choler until it too was at once both red and white. His fingers fiddled at his collar, his brow frundled into rows. 'And you subscribe to this Geneva nonsense do you?'

Hackett's smile arced until it became arch. 'I'm not so sure,' his eyebrows waggled. 'The question, it seems to me, is how do you fix the value of a notional term.'

'In plain Engelish?'

'Precisely. How do you define words in such a way as to fix their value?'

'But that's what a dictionary is for,' squinnied the Cultural Attaché, suspicious.

'Is it?' gruffed Hackett. 'I'm not so sure about that, either. Perhaps our friends in the Academy of Letters can help us out.'

'Help us out how? I don't see the problem.'

'No, I daresay you don't. But you do see this?' Hackett, opening his wallet, pulled from it the last remaining 10/- banknote. This he unfolded diligently and laid atop the Attaché's attaché case. 'What would you call that, now?'

'That? That's ten bob.'

'That's how much it is. But *what* is it,' he tapped the 10/- note three times, '*really*?'

'What is it,' Chapman too sat forwards, 'really?' He guffawed, not with mirth. 'It's money. Lucre. Pounds sterling.' Pause. '*Money*!'

'Ah! But what's money?'

'You're asking me what's money?' Chapman deflated like a tyre. 'It's… legal tender. Coin of the realm. Pounds, shillings and pence.' He gasped. 'Money is money!'

'What if I was to tell you,' pondered Hackett, 'that this 10/-note wasn't money at all?'

Chapman shook his head, his panic growing. '*Not* money!' Then, with a snap of the fingers he sprang forwards, springs detonating in the seat beneath him. The penny had dropped. 'It's counterfeit!' he calloohed, triumphantly.

'You misunderstand my meaning.'

'Melancholy Christ,' whimpered Chapman, as though he hadn't the heart to pronounce the dubit out loud, 'aren't you after saying to me it's *not* money?'

'What if I was to put it to you that any bank bill is the *symbol* of money?'

'Stop!' cried Chapman, so loud that the chauffeur started. 'Stop!' he cried. He swallowed hard to quell an uneasy vertigo. 'You might just as well say, with the knight in the fairy-tale, that it's the *name* of what a song is called.' Because bedamned if it wasn't some class of a trap his accursed Secretary was setting.

'You don't believe me? Take it up,' a sweep of Hackett's hand invited. 'Please!'

Desperately, for it just might be counterfeit after all, he raised the orange bill and examined the portrait of the past king. The one that had passed on, not the one that had passed up the chance.

'What does it say? Read it to me.'

'*I promise to pay the bearer on demand the sum of ten*

shillings sterling.' That much was plain sailing. Unless he was about to ask how a dead king could be expected to pay anyone anything. Though you could still pay him your respects.

'So tell me this and tell me no more. If you brought that note in to the Old Lady of Threadneedle Street, would you be happy if she just gave it back to you and said "there's your ten bob, sir"?' A pause, for effect. 'Of course you wouldn't! You might just as well say that a bankrupt might clear his overdraft by writing a cheque. Why, it'd be another case of Baron Munchausen pulling himself from the swamp by his own ponytail!' If the secretary noticed the waxing despair on his superior's face, he gave no indication of it. 'But tell me,' he continued without mercy, 'what would make you happy? Would you be content if he passed you four half-crowns?'

Chapman was stumped. It wasn't the mathematics that was causing him the difficulty. It was that he could see that no matter what way he answered this question, another was sure to follow. And if he answered that one? So he let out a snort, as much as to say I know what you're driving at. Eight half-crowns made four crowns made twenty shillings the pound, so that four half-crowns made up a 10/- note. A child could do the sums. But this Mephistopheles had something besides arithmetic up his sleeve. He smiled, weakly. Blinked affably.

'You'll tell me, Ah-ha! But the half-crowns are silver. The bank-note is only paper.'

Chapman paused, considered, nodded desperately.

'But if it's silver itself, it's debased silver. Diluted. Watered down. But let's suppose, just for a moment, the cashier hands you a gold half-sovereign.' A pause for effect. 'Are you satisfied?' Like a punch-drunk fighter, Chapman nodded. 'Of course you are. Very good. So now a new problem presents itself. What will you do with your gold? What *value* has it?'

Something low, a whimper, emanated from the Cultural Attaché.

'Well, you can readily exchange Troy ounces for the equivalent in…?' he prompted.

Like a punch-drunk fighter, Chapman winced. 'In…?'

A whimper.

'In pounds, shillings and pence?'

'Stop!' cried Hackett's superior. 'For pity's sake, stop!' It was a sobering moment. It was a moment when Hackett realised that, as was his wont, he'd allowed the imaginary mice to lead his thoughts every which way. But it also coincided with a logistical resolution, as it were. Because if the unfortunate Cultural Attaché was no nearer to comprehending a blessed word of what he'd been perusing, the diplomatic Bentley was much nearer to its destination. Indeed, it was just at that moment passing a great red-brick Victorian building upon the gates of which was chiselled the grim legend:

Parolles' Mental Asylum

Had the Cultural Attaché been less bamboozled, he might have derived an obscure pleasure from the involuntary wince that the chiselled words appeared to occasion in his travelling companion.

Within a half-mile, the Bentley pulled into a dusty courtyard off Ealing Broadleaf and puttled to a halt where a footman in somewhat shabby livery stood attentive.

'Could I have my ten bob back?' asked Hackett.

CHAPTER THE SEVENTH

in which a meeting is convened in the bowels of the Academy of Letters wherein many interesting and heretofore unimagined matters are discussed

The building into which the two visitors were butlered had all the appearances of a ramshackle affair; a tenement perhaps, that had been earmarked for refurbishment but from which the decorators had departed leaving the job half done. The windows had been whitewashed on the inside, but in an uneven manner, with translucent brushstrokes clearly visible. The floorboards were uncarpeted; the paint on the walls discoloured and peeling; the light bulbs naked. Even the brass plaque, which was on the door's interior, and which bore the impressive legend:

Royal Academy of Letters
MDCCXIV
Legere, et non intelligere, neglegere est

was so tarnished as to have become difficult to read; and if read, difficult to understand. An illegible sign screwed to the reverse side of a door — that was taking the Engelish flair for understatement just a tad too far! Their shabby escort, whose bulging eyes high on a forehead and downturned mouth gave him the aspect of a newt, coughed invitingly into an off-white glove before submerging into the gloomy interior. Before long, the heroes found themselves in a large if not much more impressive boardroom, dominated by a mahogulous table. This was more in line with what Hackett had been expecting. So, too, the cetaceous Home Secretary, in dress-suit and great white whiskers, who was dominating the head of the table. 'Good of you to join us, Chapman. This the chap you wrote us about?'

'It is, Sir Æthelred. Ignatius Hackett.' Without rising from their places, the other figures made themselves known. In place of a certain O'Brien, the Academy's Hereditary Director, there were McTurcaill and Hastings, the one Commissioner, the other Decommissioner. Or vice versa. Opposite these in voluptuous paisley waistcoat and open ulster sat Sol Isaacs, the orgulous press baron. There was an ancient, tweedy Professor Emeritus from Oxenford, a gaunt and bewhiskered linguist whose name was misplaced. There was a Tipperary Viscount by name of Bracken, though his hauteur could scarcely have been more Etonian. An ally of that maverick Churchill,[31] he'd come merely to listen, he declared, and his one intervention during the proceedings was to annunciate 'quite right!' anytime anyone underscored the present danger. And there was a conspicuously empty seat in which an Inspector Quibble of the Yard had failed to materialise. His absence hovered like

31 A Liberal and then Tory politician largely remembered for his restoration of the gold standard at a ruinous rate of £1=$4, for his foolhardy foray into the Dardanelles some years earlier, and for his advocacy, as First Lord of the Admiralty, of a policy of "rum, sodomy and the lash". During the Second World War, he gained notoriety for giving journalists the two fingers.

a question mark punctuating all the proceedings that followed.

An advisor who was dandering imperturbably behind Sir Æthelred's chair leaned forwards and whispered into the latter's venerable ear. The Home Secretary snorted and motioned him away. 'Heard a good deal about you, Mr Hackett. Read a thing or two, too.' Hackett was unsure if something was being asked of him, so his gag-reflex kicked in. 'As the postman said to the typesetter, I am a man of letters.' The Home Secretary stared hard, as though he dubited the evidence of his ears. Was this Eirishman pulling his leg? When the dubit began to extend over the entire mahogulous surface, Isaacs, whose inflection made one think of a West End theatre promoter and whose cherub lips seemed formed to suck on a Havana cigar, picked up the thread. 'Hackett. Yeeees. Used to write a good line in your day.' Hackett eyed him as he would a goer in a parade ring before risking a few bob. Sol Isaacs had been editor of the *Sun* and *Star* before they turned tabloid. A contemporary quip ran "we're all of us writing for the gutter, but some of us are looking to the *Star*." Was it out of tact he made no mention of Hackett's hackwork for the *Peerglass* and the *Evening Exposure*? The press baron flashed a gold-spangled smile. 'In his day, this man commanded the ear of Smyllie himself! And to think, he never mastered shorthand.' The gold spangles were directed now at Hackett alone. 'The Grimaldi fiasco, eh? "Settling Old Scores", very clever. Word is, you have… connections.' A strubbly finger tapped a conspiratorial nostril. 'You must call on me. Maybe you can write something for my people.' Deft as a prestidigitator, he conjured a business card from the sleeve of his ulster and slid it across to the journalist.

'Let's cut to the chase,' gruffed Sir Æthelred. One flipper-hand flapped over a large green tome on the table before him. 'I told you I smelled a rat, and what we need to do is to nip it in the bud! Tell me, Hackett, you're familiar with this man Dinneen?'

'Dinneen,' he considered. 'The long-jump man played half-back for Offaly is it?' Something resembling a gruntle emanated from the throat of the Home Secretary, and a side-whisper from his compatriot hissed: 'ná bí i do bhrodach a mhic-ó,' a phrase which might be glossed *don't be acting the eejit, sonny Jim*. 'If I may,' put in the Professor Emeritus, whose mane of white hair lent his elongated features an equine mien, 'the Dinneen Sir Æthelred is referring to is Dinneen the lexicographer.'

'Damnation!' blustered Sir Æthelred, his moustaches working like the tusks of a walrus, 'say it in plain Engelish blast you!'

'Dinneen,' echoed Hackett, ribbling his chin after the manner of an actor in repertory. 'Poor Paddy the Priest, is it? The late and lamented compiler of the Foclóir Gaedhilge that's been raising so many semantic eyebrows...'

'The...?' queried McTurcaill, or Hastings — one of the two Wardens at any rate, who resembled one another not so much with a familial as with an institutional likeness.

'Foclóir, gentlemen, is the Gaedhilic for dictionary,' smiled Chapman, his vexation with his old classmate peeking through the tatters of his smile and taking much of the good out of it. It was his candid and considered opinion that Hackett's cleverality was too clever by half. Hastings, or McTurcaill, the other one in any event, evidently hadn't been attentive. 'Sorry, what did you say your folklore was?'

'A dictionary.' Momentarily caught off balance, Chapman made to explicate. 'Everything from *aardvark* to… ahm,' he floundered.

'*Zymurgy*,' put in Hackett, who always liked to have the last word.

'Tell us, Mr Hackett, are you very familiar with this new… dictionary?' This was the other of the two. 'If I may,' he went on, pulling a bulging notebook from his breast pocket, licking his left thumb, and leafing through it with eyebrows raised like citation marks, 'these are just a few of the entries for 'Fa', mind. You'll have to bear with my pronunciation; your alphabet is strange to me.' The eyebrows executed a facetious little skip. '*Fadarcawn*: the remains of a branch on a tree, or the hole left in wood when the knot falls out.' He tilted his head, as though weighing the definition, and appeared to agree with it. '*Fawrbre*: the mark on a cow's horn, indicating her age, and hence *Fawrbreach*: old, as a cow.' He raised a right hand as though to forestall interruption, though none was forthcoming. '*Fawsach*: either a desert wilderness or else a pasture with particularly luxuriant grass.' He repeated with italics, '*either* a desert wilderness or else a pasture with *particularly* luxuriant grass!' He snorted. '*Falaracht*: the flaw in horses of moving both legs on each side alternately; also, the gait of a spancelled goat; *Fatea*: a striking of the arms and hands against the chest and sides…[32] gentlemen, do you begin

32 In the case of *fawsach* McTurcaill, or Hastings, is embellishing. The actual entry reads fásach, -aig, *m.*: *a desert; a wilderness; pasture; luxuriant grass.* It might be added that *fadarcawn* (sic) also includes the notion of a corn on one's foot; *fawrbre* can be used for any kind of notch on a tally-stick; while *falaracht* is more frequently the gait of a spancelled goat rather than a flawed horse.

to see what I'm driving at?'

Hackett's eyes narrowed and eyed the narrow eyebrows, which remained interrogatively hoisted. Then, with arms and hands, he executed the precise gesture known more correctly in the Eirish tongue as faiceadh. The second Academician, McTurcaill on balance, made a less than effusive gesture in reply, and pulled a notebook from his own breast pocket not a whit less pregnant than his companion's. He licked his right thumb. 'And what are we to make of *cuilith gwarne* which purports to mean "the rippling of the mid-current of a stream," but which may also be "the heart of a cabbage" or the "mid-sheaf of a cornstack"? What sort of currency has a term like *cuilith gwarne*?' Now that Hackett began to look at the pair more closely, they were no more alike than a rabbit is like a hare. Where the one was domestic, docile, and daft, the other was bug-eyed, buck-toothed and scatter-brained.

'Perhaps in an age more pastoral…?' suggested Chapman. 'Ours is an ancient tongue.' With one eye to Hackett, who might easily pull the rug out from under him for pure devilment, he chanced an elaboration. 'The strange alphabet you mention…'

'Whose letters have been found among the casts of the Rockchester cache,' gruffed Sir Æthelred. Hackett hoisted his eyebrows. Realising he'd been ill-advised to mention the cache, the Home Secretary squinnied at Chapman. 'The alphabet, you were about to say?' Chapman, for his part, kept a weather eye upon Hackett. '…is itself fashioned from umpteen varieties of tree.'

'Eighteen,' specified Hackett, whose mind was on the Rockchester cache. The police had stumbled upon bagfulls of counterfeit and nefarious terms, by all accounts. But why on earth would they include the types of Gaedhilic characters? 'Eighteen,' he went on, woodenly, 'all Eirish school kids have to master their *elm, birch, hazel* from an early age and frequently receive the birch when they fail to do so.'

'But have you people no notion of a Decommissioner?' asked the Decommissioner.

'Enough!' gruffed Sir Æthelred, pattling the green tome and simultaneously motioning towards the vacant chair in which Inspector Quibble of the Yard had singularly failed to materialise, 'Dinneen is a matter for Semantics. It's their baby. Let them get to the bottom of it.' The Home Secretary's red-rimmed eyes had been scrutinising Hackett for some time now and had come to the less than satisfactory conclusion that it would be best after all to trust to the Eirish to vet their own private secretaries. He consulted a fob watch, which appeared to have stopped. 'Seymour!'

The Oxenford Don started out of whatever academic reverie he'd been meandering in. 'Seymour! What the deuce is it you call it that the blighters seem to be up to? DDT was it?' Any ecclesiastical reserve fell from the Professor Emeritus' comportment as he stood up to reply. While everyone's attention turned to the Don, at the word 'Seymour' Hackett's was set scurrying in pursuit of an imaginary mouse. So this was the renowned Seymour Doolittle, whose doctoral thesis had demonstrated the futility of the search for the perfect tense.[33] If this was the same Don, he'd made a remarkable recovery.

33 Doolittle was the original for the phonologist Col Pinkerton in Pshaw's 1912 play *Pygmalion*. Due to a typesetter's error, the surname got transferred to the flower-girl, Eliza. Pshaw was evidently tickled by the error. When asked by his publisher if he wished to correct it, he replied 'not bloody likely!'

Because everyone who had a love of words knew that in the middle of a most illustrious career, the fruitless search for the cenologos,[34] the elusive signifier that was said to be empty of all meaning and therefore infinite in its applicability, had dried out his wits and sent him tilting at windmills…

'Systematic Semiotic Decentring,' he declared, returning Hackett's errant attention abruptly to the present. 'The decentering of semiotic meaning carried out in a systematic or systemic manner,' he concluded.

'Damn it all, man, say it in plain Engelish can't you!'

Unperturbed, the Don cleared his throat. 'In his crowning *Third Treatise on Government*, Locke tells us that just as Euclid's geometry rests on a number of axioms, there are just such a number of conventions upon which every civilisation must be founded. There is the convention of social hierarchy. The convention of marriage. The convention of private property. The convention of monetary exchange. The convention that there is a set of natural laws which are prior to interpretation. The convention,' he peered at the two Eirishmen, 'of patriotic duty. But beyond any of these conventions, prior to any of these conventions, is the convention of language. Language, if I may put it this way, is the Ur-convention. Language is the *a priori sine qua non* of all posterior conventions.'

'Yes I daresay Hackett knows all this,' muttered Sir Æthelred gruffly. 'Daresay he's not entirely green, you know.' The Don nodded, a gesture which somehow reserved judgment

34 A search famously described by Pshaw as 'the unspeakable in pursuit of the ineffable.' A comparable search in the realm of mathematics led to Lord Kelvin of Bailfast discovering what he termed 'absolute zero', as for instance the difference between knowing nothing, knowing nothing at all, and knowing absolutely nothing at all.

on all that the Home Secretary had dared say. 'The point I wish to stress is merely this. Without an agreed currency of language and a gold standard with which to underwrite the value of its terms, what do you have?' He allowed the question to hang impressively. 'Gentlemen, you have chaos, debasement, and a linguistic free for all. Gentlemen, you have the Weimar Republic!'

'Quite right!' ejaculated the Eirish Viscount while the press baron gave the table an enthusiastic palming.

'Now, the absolute value of a word, and of the language that underwrites it, varies. Emperor Charles V said that he sprake to his God in Spanish, to men in French, to women in Italian, and to his horse in German.'

'What language did he say that in?' queried Hackett.

'He said it in earnest,' replied the Don, who enjoyed nothing better than to break a verbal lance with a rival. 'In Sir Thomas More's *De Naturae Linguarum Cogitationisque*, the Renaissance scholar likens any language to a reticulum, or 'net'. The individual words form the nodes or knots of this net. The gaps between the words are the nuance of differences. Its overall structure is determined by syntax and inflexion; and rhythm and custom combine to give it its tensile strength.' As the Don expounded, his long fingers formed the pattern of a net whose mesh twisted and tightened. 'Each language nets the world in its own way. You have only to travel Europe to experience it. Every time you cross a linguistic border, it's as if you pass through a looking-glass to a world where everything is the same but not the same. Sometimes, as in the Cyrillic, the very letters are reversed. Each net has a different mesh, and each mesh nets a slightly different catch. If you'll allow me to mix my metaphors, the German's innate **Zugehörigkeitsgefühl** allows his nodes to cluster freely into enormous freight-trains of meaning, gathering terms the way the old Reichmark gathered zeros. Note too how the syntax tends to hold back the locomotive verb. "*Ve vill ze Rhineland, because it vonce a Part of ze Homeland vas, remilitarise*!"'

'Suspect the Hun, do you? Because I can tell you, if he's behind this affair, it's bound to be dastardly.' The Home Secretary's concern was understandable. Only the week before, Maulwurf and Leberfleck had been exposed as German moles.

'My point, Sir Æthelred, is, one always gets the feeling with the German that he withholds from you what action is to be undertaken until all the circumstances and justifications have been grammatically set out.'

'Just the opposite of ourselves,' put in Hackett. 'The Eirish starts by declaring what action is going to be undertaken before ever an agent has been found to carry it out.' Viscount Bracken's spectacles flashed in the direction of the journalist. Perhaps, after all, he was a compatriot? Besides the queer fact that he was named for the navigator,[35] the only thing Hackett knew about this Bracken character was that he was continually agitating for a Ministry of Information. The Don looked at the Eirish upstart with tolerant disapproval before resuming. 'Or consider the Italian. In polite Italian, 'you' is rendered as 'la' and 'lei'. The Italian gallant assumes that his addressee will always be female. Or look to the East. Our Slavonic neighbours do without the distinction between 'a' and 'the' and appear to

35 An Eirish monk, St Brendan of Clonfert (484-577) is credited equally with having accidentally discovered America nine centuries before Columbus and for keeping the discovery under his hat.

suffer no loss from it. And they have entire sentences without the verb 'to be'. *Bolsheviks — majority*, are you with me? *Politics — red*, do you see? Whereas for the Iberian there are two distinct verbs 'to be', which perhaps suggests a fickleness in his character.' He peered at Hackett. 'I think the same is true of you Eirish?'

'We're fickle?'

'I was referring to your syntax.'

'You're not wrong,' affirmed the journalist. 'You know the Eirishman has no way of answering a simple yes to that question?'

'But is that true?'

'It is.'

'And no?'

'Likewise.'

'Really?'

'I wouldn't tell a lie.'

The Don smiled. Almost. 'Try to catch a thought without the *reticulum linguae*, without the net of language and you'll find you've a haul of nothing but impressions and sensations. Colours. Sounds.' He looked to the Eirish duo. 'Smells.' Hackett winked at Chapman. Chapman frundled at Hackett. 'Gentlemen,' soared the Don, as he approached a climax, 'there are enemies of civilisation who are intent on snipping holes in that net. Pushing the nodes apart, slipping in false nodes to throw the whole lattice out of kilter. Purveyors of gammon, of slang, of acol, of jargon, of verlan, of polari, of shilta, of argot, and of cant. Fomenters,' he pronounced impressively, 'of discord. They've always been there, lurking in the shadow of the Colosseum, the Parthenon, the Globe, the Comédie-

Française, and the Crystal Palace. And every civilisation spawns them, as surely as it spawns thieves, con-artists and prostitutes. Now, one of the glories of the Engelish *reticulum linguae* is also one of its weaknesses. As our colleague Harry Hastings has always attested, its woof and warp have been synthesised by combining two distinct nets, of French and German manufacture. This makes for a particularly fine grade of mesh.'

'That should render it less vulnerable to attack, surely?'

'Careful, Sir Æthelred! The finer the mesh, the more plentiful the holes.' The Don picked up the thread of his argument. 'It's a danger that has long been known. Centuries before the present age of mechanical reproduction it spawned, among other cavils, the Inkhorn Controversy.' This mention conjured before Hackett's wayward imagination a woodcut he'd encountered a bare week since in the British Library. During the Elizabethan period, the spat between Saxophonists and Latinisers got its name from a notorious incident when Sir Philip Sidney hurled an inkhorn at the head of Thomas Kyd after the latter had called him a tosspot. When his errant mind returned to the mahogulous table, the Professor Emeritus was impressively reciting from memory an entire paragraph from Locke's *Third Treatise*, from the section that begins with language as the first term in the social contract and concludes with the desirability of proportional representation. 'It follows, gentlemen,' he concluded, 'that an attack on the language is an attack on the very fabric of civilisation. Jargon and argot will always persist in the recesses of the demimonde. Shadow, rather than substance. Prior to the era of mechanical reproduction these were short-lived, due to the low vigency of their component terms. The great exception to jargon remaining in the shadows is, of course, Dutch, which began life during the medieval era as a sailors' crude addendum to Low German. In East Anglia, the guttural impenetrability of the maritime language led to it being dubbed 'phlegmish', a name that stuck. But what I have in mind is a *methodical* attack. What I have in mind is linguistic terrorism. What I have in mind,' he drew to an even more impressive climax, 'is Systematic Semiotic Decentring. Gentlemen, from what Inspector Quibble has said to me in private in relation to the Rockchester outrage, I believe that just such an attack is at this very moment being perpetrated on the King's Engelish. The Engelish of governance. The Engelish of Shakespeare. The Engelish of the Bible.'

The effect on the table was gratifying, and the Don took full advantage of it to resume his seat. At this, the advisor, who'd been standing erect behind the Home Secretary with that furniture-like discretion peculiar to the Engelish butler, leaned forwards and once more whispered a few private words into Sir Æthelred's shell-like ear. The latter nodded and turned to the Academicians. 'You're intending to go out to Rockchester once we're done, Hastings?'

'McTurcaill,' said McTurcaill. 'This is Hastings.'

'I wasn't… well, I suppose I was thinking of possibly going out later this evening,' Hastings affirmed, replacing the notebook in his breast pocket and lowering his eyebrows into a frundle which suggested that he'd entertained no such thought.

'Then I suggest you take Mr Hackett along with you. He is newly arrived from Dubilin. I daresay he's ignorant of the seriousness of the present threat. As you sit together, you can bring him up to speed.'

A trip out to Rockchester suited Hackett. He was determined to find the blaggard who had dared use his cypher at the bottom of the Bisharp of Botolph's report. But if it suited Hackett just fine, it did not suit Hastings just fine, and Hastings was less successful at concealing the emotion. 'Will that be all, sir?' he muttered. The Home Secretary's brow frundled, to face off the Warden's frundle. He could never be quite sure that a rise wasn't being taken out of him. 'No,' he declared, once more palming the great green tome before him. 'You can warn Quibble from me that all we've seen so far is the tip of the iceberg, so it'd better be full steam ahead.'

When they were once more alone in the Bentley as it muttled back in the general direction of Belgravia, Hackett took hold of Chapman's elbow. 'Tell me this and tell me no more. What in the name of the Melancholy Christ has Paddy Dinneen done to the Sassnachs that's ruffled their feathers?'

Chapman blew out. 'It's a long story. And it's a complicated one. I only know the half of it. But if you want my candid and considered opinion, Dinneen is nothing but a blind. It's more than Dinneen has their feathers ruffled, I can tell you that much.' And over the remainder of their journey, Chapman told him all the much that he could. 'So do you mean to tell me,' exclaimed Hackett as they finally puttled into the Consular Buildings of the Eirish Free State, 'they seriously consider there's an existential threat to their precious language?'

'That,' declared Chapman, 'is precisely what I mean to say.'

'Their reaction strikes me as altogether… what's the word

I'm looking for?'

Rising to this unexpected challenge, Chapman mobilised the standing army of his technical vocabulary. 'Hyperbolic?'

'That's over the top.'

'Superlative?'

'Too strong.'

'Comparative?'

'More or less.'

'Exaggerated?'

'The very word!'

If there was irony in his secretary's affirmation, Chapman was unaware of it. 'And this supposed attack on their blessed "language of the bible",' Hackett pursued, 'what makes them think it's our people is behind it?'

'That I can't say. Keep it under your hat, Hackett, but word is, they seem to think it might be one or two of *your* old acquaintances.' Chapman looked around him, then confided into the car, 'I daresay that's why Dubilin sent you over.' Hackett squinnied. His old acquaintances? And who would those be, now? Card carrying members of the League of Has Beens and Ne'er Do Wells?

Chapman's face became serious. 'By the by, have you heard tell,' he asked, 'of a man by the name of Quinn?'

'Quinn, is it?' Hackett ribbled his chin. 'Quinn, you say?' Hackett scrummeled his ear. He knucked a finger. 'There was a character by the name of Quirk in the Records Office helped put my papers in order. It isn't him you mean? Quirk?'

'Quinn. Quinn.'

He shook his hoary locks. 'Can't help you.'

Chapman stood out of the car. He was vexed. Whether he

was vexed at Hackett's flippant evasions or at his own lack of discretion in positing the question was less clear. 'I have to tell you, Ignatius, if you want my candid and considered opinion, I'm surprised, not to say chagrined, that Dubilin haven't been a bit more flúirseach[36] in their briefings prior to sending you over.' Hackett looked up at him and, suddenly aware that all had been said within earshot of the chauffeur, on the instant came to a decision to vacate the diplomatic Bentley.

'Who are you telling, Chippy? Who are you telling!'

36 'Spendthrift, prodigal, or loose-bowelled.'

CHAPTER THE EIGHTH

in which Hackett sets out on a frabjous railway journey; and of the curious thoughts that railways occasion in him

Harold Hastings hated railway stations. It wasn't merely on account of the soot and condensation that fouled up one's tweeds and bothered the roof of one's mouth. Nor was it just the relentless clanking and shunting, the shrieking whistles and squeal of steel on cast iron that so tested one's mettle. These were the condiments, as it were, to the more general distaste he had for anything that smacked of the tyranny of the timetable. As he jostled past the match-sellers, cripples and newspaper vendors that thramawled about the entrance to Victriola Station, his little eyes automatically lit upon the great lunar clock-face that was suspended between platforms 3 and 4. The minute hand was just shy of **XI**, which was to say fifty-five, so that he calculated he had ten minutes to spare before the 17:05, which was to say the five-after-five, to Medway Towns, pulled out. Good. His eye scanned the Departures Board, to ensure that there had been no last minute change of platform. There had been none. Satisfactory. Now, where the deuce was that damned Eirishman?

With his right hand, Hastings slapped his white kid gloves

repeatedly against the palm of his left. Damned nuisance, having to cancel an engagement at the Scribblers Club at the very last minute. Damned, damned nuisance, having to rush down to Rockchester, as if Quibble couldn't be asked to submit a report by telephone like anyone else. And thrice be-damned, the nuisance of having to rendezvous with this dubitous Dubilin character who you may be quite sure could not be depended upon to distinguish one Logdon Station from another. Now where the devil had he got to?

Every thirty seconds, Hastings' reluctant eye was drawn as though by a magnetic field to the great white clock-face. Every sixty seconds, which is to say on every second glance, he was dismayed to find that the minute hand had advanced through another 6° of azimuth, the precise tally of degrees that corresponded to the rising pitch of his anxiety. Five o'clock had already blanged through him and fallen silent and his gaze had already three times pleaded with the now falling arm since that ominous knell, when a ludifarious, garmungling figure, his own arms flailing like a clock gone mad, saluted him from over by the newspaper vendors. 'Hullo!' issued a voice which somehow carried over the clamour and bustle of this teeming hub of the Empire upon which the sun would never set. 'Be with you in two ticks!'

The Decommissioner of the Otiose made no reply, but gesticulated exaggeratedly towards the impatience of the train. Then, on legs somewhat short for his body, his briefcase careening off his calf, his free hand securing a perfidious bowler, Harry Hastings hastened down a platform that was by this time quite deserted but for a porter who, with green flag lethally unfrabbled and whistle in the leer of his mouth, was staring after his progress with maleficent glee.

Thirty yards behind, and moving at a comparable pace but, in spite of a mild limp, at infinitely greater leisure, strode the bally Eirishman who, so help him, would soon feel the Arctic ice of Hastings' displeasure. Wagon D, Wagon C. By God sir he would! Wagon B. After a horrible dilation of time and space, Hastings hoisted himself onto the step of Wagon A and fired a backward, basilisk glare. The sauntering fool was barely level with Wagon C, and the minute hand on the clock was trimbling on the very brink of **I**, which was to say, *5*. Muttering scarcely coherent words, he pushed into the narrow corridor, manoeuvred past loutish men in shirtsleeves and impriable, snot-nosed families, twice mistook the compartment, (twice!), and finally dropped into seat 14B just as the whistle shrilled outside. His breath was short, his temper out, his complexion high. Indignation contended with exasperation as he looked ferociously about him, one hand pressed to his heaving chest, the other still pressing the bowler into his hair. He was out of three things: of sorts; of patience; of puff.

Ignatius Hackett waved his frabbled newspaper after the avuncular figure who'd squinnied from the step of the first carriage before disappearing inside. From the earliest memory of his father begrimedly smiling as he shovelled coal through the furnace door on the Dubilin to Kingstown Atmospheric Railway to the evenings they'd operate on the clockwork replica engine, railways fascinated the boy. Cathedrals of a secular age, someone had called the great stations. As the adult now gazed from the high, vaulted ceiling to the great clock that was raised like a host over the multitude, he found himself concurring. But it wasn't so much the ecclesiastical scale of the architecture that held a fascination for Hackett. It was the idea of simultaneity. Wasn't it the case that it was the railway timetable of Mr Bradshaw, with its logarithmic hunger for precision, which had first required the standardisation of time across the pink imperial map? The very standardisation the anarchist Δ had tried to destroy!

With flawless choreography, the minute hand dropped onto the I, which is to say the 5, the engine coughed a billow towards the great glass ceiling, the carriage shunted and lurched, the Eirishman skipped aboard, and then, consistent with the laws of parallax and of relative motion, the entire station began to ease majestically rearwards. Not at all bad for a democracy.

Still not entirely inside the accelerating carriage, Hackett stared at the retrograde station whose dimensions had begun to decrease according to Brunelleschi's inverse-square law of pictorial perspective, the law Sir Isaac Newton had filched to account for the fall of an apple. In his grasshopper mind, the inverse-square law had somehow become entwined with Mr Einstein's Theory of Relativity. What's this now that that theory held? A ray of light (was it?), that if you shone it at a moving train, no, if you shone it *from* a moving train, meant that time slowed down. Or sped up. (But compared to what?) Well if that little scientific paper, which had stood Sir Isaac on his head, had had no discernible effect on the dependability of Mr Bradshaw's railway timetables, it was hard to see how Δ's bomb thrown into the First Meridian would have upset the apple cart. Ach, this was hopeless. Hopeless! Who was he trying to kid? After all, it was said the present Taoiseach was one of perhaps a half-dozen people in the entire western hemisphere who grasped the nuances of Mr Einstein's thesis.

Hackett pushed inside the carriage, opened a window, and stuck his head out into the torrent of smokey air. And now there was supposed to be some class of attack on the language. On the *language*, bedad! Still, Dubilin seemed to think so, too. And the great R. M. Smyllie. He reviewed in his mind the 'much' that Chapman had confidentially imparted on their journey back from the Royal Academy of Letters. It would appear that the recent verbal outrage perpetrated in the city of Rockchester, towards which their train was at present hurtling with no discernible distortion of space-time, was merely the latest in a series of such outrages. Outrages which, Chapman assured him, put beyond reasonable dubit the existence of at least one counterfeit cell operating in and around the Medway region.

His boss had recounted two of these. Prior to the Bisharp's bungle in Botolph's, there had been the bizarre incident in Coalchester when the Chamber of Commerce had brought out a publication in which were extolled, not 'the cardinal virtues of thrift, industry and investment' as one would have anticipated, but rather 'the crumnjal virtues of tripe, forstyn bgrrgl and investestament.' Now even this might have raised relatively few semantic eyebrows and been put down to the shoddy proofing that so frequently attends upon semi-official publications were it not for the fact that the very tripartite phrase was also delivered verbally and verbatim during the annual address to the Guild of Glovers, where it had been not merely comprehended but applauded.

Then to put the tin hat on it, on the same day there had been the unfortunate BBC report, transmitted live from Bradfjord

Cathedral, in the course of which the Bisharp had bluntly referred to Edward Windsor three times as His Travesty the King! Too late, an apology was issued from Yorvik Minster. To contend that such a concatenation might be coincidental seemed to stretch credulity.

Hackett wondered where Harry Hastings had settled. His host. In his haste. Decommissioner, wasn't that it? Which would make the McTurcaill character Commissioner, as though the one demanded the other in accordance with Newton's Third Law of Motion. Back to Hastings. There was the joke about the Engelish gent drops into the Irish Pavilion at the Chicago World Fair to pick up a bottle of whiskey. Stall is run by an oul couple from Bailfast.[37] *That'll bay tayn saxty sax*, says the woman. *Ah*! replies the gent, *Battle of Hastings*! Woman looks at him. *Ay don't know, sir. Billy! Do we have ere a battle of* "*Hastings*"? Would his travelling companion find it amusing, that was the question. Be nice to set off on the right foot.

Hackett pulled his head in from the rushing air and tugged up the stubborn sash-window. It was difficult to believe he was standing here, swaying gently as the Kentish countryside, by relative motion, sped past him. It was hard to credit not so much from an Einsteinian, or even a Newtonian, point of view. What was remarkable about the entire set up was that not a fortnight since, Hackett had been down on his uppers, penniless, jobless, friendless, and squatting in a doss-house at the mercy of the avarice of a Cavan man, the very man who'd delivered into his hand, with an uncharacteristic degree of

37 A city in Co Antrim famed for its ship-building. The words Bailfast and Titanic are indelibly associated in the public mind.

deference and an unredeemed outlay of 3ᵈ, the manila envelope with reversed harp that had set the whole train in motion.

And if that was strange itself, it wasn't the half of it! Chapman had been quite wrong to say that he'd not been briefed prior to his arrival. What had happened over the next few days would have set the head spinning of a man many times more sober and secure than the likes of Ignatius Hackett. He was shunted from Billy to Jack and back by a handler by the name of Chandler. This Chandler was a taciturn individual with an equivocal handshake whose office was unclear. One of the few utterances he made, on first taking charge of Hackett, was: 'You seem to have… connections.' Later, the phrase was precisely reiterated. It struck Hackett obliquely, and stuck in his memory because of this unusual feature: the emphasis, which was unmistakable, fell squarely on the ellipsis. But nothing would make the man elaborate as to who or where these… connections might be, nor what was intended by the evocative pause. Smyllie? But how could Chandler & Co have factored in a fortuitous encounter in the PALACE BAR on the day he'd received the summons? And then earlier, as he passed him his business card, Sol Isaacs had repeated the very ellipsis…

The handler imparted one instruction that was most curious. While Hackett was to be attached to the Cultural Attaché, his official brief was to provide his erstwhile classmate with general information only. Gossip; hearsay; tittle-tattle; in brief, the very stuff of hack journalism. When it came to anything touching upon the perpetrators of the verbal outrages, the methodology of Semantics or the workings of the arcane Royal Academy of Letters, he was to deal only with

Chapman's secretary, a Miss Maloney. Was that understood? Only Maloney, repeated Hackett. Chandler was pleased. But was he, Hackett, not to be Chapman's secretary? His private secretary. And Miss Maloney? His office secretary. Then, as he was taking his leave, the handler extended his hand. 'Rooney,' an eye half-closed, 'go n-éiri an bóthar leat.' There was nothing untoward about the blessing, which translates as 'may the road rise to meet you'. It invariably does. After a moment's hesitation, Hackett understood 'Rooney' to be rúnai, 'secretary', just as rún was 'secret'. But was there anything more in it, an allusion to the old Banna Strand rumour, perhaps? Whether Chandler was being ingenious or ingenuous remained a moot point.

Over the course of a hectic couple of days while he waited for his travel documents, Hackett was handed from handler to civil servant, from diplomat to g-man and from secretary to lexicographer and back to handler until he could have hardly said any more if he was coming or going, much less worry about whether he was up to the task. The letter Q? was bandied about, always in the interrogative. No-one knew who or what Q? might be, but somehow, Q? was instrumental to the whole nefarious business. A thought struck him. Could Q? be Quinn? And if so, could Quinn be the scurril who was passing off bogus articles under his six-footed glyph? Hackett had been briefed and debriefed, questioned and catechised, brought up to speed and given crash courses until he could scarcely have told his own name with any degree of confidence, and all that he knew for certain as he stood on the mailboat and watched Kingstown Pier recede into the twilight was that he was to vouchsafe to his former classmate and future boss as little of the above as might be consistent with his sudden elevation to the position of rúnaí. For anything of substance, Only Maloney was the word.

But *who* had sent for him? And why had he been sent for? And in God's name why him, and not another? Throw a plumstone from the top of the Pillar and if it doesn't strike a poet, a *tanner* to a *make* it'll hit a freelance hack. True, he'd been a reporter in his day, a correspondent of considerable note at his apex. But if he'd pulled off the occasional scoop or unlikely interview, he was, as his detractors said, only ever a columnist. In every field you'll find detractors, that was an Eirish axiom. As for his celebrated knack of being in the right place at the right time, Hackett knew well there had always been something more than fortuitous about that. Ever since that Easter morn when McCann had singularly failed to inform him that the Cervantes cavalcade had been called off, he'd had the uncanny suspicion that a clandestine hand had been guiding Lady Fortune's.

The head head-doctor in Swift's Institute for the Insane had spoken of Imposter Syndrome, a professional hazard among the writing classes to which the standing army of poets alone remain immune. From the moment he'd stepped off the mailboat at Holyhead into the imminence of once more taking up the pen, he'd had the syndrome in spades. All very well to swagger before a bantamweight like Chapman, but as to that 'Settling Old Scores' Grimaldi article that had his boss' nose out of joint, well. He'd been as surprised as the next man to read it in the *Munchester Warden.* A fortnight in, he hadn't even blown the dust from his *Underwood.* But before the emulous squint of the Cultural Attaché, he couldn't let on his trademark Ж had been filched. Damn it, he almost admired the usurper, how he'd given that Grimaldi pinesse the old Hackett treatment. No, the present Hackett was a fraud, out and out. At the drop of a hat he was ready to chuck it all in, hightail it back to Lr Dorset St, sink once more into the slough of oblivion.

Back to Hastings! Neither man greeting the other, Hackett dropped into seat 14C. The two were directly facing one another, and if their eyes didn't meet, the jostling of the train ensured that their knees continually did. Hackett was vaguely aware of having done something that had put the other out of sorts, but he was damned if he knew what it was and he was twice damned if he was going to take the trouble to find out. So he stared into the middle distance and he began to whistle *Lilliburlero*.

The stratagem of gazing and humming, if stratagem it was, at length paid dividends. Hastings had removed his bowler and was running a finger along the inside rim. 'Can you tell me,' he asked the hat, without seeing any necessity either to go through the formalities of a second introduction, 'the names of the two most powerful men in the Empire?' Hackett scrundled his forehead and glanced about the carriage, to see if anyone was in a position to follow the conversation. A man in unbuttoned military uniform sat daydreaming by a window. Further up, an elderly vicar was raising his Anglican eyebrows over the editorial of the *Ecclesiastical Epistle*. 'Their names,' gruffed Hastings, staring hard at thumb and forefinger, 'are Harmsworth and Aitken. You've heard of them, I daresay?' For the moment, Hackett chose to keep his cards close to his chest. Harmsworth's distorting *Mirror* had done its harm's worth. Showing scorn her own image, one tabloid to be taken before sleep. But who Aitken was was anyone's guess. He smiled ingratiatingly.

'Then, sir, I shall tell you. They are barons of the press. I'll grant you that in times to come, a broadcaster in the position of John Reith will wield even more power, because the public is eternally lazy. You'll agree with me that it takes considerably less effort to listen than to read?' Hackett agreed with him. Hastings made a gruntle, and returned his eyes to a perusal of the bowler. 'I shudder when I think of what's to come. You only have to look across the channel! Dr Goebbels is only too aware of it. That, sir, is the power of the Marconi wireless. That, sir, is the power of the ear. But for the present, in this country, it's still the newspaper that rules the roost.' He pointed to the paper scrundled up in Hackett's hand, reassured. 'Printed matter, sir.'

Until that moment, Hackett had forgotten all about the paper. Taking Hastings' words as invitation, he unfrabbled the pages and found that he was looking at the *Daily Yob*. He scanned the headlines and then inquired by means of raised eyebrows. Hastings tapped the now unfrabbled tabloid. 'Your friends in the *Yob*, Mr Hackett, had quite the field day over the Mayor of Gillingham. Quite the field day!' Harry Hastings glanced about the carriage, suspicious. Ignatius Hackett glanced about the carriage, supercilious. The vicar was absorbed in the crossword of his *Ecclesiastical Epistle*. The soldier was dozing. Hastings momentarily winced, for the cryptic crossword was the very bane of his life as Decommissioner. He leaned forward and dropped his voice. 'It's that that has Semantics interested in all this.'

'I see,' said Hackett. He didn't see. Whether Hastings saw

that he didn't see he couldn't say. Harold Hastings sighed. His little eyes left the bowler and tried to take the measure of the man opposite him. 'In the first place, during his unfortunate sprake, the misfortunate man had a bad case of the bgrrgls. I heard the recording with my own ears! It was quite remarkable. Every so often bgrrgl would just... jump out of a sentence. Once it even paired up. Bgrrgl bgrrgl. You must have read the example that was crowed in every edition of the gutter press?' He raised a theatrical hand. 'I shall now turn to the bgrrgl bgrrgl matter of public floonances.'

'No! He said that?'

Hastings frundled. Or grimlied. In any event it was an affirmation. Then he sat back, the eyes again in the hat. The brief intimacy was ended.

After a pause, Hackett picked up his *Daily Yob*, scanned it, and turned to page five.

What a Holy Show!

St Botolph's in Chat'em has rarely had a sermon qu-quite like this one! Dr Co-coyne, the Bisharp of Rockchester, had his co-congregation in stitches every time he ca-called on them to co-consider the evils of ca-calumny! What will the Archbisharp of Ca-Cantbury have to say? And, like the Major of Gillingham before him, it seems our Bisharp was also victim of a bad ca-case of the bgrrgls! And if all that didn't have his co-congregation falling about the aisles in co-convulsions, bgrrgl, what in heavens did the ce-cleric mean by 'lali perpengi'? We're left ca-calmanning is there something in the waters down in Medway that's ca-causing all this verbal cha-chaos!

Relieved to find no sign that Ж had claimed authorship, he laid down the tabloid. 'You say Semantics are interested. What I'm not clear on,' Hackett bluffed, 'is what has Semantics interested in a piffling incident like this?'

'Didn't you read the article?' Harry Hastings glanced surreptitiously at the vicar, who was angling a fountain pen over the ecclesiastical crossword as if he wanted to harpoon an arcane word there. No danger from that quarter, though the word he was hunting was bound to be recondite if not recherché. The soldier continued to doze. 'What has Semantics interested, as you phrase it, is that this doesn't appear to be a common or garden case of verbal counterfeiting.'

'I daresay not.' Hackett hadn't the foggiest what his travel companion was talking about. For a while they were silent. Hastings put on a pair of reading-glasses which made his eyes balloon out to fill them, and took a neatly frabbled newspaper out of his briefcase. The *Morning Decorum*. His briefcase acting as a table on his lap, he spread the broadsheet out. For a time he remained absorbed in it. 'You've read Chaucer,' he suggested, just as the train at last erupted into open fields. Hackett, startled by the enlarged eyes, confessed he had not. Hastings frundled, harrumphed, then he suddenly beamed, for the first time since he'd had to cancel the evening at the club. 'I say! We're actually following the route of the pilgrims! The marvellous thing, you can tell the precise *estate* of every single pilgrim simply by the register.' He tapped his *Decorum*. 'The lexicography, don't you know.'

Now when Hastings mentioned pilgrims and estates, he might just as well have been talking Greek. There were pilgrims on the Mayflower and they went to the States. But it was hardly them! Then, considering the word 'register', a figurative light bulb lit up over Hackett's head. He unfrabbled the *Daily Yob* and tapped the Botolph article. 'The report I read in the *Gravitas* had a deal more *dignitas* about it,' he tried, with an alarming smile.

Hastings winced. 'I mean, sir,' the Academician clarified, 'the *great poet's* balance of the Engelish to the French. Saxon,' Hastings laid one hand flat, 'and then Norman.'[38] His other hand slid over the first. Then he began to ripple the one over the other. 'Language has its fault-lines,' his left hand slapped the right, 'its tectonic plates.' Hackett ribbled his chin. Tectonic, bedad! Twenty years ago there'd been a fault-line of trenches running through Europe, all the way from Flanders to the Alps. It was excavated to keep the Germanic from the Romance. Another fault ran down the east, where the Germanic collided with the Slavonic. According to his erstwhile pal McCann, the entire catastrophe was due to the movement of Teutonic plates. But what had any of that to do with pilgrims?

The train was making faster progress. Its rhythm had rattled through a wrought-iron structure and the right-hand windows were suddenly clear of hedgerows. Hastings tilted forward and their knees became intimate. 'Semantics are interested, as you put it, because what we're threatened with is nothing less than cleavage.'

'With?'

---

38 Norman, a corruption of Norsemen, designates a group of French speaking adventurers and ne'er-do-wells bent on conquest. In Eirland, the Normans, who found the native hare too wily to hunt, are best remembered for having introduced the rabbit, in what was to be an ecological game-changer.

'Cleavage,' insisted the man. 'It's a curious word,' he went on, sitting back and surrendering to reverie. 'To cleave together.' His hands came together. 'But then, to cleave apart.' His hands came apart. The train plunged into a tunnel and Hastings sprake from the shadows.

'McTurchaill has yet to ascertain the technical term.'[39] He sat forwards, but the shadow persisted. 'Another example would be to dust. You dust the table with a powder.' His fingers made as if to sprinkle his case. 'But then you dust the table with a cloth.' The back of his hand swiped the surface clear. The train emerged into the fading daylight. Hackett remained in the dark. 'But… threatened?'

'By cleavage, sir. Cleavage! Can you imagine the chaos that would follow?' Never a man to put his ignorance on display, Hackett articulated the word 'pan-de-mo-ni-um'. Or more accurately, he disarticulated it. At that moment it was the longest word he could think of. It was a word whose five slow syllables might give him five fleeting seconds to consider what the hell the Academician was raving about. Beyond Hastings' hairline, which still bore the impression of the bowler, interminable telephone lines fell and rose, fell and rose. 'Pandemonium is precisely the term, Mr Hackett!' They whacked through a sudden tunnel, rattled another wrought-iron bridge. The glasses with the enormous eyes were now

---

39 At the time of this conversation, Neologistics, under the charge of McTurcaill, was examining several contenders for this technical term, among them *antagonym*, *contranym* and *autantonym*. Other slippery examples include the verbs *sanction, overlook* and *endorse*, as when the League of Nations failed to sanction Italy's invasion of Abyssinia; their consequent decision to *overlook* the occupation; but not to *endorse* it, (a *contranym* which anyone who's had their driving licence endorsed will appreciate).

staring at the antimacassar behind Hackett's head. 'Look at the case of meats. It's a well-known example. 1066 and all that. Every schoolboy knows the example of the animals and their meats…'

'Every *Engelish* schoolboy,' Hackett corrected, for fear he'd be discovered a dunce at history. Harry Hastings removed his glasses, wiped them, returned them, removed them, replaced them in his breast pocket. 'I daresay you Eirish *do* know that Engelish is an amalgam of several older tongues?'

'We've heard rumours.'

'Anglo-Saxon and Norman-French, but with a good smattering of Church-Latin in the mix. Look!' he calloohed, so loud that it startled the cleric and woke the soldier from his slumber. Fortuitously, the train was rounding the great arc of the Medway, and over the water the windows of Rockchester had begun to crowd the far bank. 'Do you see how the city is dominated by that castle? And do you see the spire of the cathedral beyond it?' Hackett looked. Across the dusky estuary, the streets resembled nothing so much as a flotilla of fishing boats bobbling about the great twin flagships, cathedral and castle. The effect was accentuated by the apparent motion imparted to the vessels by the law of parallax as their locomotive approached. 'I want you to imagine how it must have looked eight hundred years ago. Between castle and spire there would have been narrow streets, single-storey hovels. Timber-frame, wattle and daub, straw and muck on the ground where pigs and children are scavenging. Do you have the picture?'

'I have the very smells.'

'Now, that,' he tapped Hackett's knee impressively, 'is the pattern of how the Engelish language was cobbled together.

Middle Engelish. Chaucer's Engelish! You had the villains and the artisans, getting by with their guttural Saxon. Trading on it, like so much copper coin. That was the base metal. Then you had the second estate, the clergy, the monks and the clerics, illuminating the profane world with the silver of church Latin. Their sentences were more highly wrought, and had currency all through Christendom. And lording it over them you had the gentility, inside their demesnes of golden governance with their refined notions of chivalry. French, sir, was their medium! Over the centuries, these three currencies came together. Cleaved together.' Hastings tried to mirror the three-way coalescence with an all-embracing gesture, but he lacked a hand to do it. The train had begun to slow into Rockchester station.

'But rather than mere duplication, and rather than mere displacement, what this cleaving together made for was great discrimination. Discrimination that is unparalleled in the history of language! You have your *laws*, do you see? But you also have your *rules*, and your *regulations*. You have *royal*. But you also have *regal*. And then, too, you have *kingly*. The Saxon *ask* is not the same as the French *demand*, nor the Saxon *answer* the same as the French *reply*.'

'I see.' As the carriage cleared, Hackett was perhaps beginning to see. But he was also beginning to see that his companion was as mad as a March hare.

'The danger is, you uncouple the languages, you cleave Engelish apart, and, in place of discrimination, what do you have?' Hackett shook his head. 'You have duplication, sir!' He slapped the briefcase. 'Doubling and duplication of all and sundry. Can you imagine it?' Hackett couldn't. The train had been stationary for upwards of two minutes. The Decommissioner peered out along the platform at a sausage vendor and an image lit up his face. He beamed straight into the Eirishman's ignorance. 'You walk into your favourite restaurant. You've brought someone with you whom you want to impress. A lady friend, we'll say.' Hastings eye narrowed louchely. 'So you take your seats, and you run your finger fondly down the familiar menu. But wait! What's this?' Hackett shook his head, concerned. They two, alone in the carriage, had failed to disembark. Even the sleeping soldier had gone. Melancholy Christ, were they to miss their stop, and their appointment with the mysterious Inspector Quibble? 'What's this?' repeated the Academician, pleased with the theatrics. 'What class of menu can this be? You find all sorts of gaps when you come to the meats section. Item after item, quite gone! There's scarcely a dish left.'

'Perhaps we might...' Hackett had risen and was hovering emphatically.

'You see, ever since the great cleavage, the French words are no longer content to be served up as haute cuisine. They want to be back out on the farms, to frolic and gambol like their Saxon cousins. In vain you may search for your veal and your venison. In vain you may search for your beef, and your pork, and your mutton. Where have they gone? Le mouton is out grazing the hills, le boeuf is lowing in the meadows, and as for le porc, he's as happy as the proverbial Larry, wallowing in as mucky a sty as ever greeted a Saxon pig. Mutton, beef, and pork, quite unprepared.'

'You don't mince your words.' Hackett was mightily relieved that the madman had at least risen. Before he had the chance to reconsider, Hackett ushered him to the carriage door.

'And if that wasn't bad enough, where have all your Saxon animals got to by this stage? Do you think they're content to stay down on the farm, as coarse as peasants? They are my backside! While you're still sitting with your lady friend, the galley door swings open. All within is din and racket. There are all your Saxon cows and your calves, and there's your sheep and your ewes, your swine and hens, all creating a right royal rumpus in the kitchens.'

'God Almighty!' Hackett declared. He was in the company of a certifiable lunatic. A shrill whistle tore through the station just as Hastings's feet touched down on the platform. A great, brass jolt shook the train, and it groaned and shunted into motion.

As they made for the exit, Hackett's attention was arrested by a character in a mackintosh and trilby at some fifty yards distance who appeared to be failing singularly to remain inconspicuous behind a newspaper. Could it be Quibble? Or even Q?? Could Q? be Quibble? Hackett strained to see more clearly, and the figure's newspaper rose in proportion as he strained, until all that remained above its print was the hat, angled back in such a manner as to push out the two ears so that they resembled urn handles to either side of the lowered brow. Now, where had he seen those ears before? A tanner to a make he'd seen them somewhere…

His forearm was clamped by a white glove. Harry Hastings had frozen mid-stride. He'd caught sight of a great railway clock. 'We're late!' he whimpered, already scurrying towards the exit. 'We're late!' As he was dragged out of the station, a single backwards glance told Hackett that the character in the mackintosh had vanished as entirely as a self-consuming snake.

CHAPTER THE NINTH

in which our hero is introduced to Inspector Quibble of the Yard; has a curious encounter on Star Hill, and makes a momentous decision

Chief Inspector Quibble of Semantics folded away the page, threw back his shoulders, and frundled myopically at the sparse crew who'd assembled around the Guild Hall. Along with a scattering of locals and regionals, only one national paper that he could see was represented, and that was the *Evening Exposure*, hardly the last word in reputability. As for the others, they were of the less than savoury variety. There was, too, an anaemic chap called Evans of the BBC who'd spent more time fiddling with his microphone than paying heed to the press release.

Quibble was tall, even for a plod. He stood a half-foot over six foot in his stockinged feet and the rostrum added at least two more feet to this prodigious height. His jaw was masculine, his eyes close-set and restless, separated by a single furrow as upright as an exclamation mark. Twin grooves curved like parentheses to either side of the thin line of his lips, suggesting reticence. Dubitless this combination helped explain why, for the moment, no questions were forthcoming. Instead, there was a general pisstisstitis underscored with chair-scraping, paper-rustling, feet-shuffling and throat-clearing. The hiatus came as no great surprise. His prepared statements had been anything but edifying. The platitudes could have been lifted from any number of crime scenes. Misinformation, his colleague Fraiser called it, though the correct term was disinformation. But that was Fraiser all over. For all his linguistic expertise, a careless bloody Scotsman. You might just as well say that to be unguided was to be misguided, or that to be disinterested was the same as to be uninterested.

Imprecision of any kind bothered Inspector Quibble. But in particular, it vexed him that a colleague should be careless in the matter of lexical accuracy. You might expect it perhaps among the charlatans who delved away in the arcane corridors of their blessed Royal Academy. But when one assumed the charge and honour of becoming an officer in the Semantics division of the constabulary, when one swore the oath that had been devised by Lord Bletchley himself and when in doing so one became a guardian of the linguistic integrity that underwrote the common weal, one assumed a duty that was sacred. A duty moreover that brooked no slackening of vigilance. Fraiser was a smart man in his own way, but if to date the Scot had avoided a verbal warning, he'd increasingly been on the receiving end of the Quibble stare. At a time when every shred of evidence pointed to the conclusion that a systematic and systemic attack was being perpetrated on the language of the realm, imprecision of any kind was indefensible.

Of course, his bulletin had been without interest, and the hacks had listened without interest. *The public has no need to be unduly alarmed at this point in time. The recent spate of incidents is being thoroughly investigated. The police are following several lines of inquiry. The public is urged to remain vigilant, and to report anyone acting suspiciously. No further details can be released at this stage. For operational reasons*. Halfway through, his reassuring delivery had been interrupted by a pair of stragglers who'd bumbled in at the periphery of his vision and who'd set up a calumption out of all proportion to their size. That sort of thing exasperated the policeman. His innate sense of order was needled, and although he hadn't allowed it to throw him off his stride, it was possible the irritation had revealed itself in his tone. So he waited. When no-one stirred, he pulled a briar from his pocket, ran his thumb around its bowl, and placed it empty and unlit into the narrows of his mouth. He did this not so much through any desire to smoke as because he felt it lent gravitas to his demeanour. Besides, like many of the detective class, he found the act of drawing air through it an aid to cogitation. At length a hand went up, and the pipe came out.

'Mark Dobson, *Rockchester Reader*.'

To say that Quibble smiled in encouragement would be to imbue his facial muscles with a motion they hadn't exercised since he was an infant, perhaps not even then. Something in his mien had altered, however, and it approximated encouragement.

'Is it true the Old Bill found a second cache of counterfeit words, this one in the vicinity of the cathedral?'

'I'm afraid, Mr Dobson, I'm not at liberty to go into the details of the investigation at this stage. For operational reasons.' He squinnied over the sea of yawning heads. To the left of the hall, someone waved. Female. 'Jenny Hewitt, legal correspondent, *Chat'em Chatter*. Will you be taking any action against those printers who brought out the tainted reports of the Chamber of Commerce?'

'I'm afraid, Miss, I'm not at liberty to discuss any actions we may or may not deem it necessary to take. For operational reasons.'

'Ignatius Hackett, freelance.' Heads turned. Just at the point where his vision became blurry, a garmungling figure had stood up, upsetting a chair behind him. One of the damned latecomers that instinct would have him ignore. Nevertheless he leaned forwards and put a hand to his ear. It was a surname, and an accent, he'd been expecting. 'Have the police any reason to suspect the perpetrators are of any particular nationality at this stage in your inquiry?' A mutter ran through the audience. The heads turned back round. Quibble allowed a considerable time to pass before he deigned to reply, though whether this was to allow the public to settle or the response to be weighed was unclear. 'I'm not at liberty, Mr... *Hackett* (?), to discuss what particular leads we may or may not be following at this point in time.'

'Would that be for operational reasons?'

There was a general guffaw. Quibble's weasel eyes narrowed even more, squeezing the furrow between them into an even more exclamatory punctuation mark while the brackets enclosing his mouth became square. 'For operational reasons.'

'Jack Dawe. *Medway Filth.* Is it true the Mayor of Gillingham is having an affair with his secretary Trish Saunders?'

Quibble's square shoulders ignored both the query and a

volley of sniggers from the ranks of the gutter press. Infra-dig. He'd come across that Dawe character before.

'Jenny Hewitt again. Could you reassure my readers, who are for the most part from the business community, that there are no restrictions on commercial publications envisaged for the Medway region at this point in time?'

'The investigation is ongoing, Miss Hewitt. I'll be awaiting the results of full forensic and semantic analyses of all the evidence before advising the Chief Constable as to any possible restrictions.'

'And what restrictions might you envisage?'

'It's far too early at this stage to try to second guess what restrictions may or may not be deemed necessary.'

'And when might we expect these reports to come through?'

'In the fullness of time. But sooner, rather than later.'

'Murray. *Evening Cornerboy*. Can I take it you'll be reporting back on your progress to His Travesty the King?' The meeting came briefly to life. The merriment extended to everyone except Quibble, who returned the briar bad-humouredly into his thin mouth and bit down on its stem, and Evans of the BBC, whose microphone gave out one ear-splitting caterwaul before dying a death. Soon after, the conference too died a death. When the hall was empty but for the two latecomers, Chief Inspector Quibble straightened a few papers, tapped the dead microphone, shook his head at Evans, and then bore down on the pair. His close-set eyes looked straight at the garmungler as he approached. Who are you? they appeared to ask. The other man rose and as he swam into focus Quibble recognised him for some fool warden out of the

Academy. Harrow, or Hedley, or Headway. Decommissioner, though he'd be damned if he could recall a single term the pedant had got around to decommissioning during all his years at Semantics. How long was it now that 'wassail' and 'hebdomadary' had sat idle on their books?

It was the freelancer who'd posed the question who took all his present attention. Who are you? the eyes demanded. No mere journalist, that much was obvious. A newspaper hack would never have been given access to Sir Æthelred's ear. And so it was to the garmungler he sprake. 'Who are you?'

'Hackett.' The reply appeared to give the questioner little satisfaction. 'Ignatius.'

'So you say.' The gimlet eyes bore into the Eirishman. 'Not Rooney.'

The journalist's eyebrows skipped facetiously. 'So you say.'

Quibble drew on the empty briar, then took it from his mouth and pointed its stem at his adversary. Those damned Eirish, all cause and no effect. It was time for a curve-ball. 'Tell me, "Hackett". Do you know the meaning of "foubt"?'

The journalist ribbled his chin. 'Of foubt?' He appeared to think it might be a trick question. 'Foubt?' The prolonged ribble suggested he thought the plod was trying to trap him in some way. 'Foubt, was it you said?' As the ferret eyes burrowed away, Quibble's hunter's instinct saw his quarry take refuge behind a thought. 'Maybe, Mr Quibble, it's the Eirish you're having a problem with. You don't mean "ꝼΔohb"?'

'Foubt. Foubt!'

The Eirishman considered this. 'The 'b' is silent?'

Quibble nodded, singularly.

'I can't say that I've heard hide nor hair of foubt.'

'Verb, is it?' inquired Headway, or Harrow. 'I foubt, you foubt?'

'That's just it. Impossible to say.' Even while the Academician sprake and he replied loosely in his direction, Chief Inspector Quibble of Semantics continued his scrutiny of this Hackett character. It was as though he was sure he knew he was withholding something from him and couldn't care less if he knew that he knew. 'Found on its own. No context.' His eyes tunnelled deep. 'Foubt.' Neither man blinked first.

Quibble now looked at Hastings (that was the blighter's name!), as though he knew that he knew nothing and was equally blasé about letting him know his opinion of his ignorance. Hastings looked at Hackett. 'I'll lay odds it's the past tense!' his eyes opened brightly, filling his spectacles. 'Today he fibts. Yesterday he foubt. Tomorrow… well, you see what I mean.'

Quibble's wince declared that he did not suffer fools gladly, and fools from the Academy least gladly of all; Hackett's smirk that he knew this and wasn't bothered if they both knew that he knew. 'Would you mind,' inquired the policeman in the direction of the Academician, 'if I had a private word with Mr Hackett?' Harold Hastings looked as if he'd been offended and he didn't mind who knew about it. His face looking boiled, he nodded disgruntedly and waddled out of earshot.

'I'm told you're something of an expert on languages,' said Quibble.

'I wouldn't go that far.'

The eyes became narrow, the furrow deep. 'You do seem

to have… connections.'

Hackett's eyes also narrowed. That ellipsis… 'None that I'm aware of.'

'All the same, your Tee-shock saw fit to send you over to us.'

'Was it the Long Fellow sent me,[40] *faith*?'

The ferret eyes carried out a quick calculus. It was time for a quip. 'The Devil in Eire.'

Now, it was a matter of cold fact that Quibble's levity was neither spontaneous nor warm. His close-set eyes appeared to be experiencing difficulties in processing the Eirishman's responses, that was all, and this uncharacteristic wisecrack was intended simply to wrong-foot the other. Were Hackett's quips diffident or flippant? If the latter, his lot was not a happy one. Flippancy had no place in the Quibble scheme of things. 'What game is he up to with this so-called Dubilin Institute of Advanced Studies?' he gruntled.

'Trying to prove there's two St Patricks, as the wag said. I'll tell you though, if it was Dev asked for yours truly to be sent over, it's the first I've heard of it.'

'There are strings being pulled, all the same,' gruntled Quibble. 'Where you're concerned,' he specified. 'I don't like it,' he opined. His eyes executed a quick survey of the empty guildhall. Hastings was bumbling over by the exit. 'I don't like it one bit.' The gap between his eyes narrowed, causing the

---

40 An allusion to Éamon de Valera (1882-1975), the Spanish-American mathematical genius who was Taoiseach (Dinnen (op cit), 'chief, head, leader, prince or majordomo') of the Eirish Free State from 1932 to 1948. He is best remembered for the policy of wartime neutrality and his for promotion of rural alfresco dancing. His ponderous delivery of speech gave rise to the epithet 'the Long Fellow.'

furrow to rise. 'That new cache they dug up in the cathedral's graveyard bears all the hallmarks of a Republican plot.'

'Do you tell me so!'

A brief pause ensued, during which hiatus Quibble enumerated mentally the many leads he was not prepared to entrust to the Eirishman's ken at this point in time:

Item: an anonymous tip-off suggesting four perpetrators, of Eirish provenance.
Item: a flame-darkened diagram of a lozenge on a scrap of linen of Ulster provenance, with four cardinal points designated ***M; C; F; S;*** in the centre of which was a large ***Q.***? with a mock crown on top.
Item: a pair of Saxon-genitives, whose provenance may turn out to be the Wooton-Hey word-hoard.
Item: a Harrison Cast of unknown provenance, returned forthwith to the Academy of Letters to see if it was theirs.
Item: a box filled with sundry items, viz., several lead-cast letters, upper- and lower- case, possibly of the Gaelic alphabet, together with orts sketched in half-round uncial which also pointed to a Celtic provenance.
Item: a precision mechanical rotor stamped with the letters 𝔊𝔖-2 and with an entire Blackletter alphabet which included the letter ß placed about its circumference, of unknown application, unlikely to be of Eirish manufacture.
Item: the predominance of carpals over tarsals in the present cache,[41] the SUI values of which had yet to be

41 For a summary of McTurcail's taxonomy of bogus terms and their broad division into carpals and tarsals, see Volume Two, Chapter the Third below.

ascertained, but which showed a tendency to diminish naturally according to the rhythm of the natural logarithm, with a half-life of a fortnight (est.).[42]

These items the Chief Inspector withheld despite the many strings that were being pulled by Whitehall, by the Chief Constable, by Sir Æthelred and, he winced to think, by the imbeciles in the Academy. Whoever this hack journalist turned out to be, he had done nothing as yet to merit Quibble's confidence.

As if he'd been party to the Chief Inspector's thoughts, the journalist now sprake. 'My turn to ask you something?' The impassivity of Quibble's narrow features suggested that he would be prepared to entertain a query. 'What exactly has Paddy Dinneen got to do with any of this?'

'Paddy…?'

'The lexicographer.' Pause. 'The "folklore"…?'

The eyes at once became shrewd. Quibble was carrying out another quick calculus, the result of which was to try to land a carp of truth, although the bait he used was not precisely a falsehood. Besides, he had bigger fish to fry. 'That "folklore" was found during a raid last Christmas on a flat in Cantbury. The birds had flown the nest just before we got there. Tipped off, I suspect. But there, nestled among the plates and discarded phonemes, and,' he winced in distaste, 'Eirish denomination banknotes, we found your Dinneen's folklore. Heavily scored.'

42 See entry 5.2.1 of the Appendix for the relationship between SUI values, natural logarithms and the Law of Diminishing Returns. For other recondite terms such as Harrison Casts, the reader is referred to Sir Henry Beadle's monumental *Etymologicon*, but warned that anything contained therein may be apocryphal.

The Inspector suddenly gave the metaphorical line a tug. 'How did you know about it?'

'The Academy.'

Quibble flinched.

'How else?'

Quibble's teeth clenched.

'At the round table this morning.'

Quibble's brow frundled.

'At which you didn't show.'

The vicegrip of lips tightened before 'Bunch of blasted amateurs!' broke from them.

'I'm sorry?'

'Amateurs! Always have been! Gentlemen etymologists the like of Burton and Sweetman, and Sir Henry Beadle.' The frundle almost became facetious. 'You know, Beadle actually used to pin substantives in enormous display cabinets, like so many beetles.' His weasel eyes estimated that the Academician was out of earshot. 'Director a bally Bailfastman, all Ulster bluster. Accent you could cut with a knife, and *he's* guardian of the King's Engelish?' The parentheses to either side of the thin lips winced. 'Commissioner and Decommissioner, is it? There should be a strict policy of quid pro quo operating. For every term decommissioned, one and only one let in. It means acting hand in glove, istead of which they act on the motto let not thy right hand know… like a veritable Tweedledeedum and Tweedledeedee. Worse, where Tweedledeedee over there moves glacially when the utmost alacrity is demanded, Tweedledeedum acts prodigally where the utmost restraint is warranted. Lets in suspect and dubitous loanwords by the boatful until you scarcely know if it's the King's Engelish you encounter walking the high street of any town of the realm. Let me assure you, the French would never be so laissez faire.'

It was time for Hackett to throw out his own carp. 'But in light of the Grimaldi fiasco…'

'Grimaldi fiddlesticks! What he should be doing, Tweedledeedum I mean, is exhuming and recommissioning good Saxon stock to displace those showy Italian imports. And your friend Tweedledeedee there, he should be just as adept at giving them their marching orders, instead of fiddle-faddling over every quaint and recherché usage. Do you know what principle governs their precious Royal Academy of Letters? Le Châtelier's Principle, which is another way of saying the Principle of Je m'en foute.[43] As if a language were some class of chemical laboratory which simply rights itself in accordance with Johnson's Postulate[44] to eliminate anomalies. If that were the case, how do you explain Welsh?'

Hackett stared, at a loss. Whither, this sudden venom? Le Châtelier, bedad! And Beadle? He shut his eyes, and seemed for a moment to see du Maurier's cartoon figure in pith helmet out of Punch magazine. Time of Livingston I presume. 'You don't mean *the* Sir Henry Beadle? The man who dug up the Wooton-Hey word-hoard?'

For the second time in so many minutes every feature

---

43 Long a favourite of laissez-faire economists, Le Châtelier's Principle proposes "if a dynamic equilibrium is disturbed by changing the conditions, the position of equilibrium shifts to counteract the change to re-establish an equilibrium." What the Principle of Je m'en foute proposes is anyone's guess.

44 In a debate with the cleric and wit Laurence Sterne, the lexicographer Samuel Johnson (1709-1784) postulated, without proof, 'Nothing odd will do long.' The fact that the unusual postulate has survived would seem its own rebuttal.

on Quibble's reticent face contracted involuntarily. 'What do you know about the Wooton-Hey word-hoard?' Hackett's shrug was so obviously ingenuous that the detective's growl resumed, as if to make up for an involuntary outpouring of disdain. 'I've one more question for you, Mr Hackett.' Quibble's brows pressed down so low they appeared to force his eyes yet closer together until they were on the point of mounting the bridge of his nose. His fingers briefly touched his breast-pocket, in which was folded the scrap of Bailfast linen upon which was inscribed, in orange juice that had been coaxed from illegibility by a candle-flame, the letters *M; C; F; S,* forming the vertices of a diamond, about a crowned *Q?.* This last item, viz. the crowned *Q?,* he'd copied onto a sheet of paper, and it was this paper copy that he now removed from a side pocket and passed to Hackett. 'Mean anything?'

Hackett unfolded the sheet as though it were the original, held it at arm's length, held it up to see if it was watermarked, held it as a token of faith that the Inspector had shared it with him, but felt he could in no way enlighten the latter. 'Q?' he shook his head, 'under a carnival crown.' He scrummeled the back of his head. 'Queen?'

'Queen,' dismissed the detective.

Hackett knucked his knuckles. 'It couldn't be a man by the name of Quinn?'

'What do you know,' drilled the policeman's eyes, at once alert, 'about a man by the name of Quinn?'

Late that evening, Hackett had a most curious experience. He was sitting on the summit of Star Hill, ears figuratively twitching in the manner of the old warhorse who's heard a distant bugle. His excitement demanded time alone to think. As he'd ascended the slope, he'd tried to square the bogus articles that had appeared in the *Logdon Gravitas* and *Munchester Warden*, penned with his very glyph, with any of the journalists he'd seen at the interview. He'd dismissed in turn each of the motley crowd — none of them seemed remotely to fit the bill. Good God, if that was the calibre of journalist writing these days, what on earth had he been worrying about? He sat on his hands, to quell the agitation of optimism bubbling inside him.

Like the fabled charger, the erstwhile columnist's journalistic nostrils had caught the whiff of a story, one moreover that held the promise of a scoop. At present it was a phantom triangle of roisterling sides: an attack on the language; an arcane Academy of Letters; a branch of the CID whose Chief Inspector didn't suffer fools gladly, and fools of the Academy least of all. But three questions arose that were bothering him. He determined to address them by turns. The trouble was, they refused to cooperate, and jostled and intruded on one another like so many children. He tried once more, focusing on the darkening sky that separated the castle's castellation from the spire's aspiration.

Perhaps Harry Hastings had a point. Who knew? Dubitous their language had come about in the way he'd said. Latin, how did it go? And Saxon, and then French. The three of them cleaving together. He removed his hands from beneath his thighs and moved them together. But if you hit them with a hammer, would they cleave apart? Melancholy Christ! What class of nonsense was that? And what could it possibly have to do with bgrrgl and lali perpengi? His hands cleaved apart. Like as not, Hastings was an amadán, pure and simple.

Quibble seemed to think so. But that led to the second side of the triangle. What class of animal was this Royal Academy of Letters? Why had no one heard of it? And how much was he in a position to reveal, given Dubilin's injunction: only Maloney?

Then there was Semantics, which was at least squarely in the public eye. Even if he'd misheard or misunderstood the plod, his journalist's nose was still sensitive to bad smells. Why was there so little love lost between them and Semantics? Were they pups of the same bitch, or were they like the Lion and the Unicorn who were forever battling? Which led back to question number two, whose obtuseness almost instantly gave way so that he'd find himself staring into the middle distance. Then he'd fix on the first stars appearing between the spire and the keep, and thus be returned to question number one, his mind a counter caught in an unending game of snakes and ladders.

Words, too, buzzed about his head like a cloud of gnats. But this was the old way. This was how the great articles of his heyday had come about. Words, goading like so many gadflies. They'd alight, line up in phrases, dispel. They'd taunt his vision, buzz in and out of earshot. It was an ecstasy of creative torment as exquisite as any torture dreamed up for Tantalus. But he remained wary. Words had been his downfall once before. If he could just find the words to begin, to allow thought to alight with them, and argument…

There was a fine, elderly gent in tweeds exercising a couple of gundogs on the green, and as much to distract his mind from the circles it had been turning as anything else, Hackett called over to him. 'Do you have the right time, sir?' Funny, he mused, how you always ask for the right time, as if you might be just as interested to know the wrong time once in a way.

'I beg your parlind?'

An eccentric. Hackett might have bloody known. 'Would you have the right time I wonder?' The question was entirely by the by. True, Hackett did have a return train to catch, at twenty past something or other. Nine, on balance. But Hastings was sure to fetch him. The elderly man stopped, reached into a waistcoat pocket, leaned forwards, consulted a half-hunter he held to within an inch of his nose, and leaning back, approached. The elder dog kept a mistrustful distance, the younger began to nose Hackett's hand.

'Cocoming on for ten to.'

'Ten to which hour would that be, sir?'

'What what?' He glanced at Hackett with what might have been suspicion or might have been myopia. 'Eirish, are you?'

'I am, sir.'

The grey head gave one of those mechanical, involuntary jerks that give to the elderly gentry the aspect of poultry. 'Never been myself. Told it's quite bleauful. Wet, though.' He twitched a second time, straightened, then looked all about him with eyes narrowed to stop the breeze bringing water to them. 'Think there'll be a foubt?'

Hackett wondered had he heard correctly. Foubt. Noun, singular. Silent 'b'. Before he'd time to reflect, his mouth had asked 'with whom?'

'Bosch!'

Hackett sat up as though insulted. The cane tapped Hackett's leg lightly. 'Can never trust the Bosch. One minute he's at your feet, and the next, he's at your bgrrgl bgrrgl throat.'

Hackett sat back and eyed him from tip to toe. He had, indeed, a military bearing. Ramrod straight, despite his year. But he was too old by half to have served in the Great War, surely. 'What do you think yourself?'

'No dubit about it.' And then, with another tap of the cane, he confided, 'Versailles.'

'Versailles?'

'They're grodlumous you see. Grodlumous as all hell! But they're too damned Teutonic to ever admit it. Not on their nankly.'

'And you think they'll start a foubt because they're... grodlumous?'

He stared at the Eirishman from surprised eyes. 'Not the blindest dubit about it, man! In the blood you see. You mark my wurrils.' Four taps of the cane emphasised each syllable. 'Already arming the Rhineland. Before this yover is out, Herr Hitler will have bgrrgl bgrrgl found casus enough to move into the Alsace.' His eyes became slits. 'Think he'll stop there do you?'

'Well, I...'

'Not on your nankly!' With a ferocious twitch, which seemed to impart to him an irresistible momentum, he set off into the dusk. 'Good dag to you!' He was on his way before Hackett had a chance to register his words, much less decipher them. Only the younger dog lingered to lick the saltiness from his palm.

'Trajan! Heel!'

The gundog bounded away. Hackett shot up. Melancholy Christ, he was still dandering and here was a possible lead! Here was a star witness! At the very least, here was some light relief! 'I say!' he calloohed, waving. But the man was already out of earshot. His instinct was to run after him, but at that precise moment he caught sight of Harry Hastings gramping up the hill, one hand pressing the bowler to his head, the other windmilling wildly. Amused, bemused, Hackett waited for him to climb almost to the summit before letting on to notice him. 'What's up?'

'Didn't know…' he puffed, 'where the devil…' he huffed, 'you'd got to!' He placed one white-gloved hand on each low knee and bent over. After three full iterations of breath, he added, gesturing wildly at the city lights spangling below them 'train!'

Late that night, while Logdon slept, at an oil-lit desk in a backroom of the Eirish Consulate in Belgravia, Ignatius Hackett removed the case from his *Underwood* and blew a decade's dust from the keys. With hands steadier than they had been in months, he dialled a virgin sheet of foolscap into the machine's barrel. After a bare moment's hesitation, "Foubt?' he typed, the patter of keys like the first spatter of rain on parched ground. "Not on Your Nankly!" He pushed the return lever, the bell tinked, and in that instant seven years of fulmering silence were dispelled.

Hackett was back.

VOLUME TWO

THE EMPIRE STRIKES BACK

CHAPTER THE FIRST

in which Hackett visits the hallowed reading-rooms of the British Library, then enjoys the confidence of the Director of the Royal Academy of Letters

It would be a mistake to think that the columnist had been idle in the course of the previous fortnight's indecisions and revisions, his resolution dilly-dallying even as his feet were shilly-shallying. In fact he'd become a regular visitor to the great reading-rooms of the British Library. At first these excursions had been faute-de-mieux, a pretext to get out from under Chapman's shoes. Once there, though, sensing so much mental industry roiling around his indolence, he determined to profit from the sessions by scouring the recent press for further articles by that scurril who'd dared purloin his cypher, and whose identity in Hackett's estimation was bound up with the enigmatic Quinn. He found none, but found instead that he could engage in reading without any obvious risk to wellbeing.

On the third day he chanced on a book. Inside, he chanced upon the woodcut that depicted the incident which had sparked off the famous Inkhorn Controversy. Famous to all but him, that was the point. Spurred by the image with such impetus that the inkhorn might well have been tossed at his head, Hackett determined to fill the cavernous lacunae in his grasp of history, in particular, history as it pertained to the development and ascertaining of the Engelish tongue. Over the previous days he'd read extensively, it remained to be seen whether he could read intensively.

Several extant copybooks filled in the manner of Da Vinci's with scribbles, notes, sketches, diagrams, doodles and marginalia attest to the energy of his endeavour. They attest, too, to the haphazard manner of the Hackett enquiry, lured continually down every footnote and byway, shunning no bauble. Two early transcriptions suggest Hackett wasn't entirely green when Harry Hastings sprake, some days later, of a certain pilgrimage route to Cantbury:

'In the reign of Henry Plantagenet, Chancellery was an elite cartel of legal clerks, scribes and cursitors called together by the Lord Chancellor, from whose office it derived its appellation. These savants were charged with transcribing anything and everything that was to be sent out under the royal seal, thereby standardising usage and orthography. At the time of the Peasants' Revolt, Chancellery was shorn of its 'ell' and became Chancery. Its staff consists of twelve senior clerks, or masters, and twelve junior. It is only the twelve senior scribes who are correctly termed Chancers. Once the Royal Academy of Letters came into being, it assumed many of the functions of Chancery, but in the utmost secrecy.' (Filmer's *Secret History*)

On the facing page was noted:

'Following the Peasants' Revolt, a certain Geoffrey of Southwalk was charged by King Richard II with taking the helm of 'Chancery', as it was now to be called. On assuming the unassuming office Geoffrey assumed the title of 'Chancer',

though in a copyist's error the 'n' was subsequently inverted. To his detractors, his incomplete Cantbury Tales *is little more than a repository for 'buried cant'. The Medway got its name as it was 'medway' along the old pilgrim's route South-walk to Cantbury.'*

Not all the entries are so coherent. Many are gnomic. Thus:

'Richard III — not the first Richard to have been harried out of office!'

Or the following:

'Manuscripts of unknown authorship, some of which marked NN, more of which anon.'

One entire copybook consists of a topic that came to fascinate the journalist:

'The Civil War — the Engelish brand (!) — was not so much about taxation and the Divine Right of Kings as the eruption of the Inkhorn Controversy onto the streets and fields. The Saxophonists were instrumental in instigating hostilities.'

Beside an elaborate cartoon of a plumed hat, a note runs:

'Cavileers — So-called because they would 'cavil on the ninth part of a hair' when it came to lexical disputes. From the Latin cavilla — mockery.'

On the facing page, annotating a minutely copied engine, the entry runs:

'Ironside: a portable press on which the Roundhead broadsides were printed. The Baroque broadsides favoured by the Cavileers were seen as 'so much frippery.' From iren and sade, Saxon stock as solid as Beowulf.'

The centre pages contain elaborate scripts and fonts, serif and sans in equal measure. One entry in childish roundhead reads:

'Roundheads took their name from the simple 'roundhead' font

that they favoured. Together with terms of French and Roman derivation, the many fanciful fonts embraced by the Cavileers were seen as 'so much Popery'.'

In the margin, vertically, runs a coda:

'Head from heafod. *Germanic. But round from* rotundus, L., *so maybe the Puritans weren't so pure after all!'*

Nor could Hackett always keep his constitutional flippancy in check. In a third copybook, a page bearing the title "The Great Vowel Shift" contains a cartoonlike doodle of Os and As and Us sprouting wings and migrating north. Others, though, are in deadly earnest. An entry under a sketch of a dour, gangly-haired, bug-eyed, warty individual he had transcribed verbatim from the *Encyclopaedia Hibernica*:

'Cromwell, Oliver (1599-1658). Though a darling of Engelish Republicans, Cromwell has enjoyed a blacker reputation on the sister island. The arrival of his Parleymentary Army (q.v.) with their attendant prostitutes or "baggage-train" into the colony in 1649 involved the deliberate introduction of crab-lice into the ports of Drogheda and Waterfjord, an early instance of biological warfare. The painful condition has been colloquially referred to ever since as the 'curse of Cromwell.' The expression 'warts and all' dates from this time.'

Several days after the appearance of the 'Not on Your Nankly' article, Hackett found himself once again muttling along Oxenford Street in the direction of Ealing Broadleaf. Chapman, who was an early riser, had left terse word for Hackett, who was not, that the journalist was to have a 'grand tour' of the Royal Academy of Letters under the aegis of Turlough McTurcaill. Then he'd left in high dudgeon.

Miss Maloney, a redhead with a mole on her cheek that

was oddly alluring and whose scent was as overpowering as it was evocative, smirked as she remarked that the Cultural Attaché had been less than impressed the invitation did not extend to himself. Hackett might have enjoyed the conspiratorial smirk more had the scent not brought him involuntarily back to surreptitious childhood incursions to his father's bedside dresser, for the spoor was unmistakably *Lily of the Valley.*

McTurcaill, he mused. The second of the Wardens. Or the first. It depended upon how you looked at it. Tweedledum, wasn't it? Commissioner of neologisms. Licenser of loanwords. If he's half the liúdramán that other eegit was, said Hackett to himself as the car puttled under Mobled Arch, you'd've been as well to stay in bed. The thought of the diplomatic king-size he'd recently vacated, with its mattress and bolster and its sheets of Bailfast linen made Hackett stretch like a cat. It was a luxury he hadn't experienced in donkey's. He became so momentarily indolent that he turned to the seat beside him, and was surprised to find there Chapman's absence.

It wasn't the only absence to disturb him that notable Sunday. When the diplomatic Bentley disgorged him at what was surely the self-same address on the self-same square off Ealing Broadleaf, he was nonplussed to find the absence of steps and portico through which he and Chapman had been butlered on their previous excursion. Had the chauffeur mistaken the spot? Unlikely, it was the self-same chauffeur with ears like urn handles. Hackett wandered its length and breadth, retraced his steps, ribbled his stubble. Curiouser and curiouser. On his third pass, the edifice was still not where it should have been…

Now when in pursuit of imaginary mice, Hackett's Pangur Bán mentality was nothing if not resourceful. The Royal Academy of Letters had been founded on the principle of absolute secrecy. Might it not follow that it be berthed in a building that obeyed the Berkeley principle *esse est percipi*? One perhaps built entirely out of trees that had fallen in woods without anyone within earshot to hear their fall? But this corridor of thought led to a pretty impasse. He, Hackett, was searching for said building. Would that search not be the necessary and sufficient condition to conjure it into being? He was on the point of refuting that line of thought when his attention was drawn to one of the two Wardens scurrying up a set of granite steps to the very portico he, Hackett, had been looking for. 'We're late!' he calloohed.

McTurcaill ushered him down corridors even dimmer and more decrepit than they'd appeared on Hackett's previous visit. The place really did have an aura of Dickensian dereliction about it, out of all keeping, one would have thought, with its national importance at so fromulous a time. They pattered past the double-doors that had led into the boardroom with the mahogulous table, turned a tight corner, all but collided with a bucket and mop. Finally, they arrived at a door one might have mistaken for a lumber room except that it bore a number, 404. 'We're late,' repeated McTurcaill, hurrying a fob-watch back into his fob-pocket. He tapped, hesitated, tapped again. Then he opened the door onto a vacant room where he abandoned Hackett.

The room was divided by a screen, or scrim. On his side of the scrim stood a chair and table on which stood a glass, a carafe of clear water, the newspaper in which the 'Not on Your Nankly' article had appeared, and an ancient, yellowed folio. Hackett squinnied at the water. Drink me, it appeared to beckon. He furtively looked about then poured until the glass was half-full, for he was feeling nothing if not optimistic. He then passed the glass untried to his right hand, picked the folio up with his left, and ran his eye down the frontispiece:

A TABLE ALPHABETICALL,
CONTEYNING AND TEACHING THE TRUE WRITING, AND VNDERFTANDING OF HARD VFUALL ENGLIFH WORDES, BORROWED FROM THE HEBREW, GREEKE, LATINE OR FRENCH, &C.
WITH THE INTERPRETATION THEREOF BY PLAINE ENGLIFH WORDS, GATHERED FOR THE BENEFIT & HELPE OF LADIES, GENTLEWOMEN, AND ANY OTHER UNSKILFULL PERFONS.
WHEREBY THEY MAY THE MORE EAFILIE AND BETTER VNDERFTAND MANY HARD ENGLIFH WORDES, WHICH THEY FHALL HEARE OR READ IN SCRIPTURES, SERMONS, OR ELFWHERE, AND ALFO BE MADE TO VFE THE FAME APTLY THEMFELUES.
LEGERE, ET NON INTELLIGERE, NEGLEGERE EST.
AS GOOD NOT TO READ, AS NOT TO VNDERFTAND.

Ladies, Gentlewomen, and any other 'unskilfull perfons', bedad! Now you had it! Though why not unfkillful? He flitted through, then looked again at the cover. "As good not to read, as not to vnderftand" That summed up his case. But had he not seen the self-same saw some place? A tanner to a make the book had been left there deliberately, as a test to see if he mightn't peruse it.

He now saw that a second volume had been concealed beneath the **TABLE ALPHABETICALL**, and setting the glass which was now half-empty on the table and passing the **TABLE ALPHABETICALL** into his right hand, he picked this up with his left:

A TABLE ANATOMICALL
OR THE ANATOMIE OF LANGUAGE
BEING AN ORIGINALL TREATIFE BY SIR ROBYN PLAIGER OF CAMSBRIDGE,
CHANCER AND PHILOFOPHER ROYALE,
WHEREIN THE NOUNS ARE SHEWN TO BE THE BONES OF THE LANGUAGE,
THE VERBS THE MUFELLS, THE CONJUNCTIONS THE JOINTS,
THE PREPOFITIONS THE LIGATURES, THE ADVERBS THE NERVES,
AND THE ADJECTIVES THE COMPLECIOUN.
PRINTED BY MERCER & SONS, LOGDON, MDCIV

This too he flicked through, pausing only to admire one or two ingenious figures that were contained therein. He then replaced the two on the table, being sure to conceal the **TABLE ANATOMICALL** underneath its fellow, and fell to examining his surroundings. Examining is too transitive a verb. The room was entirely bare but for the screen or scrim behind which stood, as though reflected, an identical desk and chair, flanked by what appeared to be batteries of lights. A door behind the scrim opened and a rotund silhouette entered the reflected area. Abruptly Hackett's half of the room was flooded with light, all but blinding the journalist. 'Sorry toy have kept yoy weetin',' the figure called out jovially in a voice that had a soupçon of Ulster in it. 'O'Brain.'

'Hackett,' countered Hackett, playing for time. The lights were so intense that each bulb was butterflied with its own blue afterimage. All he could make out of the pendulous figure behind the scrim were round, wire-rimmed glasses that had the disconcerting knack of flashing opaquely. 'Forgav the exsassive precaution, they teek secrecy to absurd lengths in here so they doy. But than, afore you wrote yon wee article, you'd naver heard tale of our Academy of Latters ay teek it?'

Hackett's head assented. Equivocally. He had and he hadn't. But if his vision had been bedazzled by the lights, his mind was bamboozled by what came next. 'You were rayt, Masther Hackett, to tray to expleen to your wee friend with that teyn shilling noot, so ye were. Very clavver.' The 10/- note, the one Chapman had taken to be counterfeit! But that had been inside the diplomatic Bentley, surely? How…?

'So than, high *does* one go aboyt ascerteening the value of the paynd starling?'

His mind in rapid pursuit of a thousand skedaddling mice, Hackett dispatched by reflex a phrase from Doolittle's disquisition. 'The gold standard.'

'The gold stondard? Aye. The gold stondard is something that we dad have until one black dee in Septamber of naynteen hundred and thirty-one, when they saw fat to throw it awee! The gold stondard, Masther Hackett, is something that gave yee a floor upon whach to pleace your furniture! The gold standard was something yoy could tip your hat toy. Do yoy know what it is that we doy here in the Academy?' The Director paused, but only for form's sake. For form's sake, Hackett made no attempt at this poser but hoisted his eyebrows invitingly. 'Ay'll tell ye. All langage is beesed upon the aydea of excheenge. Avery santence is a bill of excheenge, and the *raison d'être* of this pleece is to underwrayt such bills of excheenge as are in circuleetion. In the Academy, we provade the gold stondard upon whach the Angelish langage has built its foyndeetions. In the Academy, we promise to pee the barer the full valyee of whatever word the bearer wants to use, just so long as it's still in circuleetion. Still legal tander. That, Masther Hackett, is the seecred dyuty of the Academy.'

'And tell me, Dr O'Brain, how precisely do you go about doing that?'

'The name's O'Brain, not O'Brain.' The glasses, a bicycle perched on a traffic cone, retreated into opacity. 'That, Masther Hackett, is what ay have invayted yoy oyt here toy discover. Because we can't have ye writing any more of your wee articles withoyt ye at least know that much aboyt us. Can I ask yoy noy. Whenaver ay came in here,[45] yoy were examining that wee book?' Hackett hesitated. 'It's perfectly fane, Mr Hackett. Ay had it left here on purpose so ay did.' Something in the Ulsterman's demeanour — though to Hackett's ear the accent was just a tad *too* Ulster — invited him to pick up the **TABLE ALPHABETICALL**, 'That, sir, is the very furst Angelish dactionary so it is!'

'Ah! And the other?'

'The other covers santax. Because let me tell you one thang. Passing off bogus words is all vary well. But if they ever saw fat to pass off bogus santax, that'd really give Inspactor Quabble something to worry aboyt! But nevermaynd th'other for nigh. Th'other was written bay Robyn Plee-giar. Bay 'Sir' Robyn Plee-giar.' A metaphorical light bulb went on above the

45 In Ulster usage, whenever whenever is used it may generally be understood as when rather than whenever although, confusingly, whenever is also used to convey whenever.

Eirishman's skull. The name had been much bandied about twenty years before when the Royal Shakespeare Society and Dubilin Cervantes Society were preparing to break lances. 'Wrote... what was it again?'

'What it was agayn was *Cardeenio*. Beesed on Donkey-Whotay, whenaver he fainds ite the bogus second part by that roogue Avellaneda. Except it wasn't Robyn Plee-giar that wrote it so it wasn't. It was Sheekspar, with meebe a wee bit of halp.[46] And that's far from the only thang Robyn Plee-giar trayed to pass off as his own.' Another light bulb, of higher wattage, had lit. 'Hence the term...' Hackett knucked his fingers. Another penny, of more tested metal, had dropped. 'So the Academy commissioned these two primers, is that your point?'

The silhouette of O'Brien opened its mouth wide and emitted an aspirate hiss, as if Hackett had just cracked the best of jokes. 'This wee volume deetes from the tame of King Jeemes!' he crocodile-smiled. Hackett's mind raced. The only King James he could think of was the James of the taunt he

46 Very little of this manuscript is extant. The much-anthologised fragment:

2nd Shepherd: Is't possible?
Lucinda: I warrant you.
1st Shepherd: Go to! Go to!

has been shown by Granville-Barker to be an interpolation, probably by Middleton. Half a century earlier, another Middleton interjection, the melancholic Jaques': *'Let us foreswear venison, 'tis mete,'* found in the 'Bad Quarto' *As You Like It*, was discredited by Hazlitt. Middleton's career as an interpolator of dubitous texts was brought to a halt when he was outed as the author of the infamous addendum to *Ezekial:* 'Woe to the horse that will not stop.' Ironically, Middleton is himself the subject of an apocryphal story which goes that when he asked his mistress whether she'd permit him to immortalise her in a sonnet, she replied she wouldn't be averse.

used to throw at Chippy when they were in school. **Seamas an cac a caill eire.**[47] Beaten by King Billy-at-the-Boyne. 'So your **TABLE ALPHABETICALL** precedes the founding of the Academy. Is *that* your point?'

'That is *presaysely* my point. Back in those tames, words were brought in wally-nally, left, rayt and santre. There was no supervasion. Ay tell a lay! There was Choncery, ay suppose. But what kaynd of supervasion did Choncery ever provade?' In spite of recent excursions to the British Library, Hackett was at a loss to say what kind of supervision Chancery might have provided. So instead he shifted in his seat and shifted the fulcrum of the conversation. 'Can I ask, is Harry Hastings right to be worried,' he made an illustrative movement with his hands, 'about cleavage?'

'Cleavage!' ejaculated the Director with a wheeze approaching mirth. Ignoring the question, he sat forwards and raised three strubbly fingers. 'Latin, Saxon, Franch, am ay rayt?' Hackett nodded. 'Nigh,' the Director resumed, sitting back, 'let's examine Latin, Franch and Saxon. Latin, you mayt think, would be a fixed entity. Latin, you mayt think, would be the terra firma of langage. But there's the Latin of the Rooman centyurion, and then there's the Latin of the medieval monk. Bear that in maynd.' A fourth finger was raised. 'Nigh, when you take into accoynt all the dalects of Saxon Engeland, not tee mention the Juts and the Angles, and then whan ye throw the Deenelaw into the max, and Norweyan Yorvik, you begin to see the complaxities. Angelish, Masther Hackett,

---

47 Literally, 'James the shite who lost Eirland.' Proverbial of Eirishmen called James. King James, who fled to France, went into immediate and persistent denial about the defeat, earning him the sobriquet the Old Pretender.

is no sadimantary rock, built up oyt of two or even three deposits! Angelish, Masther Hackett, has an entare geology: metamorphic; igneous, yoy neem it. It's vulnerable, that I'll grant yoy, you could split it apart with a few well choosen bloows, but not quate in the sample wee that Mr Hastings imagines. He warns of the greet cleavage. Bay rayts he should say cleavages.'

O'Brien shifted, a spring detonating beneath him. 'Have yoy heard tell of what they term, in legalese, the laxical doublet?' Hackett shook his head. The only image the term evoked was of an outmoded garment with as scant a bearing on legalese as the accompanying hose had on the Elizabethan fire-brigade. O'Brien's shadow raised two strubbly fingers. 'Two words, where bay and large, one would doy just as well?'

Hackett thought for a minute. 'To have and to hold?'

'To have and to hoold,' he assented.

'Breaking and entering?' Hackett sat forward. He was getting enthusiastic.

'Breeking and antering. Good mon!' Hackett was on the point of crying 'assault and battery!' but the other's hand forestalled the cry. 'That tradition of the legal laxical doublet deetes back to the reen of Kang John. That's what we call him, nigh. At the taym of Robin Hude, he was Jean Sans Terre. Though Jean Sans Terre didn't remeen *sans terre* for all his lafe. High could yoy have a Prance with noo londs? Ye mayt as well have a feshmonger with no fesh. You mayt as well have a pranter with no prantin-press, or a hatter with no hat! So his father Hanry Plantagenet, in a rare fat of generosity, gronted the seeme Jean Sans Terre the Lordship of Ayreland. That's high come ye have a John's Castle in Lamerick.[48]

'Nigh, the seem Kang John was a greet mon for the books. No sooner had he sayned the Magna Carta than he desayded to codify the laws of the lond. But high to doy it? In what tongue to doy it? Magna Carta had been devaysed in Latin, but would that doy to settle a dispyut over a pag between toy peasants? The Chancellor at that tame was what ye'd call a cyut hoor. He advased His Hayness that it would be "fat and proper", if he wanted to "keep and mainteen" the "peace and quiayt" of his Ralm, to couple words together. To yoke them, like oxen. He should teek one from each tradition, d'ye follow me? He'd foreseen, before aver the mongrel langage had properly emerged, the sort of cleavage that our frand Heastings stall fears.' A latter spring detonated beneath O'Brien's bulk as he shifted in his chair. 'If the Franch was ever to feel, you'd be laft with the Saxon to fall back on. If that feeled, there'd be the Latin. And all the whale, the laxical doublet would act like a steeple across the linguistic breach, helping the langage to cleave together.'

'For fear it'd cleave apart?'

'Pracicely. That's whey, for the purposes of the law, the scheme was "fat and proper", *fat* from the Maddle Angelish, d'you see, proper from the Old Franch *propre*, meaning mane own. Ay'll give yoy an example. In law, you leave your last will and tastament, don't ye? Either word would serve very well on its oon. They're both respactable words, with gude long padigrees. 'Will' from the Old Engelish *wylla*; 'tastament' from

48 A city on the Shannon river immortalised by the poetic form to which it gives its name. A Limerick is any five-line rhyme the second line of which begins with the pronoun 'Who'. The granting of the Lordship of Eirland by Henry II, on April 1st 1177, to his doltish son John was intended sarcastically.

the Latin *testamentum*, so everyone from priest to pauper knyoy what you were talking aboyt. And af you neglact to leave your last will and tastament, your relatives meyt very well squabble over your "goods and chattels" if they don't want to go to "wrack and ruin". Nigh do ye see? Wrack from the Saxon *wraec*; ruin from the Old Franch *ruine*. Am I getting through to you?'

'Loud and clear,' said Hackett. 'But...' the Dubiliner raised one finger aloft in the manner of the Punch cartoon of Edward Carson at the trial of Oscar Wilde, 'why all the hugger-mugger? Why hide the Academy out in Ealing Broadleaf in what I take to be a Berkeley building? Why deny its existence? The French and Germans and Italians see in their academies a source of national prestige, not to say rivalry.' In silhouette, O'Brien's face cracked into its Cheshire grin. 'You ask me whey. Ay'd have thought the reasons are obvious, Masther Hackett. Ay'd have thought the *deenger* is obvious. Ay'd have thought the *necassity* is obvious. What ay would not say is at all obvious is, the *high*.'

'The how?'

'Aye. The high. You've heard, ay teek it, of the Scrabblers?'

Hackett ribbled his chin. 'The Scribblers, is it?'

'Aye. The Scrabblers.' O'Brien's shift in bulk corresponded to another sudden shift in the ballast of his conversation and in the distribution of springs beneath him. 'Masther Hackett, ay'll give ye a wee hastory lasson.' Hackett's ballast also shifted, to accommodate what he intuited would be a sustained delivery.[49] 'What ye need to understond is, all

49 The reader familiar with the history of the Academy need feel under no obligation to follow O'Brien's summary, and can with clear conscience omit the remainder of the chapter.

langage is first and foremost a polatical beast. Let me ask yoy, could ye have had a Rooman Empaire withoyt a sangle and unitary Latin langage, each decleynsion and conjugeetion as ordered and dasciplined as a malitary legion?' The question was rhetorical. 'Isabella of Aragon, on the eve of carving out for Speen greet sweethes of tarritory in the Amaricas, declared to her conquistadors,' one of O'Brien's fingers rose imperially, 'langage is the parfect instrument of Empaire'. And she was rayt! Of course the Cotholic and Apostolic Church needed no upstart Sponiard to school theym in the theory of Empaire! That's whey for santuries they clung to their yoyniversal Latin. That's whey men like Weycliffe and Tollund were far more deengerous than a thoysand heretics could ever be. What ameezes is high long it took for the realiseetion to dawn on the polatical classes.

'But it did feynally dawn on them. Having spant the whole of the Reneessance squabbling insade the walls of their city-steetes, the Itollians were the first to realise the need to stondardise, if there was aver to be a somblance of unity on the peninsula. Fafteen eety toy! It's a year avery bit as important for linguastics as fourteen naynty toy is for navigeetion. Fafteen eety toy. That's the year the Itollians feynally got aroynd to foynding their *Accademia di Linguaggio*, and still it was the first in Chrastendom, would you believe that nigh? *Unità pela lingua*! A nooble ambition, like the Matric Sastem in Saynce. Standardiseation! There'd have been noo Cavour nor Garibaldi withoyt *unità pela lingua*, believe yoy me. And Jarmany followed. It's the self-seme varayty in the argot that held back the Hun all those santuries. The map of Narn Yurp, once yoy crossed the Rhane, was a patchwork qualt of squabbling principalities so it was. Hey Jarman and Loo Jarman and the davil knows what Jarman. But look at them nigh!'

'You're holding up Germany and Italy as models of social organisation?'

'But look at their langages, mon. *E pluribus unum*! That's the only wee. Ein Reich, Ein Volk, Eine Sprache. Divarsity in spreech is nothing but a racipe for jalousy, misunderstonding and disaster. That's what put peed to Austro-Hungary. That's whey you'll never see a Balgium or a Swatzerland a greet par.' Hackett nodded. Though his eyes were dazzled, the entire argument was becoming clear. Also, perhaps, the nature of the attack, if attack it was. 'Nigh we come to the Restoreetion. Saxteen Saxty. Yoy had the death of Angelish Republicanism. Yoy had the Greet Fare of Logdon, and with it, the *tabula rasa* upon whach Hooke and Wreyn would bald a capital worthy of the Angelish tongue. And, in tondem with the foynding of the Royal Sosayty, you had the foynding of this vary Academy. There was greet debeete aboyt it. Mony a mon wanted it to be the flagship of the Restored Monarchy. But whenaver it was foynded, the Academy of Latters was to remeen the best kept of secrets!'

'But what has this to do with the Scribblers?'

O'Brien sat back, satisfied in the manner of a schoolmaster who has been asked to exercise his hobbyhorse. Through the opacity of his glasses, the eyes could be inferred to have half closed. 'What has any of this to doy with the Scrabblers. Well mate yoy osk.' He set his shadow hands on the shadow table and set about examining their backs. 'Ay'll expleen. But ay have to insast that none of what ay sea goos beyond these four walls.'

'It goes without saying.'

'Very goode. In the tame of Queen Onn, the Scrabbler's Club was meed up of men the lake of Pope, and Gay and Congreve. And theyn of course there was Swaft.'

'Swift?'

'Aye, Swaft. He was the cyutest of the whole domn bunch so he was. Nigh, what ye have to understond Masther Hackett is that the Academy was already in pleece from the tame of the second Charles. Of course, it had no charter. That didn't hoppen until the reen of Queen Onn. From the first, what yoy had were repeated *calls* for an Academy. That was always part of the deception. There was noo Academy! There never had been an Academy! And so there were demands toy *establish* an Academy! Most of the Scrabbler's Club were in on the jooke. Pope, and Gay and Steele. Swaft even went so far as to *demond* an Academy be set up in an open latter! The cheek of the mon. In saventeen hundurd and twalve, he penned his feemous *Modest Proposal for Ascerteening the Angelish Tongue*. There's wit for ye! There's effrontery! Ascerteen, from the Franch, to fax.'

'To fax?'

'Aye, fax. Swaft was a Tory to the marrow of his bones so he was. So that whanaver the Whags came to par under Jarman George, the Academy had no other course but toy goo undergroynd. And that, Masther Hackett, is where it's remeened to this dee.'

If Hackett was dazzled by the plethora of royals thrown out by the Hereditary Director, he didn't let on. The time had come to cry havoc and let slip the keenest of his questions. 'If you're so wedded to secrecy, why invite me, a journalist, out here.'

'I'm glod ye osked. We survave, Masther Hackett, by

hiding in pleen sight. We survive, Masther Hackett, on the principle of deneyability. The trouble is, we're too damned gude at it. Deneyability is all very well, but it's a double-edged sword so it is. Too much deneyability and our funding gets cut. High does a Manasther justifey a budget for an Academy that isn't thar? So that's whey, avery nigh and then, we invite the lakes of yourself oyt here. We're gude at hiding, betimes it's the plain sight that goes massing! All ay ask is that in your next wee article and the ones to follow, you keep what I've said in meynd.' The Hereditary Director shifted once more in his seat, hand aloft. 'Yoy asked me what we doy here in the Academy?' He sat forwards, his teeth bared into a crocodile grin. 'Ay won't teek up any more of your tame, Masther Hackett. Whenaver Masther MockTurcaill is taking yoy on your tour,' he jovially wheezed, 'be sure to ask ham what we doy here in the Academy, won't yoy.'[50]

---

50 For a redacted account of what Hackett learned from McTurcaill's tour of the Academy, as presented in his dossier passed on to Miss Maloney, see the Appendix.

CHAPTER THE SECOND

in which an account is given of the Phoneme War, *during the course of which Hackett's reputation steadily advances*

Our story now moves on some eighteen months. It is the year of the Munich Crisis.[51] A great deal has happened in the interim. Shanghai has gone up in smoke, the Hindenburg has gone down in flames; and somewhere in between Amelia Earhart has gone off the radar. In Spain, the Nationalists have the Republicans on the ropes, a feat replicated by Joe Louis in his return match against Max Schmeling; in the Netherlands, Alekhine has recovered his chess crown from Euwe; and in Great Britain, the verbal outrages have continued, but without sowing the chaos and confusion that Sir Æthelred, who will shortly succeed to the hereditary title Lord Bletchley, predicted. It is a hiatus that will come to be known as the Phoneme War.

---

51 Named for a conference held in the Bavarian capital in Sept 1938, of which Neville Chamberlain was warned by Edvard Benes, the Czechoslovakian president 'This means appease in our time'. An offhand comment to an aid in which Benes purportedly called the Prime Minister 'Neville Chamberpot' was notoriously reproduced by the gutter press. There is no evidence that Chamberlain ever actually retorted 'Mr Benes is a far-away c*** about whom we know nothing.'

All this time, Hackett's star has continued in the ascendant. It's said 'the more complaisant the mistress the more complacent the man', and for a time Providence was beyond complaisant. Hackett, to his credit, never became her match in complacence. Nevertheless, with his uncanny knack not only of being in the right place at the right time, but of anticipating which bogus terms were about to gain common, if counterfeit, currency, he was the one man in the realm with the instinct to remain one step ahead of the game. Weeks before the term caused havoc in sixth-form maths classes countrywide, when the Minister for Education startled a geometry class in Greenwitch Grammar with his question on the area of 'quomboids', it was Hackett who broke the story. In early 1937 there was a by-election in Gloucestersauce, and when the good people of Bath were heard to employ the verb 'to podiate' to designate the taking by a politico of the podium, it was found that they had been anticipated by Hackett in an article entitled 'The Battle of Hustings' in the *Speculator* under his pen name Ж. More famously, or infamously, when during the Autumn Sales of the same year Barchester High Street was cast into confusion by the appearance of the collective noun 'baggerack', when almost overnight you had plumbers stocking cow's intestines, when saxophones and flutes started to be sold in hardware stores, and carburettors to put in an appearance in the window of the family butchers, at a time when, on account of 'baggerack', if you wanted to buy a length of hose, or a tundish, you were as likely to go to the music store as anywhere else, once again an article penned by Ж, this time for the weekend supplement of the left-leaning *Munchester Warden,* was found to have anticipated the pandemonium. In it, Hackett traced the history of such fromulous terms all the way back to the time of Albrecht Durer, when "*with pachyderm, the unknown hoaxer managed to corral the armed rhinoceros in with the recalcitrant elephant and the preposterous hippopotamus*". In its remarkable prescience, appearing a bare fortnight before the Barchester High Street outbreak, the opinion piece has become something of a collector's item. Small wonder, then, that when 'baggerack' made its short-lived but disruptive appearance during those Autumn Sales of 1937, Ж was lauded as a latter-day Cassandra. Of course, in the shadow of this admiration the columnist aroused suspicion. It is its natural corollary. Chief Inspector Quibble, in particular, began to keep an ever closer eye on the Eirish journalist.

An account must be given of Hackett's living conditions during the long months of the Phoneme War, months characterised by rumours, scares, mockery and uneasy laughter; for if Viscount Bracken, Lord Bletchley and Chief Inspector Quibble have been tireless in urging the utmost vigilance on the public, the public has heard the boy crying wolf once too often. Yes, the bogus words of what has come to be known as 'contervoc' have continued their sporadic and spiteful appearances. Nevertheless, either their effect has proved less than nefarious or their longevity short-lived.

Hackett himself has played a somewhat equivocal role during the course of the Phoneme War. Ж's articles were cited, and misquoted, on either side of the house in the debates on public safety, none more vocally than his evocation of Le Châtelier's Principle, a laissez-faire policy named for the late French chemist and amateur linguist whose retrospective study 'Le Z à A de Verlan' had become the standard text on the subject. To those of a Liberal outlook, the principle suggested one might 'leave well enough alone'. But for the hawkish advocates of public vigilance who flocked to Bletchley and Bracken, the inference was quite the opposite. Le Châtelier's Principle applied to closed systems only, whether chemical, ecological or semantic. It was therefore desirable to close the entire semantic system by introducing draconian measures in the five Channel ports, a policy that ran to an injunction on 'foreign loanwords' (sic). Moreover, the airwaves were to be policed, and jamming posts hastily designed by Robert Watson-Watt were constructed post-haste along the coast. By the slenderest of Westminister majorities the party advocating the 1st Linguistic Integrity Act won the day, but the measures were so watered down that, in the words of the Chief Inspector, Operation Babylon was scarcely worth the paper it was written on.[52]

As to his living quarters, immediately upon his return from room 404, Hackett found that the luxurious bedroom in the Eirish Consular Buildings that had been at his disposal was no longer at his disposal. If he was surprised, he wasn't overly so. Chapman had ever been an emulous character much given to pettiness, and if his nose had been put out of joint that he hadn't been included in the jaunt out to Medway Towns, it was doubly so that he'd been excluded from the second jaunt out to the Academy. The postcode of the boarding-house on the card

---

52 While Quibble may have had a point in regard to the suppression of 'contervoc', the series of radio-jamming stations played a pivotal if fortuitous role in the Battle of Britain, when it was found that their transmissions bounced off incoming aircraft.

that the rather saucy Miss Maloney furnished the journalist the following morning, and that smelled so evocatively of her *Lily of the Valley*, did not bode well.

Evening found Hackett listlessly pursuing the address his feet carrying him down the tedious argument of certain half-deserted streets. *Brigid Waddington's Boarding-house for Gentlemen* scarcely portended luxury. In proportion as the distance from Mayfair grew, the public squares and places grew less salubrious, another illustration of the inverse-square law. This was particularly the case once he'd passed under a pigeon-infested railway-bridge that shook abominably under every passing locomotive. Washing now hung like drab bunting above dark-eyed, gossipy women in curlers and aprons; grimy children cavorted in snot-nosed cohorts; and idle men in shirt-sleeves stared blankly over their pipes from yawning casements.

Hackett had nothing on his mind. It is a phrase that needs to be clarified. The nothing the columnist was thinking about on this occasion was neither the nothing that poetry makes happen nor the nothing that philosophy makes happen. It was, rather, the nothing much that the circulation of the bogus words, which were coming to be known collectively as contervoc, was making happen. One would assume that the terms should propagate according to Huygens' Principle, a model by which each point source gives rise to a wave-front of new point sources.[53] But something was preventing that from happening with the bogus terms. Now, if the island of Britain could be considered a closed system, one would

53 The Dutch astronomer famously developed the principle while observing how, every night, his neighbours' dog set the entire neighbourhood barking.

have thought that a Law of Conservation of Semantic Value might obtain. The terms should be self-propagating, whereas instead, something along the lines of the Law of Diminishing Returns was curtailing their vigency, which is to say, their longevity. At length, his mind wandering wildly in the manner of the mad Sweeney among the birds, his legs wandered up to a dingy junction with a dingy street-sign that corresponded approximately to what had been scribbled on Miss Maloney's lily-scented note. About halfway along was a pawnbrokers beneath whose three brass balls was idling a beggar in army coat and beret, bearing a tray of laces and lucifers. Bedamned if the journalist wasn't seized by a queasy feeling of déjà vu.

As Hackett bore down on him, he found the man's protuberant lips were whistling *Lily Marlene,* though there wasn't a lamp post in sight. That a demobbed beggar should be whistling *Lily Marlene* was not in itself surprising. It was a tune popular on both sides in the trenches of the Great War. But it put Hackett briefly in mind of the garmungling carpenter who'd been whistling *Lilliburlero,* and that may explain his thoughtlessness, for Hackett was about to show him the slip of paper when he took in the dark-glasses and white stick. A few rainbow-coloured medals decorating the chest suggested a war injury. He nodded, as if to bid the unfortunate the time of day.

'♪♫♫♪, ♪♫♫,' came the response, or lack thereof. Not having given the man's affliction proper consideration, Hackett now nodded again towards him as if to bid him adieu, replaced the note into his pocket, and would have continued on his way but that at that moment the man gruntled: 'You're looking for *where*?' Hackett was taken aback, not least by an Eirish inflection in the man's query. If Eirish he was, he was a long way from Tipperary. 'A boarding house,' he replied. Then, since he wasn't sure that the blind man mightn't have understood 'a *bawdy* house', he specified 'for *gentleman*.' Still unsatisfied, he concluded 'a widow runs it.'

'It's looking at you,' sprake the veteran. Definitely Eirish and possibly Jackeen.[54] And there indeed was Mrs Waddington's Boarding House, directly opposite, as plain as the nose on his face. Hackett winked his thanks, which he'd heard was as good as a nod, and not entirely satisfied, he muttered 'go raibh mile' before crossing. The man gave no reply, unless '♪♫♫♪, ♪♫♫,' might be construed as a reply.

Hackett didn't advance immediately into the open gateway. This was for two reasons. In the first place, a dog worrying a marrowbone was worrying a cat whose raised hackles were worrying the journalist. The world, he mused, divides into those who like dogs and those who prefer cats. Hackett belonged squarely to the former camp. A dog was what it seemed to be, no more and no less. It liked to chase things. It did not like postmen. It was suspicious of all things electrical. Whereas the cat always knew more than it let on, or let on to know more. And this tabby was no exception. It purled at the dog, its back arched in the manner of the Ha'penny Bridge, whilst its pupils narrowed in unfathomable insouciance. Walter Hackett had been no amateur of the feline class. A cat, he told his son, is the true sphinx without a riddle. Besides, cats were unlucky, particularly those of the black variety. He studiously avoided them. But here Fate, which

54 A native of Dubilin supposedly alluding to a penchant of the natives for waving Union Jacks, though more likely a reference to the communal outdoor privies that characterised the tenements that blighted the capital.

delights in irony, had the last laugh. For it was the railway fireman's very superstition that had him step out under a van in the livery of the Swastika Laundry. So that he was right to have been superstitious of them. Although had he not been, he'd equally have been correct, not having been impelled to step from the pavement.

The second reason that Hackett hesitated to enter was that his mind had characteristically set off in chase of another imaginary mouse. The war cripple. Now, several months before, he'd collided with a war cripple outside the doss-house off Dorset St Lr, though he was sure the man had a beard, beaked nose and coal black bushy eyebrows. A couple of days after that, he'd got the uncanny feeling a blind veteran was staring at him from under the portico of the GPO, though he was beardless and had worn a regimental cap. Later the same day, he'd encountered a blind man in a beret playing chess with another inside a looking-glass. And here, too, a blind war veteran had been fortuitously at hand, watching him. Now, blind men behind their dark glasses can resemble one another with a family resemblance, that much is well known. But suppose these were the same person? Suppose the beard and bushy eyebrows and the change of hats had been some class of a disguise?

But how to put it to the test, that was the rub. In any other circumstance, Hackett might have made use of the de Broglie Hypothesis. This was a hypothesis his erstwhile companion Malachi McCann had attempted to apply, with limited success, to horse-racing. Now as is widely known, according to Louis de Broglie, every mass moves with its own characteristic wavelength. The stork moves with a different rhythm to the skittish sandpipers who dart like animated sewing-machines between its garmungling legs. And the cooing pigeon, when courting, canoodles at a purling rhythm. That said, there were several caveats in applying the hypothesis to horseracing. In the first place, the de Broglie Hypothesis does not imply that every body should move with a characteristic *velocity*, velocity being the *product* of the fundamental frequency **f** with the wavelength λ. Secondly, though the fundamental frequency is a given, the motion might jump to any related harmonic frequency, as when a horse moves from a walk (fundamental) to a trot (1st harmonic), a canter (2nd harmonic), or a gallop (3rd harmonic), a phenomenon known as harmonic motion. From timing the fundamental frequency in the parade ring, you'd have to estimate the fancied horse's 2nd and 3rd harmonics. Thirdly, the medium through which the body is propagating would also have an effect on the velocity, as when the going is good or soft or yielding. It's a curiosity of harmonic motion that when acceleration is at a maximum, velocity is at a minimum, illustrating the well-known dictum 'the more the hurry, the less the speed.'

Now, a footpath upon which a footpad might scarper should have a consistently firm going. It followed then that regardless of what disguise a character might don, the one characteristic he could scarcely shake off was the fundamental frequency at which he walked. On the other hand there was this to consider. Just as a horse might move through a walk, trot, canter, or gallop, so too a dubitous character might make themselves scarce at a sidle (fundamental) a slink (1st harmonic), a scarper (2nd harmonic), or a skedaddle (3rd harmonic). But even assuming a sidle, to calculate from first principles a body's fundamental frequency you'd need to know not just their dimensions — their height and weight and inside-leg — but also their temperament and even their metabolism. All at once Hackett knucked his knuckles. Because of course he'd have no need to calculate anything! All he'd have to do was *observe* and then compare frequencies. The trick was to coax the character into motion. By the time he made up his mind to do just that, the blind man was nowhere to be seen.

The next few days passed in disquieting silence. There was no word from the Eirish Consular Service, much less from Chief Inspector Quibble or the Academy of Letters. Hackett grew restless. Then, idly, his fingers encountered in his rear pocket the business card of Sol Isaacs, and he recalled the press-baron's invitation to pay him a visit. Why not? Isaacs had presumably now read his 'Not on Your Nankly' article and with that recent triumph in mind, he leapt up from the bed and set out for Grub St. Having consulted the venerable Brigid Waddington, a woman 'of a certain age' — though there is nothing less certain than the age of 'a woman of a certain age' — as to Grub St's whereabouts, he set off at a good pace and in no time at all was mounting the stairs to the editorial offices. The meeting was a disappointment. The press-baron was busy, and Hackett was kept waiting for upwards of two hours before an opportunity to meet the great man at last presented itself. But even then the telephone scarcely stopped hopping, the intercom buzzing, the tickertape tacking, the door swinging, and in any case, to put the tin hat on it, any news of the love lost between Semantics and the Royal Academy was by this time old hat. So that Hackett finally left the building with little more than a hatful of platitudes, a lungful of cigar smoke, and another vague entreaty to 'write something for us.'

Big Ben's bells blanged. Big Ben's bells blanged. It was half past something. He was shundling listlessly, his mood lowering with the lowering sky, when he quite literally collided with a be-capped character in dark glasses and moustache ensconced inside a sandwich-board[55] who was trundling at some speed, head down, in the opposite direction. 'I say!' griped Hackett, 'watch where you're going!' He would have set off after the figure, too, but he was held from moving by the sudden conviction that something or other had been thrust into his coat pocket. Sure enough, his curious fingers encountered there what appeared to be an envelope. Standing as still as the proverbial rock in midstream, for it was a busy street, Hackett ran a finger inside the envelope and pulled out a brief, typed note. 'Tory politico to visit Greenwich grammar school tomorrow noon, **ꝏ**.' It was during this visit that the infamous 'Area of Quomboids' debacle unfolded — a quomboid, insisted the Minister to the bemusement of the form teacher and the amusement of his students, being "any polygon with two and only two right angles contained therein". Before the cameras he'd morsed it out in chalk across the blackboard, an iconic photograph giving Hackett his headline: "Writing on the Wall for Tory Minister". The story was to be his first scoop that actually related to the propagation of false and dubitous terms.

---

55 An advertising device first concocted by John Montagu, the 4th Earl of Sandwich, when he stood for election in 1744 on the Tory ticket. His constituency of Sandwich, in Kent, was so-named because it was squeezed in between Ramsgate and Deal.

But we're getting ahead of ourselves.

The tip-off he was now fingering must've come from someone in Isaacs' office. The secretary, or a sub-editor. Who knows, maybe even Isaacs himself? Could the cypher, **ꝏ**, be his? It seemed oddly familiar. Maybe the press-baron couldn't be seen to be favouring Hackett with an overt commission. He turned the note over, held it to the light, turned the envelope upside down, tipped out its vacancy, peered about him over the heads of the gruntled public, and many minutes too late, set off in the direction in which the sandwich-board man had been muttling. But the street was moiling, the crowd madding, and all he could do was watch the cap bob rhythmically above their number as though in illustration of de Broglie's Hypothesis.

CHAPTER THE THIRD

in which an account is given of the Second Law of Thermodynamics, and Hackett's informed discourse on McTurcaill's Taxonomy of bogus terms

Months passed. Sporadic instances of lexical contamination occurred. But the linguistic mayhem that had been forecast failed to ensue. Operation Babylon's restrictive measures were seen to have been, in the expression popularised by demobbed soldiers, 'over the top'. One that came up for general derision was a *British Movietone* documentary which highlighted the threat to the average citizen of linguistic contamination. Up on the silver screen, crowds were seen going about the normal range of social activities — on the High Street, on the omnibus, in the public-house. But in each locale, ominously, and to an ominous strain of music, a figure, low-hatted and high-collared, would slip from pocket or portmanteau[56] a bogus term and pass it to the unwitting citizen. Then the last word in

56 There is a long-standing association between bogus terms and portmanteau travelling cases, whose double compartments are thought to have helped conceal such linguistic horrors as smog, brunch, bedward, slithy, ginormous and guesstimate. Satisfyingly, portmanteau, a case designed to 'porter manteaux', is an illustration of itself, and thereby of the Munchausen Principle.

special effects offered speech bubbles of gobbledygook which sprang up like mushrooms throughout the map of Britain. And all the time, a doom-laden voiceover gave ominous warning:

'Avery lavin' langage in tha woruld is meed up o' lavin' wurds. Your boogus langage isnae, so it follows your boogus langage isnae a lavin' langage. Your boogus terum doesnae exast withoot what they terum a hoost santance. What your boogus terum does is, it utilases the hoost santance to raplicate. Raplication is just a foncy terum for copyin'. That's all your boogus terum does. It copies and it copies untal the hoost is overwhalumed. Af the false terums of contervoc ever get a foothold, meek noo misteek, that's wha' may happen tay Anglish atself. Be vagilant!'

Then the screen would flicker white to the *thrum-slap, thrum-slap* of the projector. The first few times it was shown, the government warning caused a stir. Then it was met with murmurs, then indifference, then finally ridicule. Outside the cinemas of Engeland — for there had not been a single instance of a bogus word west of the Severn nor north of Hadrian's wall — dodgy Highland accents proliferated. *Be vagilant o' boogus terums!* became the catch-cry.

There was not the slightest sign of any of the counterfeit terms 'overwhaluming' anything. During his leisure hours, Hackett pondered why. About this time, a traveller lodged for several nights at the Widow Waddington's. There was nothing unusual in this, it was after all a boarding house. What was noteworthy was that the itinerant guest was known to Hackett. He was known, indeed, from Hackett's darkest days, when the two had been fellow lodgers at Swift's Boarding House for Lunatics. Here in the flesh was the hare-eyed veteran veterinarian who'd lived in mortal fear of being bowdlerised. If his demeanour was now almost jaunty, the years had done little to curtail the man's hypochondria. The linguistic contamination he compared with grim satisfaction to the Spanish Influenza of 1918. Now, the young Ignatius had never been any great shakes at biology. The science of plants and animals had never stoked the curiosity of his railwayman father, and Hackett *fils* had never acquired a taste for it. He was ill-equipped then, to follow the niceties that distinguished the epidemic from the pandemic; nor could he quite relate to the gloomy triumph in the eyes of the valetudinarian when he sprake the word plague.

So much for pathology. But the vigency, and the concomitant half-life of the counterfeit term, that was another matter. Walter Hackett considered physics the king of the sciences; and of all the provinces that made up the great realm of physics, the fireman held that thermodynamics was, like Meath, the most royal. From an early age, as he rode behind his father on the Dubilin to Kingstown line, young Hackett was equipped to estimate how much thermal heat might be released from each hundredweight of coal, based upon its calorific value. Given the specific heat capacity of water and its latent heat of vaporisation, he was able to convert this thermal energy into the maximum quantity of steam said hundredweight of coal might generate. Then, by an application of the First Law of Thermodynamics to Boyle's Law, it was a doddle to calculate how much work was available each time the engine's pistons went through their strokes. But that was in theory. The spanner in the works was a malevolent little fire-sprite known as the Second Law of Thermodynamics —

and the worst of it was, it was framed by an Eirishman! It was on account of Lord Kelvin of Bailfast, the stoker lamented, that even were you to design the perfect locomotive engine, with the purest of mountain water and the most well-oiled of pistons, you could only ever recover a fraction of the energy you put in. It was as if you were to go to the *Munster and Leinster Bank*, and all they gave you for your pay-slip was seven and sixpence in the pound.

As to why this should be the case, Walter Hackett was less clear. Nevertheless, from the earliest age Ignatius Hackett grew up in a world that he knew was governed by the Second Law of Thermodynamics. It was the Second Law of Thermodynamics that said that clocks wound down but never back up again; that the toddler with jam on her fingers would always find the whitest of trousers to press against; that year on year, the half-crown in your pocket could buy less and less; that as they aged, people grew slower and more wrinkly. That was why, once he'd fallen, Humpty Dumpty could never be put together again. To put it in a nutshell, the Second Law of Thermodynamics was none other than our old friend the Law of Diminishing Returns in a more respectable guise. It followed that, as time went on even the choicest of words lost their precision. Despite the best efforts of the Academies, turns of phrase, once pristine and inventive, would by degrees lose their contours and become debased into empty cliché. As words proliferated, the total sum of meaning, even assuming that the island was a closed system, ineluctably diminished.

Having set out on foot from the reading room of the British Library, Hackett was, by this juncture, already turning onto the shabby street with the three brass balls. There was a cat stretching indolently on the wall outside the digs, taking the last of the sun. Hackett's squint resolved it into Oedipus, the landlady's tabby. Now Hackett was no great lover of cats, and cats were no great lover of Hackett, and this particular moggie was regarding the journalist with that smug suspicion that naturally arises out of antipathy. Hackett eyed up the manxome foe. What was it the fellow said about you could have a cat without a grin, but not a grin without the cat? Then, since his mind was enjoying one of those Pangur bán evenings where it ran in all directions in pursuit of imaginary mice, what's this the other fellow said about if you put a cat into a box and didn't open the lid, you wouldn't know the state it was in? Or wasn't in.[57] The Uncertainty Principle that one was klept. That cat was alive and dead at the one time. Or else it was neither alive nor dead. At the one time. On account of the wave isn't a particle, or else the particle isn't a wave. Not until such time as you looked at it. The particle, not the cat. It was only once you looked that you let the cat out of the bag about whether it was alive or dead, though in the latter case, you could say that curiosity *had* killed the cat. Another German said you couldn't know two things at the same time, though the more precisely Hackett tried to nail down the identity of that German, the less certain the quote became. McCann, his college bedfellow, had always maintained a paradox is nothing but a shadow cast by language. The German 'da' means both *there* and *then*, and that conflation suggested to Mr Einstein the notion of 'space-time' — the same Einstein who famously posited: 'God does

57 An allusion to Austrian scientist Erwin Schrödinger, who, once Austrians became Germans, moved to the Eirish Free State. There is no evidence that he ever had a cat.

not play dice with the Universe, as in an infinite number of throws He'd always lose'. Because of our friend the Second Law of Thermodynamics, needless to say. And the wimbling Planck was a German, though where was Max Born? Hackett threw up both hands and let out something midway between a gasp and a guffaw. Whichever it was, it startled the tabby and must have caused it to slink away, because when Hackett looked up again the cat, like Macavity, wasn't there.

McCann had a point all the same. Suppose one of these counterfeit cells put into circulation a word that meant alive and dead, at the one time. *Delive*, for the sake of argument. And another that bore the meaning of both a wave and a particle at the one time, or neither the one nor the other until such time as you looked at it. A *wartick*, say. Then you wouldn't have a paradox at all. All you'd have is a statement, and a statement of the bloody obvious. Except you'd still have the original situation in the original German. That went without saying. But where would that leave the cat? For all he was getting anywhere, Hackett may as well have been the proverbial blind man in the dark room looking for the black cat that wasn't there.

It seemed to the columnist, who had been looking for some time at the absence of his landlady's pet feline, that there was nothing intrinsically Boolean about cats.[58] The owl,

58 The reference is to the Cork mathematician George Boole (1815-1864), who was either a genius or a charlatan depending on how his contribution to binary logic is assessed. Boolean algebra is itself derived from the 'now you see it, now you don't' philosophy of Kilkenny Bishop George Berkeley, friend and contemporary of fellow 'Clonmel Anglicans' Jonathan Swift and Laurence Sterne, though these weren't themselves contemporaries (as might, if space had permitted, have been best illustrated by a Venn diagram). The long association of Kilkenny with cats dates from this period.

now, was a different beast entirely. An owl's hunting instincts were strictly Boolean; it either caught a mouse or it did not catch a mouse, and there was an end of it. But a cat? Hackett had watched Oedipus toy with a doormouse for hours on end, catching it, letting it go, catching it, letting it go. Like the Engelish parleyment, which for years had granted and had not granted Home Rule, it was constitutionally indecisive. 'I can and I can't,' M^c used always to say. By God, it'd be a useful trick to pull off all the same, to coin a word that would cover a case like 'I can and I can't'! The way a shameless act is shameful, or the manner in which Dev had both taken and not taken the oath of allegiance.

His errant thoughts had by this time taken him inside *Brigid Waddington's Boarding House for Gentlemen* where he was surprised to find a message awaiting him. It had been left, said the gallous widow with a glance both deferential and louche, by a chauffeur. In uniform. A Bentley would call for Mr Hackett first thing in the morning.

'Sorry,' said Hackett. 'At what time?'

'First thing,' she said, nodding sagely. Then, marking his consternation, she specified, 'in the morning.'

First thing in the morning, Hackett slept on. But at eight his landlady tapped at his door. Second thing in the morning, he breakfasted. Then he returned to his bedroom window. There was sign neither of car nor of chauffeur. Finally, when he was just on the pop of dispatching copy to the *Speculator* — for it's a sad fact of journalism that a scoop has the self-same shelf-life as shellfish — he heard the diplomatic Bentley puttle to a halt beneath the three brass balls. Hackett allowed three long minutes to elapse before he approached. Chapman was sitting in the rear seat, his nose stuck inside the *Logdon Gravitas*. It wasn't one of Sol Isaacs' papers, so it was unlikely that another of Hackett's articles was in it. The journalist climbed in, and laying a finger atop the paper, depressed it just sufficiently to be annoying. 'Why the mystery ride?'

'No mystery.' The Eirish Cultural Attaché deftly flicked the *Gravitas* back to the upright. Hackett paused just long enough to allow him to resume the interrupted paragraph, then tipped down the top edge with the tiniest bit more insistence. 'So where are we off too, if there's no mystery in it?' Chapman gruntled and flicked out the paper, peered into it, brought the print to focus, drove through to the end of the paragraph without registering any of its import, and only then gruffed, 'Oxenford.'

'Ox-en-ford!' calloohed Hackett as though delighted. Seeing that Chapman had grumpily frabbled up the paper in expectation of further questioning, Hackett fixed his eyes on the terraced houses outside and began to whistle '♪♫♪,♪♪♫♪', which is to say *Lilliburlero*. Prompted by the tune, his imagination set off down the corridors of memory. If only, in place of this ginger-haired dunce, he had beside him the one man to whom he'd ever doffed his hat when it came to matters linguistic. In his mind's ear, he heard again Malachi M^c^Cann holding forth inside a fuggy **MULLIGAN'S** of Poolbeg St on the mechanics of the cloud-chamber. Let a charged particle drop into a cloud of vapour, droplets condense about that particle. That, my friends, is how vocabulary works. Mulcahy drank deep and was silent. Hackett was silent and drank deep. The world, declared M^c^Cann, scrummeling his head, is a cloud of possible meanings. What were you fellas talking about before I got here? Just talking, M^c^. About what? This and that. You know yourself.[59] Anything in particular? Horses, says Teddy Mulcahy. We were swapping stories about the gee-gees. Suppose I was to tell yous[60] you were engaged in fraddling? I wasn't here, boys, but I'll engage that's what yous were at. McCann's pianist's fingers invent inverted commas.

Fraddle. *vb. intrans.* To simulate interest in someone's anecdote while actually trawling one's own store of related anecdotes in anticipation of the meanest opportunity to launch said anecdote, thereby trumping the anterior.

They look one to the other, blush, admire, laugh, you're a dangerous bloody man! Now that you know what fraddling is, you'll find it'll condense out of the fug on all sides. *Circumspice*! Mulcahy looks around the bar, but his eyes narrow, and it wasn't the case before? It was and it wasn't. It's our old friend the chicken and the egg. Zeno of Citium advises: take away the complaint and you take away the injury. Contrariwise, you pronounce the verb to fraddle, and presto! Meaning condenses out of the void. Suddenly everyone's at it. "**Ἐν ἀρχῇ ἦν ὁ Λόγος**". Hackett watches him, a thought condensing. Could we make a few bob out of it, d'you think? McCann shakes his wistful head. I pull meaning from the world like a rabbit from a hat, and the price of a pint is all the beauty you see in it. Idle chatter, such as students have on

59 One of a number of untranslatable phrases dating from the time of the Land War, when Eirish Secret Societies tried to oust Engelish spies and informers with such arcane usages. Another dating from this period is the (rhetorical) "Is it yourself?" Much sport was had confounding foreign infiltrators by nominally acceding to a request in the form "I will, yeah."
60 Colloquial second person plural, not to be confused with you(s).

any licensed premises in Dubilin. But wasn't there the grain of truth in it?

To coin a phrase wasn't so straightforward. As he'd learned from the Commissioner himself, to have a term bonafide you'd have to specify the domain. You'd have to account for the spelling and invent an etymology. And then it would have to go through every class of field trial. And does any other crowd have a word that'd do the job just as well? The Germans, say, for they're great men for the contradictory impulse: **liebestod**; **und weltschmerz**; **und schadenfreude**; **und selbstgerechtschuld**. And what would it be worth to you, even supposing you were to finally get a patent? Thirteen Eirish miles had gone by in fulmering silence.[61] At long last it was the Cultural Attaché's patience which gave out. With ill-grace in direct proportion to his ill-humour, he curmudgeoned: 'Would you mind explaining to me in plain terms that last damned dossier you sent on to me?'

'Carpals, tarsals, and contervoc, is it?' Chapman frundled rather than nodded, but it was affirmation enough. 'It's all so much…' Hackett searched for the substantive adequate to the taxonomy, 'nomenclature.' Chapman's eyes narrowed. 'Nomencla-*what*?' His secretary decided to be expansive. 'As

61 Just as the Eirish measure of spirits is more generous than the Engelish, viz. ¼ rather than 1/6 of a gill, so the Eirish mile is longer than the Engelish. In Elizabethan times 4 Eirish miles approximated 5 Engelish. A 1593 Act of Parleyment defined the Engelish mile by statute as: "A Mile ſhall contain eight Furlongs, every Furlong forty Poles, and every Pole ſixteen Foot and a half." Although the statute mile was intended also for the neighbouring kingdom, the Eirish Pole exceeding the Engelish by a matter of 5:4, the superiority of the Eirish mile was unaffected by this decree. The situation is further complicated by the country mile, which exceeds the Eirish mile by an undefined ratio.

well I give you a bit of background. It all came about on the back of one of their interminable press conferences. One thing you'll have to say for your Bobby, he's a great man for the press conference. Chap by the name of Fraiser. Scotland Yard Scot. Now, all this dates back to before Christmas '36, mind. And it was Dorchester, not Rockchester. It wasn't that any of these words was particularly vigent or virulent. Not in the way the Rockchester batch seem to…' Hackett searched for the adequate verb. 'Proliferate,' he nodded, satisfied. 'But on the other hand, they weren't exactly what you'd call benign either. For instance,' pulling a bunch of papers from his coat pocket he checked his figures, ' 'brandlr' began to displace 'bargain' at the rate of about 4% per day oral. Oral, mind. There's no record of any written displacement with the Wessex[62] batch. Still, in the run up to the Christmas sales, you can imagine the kind of confusion a chap the like of 'brandlr' could cause.' Chapman frundled. He'd begun to pick at his thumb. 'Now here's the point. Evans of the BBC asked on live radio if there mightn't be something more sinister than the palming off of a few bogus words going on. "If ye mean, does this represent a verr-bal cluster," quoth Fraiser, "then it's far too early for anyone tae ken." Then he ends up throwing oil onto the flames. "If I can mehbe give ye a wee *meh*-taphor," says he, "when it comes tae semontic analysis of a very few terums, such as we hae in thas case, can I liken the task to the problem of reconstructing the entire *skeh*-leton of a *mah*-stodon from a mere handful of tarrsals?"

62 Following the arrival of the Saxons, their four constituent tribes dispersed in the four cardinal directions, giving rise to Essex, Wessex, Sussex and Nossex, the population of the last of which declined catastrophically within a generation for reasons unknown.

'A *mah*-stodon?' queried Chapman, in dismay. Hackett's eyes narrowed. 'I thought you'd read the dossier?'

'Go on with your story.'

'"A *mah*-stodon," says he. The metaphor was widely reported. Or is it an analogy? In any case, the word 'tarsal' gains common currency. Initially, it describes any of the constituent terms of contervoc, with no distinction.'

'Contervoc?'

'*Man dear*, did you not read…' In the face of a hostile stare, Hackett aborted the question which was, in any event, shaping up to be rhetorical. 'Contervoc is the name they give to the counterfeit language. For by all accounts, that's what it is. It's no matter of a few bogus words. This contervoc appears to be governed by rudimentary rules. That's what has the pants scared off the Operation Babylon brigade.'

'So contervoc is made up of tarsals, is that it?' gruntled Chapman. He was fast becoming disgruntled. '*Man dear*, that's only the start of it! Now, tarsal was all very well to begin with. Tarsal was all very fine when there were a few dozen spurious words being foisted off on the sly. But what words were they? And what kind of words were they? Are you with me?' Chapman's gruntle by now approximated a growl. The quick of the thumb was back between his canines. 'So the next thing, another batch appears. This one in Barchester. What do you think the Bill proposes? You have it! Another press conference. Now, all this time, behind the scenes, Semantics are working frumiously to get to grips with the Wessex batch. Inspector Quibble brings in an outside expert, though I'd go bail his arm was twisted. It's our friend McTurcaill, and you know how much time Quibble has for Academy folk. And it's soon clear there was no love lost between himself and Fraiser, either. Two Scots, but one a Catholic and one a Protestant. Or vice versa. As a highlander, Turlough McTurcaill has a passing acquaintance with Scots Gallic, whereas your lowlander Fraiser doesn't know his Erse from his Alba. But the Commissioner was in the process of commissioning the very term contervoc, so they could scarcely leave him out.

'Just prior to the press conference, a round table was convened between Semantics and the Academy, and it's on foot of[63] this meeting that you got your dossier. So to begin, McTurcaill distinguishes between what he dryly terms Type I and Type II exhibits. Fraiser suggests, not altogether joking, that since 'tarsal' is already in the public domain, why not use it to designate the former, and then 'carpal' could be used to designate the latter. McTurcaill, a humourless bloody Scot[64] — I daresay he must be the Protestant — goes on with his exegesis as though nothing has been proposed. The classification sticks, that's the power of the popular press for you. Fraiser now follows McTurcaill, though if your man took the high road, he'll take the low road. Not to be outdone, he proposes the division should be refined into sub-divisions. Are you ready?' Chapman's face ill-disguised his ill-humour at being so ill-equipped to follow his secretary down whatever rabbit-hole he was now scampering. 'Tarsals consist entirely of neologisms. New words, not corruptions. Now, here's

63 A useful Eirish expression implying a causal as well as temporal relation. '*Richard of Yorvik was thrown from his horse, on foot of which he was readily vanquished.*'— Annals of the Four Masters.

64 Unlike his ancestor Dougal McTurcaill, head chef at Balmoral, who on April 1st 1847 passed off an eponymous soup made with a calf's head on Queen Victoria, who was 'not amused'.

where it gets interesting. 'A'-tarsals substitute directly for existing words (*barbak* for jam, *brandlr* for bargain, *indegar* for both feather and to alight); 'B'-tarsals also take the form of what McTurcaill termed paradigmatic substitution, but where no equivalent has been identified in the original (such as *nang* or *fraddle*); and then there's 'C'-tarsals, which interpolate into the syntagmatic order of the sentence but without replacing any existing word.'

''C'-tarsals!' retorted Chapman, deflating. It was abundantly clear to both men that when Hackett sprake of syntagmatic and paradigmatic, he might as well have been spraking of simians and pachyderms. 'Only four 'C'-tarsals have surfaced, all of them entirely lacking in vowels. Of these, *bgrrgl* is particularly virulent. It displays a nasty penchant for proliferating in such a way as to both split the infinitive and the inseparable phrasal verb.' Chapman looked up at his secretary pleadingly. Hackett didn't smile as such, but his crow's feet had become crows' feet. Another page was flippantly flipped. 'Carpals Fraiser considers particularly insidious. Once more, a sub-division refines the taxonomy. Tarsals, you'll remember, are neologisms. Entirely new words. Not so carpals. Now, 'A'-carpals are existing words which have been corrupted in such a way that they exactly duplicate that word. They're therefore unlikely to cause confusion (*parcark* for carpark, *emnity* for enmity). On the other hand your 'A'-carpal displays a high level of infectiousness. However, it's your 'B'-carpal which, according to the Inspector, poses the greatest risk to the public order. Why so, you ask? I'll tell you. Your 'B'-carpal is a corruption of an existing term in such a way that it becomes indistinguishable from a second term, itself already in the language. Fraiser cited the recent embarrassment of Lady Gresham, who'd welcomed a number of debutantes into Barchester society with the unfortunate 'how *roughly* you're all looking this evening.' Then there are 'fulsome' apologies. Or think of the Mayor of Barchester's much-quoted remark. You've forgotten it I suppose.'

Chapman's weariness fell briefly away and he looked about in triumph. 'His Travesty the King!' he calloohed. Hackett let on to be impressed. It was the most effective of put downs and Chapman deflated accordingly back into his seat. An Eirish country mile went by in fulmering silence, and for the remainder of their journey, they muttled on in antagonistic reverie.

CHAPTER THE FOURTH

in which an account is given of the confidential Oxenford Council, of Seymour Doolittle's incomparable disquisition and a dire warning

Oxenford was bustling. As a result, it took the chauffeur, a novice to the City of Aspirers, some time to arrive outside the august institution where the briefing was to take place. There's no way he's the self-same driver. That last fella had ears the like of handles on a Grecian urn; whereas this buck has scarce any lugs at all to sprake of, or into. Hence the way the chauffeur's hat sits low as a visor on his head. Hackett tugged at his own lobe. Those anterior jug ears must have been the source of O'Brien knowing about that 10/- note he'd shown Chippy. He'd encountered them before. Damn it, but where? On the blind man, was it? Or the carpenter back at the Book of Kells? Or the sandwich-board who'd set him off on the quomboid scoop? Were these three one and the same, the way the three foils on the shamrock made up the one leaf?

Setting aside the question of identity (in both senses) until such time as he might finally be able to put it to the test by the de Broglie Hypothesis, the next question was, who was having him watched. Cracking this particular nut might lead on to why. Here was the point. The war veteran had been positioned opposite the *Widow Waddington's Boarding House* prior to Hackett's arrival there. Ergo, he had not simply followed him to the premises. Based on these premises, he'd been apprised in advance of the address. Now, who knew the address? One of the boarders might have been tipped off. But who needs to engage a blind man to spy on him, if one of the boarders might perform the office? Chapman knew the address, to be sure. Hackett glanced at the man. Not Chapman. Miss Maloney had scribbled it out for him, and she presumably had the ear of Chandler the handler. Hackett tugged harder at his lobe. But why would Dubilin have him shadowed? He had little time to fondle either the ear or the question. Having arrived late, Chapman was eager to make amends, and did so by charging conspicuously into the building and then the auditorium, disturbing such attentiveness as had descended upon the mahogulous table. A dozen paces behind him, Hackett exchanged 'you know yourself' glances with all who'd turned to frundle at the disturbance. A quick survey discovered a surprising absence of anyone representing the Royal Academy of Letters.

For their benefit, the Oxenford Don, who was on his feet, recapitulated an anecdote with which he had just regaled the company. 'I was saying, gentlemen, in my youth I was once running late for the Albert Hall,[65] and in my desperation, I hailed down a hackney.[66] Can you get me to the opera on time, I inquired of the driver. Sir, you behold in my cab

65 A musical venue named for Albert Hall, who founded it.
66 A popular public conveyance which got its name from the characteristic conversation of cabbies.

Caruso's very Phaeton! It was a striking metaphor. But I am led to ask, which was the vehicle, and which the tenor?' 'The tenor! Very good!' nodded Hackett, mirthful as much at Chapman's disgruntled incomprehension as at anything else. To Chapman's further displeasure, as the two latecomers took their places in front of a large capstan upon which stood a film projector, several present muttered their congratulations to his erstwhile schoolmate on his remarkable sequence of ground-breaking scoops. Damn it, whatever else you might say about him, and you might say a great deal, he still had the happy-go-lucky knack of being in the right place at the right time.

'Gentlemen!' gruffed Sir Æthelred. 'Doolittle here was just bringing us up to speed on the latest fashion in linguistics.' In a lower voice ostensibly directed towards his own private secretary's ear, but which was for all that entirely audible, he gruntled, 'all so much balderdash if you ask me.' Professor Doolittle, who was standing beside a flip chart at the far end of the table behind which stood the projector screen, ignored the scurril remark and, once the cursory round of courtesy nods had run its course, resumed his disquisition. 'Centuries before the Copernican revolution displaced the earth from the centre of the cosmos, playing such havoc with the calendar, the Moorish polymath Averroes challenged the Aristotelian view of language which underwrote the entire Ptolemaic system. From time immemorial, man had placed the world of fact at the centre of experience. Language, in the form of Sol, was simply the most brilliant of the planets to illumine this terrestrial world. The lunar imagination worked by its reflected light. Such other planetary worlds of human intercourse as the Mercantile, the Marital, the Martial, the Magisterial and the

Mensural circled within their respective spheres around our Mundane ground of solid fact. Averroes stood this geocentric model on its head. What the Moor averred was that at the centre of experience there was no world of fact. In its place he located language. Words, words, words. Words not only determine facts and conjure them into being, they are in *excess* of the facts.'

'Meaning?'

'When all is said and done,' said Seymour Doolittle, 'there's more said than done.'

'That's easy said,' said Hackett, whose **pangur bán** mind was running after whether McCann's verb 'Fraddle' had anticipated the play. By God, there was the man that could've got to the bottom of this! 'But steady on!' blustered Sir Æthelred. 'That contention was Sir Robyn Plaiger's, surely! When I was a Fellow in Maudlin Camsbridge,[67] I read his *De Revolutionibus Orbium Experimentorum.*'

'A translation of a translation, I'm afraid.' The Professor's eyebrows executed a facetious skip. 'Unattributed.' Sir Æthelred fulmered in silence. How like an Oxenford Don to disparage Sir Robyn, simply because, like Sir Æthelred, he had attended Maudlin Camsbridge. After all, what had Oxenford ever given the world besides the first newspaper, and a dubitous honour *that* was proving to be!

'I don't see where any of this is getting us,' gruntled Chief Inspector Quibble of the Yard, who was sitting directly

67 The old spelling of Maudlin is occasionally still preferred, as is that of the riverside Quays. The college itself, founded in 1428 on the site of a notorious brothel, was so named for the 'maudlins' or sentimental prostitutes associated with the area.

opposite Hackett and whose eyes appeared to have shifted ever closer together. The figure beside him, who was also dressed in an unbuttoned mackintosh, Hackett took to be Duncan Fraiser. Though a lowlander, there was something of the highland terrier about his Presbyterian eyebrows. The eyebrows executed a skip. 'Aye but any wurrd is itsalf only a wurrd.' Fraiser sat back. Hackett paled. Momentarily he was at the edge of the precipice of mise-en-abyme. The Don nodded benevolently, as though welcoming both the question and the assiduity which had given birth to it. 'The word 'word' is tautological.'

'Tautological?' whispered Chapman.

'Like the Baron Munchausen,' whispered Hackett.

'?'

'Who pulled himself out of the swamp by his own ponytail, man.'

'And wha' is yer point, Profasser?' put in Fraiser. 'Wha't has any of tha' tae doo wath conterrvoc, if ye don't meend me askin'?'

'Mind you asking?' calloohed Doolittle, a repertory actor feigning surprise. 'Of course I don't mind you asking. I wouldn't be here if I minded you asking. You might even say I'm here precisely *because* I don't mind you asking. But let me ask you. In any language system, will one term not do just as well as another term?'

'That'd depend on its vagency,' suggested the Scot.

Chapman's elbow nudged Hackett's rib cage. 'Vagency?'

'Vigency.'

Chapman audibly exhaled.

'Or af ye prefer,' supplied Fraiser, 'its half-leefe.'

Chapman's elbow nudged Hackett's rib cage. 'Half-life?'

'$N(t) = No\ (1/2)^{t/t1/2}$.'

Chapman audibly deflated.

'Time enough to talk of vigency, Fraiser,' gruntled Chief Inspector Quibble. 'I don't believe the Professor has quite finished his point?'

The Don nodded. 'Permit me to ask our Eirish friends a question. Has either of you gentlemen ever heard of aspirate migration?' An exchange of shrugs suggested they hadn't. 'The migration of the letter aitch. Or, as you people would have it, haitch. It's a curious creature, your Eirish haitch. Breathes down the necks of witch and weather and Wales until they're bullied into which and whether and whales, then like a bully it hides entirely when you look for it in thirty three and a third…'

'And a turd,' assented Hackett.

'Then it pops up uninvited at the end of a word. Heighth, say, or drouth.'

Sir Æthelred's frundle once again invited the Oxenford scholar to come to the point, but it was Quibble who gave voice. 'What has any of this got to do with contervoc?'

'The point,' picked up the Don, 'is that not only did you Eirish invent the spaces between words, but actual letters disappear in the lexicography of your Fr. Dinneen.' Hackett knew of old that, in an attempt to save ink, the medieval monks had left spaces between words. But Dinneen's dictionary? 'What's particularly interesting is the methodology by which your Dinneen carries it off. The meddlesome priest titles his seditious work,' and here the Don demonstrated considerable dexterity in the uncial script as he scribbled: "Foclóir Gaedhilge." He turned to Hackett. 'Would you pronounce for us the — "Foclóir Gaedhilge"?'

'Fucklore Gaylga,' he shrugged as though it were the most natural thing in the world.

'Indeed. You took the mailboat over, I assume? Good. Yes. Now. Can you tell me the new name they've put on the port of Kingstown over there?'

'Dunleary.' Hackett obliged. The Don was much obliged. "Dún Laoghaire," he scribbled, deftly. 'Excellent. Now here's the trick.' He thumbed out the two aitches, or haitches, and placed instead a tittle — in mathematics, the symbol recurs — above the d of Gaedailge and the g of Laogaire. Then, tapping the pen beneath the newly modified letters, he pronounced '*Gaylga. Leary.*' He then tapped the dot above each consonant. 'The tittle makes the letter inaudible, giving it a licence to proliferate. Since it's so deuced hard to hear, it can crop up in all sorts of unlikely places…' A mutter of disapproval ran around the table at so underhand a trick. 'Wait now a second!' said Chapman, shifting about to glance at Hackett. 'What about the k in knight, or the b in debt?'

'A subtle knot,' opined Hackett, whereupon he recited from memory one of the entries he'd copied out in the British Library's reading room. '*During the Inkhorn Controversy, many were indicted or impugned for such malign additions.*'

'I think you miss my point. What you are referring to are *irrational* letters, which is to say letters that misbehave. What I am referring to are *imaginary* letters.'

'Imaginary?' blustered the Home Secretary, his moustaches working like tusks.

'In mathematics you have *irrational* numbers, such as the number of inmates in the Parolles Mental Asylum; and you have *imaginary* numbers, such as the number of afflictions they have. In analogous manner, in linguistics, so the theory runs, you should have irrational letters and you should have imaginary letters. Now, as Bernard Pshaw has spelled out time and again, there's no shortage of irrational letters in Engelish orthography. But strictly imaginary? In Dinneen's dictionary, for the first time, by virtue of his little tittle, the imaginary is made real.' After a brief hiatus, a satisfactory round of aspirate gasps circulated the mahogulous table.

With a loud slap of his open palm on the table, Sir Æthelred bumbled to his feet. 'Inaudible or invisible or, or, or… I fail to see what any of this weather or whether they're Wales or whales has to do with contervoc. *Contervoc*, gentlemen!' So gruntled was this outburst, so apoplectic the Home Secretary, that embarrassed silence descended over the company. It was Fraiser who broke it.

'If ah may be allood, Sir Æthelred. The peent is thas. As ye ken, Foransics hae carried oot extansive and intansive tasts on a larrge sample of the counterrfeit terums that came to leet in the Rockchester cache. As of todee,' his hand motioned towards a frundling Quibble, 'we hae the corresponding analyses undertaken by Semontics. The peent, gentlemen, is thas. Booth sets of tasts concurrr in the moost likely provenance of the cache. At the 95% confadence level, the terums bear all the hallmarks of an Hibernian provenance.'

Hackett's elbow tickled Chapman's ribs. 'My colleague Inspactor Quabble…' resumed the dour individual who was at the 95% probability level Duncan Fraiser, but he was anticipated and arrested by Quibble's hand. The Chief Inspector looked directly at the Eirish journalist. 'We've long suspected it. These results put it beyond any dubit. You Eirish are behind this!' His eyes narrowed, forcing up the vertical frundle. 'It wouldn't be the first time. I hardly need to mention, Sir Æthelred, the Munchester Outrage of the Coronation Year of the previous Edward, which was so ably handled by the first Lord Bletchley.'

'Hmmmph,' gruffed the Home Secretary, petulantly resuming his seat. Feeling that in some way he was being upstaged, he countered 'and which led directly to his founding *your* Semantics Department, Quibble.'

'Indeed. And I thank him for it. But my point is, there was a Fenian hand behind that outrage, too.'

'Outrage?' smiled Chapman, the career diplomat. 'That's a bit strong isn't it? A few bogus words…'

'A verbal outrage, gentlemen! A semantic outrage! An outrage,' his close-set eyes did another tour of the mahogulous table, 'to comprehensibility.' A low, incomprehensible hum, as of insects, followed on this seven-syllable substantive.

'What's incomprehensible to me,' picked up Hackett, who looked as though he was being richly entertained by the roundtable, 'is how in the name of the Four Ancient Masters you derive a Hibernian origin for the like of 'grodlumous' and 'foubt', to say nothing of 'lali perpengi'. You won't find 'lali perpengi' anywhere in Paddy Dinneen!'

The room became alive with mutters and mumbles, and a persistent pisstisstitis poisoned the air until Quibble's palm slapped the table decisively. This was so entirely unexpected that to a man, everyone shut up. Everyone sat up. 'You miss the point,' growled the redoubtable Chief Inspector. 'Fraiser?'

The Scotsman leaned back in his chair. 'In terums of morphology I daresay you're reet. The morphology has nothin to doo with the Gallic tongue. Such declansions as MockTurkill tells me you hae in the Eirish are noowhere to be foond, I grant you tha'. But as Inspactor Quabble talls ye, you mass the peent.' It was the same Quibble who now took over the delightful task of enlightenment. 'What my colleague stated is that forensic and semantic analyses have shown the terms to be of Hibernian provenance.'

'Aetiology,' corrected the Scotsman.

'Of Hibernian aetiology. He never said that they were of Gay-lick aetiology.'

'But Dinneen's dictionary…' sputtered Chapman. 'That's Gaedhilic, surely!' He glanced hurriedly at Hackett as though he momentarily dubited the assertion. 'Where does Dinneen's dictionary fit into any of this, this…?' he waved a hand, unable to find a noun adequate to the state of verbal pandemonium.

'The provenance of the terms is Hibernian,' continued Quibble, unperturbed by Dinneen or by anyone else, 'but it may surprise you to hear that their morphemes are based upon the Wooton-Hey word-hoard.' The Chief Inspector surveyed the table, gratified at the almighty calumption his words had unleashed. When finally it subsided he resumed. 'It has long been suspected that the infamous fire at the Ashmolean was nothing more than a cover-up. As the Home Secretary is aware, at least a half-dozen terms which were supposedly destroyed in that fire have since come to light. I myself,' the ferret eyes weaselled out the two Eirishmen, 'headed the team entrusted to examine them. Two years ago, our report was circulated. Until today, its findings have been kept secret. Home Secretary, you have a query?'

'The Academy knows nothing of this report?' squinnied the Home Secretary.

'The Academy, *especially*, knows nothing of this report.' Once more, the weasel eyes ferreted out the two Eirishmen. 'I'm not at liberty to go into it in any detail in public. Suffice it to say that the morphology of a number of the bogus terms in the Rockchester cache can only have been derived from the morphology apparent in the extant terms of the Wooton-Hey word-hoard. Suffice it to say, gentlemen, that once a process analogous to aspirate transposition as it occurs in the Gaylick is added into the mix, we are talking of a morphological derivation at the 95% confidence level.' The round of calumptions that overtook the roundtable was even more gratifying. 'Suffice it to say,' concluded the Chief Inspector of Semantics, a raised palm putting paid to the pisstisstitis that followed the ebb of the calumption, 'that it is precisely this derivation from the Wooton-Hey word-hoard, which is to say, from the embryonic stage of Old Engelish, which *allows* the counterfeit terms of the Rockchester cache, and of contervoc as a whole, to persist so perfidiously in the present day language. What the Academy,' he shook his head distastefully, 'have termed "vigency". Gentlemen, vigency is not the worst of it! I hand you back to my colleague.'

Duncan Fraiser gravely rose. Duncan Fraiser gravely walked over to the flipchart. 'If I may?' His terrier's eyebrows coming together as if to darn in the stray hairs, he moved the flipchart to one side so that the screen was unblocked. 'Thar's two wees in whach terums of even low vagency may be spread far and weed. The furst is mechonical. There was yon Prussian philosopher who treed tae patent a steam-powered prantin-press tae manyifacture santhetic a priori statements., can ye recall, Quabble, what's thas his neem was?'

'I can't,'

'Aye, Kant. Anyway, that didnae work. Far too mony category errors. Zammerman tried tae revive the dastardly process toward the end o' the last war, but tae no avail. Tis nae harum. I needn't tell ya the pan-de-mo-nium that any mechanical devayce…'

He was interrupted abruptly by Quibble, whose glare forestalled any elaboration. 'All the same,' continued the Scot, admonished, 'we all meend at the close of the woruld war, the Sponnish influenza that came oot o' the tranches?' In the darkened room, a shudder ran around the table. They did mind it. 'What ye'll meybe no meend is the *mechonics* be whach the influenza spread sae fast aroond the woruld.' A shiver ran around the table. They didn't mind that. If Hackett was minded of the Huygens' Principle, which he was, he kept the thought to himself. Besides, Huygens' Principle took small account of vigency, and appeared to neglect entirely the universal Law of Diminishing Returns. He was startled out of his reverie by a newspaper being slapped onto the table before him. It was the *Speculator.* The question that accompanied it carried, if not a question-mark, at the least an edge of inquisition. 'Mr Hackett. Ye talk in thas wee article o the threat o' terums "gooin' varrul".'

'Do I?'

'Aye, ye do. And it's no' the furst teem yav been ahead o' the curve whan it comes tee the spread of contervoc.'

Hackett lifted the *Speculator* — it was several weeks

old — and examined the article that had been underlined with a red pen. It was a speculative piece he'd penned on foot of the talk he'd had with that hare-eyed traveller who'd lodged temporarily at *Widow Waddington's Boarding House for Gentlemen*. 'Is that an accusation?'

'That's an observation,' said the lowlander, while Quibble levelled at him the Quibble stare — 'I'm watching you', it declared. Fraiser meanwhile executed a signal with his eyebrows, and a figure who had been standing innocuously by the wall extinguished the lights while another manned the capstan upon which the projector stood. Fraiser nodded imperatively, and with a sound like the purring of an indefatigable tabby, or of a deck of cards being allowed to singly drop, the projector threw a white light over both inspector and screen. In rapid succession, circles and numerals flittered over both their surfaces. The Scotsman stood to one side. 'Thas filum should scare tha ponts off ye.'

What followed was shaping up to be yet another showing of the *British Movietone* presentation so familiar and so decried. But almost at once, the scenario changed. Now, on the silver screen, doctors and lab technicians in white coats peered down huge, lumbering microscopes whose slides showed the division of cells and the circulation of blood and lymph; scientists and epidemiologists scribbled on blackboards and pointed to projections, graphs and charts; while the last word in special effects offered a stick inside a bubble which multiplied and divided, multiplied and divided with frightening rapidity while a black stain spread ominously over a map of Europe. All the time, a doom-laden voiceover from the Scottish highlands gave ominous warning:

> *'Avery lavin' organasm is meed up o' lavin' salls. Your vayrus isnae, so it follows your vayrus isnae a lavin' organasm. Your vayrus doesnae exast withoot what they terum a hoost sall. What your vayrus does is, it utilases the hoost sall to raplicate. Than it can take oover. That's wha' we terum "gooin' vayral". Raplication is just a foncy terum for copyin', and vayral is a foncy terum for raplication. That's all your vayrus ever does. It copies and copies until such teem as the hoost is overwhalumed. And if the false terums of contervoc ever "go vayral", meek noo misteek, that's wha' may happen tay Anglish atself.'*

Thrum-slap, thrum-slap, thrum-slap went the machine. The lights flickered on. To a man, everyone blinked and looked at the Scotsman in appalled expectation. The Inspector's eyes moved slowly and methodically about the still mahogulous table, to see if his listeners had been likewise overwhelmed.

'Gentlemen,' he said at last, his Old Testament eyebrows twitching like antennae, 'what I hae to tall ye is thas. As of todee, we *knoo* the terums that come oot of the Rockchester cache hae finally gone vayral.'

CHAPTER THE FIFTH

in which an account is given of a remarkable encounter with an old acquaintance

Fraiser's pronouncement changed everything. It was splashed across the front-page of broadsheet and tabloid alike. It was repeated in bulletins on the wireless-set in every living-room in the land. In every picture-house, the new *Movietone* short was played before the feature, to chilling effect. Overnight, the term 'gone viral', which once again had been anticipated by the inimitable Ж, was on everyone's lips. Worse, it seemed to have precisely the effect of a mote of dust in a cloud-chamber as outlined by Malachi McCann all those years ago in relation to *Fraddle (vb. intr.)*. No sooner would the phrase be pronounced than an instance of verbal contamination going viral would be conjured into being. Anxieties, that had long been latent or coated with irony, condensed about the fromulous term. It was as if society itself were succumbing to the Cartesian Proposition 'J'y pense, donc j'y suis.'

On foot of the panic, emboldened by it, Æthelred Lord Bletchley tabled a motion which would lead in no time to a white paper entitled the Linguistic Integrity Act — it was to garner cross-party support. On foot of that paper, Chief

Inspector Quibble would make his case for wider powers of search and detention; on foot of the Linguistic Integrity Act, Bracken would make a down-payment on the Bloomsbury skyscraper which would house the future Ministry of Information, though it would be two years before the Viscount became Minister of Information. Operation Babylon had been a hit-'n'-miss affair, half-arsed measures of stop-and-search enforced half-heartedly. Operation Babel, its fearful successor, would be no such thing.

But once again we're getting ahead of ourselves.

On foot of Fraiser's pronouncement, Hackett returned from the Eirish Consulate on foot. There, he managed to slip Miss Maloney his report on the Oxenford Council without his hapless superior noticing. So much had happened since his arrival here, and still he was no nearer to solving the old conundrum: who was the bogus Ж? Was he ***Q?***, and should that query have an extra interrogation mark? From there his imagination went to a curious slip of linen that had been slipped to him by that hare-eyed individual who'd lodged briefly in the boarding house. Mentally he examined it: a flame-darkened diagram of a lozenge on a scrap of linen of Ulster provenance, smelling vaguely of eau de toilette. It had four cardinal points designated ***M; C; F; S;*** in Bahnschrift font, and like the scrap of paper Quibble had once briefly shown him, in the centre a large ***Q?*** with a mock crown on top. It was just the sort of enigma to fire his imagination. Now, there were four corners to a square, as to a lozenge, rectangle, trapezium or quomboid. There were four cardinal directions; four seasons, four provinces, four Masters, four suits, though none of these quartets was begun by the letters to hand. But in any case, where did that leave ***Q?***? And was ***Q?*** related to Quinn, who was said to be the Moriarty behind the whole nefarious affair? That quintessential question remained.

His errant thoughts were about to take him inside *Brigid Waddington's Boarding House for Gentlemen* when he chanced to glance across the street. There, beneath the three brass balls, Hackett thought he could make out the figure of the war-cripple. He squinnied. It was a suspicious character, one way or another. Or no. He himself was the suspicious character; that other character was the occasion of the suspicion. Damn it, I'll set the fella in motion, test the de Broglie Hypothesis once for all. Seeing or hearing what was fast bearing down on him, or perhaps using that sixth (or more correctly fifth) sense which the blind are said to possess, the war-cripple began to slink away. 'You! Hey!' calloohed Hackett. 'Hold on a minute!' Suspicious, the suspicious figure continued along the road as though he hadn't heard. Hackett stopped fast. The receding head was bobbing at regular intervals. Hackett began to count. But it wasn't the number of crests and troughs in the bobbing motion that Hackett was counting, it was rather the interval that separated them. After all it was the Eirish who'd invented the spaces between words. Now, the frequency required by the de Broglie Hypothesis should be inversely related to the interval. So perhaps he'd do better to count the number of crests or troughs (f) in a given interval (t), and then to average the duration as (d) = (t)/(f)? One elephant, two elephant, three… Ach! It was too difficult. Besides, what was the figure to which the result might be compared? 'Stop!' calleyed Hackett, dismissing de Broglie and all his blamed hypotheses! If the war-cripple failed to answer, he had no answer either for Hackett's longer stride. Before he'd gained the corner, the garmungling arm of the Eirishman was laid on his stooping shoulder, arresting him. 'Not so fast, a chara!' said Hackett.

'What d'you want?' The man pivorted about until the dark glasses were on a level with Hackett's Adam's apple. All that separated the two men was the tray about the mendicant's neck upon which were laid out sundry shoelaces and lucifers.

'I want to know why you've been spying on me.' An instinct made him draw back his hand as though he was about to strike. The blind man instantly flinched. 'You cowered!' calloohed Hackett, triumphant.

'Coward?'

'Cowered.' He laughed a low, fromulous laugh. 'You're no more blind than I am!' A hiatus followed. 'So?' said Hackett, resisting the delicious pleasure to test if the coward cowered a second time. 'What have you to say to that?'

'You have me mixed up with the brother,' retorted the cripple, the accent unmistakeably Jackeen 'It's the brother as is blind.' A vision from the PALACE BAR came to Hackett, who knucked his fingers. 'You're both chess players!' Then he checked himself. 'You and your brother have been shadowing me from the minute I got here. Even before. Why?' The mendicant ignored the question. 'Who put you up to it?' Behind his shades he frundled, or grimlied. 'Was it Semantics?'

'Huh!'

'The Academy?'

'The "Academy", a deir sé.'

'Chapman?'

'*Who*?' Not Chapman.

'Dubilin, then?'

In place of answering, the man made to shundle away,[68] but dawdled. 'There's a message.'

Hackett was unsure he'd heard aright. 'Message? What message?'

'You've to be at the PUNCH & JUDY at three o'clock this coming Saturday.'

'What Punch and Judy?'

'Covenant Garden.'

'Wait!' The man waited. 'Who says I've to be there?'

'Mulcahy.'

'Mul-*cahy*!?' Hackett reached out as though to again arrest the beggar's progress, or egress, but something held him back. The blind man shundled away and was gone.

Mulcahy! Hackett shook his hoary locks. There was only one Mulcahy that he knew of. But that was years ago, man! Ignatius Hackett, whose journalistic name was once of such standing that he could command a stool in any licensed premises from the OVAL to the PALACE, was dumbfounded.

As Hackett climbed the stairs up to the balcony of the landmark Logdon public house, his heart was beating as much from anxiety as from the unaccustomed exercise. But it was not Teddy Mulcahy that Hackett found waiting for him. It was little Willy Clarke.

Clarke's appearance turned everything on its head. At one time, he'd been Mulcahy's nemesis. At the time of the Dubilin Lock-in, he'd been directly responsible for placing

68 A shundle lies somewhere between a shunt and a sidle. What its fundamental frequency might be is anyone's guess.

the printer's son and his printer father behind bars. A latterday Hobbes, he was nasty, brutish and short. Now, Hackett hadn't set eyes on the little man in nigh on twenty years, but so little was he changed that the journalist unwittingly burst into a guffaw. There, rising a good fifteen inches over the gnarled face and malevolent eyes, was the very topper that had ever lent the DMP G-man the look of an undertaker for dwarves. 'Willy Clarke!' he exclaimed.

'Liam,' gruntled the little man. A grim companion stood next to him, a man almost as short, though his eyes were on a level with the brim of the topper. They might have been a pair of jockeys. They were standing outdoors on a balcony that overlooked the stalls and crowds and jugglers. As Hackett extended his hand, it came to him why the venue had been chosen. From this vantage, no peeler nor plainclothes detective might approach them unobserved. 'Been donkey's, Willy. How have you been?'

'I told you. Liam.'

'Suit yourself. I'm here to meet a man by the name of Mulcahy. I wonder would that be the same Teddy Mulcahy whose printing press you wrecked?'

'Never mind about that,' he snapped. 'Did you come on your own?'

'You saw me come on my own.'

'You weren't followed?'

'You tell me.'

Out of his hat, Clarke conjured a set of dark glasses. 'Put these on. We're leaving.' Hackett, whose hand remained unshaken, accepted the glasses. 'Can't be too careful,' said Clarke's companion with something of a sneer. The two took position, one at each of Hackett's elbows. It was only after he tried them on that he found they were no conventional dark glasses. These glasses had been painted opaque black. Simultaneously he felt a hand under each elbow. 'Walk.'

Hackett felt something being pressed into his right hand. 'What's that?'

'It's your white stick,' guffawed Clarke's companion. Slowly, tenuously, the three men took the stairs. Hackett closed his eyes. He found that it made it easier to concentrate his attention on his other four senses. They stepped outside into the Saturday crowd. 'Where are we going?'

'That doesn't concern you.'

'Then why do I feel concerned?' Despite the starts and stops, jostles, bumps, turns and occasional stumbles, Hackett managed to keep a loose tally of the number of lefts, rights and straight-aheads as the threesome made tortive progress to wherever it was they were going. After two hundred and eighteen paces, give or take, they entered a building and he was ushered down a set of stairs and into a basement. Once they were on the level, his two vademecums released his elbows. Willy Clarke, the evil of two lessers, pulled the glasses roughly from his nose. Hackett was momentarily blinded by a naked bulb. For minutes afterwards, his sight was tainted by its blue afterglow. '**Dia's Muire duit**,' issued a voice from beyond the blue taint.

'**Is Padraig**,'[69] replied the journalist, bedazzled but unfazed.

'You can leave us.' The two minders lost little time in

69 A form of reciprocal greeting that can be extended indefinitely through an entire canon of saints.

removing themselves, and Hackett found he was facing a desk behind which the former companion, anarcho-syndicalist and fellow taker of Irish classes before he was expelled from Conradh na Gaedhilge for being too zealous, was seated. At the apex of a pair of forearms, set into a head that was entirely bald but for tufts of curly hair over either ear, the presence of which reminded one against one's wishes of the Great Auk's nest in the display cabinet of the Natural History Museum off Merrion Square, two lugubrious brown eyes were fixed on his. The pyramidal arrangement was curiously picked up by the red triangle in a mirror advertisement for Bass that was stuck up on the wall behind. 'An bhfuil tú go maith?' asked an Maolcathach. Uninvited, the thought came to Hackett that the surname might be translated 'bald-curly'.

'Ceart go leor, slán a bhéas tú. What's with the old language?'

'Comes in handy, when you don't want the bastards to know what you're spraking.'

Hackett looked about the room, as though any corner might conceal an eavesdropper. Behind him was another mirror. In it was mirrored the Bass advertisement, its slogan reversed. ***!ssaB s'taht, hA.*** It wouldn't make the blindest bit of difference. As a printer, Teddy Mulcahy had ever the queer knack of reading backwards. The thought made the journalist feel curiously exposed. He decided to go on the offensive. 'Thanks for the tip.'

'What tip?'

'Quomboids. Don't play the soineanta! It was your hand was behind the note.'

'Was it?'

'The war-cripple.'

'The war-cripple?'

'Or his brother.'

'His brother, faith.'

'Who played chess.'

'Chess, is it?'

'And if not him, then the carpenter.' No response. Hackett shook his head. 'As the prison doctor complained to the judge, a chara, you're beginning to try my patients.' Now that the blue afterimage had at last drifted out of view, he could see on the desk a typewriter and a quantity of books. 'Let's cut to the chase. Why did you have your two stooges bring me here?'

'Tell me this first. You've still no use for shorthand?'

'Never learnt it.'

'You must have the same prodigious memory, so. Even after your… mishap.'

'It's good enough. Why do you ask?'

'Agallamh atá i gceist againn.'

Hackett once again scanned the room, this time for a chair. None could be seen. 'An bhfuil cead agam bheith i mo shuidhe mar sin?'[70]

'Cé tá i do choisceadh?'

'Ar an urlár féin?'

'Mar is mian leat.'

Hackett sat, folding his garmungling limbs awkwardly beneath him as a carpenter might fold up a hinged ruler. He was damned if he was going to be faced down by a baldy

70 O'Buachalla glosses the exchange as follows: 'It concerns an exchange of words'; 'That being the case have I your permission to sit?'; 'Who's stopping you?' 'On the floor itself?'; 'As you wish.'

headed depressive the like of Eamon Maolcathach. Besides, on the floor, he would be beneath the scrutiny of the facing mirrors. It was just as well he sat. After an initial catechism on every aspect of Hackett's present set-up, the agallamh, or to be accurate, the wild ramblings of this wandering aongheal continued for the better part of a half-hour.

By the time the two minders had conducted Hackett back to the PUNCH & JUDY and removed his dark glasses and stick, he was convinced of one thing. Teddy Mulcahy was as mad as a brush. If he could be believed, and sure it was plain as a pike-staff you couldn't believe the Hail Mary out of his mouth, he alone was the motive hand behind the entire counterfeit campaign, everything from Rockchester to Barchester to the Bisharp of Bedford. Not alone that, but he outlined to Hackett, in the faultless Eirish of the Dubilin Gaedhaltacht, a scheme that was so outlandish in its conception that Hackett wondered how this character rather than himself had lasted so long outside the walls of Swift's Asylum.

What he had vouchsafed the journalist was this. The whole idea was to bring down the Engelish language from the inside. Fair enough. Quibble of the Yard suspected as much. But the why and the wherefore? So that back over in Eirland, if you please, they'd have no option but to fall back on the old language! *Unruly Gaedhilic, that was ne'er teased out / on the six tynes of Latin syntax...*

And not any class of Eirish, mind. Dinneen's Eirish! To that end, Mulcahy had a clandestine press set up somewhere outside of the Pale[71] that was to run off ten thousand pirated

71 A bucket-shaped fortified area around medieval Dubilin that gained the deprecation of the native population for the pallor of the town-dwellers.

copies of an abridged version of the same foclóir. And this the very minute the campaign in Engeland had passed what he called a tipping point. Now Hackett knew a red herring when he smelt one, and Dinneen's green foclóir was as odoriferous a herring as he'd smelt this many a long day. But on the other hand, there was the little matter of the hints and tip-offs he'd been garnering, and that was a different kettle of fish. If he could dismiss any suspicion that Teddy Mulcahy might be the redoubtable Quinn, nevertheless it was Mulcahy's lackey had given him the nod about the quomboid. And that tip-off had led to his first big scoop. As Sir Æthelred might proclaim, that quomboid was a difficult circle to square even if it was a horse of a different colour. And how many nods and winks had followed hard upon it? If the sandwich-board man wasn't the blind-man, he was in league with him, and it was the blind-man or his brother had sent him to the PUNCH & JUDY. So in the heel of the hunt, he was as well to keep his powder dry and to see if the tips that followed weren't mere flashes in the pan. After that the rest was plain sailing.

As the curious meeting that took place in the PUNCH & JUDY took place immediately after the general panic occasioned by 'going viral' brought the Phoneme War to an end, only one final item need be related before we take our leave of the period. Now this was not the end. This was not even the beginning of the end. But it was, perhaps, the end of the beginning.

It was a trivial occurrence, such as happens in every typing-pool the world over, particularly since women were given the vote. Soon after Hackett completed his third secret report on the inner workings of the Royal Academy of Letters and duly handed it over in a sealed envelope to Miss Maloney, the lady vanished. More precisely, the lady was dismissed. She was found to have succumbed to what French delicacy terms *le mal de mère*. Chapman was not greatly surprised to find the casual typist in the family way. It was his candid and considered opinion that to take on an unmarried Eirishwoman in a foreign city was to court disaster. It gave him a grim sense of that brand of satisfaction that derives from a mishap foretold when he informed Ignatius Hackett of the development.

And that might have been that. Except of course it wasn't.

CHAPTER THE SIXTH

in which is celebrated the extraordinary lengths to which the Foundling Fathers went in order to effect a breach with their trans-Atlantic cousins

On foot of Miss Maloney's disappearance, or dismissal if that's what it was, a telegraph from Dubilin summoned Hackett home. Evidently, Chandler the handler had not been expecting the development, nor whoever it was that was Chandler's handler. But before we follow Hackett down the august corridors of 70-80 St Stephen's Green, we must return briefly to a Logdon that no longer laughs at *Movietone* government warnings. Two events in particular merit our attention prior to the columnist's departure for the ould country — an invitation from the departing American Ambassador to the gala opening of their new premises at no.1 Grosvenor Square; and a peremptory summons to Scotland Yard at the behest of a certain Chief Inspector of the Semantics branch of CID.

The former enthused the journalist as the Ambassador was none other than Kermit Froschmann, whose lavish parties had long been the toast of the diplomatic world. Even during the driest days of Prohibition, he'd never pulled his punches. Perhaps it was the Ambassador's bibliophilia which had brought the inestimable Ж to his attention and led to his being invited. It was widely known that in the hallway of the Ambassador's residence, he had a first edition of Thorstein Veblen's *The Theory of the Leisure Class* on conspicuous display. As a parting gift, moreover, he was to be presented that evening with the annotated fair copy of Webster's *American Dictionary of the English Language* — the very copy upon which the ornery lexicographer had scored out the middle e in *Engelish.*

Lured as ever down the footnotes and byways, Hackett spent several fruitful afternoons in the reading rooms of the British Library to bring himself up to speed on American exceptionalism. As the diplomatic Bentley, which had called for him at the Widow Waddington's, puttled in the general direction of Grosvenor Sq, he decided to share his recently acquired knowledge with the Cultural Attaché. The more he informed, the more bamboozled the latter became. 'Let me ask you.' Hackett blithely ignored the appeal for clemency in his superior's eye. 'In the wake of their famous Tea Party,[72] who would you say was the most instrumental figure in keeping the thirteen colonies sundered from the crown?'

'The thirteen...?'

'Colonies. Not to be confused with the thirteen Connollys who sailed there.'[73]

---

72 The Boston Tea Party of 1773, these days chiefly remembered due to its infamous parody in Lewis Carroll's *Alice in Wonderland.*

73 Emigrants like the Connollys who took part in the 'Manifest Destiny' policy of westward expansion were given a lot of latitude. While the word 'colony' derives from Cristobal Colón, responsible for their institution throughout the New World, America itself is named for Giuseppe "Amerigo" Vespucci, an Italian cartographer whose sobriquet alludes to a childhood penchant for guns.

Gingerly, Chapman dredged his errant fingers through the ever thinner strands of his ginger hair. 'Go on,' he surrendered.

'You've heard of course of the Foundling Fathers?' Chapman failed to answer a question that smacked rhetorical. 'Figures the like of Hamiltown and Frankly and Washington Deasy, whose speeches were so on the money that they're now on the money. And Madson, whom they tender more dearly. These seccessionists were statesmen and lawmen, men of the sword, men of property, propriety and of foresight. But what's missing from these denominations? Will I tell you?'

'I feel sure you're going to.'

'To create the breach after which there was no going back, what was needed was a lexicographer. And that man's name,' he paused, as much for affect as effect, 'was a man by the name of Webster. Let me ask you, Chippy. All these bogus terms over here, proliferating like midges about a cow pat. Why haven't they the Yanks worried?'

'You're about to tell me it's down to this Daniel Webster character, Yes?'

'No.'

'No?'

'Noah.'

Hackett watched his superior's eyes turn to slits. 'A wonder none of our own republicans and revolutionaries ever thought of a ploy like that.'

An image rose before Hackett of a head like an auk's egg on a nest. 'You'd be surprised,' he supplied. 'But the greater point is. American English (sic) would appear to be distinct enough not to be at risk of cross-contamination. You follow?'

'What I do not follow is why you're telling me all this.'

'I thought you might appreciate a bit of background. For diplomatic chitchat.'

'Chitchat!' Something akin to indignation passed over the Cultural Attaché's countenance. He sat up, just as the car puttled up beside the Embassy. 'You were not sent over by Stephen's Green to provide me with chitchat.'

Quibble of the Yard did not suffer fools gladly, and there was no shortage of fools at this particular reception. As a younger man he'd cut his constabulary teeth, so to sprake, on the backstreets of the Eastend, in whose ghettos and tenements one at least encountered an honest class of felon — petty thieves and con-artists, fraudsters and career burglars the like of Alfie Briggs and Jimmy 'the Monk' McCrae. There was never any great harm in their patois and their rhyming slang, no insidious intent behind their demimonde of bogeys, narks and polonies, monkeys and ponies, tins of fruit and Gordon Bennetts. Whereas this present assault, which was fracturing into two distinct dialects…

He stood aloof, scarcely heeding the stuffed-shirt from the Foreign Office who was singing the praises of the renegade colonial who'd compiled their Anglo-American dictionary in the first place. An effusive paean for the benefit of that libertine Yank, Froschmann, who bore an absurd resemblance to Groucho Marx. No shortage of fools from the press lapping it all up. And that bally Eirish hack, too, though whether he was fool or virtuoso was a moot point. One way or another, his fingerprints were all over this present threat. Been giving him plenty of line to play with. Find out soon enough, once the line is reeled in. That gormless Sancho Panza beside him, though, there was a fool to end all fools.

Despite himself, some of the stuffed-shirt's disquisition was going in.

'Two by two, Noah Webster is determined to get a raft of modifications safe inside the language in time for the Continental Congress. To date, any changes he's carried off have been on an ad hoc basis. Pronunciation is an easy target in a land where route is rout and not root and shone is shown and not shun. Next he manages to pull off a hatful of alterations such as cutting his vest down to a waistcoat and using suspenders to hold up his pants; of substitutions, as when he turns rubbish into trash and for a tap he employs a faucet. He manages to disburden the word-hoard of a few Old World words of long standing, fortnight and fromulous and fardle; and to re-stamp a few new ones for the Brave New World. Ornery, as an honorary example. Of course he did concoct a few duds along the way: hokey for instance. But a heavy price was paid in those endangered substantives Noah left out of his ark. Abandoned to extinction the fischew, the shough, the flittermouse, the jade, and the common pard. From that time to this, no restauranteur can be quite sure if it's an eggplant or an aubergine that'll be served up, a zucchini or a courgette, nor what precisely constitutes a potato chip. And as for such dubitous terms as fag and fanny,' the stuffed-shirt risked a risqué smirk, 'the less said the better.'

The less said the better was precisely what Quibble was thinking. He watched the ripple of smutty guffaws sweep the assembled company. Old bald-head and whiskers, the frundling Home Secretary, didn't follow, and was being enlightened by a M^c^Turcaill discrete whisper.

'In addition, or more precisely, subtraction, he removed the 'and' from numbers larger than a hundred; in one bold stroke he culled three zeros from the American billion; and Maths he singularly had shorn of its s. In fact, you might say he was dealing in carpals and tarsals before ever it was popular or profitable!'

There was the point. Why were the Yankees so damned smug when it came to the risk of cross-contamination? The French were characteristically jejune, every manner of obstacle and barrier being de rigueur with them, when all they shared was a common alphabet dressed up and Frenchified in such frippery as circumflexes and cedillas. There was more to this than met the eye, and the Quibble eye was not so easily conned. His brow contracted, the vertical furrow deepening. What was it Pshaw had said about two peoples separated by a common language?

'So far, Webster's successes have been lexical. They've scarcely touched on orthography. But by a sleight of hand, he was next able to pull off the transposition of -re to -er in such a way as it would stick; to substitute *-ise* for *-ice* and *-ize* for *-ise*, though not *-ize* for *-ice,* which had I the means to hand I might illustrate using a Venn diagram; and to carry out a general cull of the letter u in all our abstract nouns — which is to say, those that end in 'our'. That wasn't so very difficult in that most had come to mean different things on either side of the pond. Humour, for instance. And neighbour. Odour, and flavour and honour bright. Favour, too, though colour remained stubbornly unchanged for another hundred years.'

The speaker threw a risky glance toward the Ambassador. Bedamned but the latter now wiggled his eyebrows like a third-rate Groucho Marx. No, these damned Americans had something up their semantic sleeves.

'To finish, the Continental Congress adopts Webster's changes wholesale for their peerless republic and enshrines them in a tome they dub, as a joke, the *American Dictionary of the English Language*. Though the printer wasn't in on the joke, apparently, and the name stuck. After that, the orthographic breach was every bit as wide as the oceanographic, and all the King's horses and all the King's men gave up all hope of recovering the House of Handover's thirteen lost colonies. Mr Ambassador, to conclude, it gives me no ornery satisfaction to return to you and your fellow countrymen the original working copy of this most seditious work.'

A raucous applause did the rounds. Quibble squinnied across to the American delegation. A dozen businessmen in double-breasted suits behind the Ambassador and every one of them smug as a bridegroom. Damn it, there was something they weren't sharing with Whitehall. Or that Whitehall wasn't sharing with Semantics. And that shady-looking galoot in the homburg hovering behind them, giving the beady eye, something something Kent, who had the ear of J Edgar Hoover® himself. Been seen hanging about the German Embassy, what's this his triple-barrel name is?

Once the speeches were made and the toasts toasted, the guests began to form and reform in clusters of common acquaintance and interest. One such grouping condensed like a droplet in a cloud-chamber about the display case containing Webster's fair copy. Quibble sidled within earshot, a model of discretion. 'Tell us, Mr Hackett,' issued from a voluble Kermit Froschmann, who only lacked a cigar to clinch the ludicrous resemblance, 'what about this linguistic divide you've been scaring the pants off us with?'

'I think, Mr Ambassador,' replied the inimitable Ж, 'that Professor Doolittle will be able to put the issue beyond any doubt.'

'Beyond any…?' gruffed Sir Æthelred, working his whiskers as though he were hard at hearing and not one bit pleased about it. 'Dubit, Sir Æthelred' supplied McTurcaill, though his tone suggested he had not complete confidence in his contribution.

'Precisely!' said Doolittle. 'But the, ah, correct word is, in fact, doubt.' Armed with an impeccable memory, the redoubtable Don recited to the assembled company the precise definition of 'doubt' as it appeared in the *Shorter Oxenford Engelish Dictionary* he'd been instrumental in editing.

'But, but, but…' sputtered the Home Secretary. 'Damn it all man! What you're saying is dubit. Dubit! Doubt means the very opposite! To doubt is to suspect that something is the case; to dubit, that it is not the case.' He frundled. 'Or am I wrong?'

'Only,' smiled Doolittle, 'in the dictionaries of the other camp.'

'By other camp you mean, sir, Camsbridge?'

'No slur intended, I assure you.' Doolittle raised a hand, as though he were standing on a stage in Stratford. *'Doubt thou the stars are fire; Doubt that the sun doth move; Doubt truth to be a liar; But never doubt I love.'* Kermit Froschmann's eyebrows hoisted and dropped rapidly in appreciation. McTurcaill discretely whispered something to which the Home Secretary nodded, pleased. 'All very well, but what about,

'*My father's spirit in arms! I doubt some foul play*'? I daresay you're not going to tell me the Dane *didn't* suspect foul play?'

'An interjection. By Robyn Plaiger. A Camsbridge fellow. One way or another it's of doubtful origin.' His hand rested on the display case containing Webster's seditious tome as though he were about to swear an oath on it. 'Oxenford publications have thus far had the fortune of being spared contamination. The same, alas, cannot be said of our pretender colleges up in Camsbridge. Their dictionaries are littered with the new terms.' He glanced at Hackett. 'That is to say, the old-new terms. That is to say, the terms of contervoc.'

'It's… not quite that simple,' interjected the newspaperman, whose articles, as Quibble could attest, had done much to put the terms old-new and new-new into circulation. 'There are new-new words in contervoc, and old-new words in what our friend McTurghaill has denominated skaz.'

The venerable Home Secretary's eyes narrowed. 'How can you be so sure it's not your *own* dictionaries that have been contaminated?'

At this, Ignatius Hackett nodded sagely, and Quibble faded into invisibility.

It was a ticklish question, just the type to excite the journalist's pangúr bán curiosity. Suppose they had been. How could one tell? It was a bit like the difficulty with Mr Einstein's theory of space-time, viz., if every ruler in the imaginary spaceship were suddenly a hair's breadth longer, or shorter, or if the hands of every clock to hand was suddenly to run a few seconds faster, or slower, what clock or ruler could you use to measure them against so as to find out?

But could a dictionary be targeted? On their most recent

visit to Ealing Broadleaf, the Eirish delegation had been met at the door not by any mere footman, but by Harold Hastings in person. His was not a happy face. Indeed, its shade was apoplectic. The cause of this discolouration became apparent only after the guests were ushered inside. 'Vandalism sir! Scurril vandalism, pure and simple!' Hackett and Chapman followed the Warden's indignant, white-gloved index to the brass plaque that was screwed into the reverse side of the door:

Royal Acacademy of Letters

MDCCXIV

Legere, et non intelligere, neglegere est

The two guests returned an interrogative gaze to the Decommissioner of the Otiose. 'Acacademy!' sputtered the Warden. 'It is the proveliest vandalism!' Vandalism or no, it was proof, if proof were needed, of the virulence apparent in the newest batches of contervoc terms. Unless they were skaz terms.

Now, if the Academy could be targeted, why not a dictionary?

His father Walter had always held a dictionary to be a repository of memory. But suppose for a minute that memory had been tampered with. Suppose the definition of a particular word inside of every dictionary had simultaneously been changed. How could you tell? In a few cases you could go back to the word-hoards, but for the vast majority? It was a good one all right, every bit as ticklish in its way as the equivocal dilemma of the Cretan liars, the incomparable challenge of the seven bridges of Königsberg, the riddle as to why a raven is like a writing-desk, the riddle of the sands, or the perennial conundrum of the chicken and the egg.

Some minutes later, as Hackett emerged into the

darkness, Quibble emerged from the darkness. 'A word,' he said, separating the journalist from his strubbly side-kick. Hackett's features composed themselves agreeably, but not without a soupçon of supercilious irony. 'See here, Hackett. At every step we've taken at Semantics, it turns out we've been anticipated by one or other of your damned pinesses. It's about time you came clean.' Hackett smiled gormlessly, inviting the plod to continue with his line of inquiry. 'I'd love to know who's feeding you all these pointers.'

Hackett ribbled his chin. 'I'd love to know that myself.'

Chief Inspector Quibble of Semantics winced. Some weeks back he'd released into the public domain his suspicion that there was a minimum of two cells operating separately, one to the northeast of the country, one to the southwest, and once again that jackanapes Ж had somehow stolen a march on him. But how much did he know? Did he know what he, Quibble, knew, viz., that all the key suspects had Eirish connections? Not alone that, but he, Quibble, could place them in Dubilin at the very time that he, Hackett, had been an apprentice hack there.

He grimlied. 'Make no mistake, Hackett. We'll get to the bottom of this. Be at the Yard tomorrow, four o'clock sharp.' He took a step back into the darkness. 'Bring your fidus Achates there along with you.'

'Are we being arraigned?' The question remained unanswered.

CHAPTER THE SEVENTH

in which our hero is hauled in by Inspector Quibble of Semantics to 'assist the police with their inquiries'

An odd assortment was ranged about the Operations Room of the Semantics branch of the CID. Representing the highest echelons of His Majesty's government was the Right Honourable Home Secretary, who had by now outlived two cabinet reshuffles and as many incumbents at No.10. Representing the forces of Law and Order were Quibble, Fraiser and an official from HM Customs who was hitherto unknown to Hackett but whose dour demeanour suggested he was more officious than efficient. Seymour Doolittle was present, and opposite him was a steely-haired woman in tweeds who stared at the journalist's unkempt locks and four o'clock shadow through disapproving pince-nez. Her position on Hackett's appearance was absolutely clear, her position in the assembly less so.[74]

As the latecomers shundled into the operations room,

74 Though the physical features don't match, most commentators identify this unnamed woman as Phyllis Winterbourne, who would shortly become Director of the secretive 5th Office of Viscount Bracken's Ministry of Information (later known as MI5. An upgrade to Logdon's North Circular Rd, which was to be called the M15, was shelved in order to avoid confusion).

Hackett's attention was momentarily drawn to a disc or rotor which sat momentarily on the desk nearest Quibble before the latter dispatched it into a drawer. He had just sufficient time and acuity to clock the letters of the alphabet placed around the circumference and, indented on the inside, 𝔊𝔖-2. To cover his discovery as it were, he allowed his curiosity to be drawn to a huge map of the metropolis in which a small number of thumbtacks had been inserted: clusters of red to the northeast of the Thames, of yellow to the southwest. Next to this was a board upon which was written the singular word 'Mamalujo'. A counterfeit term, perhaps, but skaz or contervoc? Several photographs were taped to the board beneath it. Hackett was less than impressed. Pinning photos to a board was his idea of a mugs' game.

For the benefit of the latecomers, Sir Æthelred repeated the concluding remarks of what had evidently been a peroration. 'We must all be on our guard, Quibble. O'Brien himself assures me the new generation of terms is more insidious. And although the attacks have ranged far and wide, bear this in mind. Thus far the larger cities have dodged the bullet. Greater Logdon has largely been spared. And Brumingham. And Covenantry. Your vigilance, Quibble, is to be commended. But we have to stand firm! We're not out of the woods yet.' He addressed his final remark to the entire assembled company. 'The immanent and imminent attack on our beloved language is both systematic and systemic. It follows that we need a response that is both practicable and practical, both substantive and substantial, and it must be implemented in steps at once discreet and discrete.'

A pause followed the words, a hiatus which invited the Chief Inspector of Semantics to take up the baton. He did so, and stepped as far as the board waving it. 'Mamalujo.' His vulpine eyes sized up each member of the assembly by turns. 'What does it signify?'

'Before you get into that, Quibble, perhaps you could answer me a question.' As he sprake, Æthelred Lord Bletchley's eyes bore down directly on Hackett. 'Is our friend Ж here justified in spraking about an imminent cleavage?'

'Immanent,' corrected the Chief Inspector when, to his chagrin, he was interrupted by his subordinate, Fraiser. 'I dinnae ken what yoo mean by cleavage, Sir Aythelrad. I'll tell ye thas. Sae pronoonced are the daffrences betwixt skaz and contervoc that there's aye an illacit trade on Westmanster Bradge in the terums of each.'

All eyes turned to Fraiser. Quibble allowed his cold stare to semaphore his intolerance of any insubordination. He then turned back to face the questioner. 'Far too early to say, my Lord. If you'll bear with me, this Mamalujo project has every bearing on your question about immanent cleavage.' After a judicious pause, the Chief Inspector's baton touched the first of the photographs that had been taped to the blackboard. Hackett stifled a gasp. Even from a distance, the ovine baldness atop a tuft of curls over either ear was apparent. 'Mulcahy, Edmond' the police officer stated. 'Printer. Political agitator. Syndicalist.' He aimed the next few words exclusively at Hackett. 'Eirish Republican Brotherhood.'

'No,' said the journalist.

'No?'

Hackett ribbled his stubble. 'Eirish Citizen Army. He was never in the 'hood.'

'I stand corrected,' said the Chief Inspector, who refrained from frundling, though a grimly escaped him. He instead picked up a stick of chalk and squeaked the letters ECA beneath the first of the portraits. His baton moved to the second, a man of dwarfish stature. Bringing it into focus, a jolt shook Hackett. Had he been followed to the **PUNCH & JUDY**? Then a second. Had he been followed *from* the **PUNCH & JUDY**? Whatever doubt or dubit had seized him he succeeded in concealing. 'Clarke, William. Royal Eirish Constabulary. G-division.' The Chief Inspector squealed the letters REC beneath the second photograph.

'He wasn't.'

Quibble squinnied first at the Eirishman and then at the portrait of the Eirishman. The latter was decidedly in a constable's uniform, and an Eirish one at that. What else did harp and crown signify if not Eirish? 'He *wasn't*?'

'DMP,' Hackett winked. 'The Dubilin Metropolitans. You're correct about the division.'

With the back of his sleeve Quibble erased the letters REC and replaced them with DMP. He then stood back, let on he was reconsidering. 'The point remains the same, though, don't it? They would still have been on opposite sides during your so-called Easter Insurrection.'

'Whether they were or whether they weren't, they were on opposite sides at the time of the Dubilin Lock-in, I can vouch for that. It was little Willy Clarke was responsible for putting half the Union leadership behind bars, Teddy Mulcahy among them, and for making smithereens of his printing press,' he went on, gazing into the middle-distance as though he would retrieve there the lost decades. 'Mulcahy was accused by the crown of sedition. He denied the charge, and his counsel submitted various affidavits to prove the point. Counsel for the prosecution submitted that these were forgeries, whereupon counsel for the defence submitted. Whereupon, like the unfortunate ladies who forgot to order a main course, he got his just deserts.'

If Hackett's account had been leavened with humour, Quibble failed to acknowledge it. 'So how comes it that two enemies are now working thick as thieves together?'

'You know very little of Eirish history if you have to ask that.'

The unexpected response brought a guffaw from all present. Only the thin lips of Inspector Quibble and of the woman in pince-nez and tweeds failed to smirk.

'One way or another,' resumed the Chief Inspector, 'these two are working hand in glove to spread their linguistic mayhem to the south and west of old Watling Street. Henceforth, the W-line.' The chalk shrieked a W. Their attention recovered, his baton moved on. 'Which brings me to the third figure. A Fleming. Aloysius, we think, though Aloysius may be an alias.' The third portrait was in fact a double-shot, full-face and profile, with numbers scrawled across its base. 'Ex-army. Known felon. He was picked up back in twenty-three trying to pass off old gammon as cant. Put in the Bridewell under heavy sentence, but the terms were eased two years later under the,' the constable winced, 'general amnesty. Broke parole. Disappeared from view. Was later found agitating the millworkers of Lanckershire, where he developed a taste for cotton gin. Was next seen wandering the docks of Liverpuddle talking gibberish. Disappeared again. There were rumours he'd taken the boat to Eirland. And that was the last that was heard of Aloysius Fleming. *Until now.*' His eyes narrowed as he singled out Hackett for the question to follow. 'What letters can we put under Mr Fleming, I wonder?'

Hackett shrugged. Of one thing only he was convinced, and the conviction came as a relief. The convict may have been ex-army, but his mugshot bore not the slightest resemblance to the war-cripple who'd been shadowing him. Nor to his brother. Nor, for that matter, to the garmungling carpenter with the jug ears. The high-pitched chalk executed the letters 'vet' under the third photograph. A brief pause met the execution. 'Army veteran?' dutifully tried the Officious of HM Customs.

'Army veterinarian.'

'In plain Engelish?'

'A horse doctor, Sir Æthelred. After the war he got a medical discharge.'

Even at the distance from the board at which he was sitting, Hackett was disturbed at a certain aura of familiarity about this third photo. That he should know two of the felons might be regarded as a misfortune; to know three… but *did* he know the man? Certainly, there was a paranoid trick about the eye that jogged his memory. Now what was the word to describe that look? Haunted? No. Hunted! Not quite. Hounded? The Chief Inspector resumed. 'There is one identifying mark associated with the prisoner. Here,' his fingers moved to his left rib cage, and tapped the region where the heart was supposed to be, 'this Fleming character has a tattoo. It shows a snake, in the form of a figure of eight. Or more correctly, a figure of eight on its side.' And on the board the chalk executed a deft **∞**.

'A military tattoo?' queried Hackett, the pangúr bán of his mind running elsewhere. Now an eight on its side was the mathematician's infinity. But that snake devouring its own tail, like the Baron Munchausen pulling himself out of the swamp by his ponytail. Where the hell had he encountered that before? In an instant it came to him. The fabled Ouroboros. Hadn't Mulcahy been a member of the secret Brotherhood, himself and the canny McCann? 'Thank you, Mr Hackett.' Supremely dignified, the baton moved on to the absence of a fourth photograph. In its stead there was taped to the blackboard a square of paper on which was executed in ominous black ink a singular interrogation mark. 'All that was known until now of the fourth character,' sprake the Chief Inspector, whose dignitas was in no way surpassed by his baton's, 'is that there *is* a fourth character. Another typesetter, possibly. Together, this interrogation mark and Fleming, Aloysius, have been unleashing their particular brand of linguistic terrorism to the north and the east of W-line.'

'W-?'

'Watling Street, Sir Æthelred, though the divide runs along an ancient Roman road all the way from Dover across to Wroxeter. In Sussex and Wessex, which is to say south and west of the divide, you no longer hear the word *indegar* except in its original verb form. A hen's indegar they style a quill, and make it plural by adding -age, and the hen itself is a poole. In Sussex and Wessex, it's a poole that lays your eyren and quillage fills your quilt. They're fond of their Qs. At first we thought it was just a quirk of pronunciation when in Yeovil we heard them counting thirteen, quarteen, quinteen. But that's how it's being taught in independent schools from Eastbourne to Weston-super-Mare. Logdon they've begun to call Landon, and they've started to call Moonday Mundie and Thorsday Thursdie.'

'In other words, it's a different language?'

'In other words.'

An interjection came from Seymour Doolittle, who until this point had said little. 'I say, this fourth character, I don't suppose it could by any chance be Quinn?' The name had an electrifying effect about the room. Quinn! Could it be Quinn? How was it it had occurred to no-one that it might be Quinn? It was left to Quibble to short-circuit the electricity. 'We've considered that,' he damped. 'No. Quinn, if he exists at all, exists outside this realm. This fourth…' he appeared to be searching for an epithet, '…Lord of Misrule is squarely inside the realm, aiding and abetting Mr Fleming to sow bedlam, in the form of old-new terms, to the north and east of W-line, while their counterparts spread new-new terms to the south and west. Though even that is to greatly simplify what's been going on. It goes without saying that in the absence of an electro-mechanical device, the whole dastardly project depends on an entire network of sleepers and subordinates. A distribution network. I grant you there may indeed be a puppet master pulling the strings from somewhere overseas. An unknown quantity. If you wish to give that quantity a name, I daresay Quinn is as good as any.'

'But supposing Quinn exists, why should he have chosen precisely four… what-did-you-call-'em…?'

'Horsemen of the Apocryphal?' tried Hackett. The quip was rewarded by general nods of 'that's good' and 'very clever' by all but the Chief Inspector and she of the steely hair. 'To answer your question,' intoned the Chief Inspector flatly, 'there are four cardinal directions to the distribution. Moreover, the executive governance of our State rests upon four great pillars, of which the Right Honourable Lord Bletchley is one.' The Home Secretary's face was infused with a flush of pleasure as he raised a great hand to ward off the compliment. 'Please!' he waved, or waived. 'And Mamalujo. Where does this Mamalujo fit into this mumbo-jumbo?'

'Project Mamalujo. It's no anagram that we can discover.' Over the course of the paragraph that was to follow, the eyes of the peeler never once left those of the journalist. 'We've been aware of Project Mamalujo for some considerable time now. Our information derives from a variety of sources, none of which I'm at liberty to go into. For operational reasons. In its essence, Project Mamalujo envisages two distinct types of argot, one largely old-new terms, the other chiefly new-new terms. What is more, each of these argots is itself composed of two distinct types of word, the carpal and the tarsal. That, gentlemen, gives us a total of four classes of counterfeit term, two pertaining to contervoc, so-called, and two to skaz. Perhaps we might think of them as the four suits of a deck of cards.' Deftly, he executed ♠♣♥♦ on the board — he was nothing if not deft. 'Now then…'

Hackett had been doodling on the blank paper in front of him, his mind busy chasing imaginary mice. Four suits were all very well, but what about four corners to a square or quomboid? What about the Annals of the Four Masters?[75] There were four seasons; four humours; four provinces; four elements. Four elements! Let me see now. Fire, air, (how does it go?), earth, water. How would these square with the four

75 The renowned Annals of the Four Masters (Annala na gCeithre Maistri) are chronicles of Eirish history running from the Deluge to 1616, the year of the death of both Shakespeare and Cervantes.

suspects? Let me see now… Fleming, water. Yes. Very good. Let me see now… he sensed the eyes of the room upon him, and the mice scuttling down their several mouse-holes, he set down his pencil. '♠♣♥♦,' he echoed, then played a wild card. 'With Quinn the Joker in the deck.' Quibble flitted the wild card away, as a beast flicks away a gadfly. 'Which is where this fourth character comes in,' he resumed. The pointer tapped the interrogation mark. 'We suspect number four must be another printer, or typesetter. Which brings me to the present danger. Ever since this year's Spring Offensive, the virulence of each false term has been increasing until, as my colleague Fraiser warns us, they've reached a point where they have "gone viral". It is a situation made all the more critical because our sources indicate that Project Mamalujo is about to be unleashed in full on the Metropolis itself.'

If the Chief Inspector had been anticipating a round of gasps, he was not disappointed. A general pisstisstitis seized the room. The Home Secretary leaned forwards. 'This attack is immanent, is it?'

'Imminent. Every piece of information points to it, Sir Æthelred. The problem is, the policy of containment we've been using to date under Operation Babylon is all very well in the countryside. But in a monstrous town more populous than some continents, it simply won't do. Which is why we've been working on a successor raft of measures which we're calling Operation Babel.' The stick of chalk, snapping once and setting all ears on edge, executed the word Babel.

The Right Honourable Secretary of State was temporarily lost in thought. 'There's a lot riding on this. Think you can pull it off?'

'That depends. Thus far, Operation Babylon has relied upon monitors. More than two hundred have been recruited under the Linguistic Integrity Act (1937). What Operation Babel envisages is supplementing these monitors by a task force of delators.'

'Delators?'

'People who delate.'

'Whereas monitors?'

'Monitors monitor, my Lord.'

'Quite. And where will delators delate and monitors monitor?'

'Monitors will forthwith be assigned at random not only to post offices as before, to monitor communications by telegraph and postal mail, and to newspapers,' the Chief Inspector squinnied at Hackett, 'but a select band will be sent to radio stations, and to telephone exchanges. So that forthwith we may eavesdrop on the full bandwidth of transmissions available in the modern, and if I may say, media-obsessed world.'

At this point, the query from which Hackett had been sidelined once more bubbled to the surface. He raised his hand. 'That interrogation mark. You said, "until now"...'

The Chief Inspector's eyes narrowed. They glanced towards the steely-haired pince-nez before returning to Hackett. 'How astute of you to remember.' He then nodded towards the Customs Officer. There was a large brown envelope lying on the table before him, where before Hackett could have sworn there had been nothing. The man drew forth from this envelope four photos, passing them one after another to the person immediately to the right, or left as you looked at him. As he did so, Chief Inspector Quibble enunciated: 'Mulcahy,

Clarke, Fleming… *Sangster.*'

The addendum of a fourth name had the effect of sending a ripple around the room, clockwise or counter-clockwise depending upon whether viewed from above or below. This ripple was on the point of subsiding when Quibble, with impeccable timing, reinforced it with: '*Miss* Sangster.'

A gratifying pisstisstis of consternation swept backwards and forwards. 'Miss?' 'Did he say *Miss*?' 'Was it Miss or Mrs he said?'

'Miss *Agatha* Sangster,' concluded the detective. All were impatient for the photograph of this Miss Agatha Sangster to reach them. Unfortunately, the effect of the Miss acted as a retarder on the free circulation of the photograph. Quibble, who was still staring hard at the Eirish journalist, played his next card. 'Dactylographer.' The exoticism of the profession demanded that each take another glance before passing on the monochrome desideratum, further slowing the progress. The photograph, when at long last it arrived, fell first into Chapman's hands. He stared, squinnied, held it at full arm's length from his nose in such a way that Hackett, too, was afforded a view. He then drew it into focus, gasped, slapped it down, and sputtered: 'Why, that's…' But how he had intended to finish this sentence must remain forever unknown. Rather than providing a predicate, the Cultural Attaché yelped. All eyes turned to him. He, however, held his breath, eyes bulging while his complexion ran through the full spectrum of apoplectic shades. Hackett filched the photograph from his strubbly fingers, afforded it a cursory glance, and passed it on. 'What's the next move?' he shrugged, carelessly.

'The next move? As of tomorrow, we publish these pictures at every crossroads and post office in the country, that is the next move!'

The dynamic in the diplomatic Bentley as it muttled back towards the Consular Buildings of the Eirish Free State that evening was greatly altered. For the moment, not a word was said about the cur's yelp that had cut short the Cultural Secretary's 'Why, that's…' Predicate or no, it went without saying that whatever it was that Hackett's sharp kick to his superior's shin had curtailed should, within earshot of the jug-eared chauffeur, go without saying.

Hackett silently ran through the rogues' gallery. Three of the felons were known to him. But what of the fourth, this Fleming character? Back from the Flemish front. The look in the mugshot was, what? Mentally he knucked his knuckles. Neither haunted nor hounded, or else both of the above. *Institutionalised* was the word to describe the look that was in that third photograph. This prisoner held at His Majesty's pleasure twenty years ago. There'd been a lodger at Widow Waddington's several months before who'd had just that look. Hackett had had a good gawp while he was awaiting the image of Agatha Sangster to do the rounds. Bedamned if it wasn't the self-same inmate of Swift's Mental Asylum the time Hackett had been inside. Bug-eyed, and a dribbler. He tried to add the effects of two decades in and out of institutions, and on and off the streets, to the photo of the veteran veterinarian. Was it possible? Chapman's words broke abruptly in on his reverie, 'You knew Mulcahy from way back when.'

'And little Willy Clarke.'

'Tell me about them,' pursued the Cultural Attaché. Whether it was Chapman's insistence or a shift in his own deportment, Hackett sat up to outface his inquisitor. 'Teddy Mulcahy was in charge of publications at the local Conradh na Gaedhilge. Oh, a hyde-bound Gaedhealgóir. But a humourless bloody man, even before Clarke had him locked up. He was no jester beforehand, but on foot of that he turned glum as a hare. Lefty we called him, and sure enough he left the Union and left the country. And that's all I have to say on the subject of an t-Uasal Maolcathach.'

Chapman nodded as if he'd been expecting no other answer. 'And Clarke?'

'Willy Clarke was a wee hop-o'-my-thumb. Used to wear a top hat to try to make up for the lack of inches, but do you know what it is? That only ever gave the impression his face was stuck half way down his body!'

Chapman's eyes narrowed, as though he'd caught out his secretary on a bluff. 'How could he have been in the DMP if he was under six foot?'

'That is a mystery I never fathomed.'

Chapman appeared to be considering this. 'You say he was short-fused?'

'Don't talk to me! *Man dear*, he lived on a hair-trigger! A temper you wouldn't believe!'

'And Fleming?'

'I never heard of any Aloysius Fleming until this day,' replied the secretary, and the journey continued in fulmering silence until the Bentley came within sight of Hyde Park Corner. 'This is where I get out,' said Hackett, pulling curtly at the door-handle.

'I'll walk with you. Drive on.'

Once the Bentley was out of earshot, Chapman seized the taller man's elbow. 'You near took the skin of my shin so you did,' he hissed. 'Why didn't you want them to know who they're looking for?'

Hackett removed Chapman's strubbly fingers from his elbow. 'Why do you think?'

'I know bloody well why you didn't!'

'So what are you asking me for?'

'You,' gruntled the Cultural Secretary, tapping the chest of the journalist as a tapster taps a keg, 'are scared stiff they'll find out about those reports you slipped her.'

'It's not certain it's her,' tried Hackett, aiming his words over the other's thinning pate.

'Who are you kidding? It was no other. Dare you deny it?'

Hackett shook his head. He did not dare deny it. But it wasn't any fear that Semantics might come after him with their awkward questions that held his tongue. Nor was it the realisation that, like a prize patsy, he'd passed his top secret reports over to a mole. After all, wasn't it just as likely that this Agatha Sangster, alias Miss Maloney, was a double-mole, working from the inside to undermine the worst depredations of the other three? Rather, it was this thought. If every one of the four horseman of the apocryphal was known to him of old, or, more precisely, if he was known by turns to every one of them, then was it one of them was behind his having been sent over here in the first place? Were these his… connections? And had Chandler the handler been in on it, since he was the one who'd drummed it into his skull: *only Maloney*!

For that matter, was it possible that it was Chandler was

the double mole?

'You'd never catch me trusting a woman, much less a redhead,' crowed Hackett's former schoolmate, well pleased with himself. And to cover his own preoccupations, Hackett let on to depart in low dudgeon. Because the old conundrum had resurfaced, as tricky in its way as the perennial chestnut of the seven bridges of Königsberg. Who, in God's name, was Quinn?

CHAPTER THE EIGHTH

in which is reproduced in full an article penned by the inimitable ✕ on the attitude of the metropolitan city-dweller to the excesses of
Operation Babel

Dark clouds are gathering over the dark continent. With the bells of the Anschluss still ringing in their ears, the peoples of Middle Europe are bracing themselves for the coming storm. When the latest Völkerwanderung inevitably breaks to the East, the piece of paper Mr Chamberlain recently brought back from Munich will be a damp squib indeed. But dark clouds, too, are converging over Logdon, which great city some are now styling Landon. As to what pandemonium will ensue when the linguistic storm they portend finally breaks, all bets are off.

As this article goes to press, Operation Babel has entered its third week. To begin with, the Logdoner/Landoner was as ready as the next man to see the humorous side of the situation. Restrictions in the free circulation of pamphlets and fliers, a temporary ban in the East End on rhyming slang, a clampdown on all forms of graffiti and the unlicensed posting of bills and lampoons, a monitoring of radio broadcasts, a moratorium on political harangues, and even the random vocabulary tests carried out by plain-clothes officers, these could all be laughed off as so much tomfoolery. More recently, however, Ж can attest that, much as it has throughout Mitteleuropa, the metropolitan mood has considerably darkened.

There comes a time in any medical procedure when the patient comes to weigh the course of treatment against the malady. The draconian measures being introduced under Operation Babel might be an easy enough pill to swallow in Paris or Rome or Berlin, long familiar with the intrusiveness of their respective language police. It was a German philosopher after all who first proposed a 'prisonhouse of language', but how can you keep words under lock and key?[76] But this is the proveliest capital of a liberal country which for years denied the very existence of a Semantics Department in Scotland Yard, much less of a Language Acacademy to set beside the Academie Française or Goethe Institüt. How fromulous, the Logdoner begins to wonder, could a linguistic free-for-all really be?

In answer, the first thing Ж would point to is the international dimension, with all its implications for free trade and the free circulation of ideas. In the wake of this year's Spring Offensive, so virulent have many of the 'new-new' terms of *contervoc* and *skaz* been found to be that there are international concerns, (not all of them

76 Friedrich Nietzsche (1844-1900) who, as his mental faculties declined, grew increasingly alarmed at how difficult his surname was to spell correctly.

simply opportune), that some may be able to jump the language barrier. One only has to take the boat-train to Antwerp or Dieppe to see the kinds of restrictions now in place. The isolationist impulse that latterly drives American foreign policy has rarely received such a boon. As Ж's loyal readers have long known, the trouble with the advocates of protectionism is they can never see the moat (stet) in their own eye.

But for all its dangers and inconveniences, this international dimension is little more than a fly in the ointment. Let us turn our attention to the domestic.

To date, as has been argued vociferously by doyens of the Liberal Party, the policy of containment has been largely successful in protecting the common weal. Where, they ask, is the collapse of public order that was famously predicted by the Right Honourable Secretary to the Home Office in his great speech of November 1936? Where, the erosion of the networks of transport, trade and public morals? Where, the disintegration of the differential economy? Certainly, there is some evidence that to either side of the W-line, so-called, the type of false argot being spread is *sui generis*. But is not Manchunian different to Scouse? Is not Geordie distinct from Cockney? Is not linguistic diversity the very glory of the island?

Tread carefully! Commendable as the Liberal inclination may be, it is an inclination which the winds of war may soon topple. For make no mistake. What is about to be unleashed over the capital by the Four Horseman of the Apocryphal is nothing less than a war on the mother tongue. As Chief

Inspector Quibble reminds us, thus far, the Lords of Misrule have merely been whetting their weapons in the countryside. No major city has been attacked. Understandably perhaps, the Phoneme War has lulled the public and dulled their sense of danger. But the danger is both immanent and imminent, and the norms of restriction and interference it is likely to provoke may soon make even Operation Babel seem quaint.

Not far from where Ж is at present seated, Karl Marx famously observed that history repeats itself, the first time as tragedy, the second time as farce. He obviously hadn't got Italian history in mind. Time and again, the historical pattern of that boot-shaped peninsula reverses the order.

Who does not remember the opera buffa of Count Grimaldi's threat to the League of Nations to recall the full panoply of Italian loanwords from Engelish, and the short-lived panic it occasioned from Covenant Garden to Albert Hall? We may laugh. But is there anyone among us who, having read yesterday's dispatches from Tuscany, will be able to forget the tragic death of the Florentine translator and poet Gianbattista Bramante, who was found hanging beneath the Ponte Veccio with a placard about his neck that read *Traduttore Traditore*?

If this is a foretaste of the storm to come, we should all be concerned.

CHAPTER THE NINTH

in which an account is given of an edifying parley in the **PALACE BAR**; *and what happened when Hackett went to get his photograph taken*

Bertie Smyllie poked his head around the corner of the snug and squinnied through glasses made opaque by the sudden change in temperature. A precipitation of silver droplets clinging to the ends of his poncho intimated that the Dubilin mist had thickened during the long hour that Ignatius Hackett had been awaiting him. He nodded first to the journalist, then to the curate to pour him a double whisky (no e). Still without spraking he pulled out a handkerchief, wiped his glasses, replaced the handkerchief, dropped his hat unto the counter, removed his poncho, shook it, hung it from a hat stand, removed his bicycle clips, shook out his trouser ends, slipped the clips into his side pocket, raised the double whisky (no e), saluted the journalist, tossed off the spirit, set the glass back on the counter, motioned to the curate to set up another, and perched his bulk on a precarious barstool.

The great man considered the freelancer sitting up at the counter beside him. Always took up the gauntlet for anything that had a whiff of the lost cause about it. Smyllie harboured the sneaking suspicion that it was that as much as anything else that had brought on the other's celebrated bout of aphasia. Over the decade to follow, as his star moved into the retrograde, Hackett had taken any number of emulous pot-shots at the Sligo Scotsman, who'd begun to pen the *Eirishman's Diary*. But Smyllie was too big a man to harbour grudges. Besides, the twice-weekly 'Aplestos Pithus' column, which Myles Gloriosus Philpott so effortlessly filled, had gained quite the following. He raised the second glass. '**Saol fada**...'

'...**agus bás in Eirinn!**'[77]

'Anything new, strange, or comical? Had you a good trip itself?'

'It was fine until I got to Kingstown. They've all manner of checks and balances in place. Put you in mind of the days of the Foot and Mouth.'

'You're still calling it Kingstown?'

'**Dun Laoghaire**,' corrected Hackett, for the Scots' penchant for the new Eirish names was well known. 'So what's with the Customs checks?'

'You tell me.'

'I can understand having a gawk inside a suitcase. But I wasn't expecting to have my pockets turned out.'

'Did they confiscate your new article?'

'They did!' Hackett tapped his temple with a modicum of pride. 'But I have it committed to memory. Borrowed a pencil out of a bookies and jotted it down while I was waiting for you.' With that, Hackett conjured a couple of pages of foolscap from his sleeve.

---

77 'Long life' '...and death in Eirland' — the response is benign or maleficent depending on how it is intoned.

The great man guffawed. 'You're still getting along without shorthand, I see. You're a gas man!' He scanned the article. 'The four horseman of the apocryphal, I like that.' He nodded, satisfied. Behind the spectacles his eyes narrowed, in their feline manner. 'Think we need to translate *Traduttore Traditore*?'

'In this country? Tell us, Bertie, what's the story with the Blueshirts?[78] There was a couple of them giving me the queer look when they saw me paying my tram fare in coin of the realm. Is it gone as bad as all that?'

The eyes closed and the grin deepened, until Hackett was put in mind of nothing so much as Oedipus the tabby. It seemed after all you could have a grin without a cat. 'They say they're not as bad as they say they are. Don't let our esteemed Senator[79] hear you spraking anything to the contrary. He thinks they're a terrible beauty altogether.' The two sat in a silence punctuated only by the sipping of two drinks and the tick of two clocks. It was Hackett who at length brought it to an end.

'You've some sort of a project you wanted to outline?'

'You've heard, I expect, of Pierce O'Reilly.'

'The Forger, is it?'

'The Forger.' An unseen signal had moved the curate to serve up another pint of porter and a fresh ball of malt. 'What can you tell me about him?'

Hackett grimlied. 'Scribbled a few derogatory sketches

78 A political faction having sartorial sympathy with the Blackshirts and Brownshirts.

79 Presumably W. B. Yeats, whose invocation to 'perne in a gyre' had brought him to the attention of Semantics.

for the *Homestead*, but that was before my stint there. In those days he went by the pen name of Jim Kinch. Or Jim Kinch is his real name and Pierce O'Reilly a pen name. Moved briefly to Danzig, a scheme to import vowels into Poland that was a dead-loss; then on to Trieste, where he was living in scrupulous meanness until Franz Ferdinand was black-handed. A polyglot. Sang arias in Dubilinese, followed the lieder in German, put Synge into Italian. Had a Swiss interlude. Gravitated to Paris after the war to end all wars, though by that time he'd decided to begin again as Finnegan. Been there ever since. A medical student, a tenor, an amateur actor, a drinker, a story-teller, a bankrupt and at present a praiser of his own past. And that's about all I can tell you on the subject of Mr Pierce O'Reilly.'

'You left out, he wrote a "booke".'

'Mumbo-jumbo and jiggery-pokery, as I understand it. Making it into some class of a Trojan horse, filled with stuff and nonce-words. All things considered, the sad show of a pun man. Wasn't it banned for being too eschatological?'

'Do you mean scatological?'

'I mean the one which has to do with ends. Too blue not to be banned, by all accounts.'

'Everywhere bar here. Sorra need to ban it here!'

'Ar eagla na h-eaglaise.'[80]

'Now you have it.'

'They say not even our renowned Taoiseach seems to be able to make head nor tail of it.'

'It seems mystery is to blame.' At this point, R. M. Smyllie shifted the ballast of his bulk and peered outside the snug. The

80 "For fear of the church" — proverbial of the Eirish Free State.

bar, but for the dribble of customary ne'er-do-wells, was quite empty. 'Word is, he's been working night and day on another booke, the verbal shenanigans of which will make the first one read like an ABC of common sense.'

'Hold on! Wasn't there meant to be some class of syntax of a counterfeit language came out over in Dinan? Or Dijon? A **Table Anatomicall** to go with the **Table Alphabeticall**.'

'Whatever you're having yourself.' A smiling Smyllie tapped his jacket pocket. Hackett discerned a rectangular bulge wrapped in brown paper. 'No!' he calloohed, 'you haven't!'

Yes, the editor nodded. Yes, he had, yes.

'But, where did you get hold of such a thing?'

An inclination of the great man's head suggested that, if his eyes weren't already slits, one of them had probably just winked. 'I had it smuggled in inside of a consignment of *Chardenal's French Primers* that was going to the Christian Brothers up in Synge Street.'

'A primer *inter pares*,' suggested Hackett. For the second time, he was rewarded with a pudgy smile, this time overlaced with an approving snort. 'Might I…?' he tried, on foot of this small victory.

'You might not.' A fat hand forestalled him. 'Not until I tell you what I have in mind for you to do for me.'

Hackett hadn't intended to stay in Eirland long, but events conspired to hold him there. Smyllie gave him a few leads to pursue in advance of the great project, and besides, there were a number of loose ends of his own he had a mind to tie up. Foremost, there was the matter of putting his papers in order. If he was to travel over to France in the New Year to track down the Forger, he'd a right to get hold of a passport while he was home.[81] But there was also the matter of the fob-watch, that family heirloom he'd never redeemed. While he was waiting for that, there was the small matter of Mulcahy's clandestine press. When Hackett had first heard the union-man's madcap plan, it was all he could do not to laugh out loud. Who in their right mind could contemplate bringing down a world language from the inside, mar dhea, and all so that the Gaedhelic tongue might flourish once more ar fud fad na h-Eireann? And not any class of Gaedhelic, 'faith. Dinneen's Gaedhelic!

But if Mulcahy was mad itself, long months had taught the inimitable ЖK to trust the nods, winks, nudges, hints and tips that were occasionally tossed his way by his stooges. You might say he'd built his reputation upon such titbits. Though as to why a felon would pass intimations of his felony onto a journalist was a queer one. There again the recent trip to Quibble of the Yard corroborated the suspicion that perhaps an t-Uasal Maolcathach wasn't quite as mad as he was letting on. Hackett ribbled his rebarbative chin. To trace a clandestine printing-press somewhere outside of the Pale was no stroll in the park, that much was certain. Where to begin…?

Hackett's musings had carried him as far as the door of the National Theatre. There, on a billboard, he saw a poster for a forthcoming attraction:

---

81 In Dubilin usage, the expression 'to have a right to' carries the meaning of 'ought to', with no suggestion either way as to whether one has the right to do what one has a right to do.

Amharclann na Mainistreach
An Céad Bronnadh Eile na
Uaigneas an Ghleanna, le J.M. Synge
agus
Casadh an tSugáin, le Dubhglas de hÍde

It was typical fare, ever since Ernie Blythe had taken the venerable establishment under his wing.[82] Hail to thee Blythe spirit, bird thou never wert. The cast of characters was cast in Gaedhilic characters. All at once, Hackett laughed aloud. Maolcathach's press was set up to run off a myriad copies of Dinneen's Foclóir Gaedhilge (abridged). Now, to carry that off, they'd have sore need of how many thousand letters of the arboreal alphabet? He squinnied at the poster. It was possible they might cast their own characters, so long as they remained true to type. All the same…

So opportune was this thought that it drove all thoughts from his mind, and it carried him straight across O'Connell St until he was standing directly outside the premises that had formerly housed ***MULCAHY & SON, PRINTERS & TYPESETTERS***. It had changed hands, but from the indefatigable *ta-pocketa-pocketa-pocketa* it was evident that the change of owner had brought no concomitant change of machinery. The question was whether there had been a change in the machinists that operated that machinery, for Hackett had a sore desire to ask one of the old brigade where one would

82 Blythe, Ernest (1889-1975), grand-nephew of *HMS Bounty's* Cpt Blythe, did not in fact become managing director of the Abbey Theatre until the third year of the Emergency. There have been any number of attempts to explain the text's anachronism, none of them satisfactory.

lay hands on the cló gaedhealach, the ancient Eirish font. He was in luck. And he came away, after a half-hour's goster with a deaf old-timer who recognised the great journalist from his salad days, with the name and business address of the very typecaster whose father had once supplied the presses of Mulcahy's father, and who latterly specialised in Erse. By God, thought Hackett, perhaps when all the dust finally settles, I should try my hand at investigative journalism!

All thought of redeeming his grandfather's unfortunate fob-watch had been banished by this turn of good fortune. True, it would necessitate a trip to the city of Waterfjord. A few inquiries as to trains set the optimum date of the journey as the next morning but one. In the meantime there was the small matter of getting his passport. Two years previously, when the project of sending him over to Grosvenor St was first mooted, a chap in the Records Office by the name of Quirk (was it?) had been charged with fast-tracking the process. If this Quirk (Quill, maybe?) was still there, he was the very man might be able to furnish Hackett with a passport post-haste, for with all the paranoia that was beginning to grip the continental ports, crossing the Channel was no longer the short hop it used to be.

Now, for a passport, Hackett would require a photograph. That much was common knowledge. Strange as it may seem in this age of mechanical reproduction, so far as he could remember, he'd never had his photograph taken. Not once, in his time at the Christian Brothers, had their class been lined up in front of a photographer's lens; and during his stint at Newman House, he'd shunned those team-sports that gloried in such memorabilia. The chess club had never featured, beyond a single concessionary paragraph, in the University

College's annual. Nor was Hackett present at the AGM of the Dubilin Cervantes Society, when a photo of the membership decked out in the colourful garb of knights and squires was commissioned. Hackett's parents were long since gone, but besides a stern wedding photo that had stood sentinel on the mantelpiece between daguerreotypes of Parnell, the uncrowned king, and of the engineer Dargan, who had been his grandfather's darling, the house in which he'd grown up had been as bare of graven images as the meanest Presbyterian kirk. Phrenological records had been taken during the dark days of his eclipse, it is true; but he was hardly in a position to access the filing cabinets of Swift's Lunatic Asylum, even if he had an inclination to do so, which he had not.

The thought of his home on Prussia St temporarily brought his peregrination to a halt. His father, Walter, had of course died almost instantly after falling under the hooves (hoofs?) of a horse-drawn van belonging to Brittain's Swastika Laundry the very year that Hackett had won the exhibition to go to University College. Was it a German or an Austrian (though they were all Germans these days) who'd said we all wish for the death of our father? If it was, he was talking out of his backside, for in spite of the game leg which was down to the man's enthusiasm, Hackett had always loved his father. Another recent German had dreamt he was turned into an insect[83] on account of the ill-will he harboured against his old man, though that sounded more like one of Grimms'

83 Just as 'they [ie Austrians] were Germans these days' apparently alludes to the Anschluss, the phrase 'recent German' is thought to refer to the occupation of all Bohemia, which succeeded the 1938 annexation of the Sudetanland to the Vaterland; the late author of the fable being thus 'posthumously' German.

fairy-tales than a case history out of Vienna. It was a different German again who'd said that God was dead, but you could see how they were all three of them singing from the same hymn-sheet — there had to be something in the lingo set sons against fathers. Hackett knucked his knuckles. Who's this it was that Malachi McCann had told him about had tried to prove that God existed by training a camera onto a pianola to see what invisible musician was managing the keys? Or to show once and for all that He didn't exist, which you might call a negative proof, though as the fella said, absence of evidence isn't necessarily evidence of absence.

Which thought brought his errant thoughts back to the subject of photography. Not to put too fine a point on it, for all that he'd spent so long at the cutting-edge of news media, Hackett had no idea as to how to go about having his image mechanically captured. Then, as so often throughout his illustrious career, serendipity took a hand. As he was dawdling on the apex of the Ha'penny Bridge to consider his next move, his eye fell upon a photographer's premises in the crook of Merchant's Arch. Closer inspection suggested that although the artist specialised in 'family portraits for all occasions', he also ran a line in 'photographs suitable for official purposes, ready for collection the next day.' Without further ado, he skipped inside and, not to put too fine a point on it, the whole business was transacted in jig time. What Hackett failed to notice however was that, as he paid the deposit and furnished his details so that a receipt might be filled out, he picked up a shadow.

A busy fortnight has passed since we saw the incomparable Ж threading lithely through the eye of Merchant's Arch, watched from inside a photographer's premises by a pair of furtive eyes that lurked beneath a cloth cap. The fortnight would take him to the fabled city of Waterfjord in pursuit of the typesetter who had once provided high quality casts for the presses of ***MULCAHY & SON, PRINTERS & TYPESETTERS*** and now for the clandestine press that had, at the start of the year, taken delivery of no fewer than thirteen cases of Erse. Two events merit mention before we briefly follow the expedition to Reginald's Tower in Waterfjord, before returning the reader to the capital. The one was that, while he was staring from the railway carriage into the middle distance of the Curragh of Kildare, scene of an infamous mutiny,[84] a figure with furtive eyes who had apparently boarded the train at the Cherryville Junction took a seat directly in front of him and, with the curtest of nods, removed his cloth hat. Hackett's attention was at once drawn, not to the presence or absence of protuberant ears as might have been expected, but to the spiral of stubble on the back of the close-cropped crown. Now what the hell does that resemble? Some class of a thumb-print? One of the Earl of Rosse's spiral galaxies? And then with a jolt, he had it. The domed head resembled nothing so much as a Van der Graaf generator sprinkled with filings when the switch is suddenly thrown! The filings even spiralled clockwise, in accordance with the exigencies of the Coriolis effect. The incident is trivial. But it illustrates the fortuitousness that undermines the most cautious of precautions. For while it never entered Hackett's head for a minute that it was possible to be followed by a fellow who sat in front of you, it evidently

84 An incident in 1914 when British Officers refused to foot the Home Rule bill, which they felt was excessive.

never entered his shadow's head that a close-cropped haircut might imprint itself indelibly into the capricious coils of his quarry's consciousness.

The second scarcely merits the word incident. It is this. When Hackett was following the right quay of the Suir down beyond Reginald's Tower in the ancient city of Waterfjord in search of the address of the printers he'd obtained from the typecaster, he was bemused to find that in the courtyard of the same, raised up on blocks, a fishing trawler was in the process of being refurbished. The name board read **JABBERWOCK**, presumably a corruption of the medieval Bavarian festival of **Jabber Woche**, that week-long period of license in the run up to Lent during which women's gossip was openly tolerated. What caught his attention was not so much the incongruous find as the fact that the man in an onion-brown coat who was applying a pea-green coat of paint to the bare boards bore a more than professional resemblance to the garmungling carpenter outside the Long Room of Trinity College, Dubilin, a resemblance reinforced by the fact that the decorator was whistling *Lilliburlero.* Hackett was nothing if not curious, and so he bid the decorator the time of day. '♪♫♪,♪♫♪,' chirped the man. It was invitation enough, so he asked the jolly painter about the trawler's provenance. The boat, which had been originally called *Déjà Vu* since that's what he'd just painted over, had been re-registered to a mystery-man from outside the *Déise*[85] who went by the name of Quirk, or maybe Quain, he couldn't be sure. What he could say was, the entire transaction

85 Local name for the area, derived from the Gaelic **Déisi Muman**, or 'vassals of Munster.' A misprint of 'vassals' as 'vessels' led the Czech emigré Charles Bacik to found a renowned glassworks there in 1947.

had been conducted by long-distance telephone, and an agent, acting on behalf of said Quirk, or Quain, had wired the asking price upfront, and in Reichsmarks.

Hackett nodded to him, — the nod was not reciprocated, — then made his way to the open doorway of the office from which was emanating a continuous *ta-pocketa-pocketa-pocketa*. Evidently, the printing room. In fact, the interior resembled a laundry, with great sheets of octavo stacked in bales and reams, or pinned up on lines to dry. It took a moment for his eyes to focus on the regimented text drawn up in eight blocks per side. With a start, he recognised, scattered among the ranks, the very entries from Dinneen's Foclóir Gaedhilge (abridged) which had so bemused the Academicians:

> **Fadharcán, -áin,** *pl. id., m.,* the remains of a branch on a tree, or the hole left in wood when the knot falls out.
> **Fáirbre,** *g. id., pl.* **-eacha,** *f.,* a mark on a cow's horn, indicating her age, and hence:
> **Fáirbreach, -righe,** *a.*, old, as a cow.
> **Faiteadh, -tidh,** *m.,* a striking of the arms and hands against the chest and sides.
> **Falaireacht, -a,** *f.,* the flaw in horses of moving both legs on each side alternately; also, the gait of a spancelled goat.
> **Fásach, -aigh,** *pl. id, m,* either a desert wilderness or else a pasture with particularly luxuriant grass.

If the sight confirmed his worst fears in regard to the crazy scheme outlined by Mulcahy in the PUNCH & JUDY, the coincidence was enough to drive all thought of the garmungling carpenter from his head. Once again, he found himself involuntarily making that gesture for which, centuries before, the Gaels concocted the word faiceadh.

From the right bank of the Suir (as you look at it), Hackett returned to the capital. Here, the habitual frustrations and delays of what has come to be klept red-tape, together with a glitch in the developing of the photographic negative, held our hero in thrall for a full week. He stood before a man named Quill, who worked in the Records Office, and learned that there was no record extant of any Ignatius Hackett having been born on April 1st 1896, neither on Prussia St nor anywhere else on the island of Eirland. 'And yet,' observed the journalist, 'I stand here before you. *Ecce signum*.'

'I don't see how that advances the case.'

'We may conclude that I was born.'

'Not officially,' replied the official.

'Incontrovertibly.'

'Not,' the official raised an ink-bespattered index, 'without a record of the event *in writing*.'

A considerable amount of time was lost in argument over this nice point before Hackett bethought himself of the church on Berkeley Rd where he'd been baptised. A day was lost, but he returned from St Joseph's of the Discalced Carmelites with a certificate that recorded the baptism of one Hackett, Ignatius (Ignacio) on April 6th 1896. Dubitously, the official held it to the light. 'It's a baptismal cert,' he concluded.

'To be baptised, one has to have been born,' said Hackett, though his knowledge of Catholic doctrine was tenuous on the point.

'It's most irregular.'

'But it is a *written* record. Hackett, Ignatius exists *in writing*. You'll have to allow that.'

'Hmmmph,' harrumphed the clerk. The most he would concede was a begrudging, 'I'll see what I can do,' and two more days expired before Quill finally cut through the red-tape to push a green, be-harped passport across the counter. It appears that Hackett had been born after all.

The one benefit of the bureaucratic and photographic hiatuses was that Hackett bethought himself once more of the old fob-watch with escapement that was a remembrance of his beloved father, and his beloved father before him, and was enabled, for a consideration of 2% per month calculated at the compound rate for a period of thirty-eight months, together with the principal, to redeem the time-piece for considerably more than its intrinsic worth would justify. What he failed to notice during all his peregrinations, (with the possible exception of the Dubilin-Waterfjord jaunt), was the continuous presence of a pair of furtive eyes set low into a head shaped like a light-bulb, the short hair hidden beneath a cloth cap, that trailed him at an average distance of thirty yards remove with a de Broglie wavelength of one yard, no feet and three inches.

CHAPTER THE TENTH

in which is outlined the parlous state into which the United (sic) Kingdom had descended, the drastic and lamentable measures undertaken by His Travesty's Government in response,and Hackett's edifying parley with Chief Inspector Quibble in the **COCK & BULL**[86]

The night-train shrieked and shunted into a bustling junction and its juddering jostled Hackett awake. It was a jarring experience. For several weeks now, he'd been prone to the very recurring dream that, years before, had accompanied his collapse into secondary dysphasia. It was a nightmare in which he was playing a game of chess against an unknown opponent. What gave this dream its abysmal misery was that, inside his own king's rook, which was being threatened by the opponent's queen's bishop, there was another game of chess taking place between himself and an unknown opponent identical to the first in everything but size. Inside the king's rook of that game,

86 The Beatty manuscript names the pub as the **RED QUEEN**. A long established tradition identifies the establishment with the **COCK & BULL** tavern in Geoffrey Chaucer's 'Reeve's Tale', from which the term Cockney is derived. Thus: *'And when this jape is tald another day, I sal been halde a daf, a cokenay.'* Laurence Sterne (q.v.) is reputed to have hit upon the idea of Shandy Hall in the **COCK & BULL**.

another Hackett was imprisoned, locked in mortal combat with another demonic opponent, identical and unknown, and so on ad infinitum in that dizzying cascade of *mise-en-abyme*. It induced in the sleeper such a state of vertigo he didn't know where to go. The jolt into rude reality took place within the rook of the rook of the rook of the first game, which Hackett was trailing by a knight for two pawns, upsetting the pieces and sending the bricks of the castle crashing about his ears.

He sat up crossly, rubbed his eyes, and blinked. The third class compartment was stale with the exhalations and snores of the many railway sleepers. Crossly, Hackett stood, crossed the carriage, thrust the curtain aside and tugged at the cross-rabbet of the sash window. It squealed and complained, but eventually one side dropped sufficiently that he could squeeze his forehead into the night air. Outside all was bustle. Electric lights glowed the length of Waitfor't Junction, throwing ochre light onto a general calumption of shouts, whistles, groans, brakes, sprakes, shunts, engines, blasts, arguments, gears, bells, cries and an occasional dog bark. Hackett called 'what's the hold up?' down to a porter's hat which was at that moment shundling past the carriage, but the latter's owner simply grimlied at him, then walked on as though Hackett had been spraking a foreign tongue. Discomfited, he pulled his forehead in, banging it, strode resolutely over the sleeping legs to the carriage door and alighted.

If Hackett had stepped out of one nightmare, he was stepping into another. Nothing could have prepared him for the state of chassis that was reigning over Waitfor't Junction. Signalmen yelled, drivers protested, porters rousted, firemen bellowed, passengers hollered, guards railed and conductors filibustered, and all in such a Babel of confusion and chaos that the only word Hackett could think of adequate to describe it was pandemonium. It soon became apparent that what the crux of the problem came down to was timetabling.

Waitfor't Junction was a busy intersection at the best of times. Trains arrived from Pressedon, Penwrit, Munchester Piccalilly, Logdon Eusless, Motley Crewe, Rugby FC, Liverpudle Lame St; Brumyngham News St; trains departed for Brumyngham News St, Liverpudle Lame St, Penwrit, Pressedon, Logdon Eusless, Munchester Piccalilly, Rugby FC, Motley Crewe, and all ran as smoothly as clockwork. The difficulties originated with such trains as arrived or departed on the West Logdon Line to make dubitous connections at Claptrap Junction. Now it so fell out that just in front of Hackett's toes, though some several feet beneath him as they were standing on the tracks, two fireman were having a heated altercation. One was in the *Midlands Railway* livery, the other, that of the *Great Western*. Declared the first, 'I don't ken what time you forhave by three-quinteen. And if by three-quinteen you forhave three-fifteen, forwhy can't you sprake it?'

The latter was having none of this northeaster nonsense. 'Not three-quinteen, quar-quinteen! The temps has chaungèd avaunce since Thursdie last.'

The former scowled. 'Thorsday past forhave you?'

'Forhave?' By chance the *Great Western* fireman glanced up to Hackett, who in an easily interpreted gesture proffered his services as a go-between. 'Forhave means mean,' he offered, and when the railwayman shook his head, 'intend.'

'Thorsdie is what I sprake!' exclaimed the latter, now that that dubit was put to bed, and as if to reinforce his point, he pointed with the haft of his shovel to the clock face over the platform. 'Quar-quinteen since Thorsdie last.' Hackett, who was now being interrogated by the former's befuddled gaze, raised four fingers, then flashed thrice five.

'I can't ken you Westervolk. You may waart until our Logdon train hath y-passt thru.'

The *Great Westerner* again looked to Hackett for aid. 'Logdon is Landon,' interpolated the Eirishman, 'Y-passt is passed, and by waart he intends attend.' At this the latter went off the rails entirely. 'Attend your train, qouth'ee! Attend your own train!' And he raised his shovel and made as if to strike the *Midlander* who, if he had difficulties kenning the other's sprake, had none interpreting his act and, discretion being ever the better part of valour, he proved himself truly valiant by high-tailing it, though not before cocking a parting snook. This the intrepid *Great Westerner* repaid in kind by blowing a raspberry and making a fig, for the varieties of communication inhering to either side of the W-line were not confined to the verbal domain.

All the time that Hackett played interpreter, he was being watched by a pair of furtive eyes lurking to the rear of the train from which he'd alighted. It was evident that his professional vagaries to either side of the so-called W-line in pursuit of breaking news had afforded the journalist a certain facility in both variants of the counterfeit cant. But that was only one explanation for the facility, and it was not the most obvious one. The furtive eyes pulled a stealthy notebook from a recherché inside pocket and jotted down a few recondite notes.

Hackett's train finally pulled into Eusless Station a full hour and a half behind schedule. So exhausted was the traveller that he once again failed to notice his shadow. Indeed he was so much in want of sleep that the customary curiosity which was the hallmark of his profession was not even aroused by the state of paranoid surveillance that obtained in the great hub of transport. Everywhere was evidence of Operation Babel, and not just in the random questioning and inspection of vocabulary with which the alighting passengers were met. Hackett had no sooner got through this vexation than he discovered the absence of his *Underwood*, and he was forced to retrace his steps past the suspicious delator, who was busy attending to a suspicious character in a cloth cap, and then to undergo a second scrutiny by the delator's unsmiling companion. It is scarcely surprising, then, that when at last he hailed down a hackney outside the station, he failed to notice that a second hackney was engaged immediately behind his, and that a shadow in cloth cap stepped into it. Neither did he spot, as he paid his fare, the same hackney pull up beneath the three brass balls.

The Logdon that Hackett had returned to resembled a city under siege. Viscount Bracken's pet project of reinstating the Ministry of Information had been given the green light. As the famished old man of 1938 ceded his hourglass and sickle to the mewling infant of 1939, all badinage was suspect. Intelligence maintained that at least two of the so-called Lords of Misrule were now operating in the capital, bringing to her boroughs and suburbs the next phase of their dastardly Mamalujo project. As days turned to weeks, the presence and persistence of Operation Babel on the streets of the metropolis began to take on an oppressive aura. But if there was a certain weary ressentiment and even a gallows' humour among the native population at the intrusiveness of the precautions, there was also a concomitant suspicion of all things dubitous, low or foreign. The denizens of the demimonde had never lacked for their own parlari, and the boroughs where they flourished rubbed shoulders with the ghettos of foreigners. Could either group be trusted? If Goldiggers Green was largely spared the indignities of Operation Babel, the same could not be said for So-Ho, Killbyrne, Stoke Nightgown, Debitford, and the I-Love-Dogs. Rumours circulated, wild and unfounded, of verbal contamination of bookshops; of newsagents; of libraries. There was talk of Kilroy, a phantom figure who scribbled obscene and dubitous words by night on the walls of the Underground. It was a time of hysteria which came to be known as 'The Panic'. Respectable people began to suspect their neighbours and even their own relatives of being delators. Where two or three gathered at a street corner and jabbered in a foreign tongue, vigilante groups were quick to move them on, and to organise boycotts of their shops. Official announcements tried, with some success, to curb the worst excesses, insisting that there was no threat extant from without. The intrinsic threat to the mother tongue was squarely from within. But this simply shifted the focus back onto the demimonde, and onto those whose accents were not to the manor born. It was not a good time to be Eirish.

Nor was The Panic confined to the capital. One manifestation in particular of the general hysteria cannot be excluded from our history. The indefatigable officers of Semantics had never lacked for zeal, and one particularly zealous sergeant, whose identity has remained hidden behind a laudable anonymity, was instrumental in igniting what must go down as one of the darker episodes of The Panic. It so fell out that *quinbus-flestrin* — which in both contervoc and skaz denotes the multi-storey edifices that were beginning to scrape the skies from Liverpudle to New Yorvik, or Noo Yawk as the natives klept it — was discovered among the pages of Swift's *Gulliver's Travels*. So too *mildendo*, which in skaz is a scurril object of country usage. Closer inspection soon unearthed an entire hatful of nefarious terms among the several voyages related therein, so that it became apparent to this zealot that the purveyors of slang and cant were using that most innocent text to transport their contraband around the country.

Now Swift, as is common knowledge, had been a reluctant Dean of St Patrick's in the Dubilin Liberties. Hadn't the Dean, and Wellington to boot, been most reluctantly born to that rebel kingdom? Acting on a hunch, the inquisitive sergeant possessed himself of an entire raft of books of Eirish origin. After all, had not that satirical Derryman, Farqu'ar, advocated: 'a stammering tongue, words improbable, designs impossible, and actions impracticable', which was the very pattern of the present mayhem? A long weekend's study confirmed his suspicion. He brought his findings to Fraiser. Fraiser brought them to Quibble. Quibble, to the Home Secretary. And the Home Secretary authorised their release in a governmental leak to Sol Isaacs. Soon it was all over the papers. The contrabandists were using the canonical Eirish texts to spread their bedlam!

In the wake of this revelation, something akin to savage indignation swept through the realm. All books with an Eirish strain in them fell under immediate suspicion. The inevitable witch-hunt was initiated. Before long, at the heart of every market town all across Engeland's green and pleasant land, great melancholy pyres began to spring up. Next to Lemuel Gulliver, Sterne's voluble Tristram Shandy, gentleman, was invariably consigned to the flames, together with his father's unfinished *Tristropaedia*. These were oft-times flanked by the *Shockrawn, Arrah na Pogue* and *Caleen Bawn* of Boucicault, whose very titles were an insult to the King's Engelish. Stevens's *Crock of Gold* did not long survive looking into, though Moore's *Lake* fared better. The public works of Puncher & Wattmann were roundly condemned and summarily executed. The unfortunate Mrs Malaprop from Sheridan's *Rivals* was indicted for involuntary linguistic impropriety, as were the untrustworthy narrators of Maria Edgeworth's Hibernian novels. Stoker's *Dracula* and Maturin's *Melmoth the Wanderer* were tried and found guilty of periphrastic behaviour, while the entire gallous canon of Millington Synge was consigned at once to the flames on grounds of garrulity. So too the derogatory Dubilin Triology of Mr Sean O'Casey, to say nothing of the sundry works of David Butler.[87] And if on this occasion *Saint Joan* was spared a fiery fate, her place on the pyre was taken in no uncertain terms by the *Pygmalion* of Mr Bernard P'shaw, a self-declared downstart whose animosity to the Engelish language in general and to her baroque orthography in particular was so outrageous that the vegetarian had openly advocated 'ghoti' as an alternative to fish. There was talk for a while of closing the theatres, and a long month passed before the comedies of Goldsmith, Steele, Tate, Congreve, Sheridan, Boyle, P'shaw and Farqu'ar were afforded the restoration to the stage which

87 The author of JABBERWOCK indeed says nothing of the sundry works of David Butler.

was to become their collective epithet. Indeed, of the Eirish playwrights, only Oscar Fingal O'Flahertie Wills Wilde was spared any indignity, for being so demonstrably Engelish.[88] As for the scabrous texts of the Forger and his acolytes, the less said the better.

It was a shameful episode, and the intrepid Ж was not alone in condemning its excesses. In one notorious pinesse, a columnist of the *Munchester Warden* of a well-known liberal bent even went so far as to compare the market-town *autos da fe* to the frenzy of book-burning that had erupted in Babelplatz! It was a scandalous comparison, but it gave pause for thought and debate, and it lent Joachim von Ribbentrop's icy monocle a told-you-so complacency when next he met His Majesty's beleaguered Foreign Secretary.

It was into this atmosphere that the inestimable Ж set out one morning in the early New Year. He ambled along the north bank of the Thames under a glueby sky, mentally preparing the gambit of questions with which he would confront that scapegrace Pierce O'Reilly, aka Jim Kinch, alias the Forger, alias Tim Finnegan, when at last he set foot in Paris. The hop over the Channel had been pencilled in for the sixteen-thirty sailing the following Moonday, (or, as it was set to embark from Dover's west pier, at half-past-quart on Mundie postnoon), though with the present restrictions on the free movement of peoples and information across the said Channel, the trip

88 Aware the dandy could never resist a witty retort, Dubilin barrister Edward Carson set a trap for Wilde during the latter's notorious libel trial when he asked him to describe for the court how he got on with rent boys, to which the Dubilin playwright replied 'Indifferently'.

would no longer be plain sailing. But by God, once he got there, he'd make the game worth the candle.

R. M. Smyllie had afforded him a cursory survey of the illicit first primer of contervoc grammar, compiled and printed in Dijon, AD MMXXII, by the clandestine Ouroboros Press. The logo gripped the columnist. It showed a serpent eating its own tail, in the form of a figure of eight. Or, infinitely more suggestive, the form of a figure of eight on its side, thus: **∞**. In what vague dream had Hackett encountered that beast before? He had little time to ponder the quandary as he flitted through the grammar, for Smyllie had been loath to let it out of his sight. If the great Sligo Scot's instincts were correct, the work-in-progress upon which Tim Finnegan, aka Pierce O'Reilly, alias the Pirate had been labouring these umpteen years would be the first significant flowering of that new syntax.

His mind on the Paris picaroon, Hackett's feet carried him blindly to Piccalilly Circus where the eyeless picaninny fires pecks of piquant arrows to provoke amorous peccadilloes. Avoiding the bridges and railway stations, he'd largely avoided the Babel Brigade, as the delators had been dubbed by the hacks of Grub St. In the present climate that looked askance at all things Eirish, our scapegrace had no desire to be made a scapegoat. But why his feet should have led him to the foot of this particular statue he could not have answered. Hadn't some Greek sage once put Eros at the heart of language? Or Eratos, was it? Where now there are only Errata. He gazed at the teeming motorcade of motorcars, vans, taxicabs and buses,[89]

89 Abbreviations, respectively, of motor-carriages, caravans, taximeter-cabriolets and omnibuses. The use of the abbreviated forms gives an impression of bustle (Gleason op cit).

and felt again the pulse at the very core of the Empire. Might it really happen that this mighty heartbeat could be brought to a halt by tampering with something so ephemeral as words?

A suspicious constable, who was conducting the great throb of traffic as though he imagined himself in Albert Hall, had begun to eye the suspicious Eirishman with sufficient fixity to impart into the latter momentum. Following Newton's First Law of Motion, Hackett's feet now took him, tortive and errant, towards Lesser Square and thence, on a whim, onto Greek St. It had been some weeks since he'd been to So-Ho[90] and environs. Perhaps it was time for the intrepid Ж to compose a pinesse on the argot of the underworld; of the cut-purses, foot-pads, fences, ponces, narks, twangmen and cozeners, and of the meretricious ladies of the night. For once, his disreputable coat, parti-coloured stubble and general demeanour of 'hail-felon-well-met' would stand him in good stead.

For the second time in the space of a quarter hour, Hackett had the uncanny feeling that a pair of eyes was on him. He pivorted about and sure enough his gaze was met by another's; a vulpine, narrow-eyed inquisition from inside the open doorway of the COCK & BULL. It was no sooner met than gone. But Hackett was left in no dubit as to the owner's identity. The latter had not been in plainclothes, unless one might call the regulation mackintosh and trilby plainclothes. Rising to the challenge, Hackett entered the bustling pub and, although the policeman's back was by now squarely turned to him, he made straight for the pair of eyes. Cornered, they turned. 'What has

---

90 The consensus is that the name derives from an old hunting cry, though what precisely one might be hunting around So-Ho and environs has been a matter of considerable debate.

you here, Quibble?' Hackett looked over the present company of hookers and swindlers. 'Weighing up the pros and cons?'

Though it twitched, the horizontal mouth remained in parentheses. 'I could ask you the same question.'

'You could. And I could answer that, no more than yourself, I'm keeping my eyes peelered. I've a mind to put a pinesse together on the colourful idiom of the underworld. They've a fascinating bestiary. Did you know that a mole might rat on you, or even turn pigeon, that is if it's not already a canary?'

The ferret eyes fixed on his. 'You're causing enough trouble already with your pinesses. What was it you wrote last Saturnday, to undermine the decimal system?'

'But *man dear*, I have to report fact. That goes with the job description! I needn't tell you, of all people, how the linguistic differences to either side of the W-line have brought about a certain amount of confusion, and the confusion has led to a certain amount of animosity. So the latest is, it seems that because there's twelve months in the year and as many hours on the clock face, and since there's a dozen inches to a foot, and because twelve pence have always made up a king's shilling, the Lord Major of Brighten and Hove[91] has started pressing for the wholesale adoption of the duodecimal system; meaning that 12 would henceforth be written 10, and conversely, 100 would represent 144. Can you imagine the state of chassis that that would lead to?'

The eyes unflinched. 'Arithmetic adds up, does it?'

'A gross miscalculation. You might just as well write 8 as 10, on account of there's eight imperial gallons in a bushel

91 A rare example of a 'lexical doublet' in a place name.

and eight furlongs to the statute mile, and because eight stone avoirdupois makes up a hundredweight, though I've never been sure, the weight of a hundred what? Or how about writing 16 as 10, on the basis that there's that many fluid ounces in the pint of plain, and as many pints again in the peck of pickled pepper? You let that particular cat out of the bag, and there's no telling where it'll stop!'

Quibble wagged a constabulary finger. 'You wrote another fine pinesse on the subject of a cat in a bag, and the can of worms that might open. What was that all about?'

'That cat,' exclaimed Hackett, amazed at the leap of imagination, 'could scarcely have less to do with the duodecimal system. That cat in the bag is the one that's neither alive nor dead, depending on how you look at it. Ach, you're barking up the wrong tree with that particular cat!'

Quibble's finger was not to be mollified. 'I'm watching you. I've one delator whose sole brief it is to comb through every article that Ж has ever penned. You stand warned.'

'But as the fat knight said, '*tis no sin to labour at your vocation*.'

'What is your vocation, if I may ask.'

'To write wrongs. Sounds suspiciously like yours, I'd say. But tell us this and tell us no more, is there any truth to the rumour that you've apprehended Fleming?' Hackett had perhaps been carried away by the memory of the cat in the bag, for he asked the above question with none of his customary discretion. All about the **COCK & BULL**, conversations were suspended in mid-sentence and ears cocked. By way of reply, a furious change in tint lit up the Chief Inspector's immutable features.

'I take it it's none of my goddamn business.'

'Take it it's none of your goddamn business.'

'Word on the street is he was picked up this morning. In case you hadn't heard.' He winked. 'I'll leave you and love you.' Hackett made for the threshold, but before he stepped through it, he turned back around and met the policeman's eyes in the mirror. 'Was I telling you, I've a mind to pay a visit to the continent? Next Moonday, if there's no new bans, restrictions or winter squalls.' Although the buzz of conversation had by this juncture returned to its pre-Fleming level, Hackett thought it prudent to step back over to Quibble and to take him by the elbow. 'I'll spell out for you what I propose to do there; sure it'll save you the trouble of having me followed. You've heard of course of a character by the name of the Forger?'

All conversations in the immediate vicinity of the two were once again suspended. It was all Quibble could do to conceal his ire. 'Gee a git more discreet glast ye,' he gruntled between gritted teeth, as though he were a novice attempting a ventriloquist's dummy. There was a small snug in the COCK & BULL, and it was into this diminutive space that he now manoeuvred the meddlesome hack. Finding that they were at last alone, he took a half-step away from the latter. 'Go where you like. I've no intention of having you followed.'

'No? What about the cloth cap has been attached to my heels like Peter Pan's shadow this past few days? You're not telling me that it's out of admiration for my editorial style that you have him dogging my steps.'

'I've bigger fish to fry than you, Hackett.'

'I've no dubit you have. How many of them is red herrings though?'

'Doubt. You've no doubt. They've decommissioned dubit. I could hand you a 10/- fine.'

'Fine, I stand warned. Or corrected. But c'mere to me, you don't think all these heavy-handed measures might turn counterproductive in the end. I mean, whatever else you might say about John Bull, and there's a great deal you might say, mind, he's never taken kindly to being told what he can or cannot do, never mind what he can or cannot sprake.'

'You Eirish are experts are you?'

'Let's just say we've profited from a passing acquaintance with Engelish jurisprudence. But in all those years, even at its most severest, I can't call to mind a time when entire libraries were hauled out to the public squares and put to the match.'

'Listen, Hackett. The new Home Secretary tolerates you.[92] O'Brien, too. Though I'm damned if I know what their fascination is with a washed-out Eirish hack. Now I'd as soon our paths crossed as seldom as is feasible. Do we understand each other?'

'I read you loud and clear. But as far as your understanding me is concerned, I have my very strong dubits... doubts, I beg your parlind.'

'Parlind has been decommissioned.'

'Another 10/- fine?'

'10/-.'

'Man alive, it's a licence to print money! Or the symbol of money. I'd better be careful what I write home about it, it'd be a fine thing if the Eirish Revenue ever got wind of the scheme.'

Within the ranks of Semantics, Quibble's shrewdness was

92 Here, Hoare, Lord Bletchley's seat having been elevated to the upper house.

proverbial. Up until this point, his intention had simply been to disarm the garmungling figure before him. In a trice, he sprang a question. 'What do you intend to do once you track down this Forrager?'

'Forger. I'm going to ask him what he's been up to this last umpteen years. And then I'm going to find out what he intends to do next.'

'Just like that?'

'Just like that. An interview to the death. He's already put pen to one bloody dangerous booke that your people had to throw onto the proscribed list.'

'That's common knowledge.'

'True. But did you know he's been working night and day on a sequel?'

'Is that so,' said Quibble, as though he were annotating rather than asking.

'That's what I intend to find out.'

'My colleagues in the gendarmerie. They'll want to know what brings Ж to their shores.' His eyes narrowed. 'Think they'll welcome you with open arms do you?'

'Depends on what you mean by arms,' observed the journalist. This was a question which to some extent had indeed been preoccupying Hackett. Over the previous year, he'd framed more than one pinesse against the draconian interventions of the French language police. More recently, in the wake of the Munich Appeasement, he'd been unpolitic enough to voice his suspicions of Édouard Daladier under the headline 'French-Polish Entente a Veneer'. In one mordant pinesse that had appeared in the influential *Spectacle* magazine, he'd imagined an imaginary Maginot manager managing an imaginary Maginot. So that open arms might be precisely what they met him with. 'I'll take my chances,' he said, pitching his tone between nonchalance and insouciance.

'I'd keep your degree to yourself.'

'My degree of uncertainty, is it?'

'Your BA in modern languages. They're particularly suspicious of translators at the moment.'

'You needn't worry on that score. I've no wish to be found dangling beneath the Pont Neuf with a placard reading *Traduttore Traditore* round my windpipe, or whatever the equivalent in the French might read.' Hackett's fingers involuntarily ribbled the sides of his throat.

'If you're being trailed, which I have to say I very much doubt,' pursued the Chief Inspector, with another alarming change in narrative direction, 'it's no one in Semantics, that much I can tell you.'

Hackett was not to be put off by the non-sequitor. 'No? Who, then?'

A low gruntle emanated from Quibble which, had it emanated from anyone else, might have been interpreted as a guffaw. 'Vice?'

'Hardly!' Momentarily, the figure with the van der Graaf head skipped before Hackett's mind's eye. It was only a matter of days since he'd become aware beyond a dubit (doubt!) of this newest shadow. For this was not Mulcahy's stooge. Not only did he move at a different de Broglie frequency; his ears were small; his height strubbly; he displayed no propensity to whistle. So Mulcahy's hand was scarcely to be suspected. Taking his cue from the policemen, Hackett threw his own curveball into their dialogue. 'So did you find out from the prisoner, is Aloysius an alias?'

Quibble's eyes drilled into Hackett's.

'I take it you'd rather the press kept shtum about our friend Fleming.'

'You can do as you please. You won't be getting anywhere near him.'

'Then you have arraigned the man! Say no more, a nod's as good as a wink.'

Quibble shifted. He had the uncomfortable feeling that he'd been outplayed. He did not like it, not one bit. So, as was his wont, he decided to try to land a carp of truth. The bait he would use he had kept neatly folded in his inside pocket for the better part of two years. Item, a flame-darkened diagram of a lozenge on a scrap of linen of Ulster provenance, with four cardinal points designated *M; C; F; S;* in the centre of which was a large *Q?* with a mock crown on top. He removed it, unfolded it with great care, and allowed the journalist to peruse it. Hackett nodded, and ribbled his chin. Then, to the astonishment of the Chief Inspector, he reached into his own breast pocket, removed a piece of frabbled linen, and with a deft flick unfrabbled it. It was the identical lozenge, even to the flame-darkening that had coaxed the orange-juice into an alphabet. 'But where…? When…?' he sputtered. 'How…?'

Hackett triumphantly harrumphed. 'Five, six months since. It was left for me in the Boarding House.' He shook his head dubitously. 'Passing mendicant.'

'Passing…?' An astonished Quibble compared the linen in each sample. The same woof. The very warp. Indubitably, the identical provenance. Who knew, perhaps even the self-same bandle, though there was a faint scent of eau de toilette on this second piece.

It was discomfiting in the extreme, and Hackett was never shy to capitalise on discomfiture. 'Tell me, Quibble. This Jim Kinch that's over on the continent. You don't think he could be Quinn, do you?'

The look which the detective fixed on the journalist put their words, which in any case had been proceeding at cross-purposes, definitively to the sword.

CHAPTER THE ELEVENTH

which tells of Hackett's jaunt to the City of Light;[93]
and of what he found there

Before it was an occupied city, Paris was a preoccupied city. Hackett squinnied up from his Baedeker to the lugubrious gargoyle that was pouting, head in hands, over the chimney-pots of the mighty capital. From the Galerie des Chimères on the North Tower of Notre Dame, his eye was drawn first to Sacre Coeur's clutch of meringues nestled atop Montmartre, and thence counter-clockwise through 90° to the great inverted Y of Eiffel's iron monstrosity. That's one quarter, he mentally protracted. But how many quarters make up a French city? He again consulted the guide so as to be certain that, in his current orientation, the rive gauche lay à main gauche. Satisfied, his gaze dived again over the roofs, and he ribbled his stubble. Rooves, he thought, seized by a sudden dubit, or doubt. Roofs or rooves? And then, dived or dove?

A brindled pigeon, perhaps it was a colombe, eying him

93 There is some confusion as to whether la Ville-Lumière should be translated as the City of Light or the City of Lights. The suggestion that Paris gained this epithet from the Shakespearean usage of 'lights' to mean 'wantons' is now generally discredited.

with Gallic superciliousness, brought him back to the more pressing conundrum. To track down the Forger O'Reilly amidst all this teeming humanity would be no stroll in the park. Unless of course the ex-pat boulevardier had a mind to be found. There was one small lead that Smyllie had given him, which was a bookshop by the unlikely name of *Plaiger & Co* somewhere along the rue des Hêtres (was it?) over in the Latin Quarter. Also, there had been any number of reported sightings of a scatological Eirishman in eye-patch and panama holding court in various cafés of the less salubrious class in the back-streets around Pigale. So that, like the fellow who'd at last found the public jakes, Hackett at least had something to go on.

But the fact remained that if Mr Pierce O'Reilly, formerly Tim Finnegan, who'd cut a youthful dash in inner-city Dubilin as that young blade Jim Kinch, alias the Pirate, also known as the Forger, whose work in French appeared under the nom-de-plume Juisse, (or the nom-de-guerre Juisse, if Smyllie was correct about the man's open declaration of war upon language), well one way or another, if that maddening character had a wish to disappear into the madding crowd, he could scarcely have hit upon a better metropolis in which to do so.

As if that wasn't bad enough, the ticklish matter of the lingo would only compound present difficulties. In school, he'd forever use the verb '*être*' to describe the weather, which the Brothers said showed a lack of *savoir faire*. And although later Hackett had, like his quarry, read to degree level both French and Italian while at Newman House,[94] he'd had little

94 From earliest childhood, Hackett associated each language with a colour. Engelish, as is natural, he saw as white; French was blue; Spanish yellow; Italian green; German black; Russian red; and Eirish, because her ancient alphabet was composed of eighteen trees and was in perpetual decline, was autumnal.

occasion to practise either reticulum linguae since he'd been made a Bachelor. His and hers were hard enough, God knows. In French the son loved her mother and she loved his son. But now, trawling his memory, he found it difficult to distinguish between peaches and sins, while both terms were somehow implicated in the apostolic act of fishing. A like difficulty had confounded the renowned theologians of the Sorbonne, since it was proverbial how bitterly their Doctors of Canon Law cavilled over le mot juste. And that very morning in the pension at which he lodged, he himself had balked before the self-annihilating complexity of asking the propriétaire for 'a large breakfast'. Faut pas prendre un faux pas!

The very streets were preoccupied. Once he stepped out of the pension, there was the ever-present danger of putting one's trust in the specious familiarity of the dreaded faux amis, those amicable fraudsters who, like the moneymen one met immediately upon disembarking, promised a favourable exchange between currencies but left one with worthless francs. Chance here was luck, Mercy thanks, and Deception was a disappointment. Though it was the German language police who'd advocated a prison-house of language — Ein Gefängnis der Sprache — which if you thought about it, wasn't a million miles removed from Sir Thomas More and his nets of language, always provided you saw it, with Jim Kinch, as a net you might get tangled up in as opposed to one with which you might try to net the world of objects and relations.

Not without a little trepidation, then, the indefatigable Ж descended the 387 stairs of the South Tower of Notre-Dame Cathedral, and doubled across the Pont au Double onto the left bank, as you looked west — unless the designation referred to the political inclination not of the river but of her riverains. *Plaiger & Co* on the rue des Hêtres (he felt sure it was Hêtres) should be his first port of call, that much was self-evident. What was less evident was how precisely to hit upon the said rue des Hêtres, because no such rue was apparent in the Latin Quarter of his Baedeker. There was a rue des Étriers and there was a ruelle des Huîtres. There was even a bustling avenue des Heurts, though this seemed to correspond in some way with the busy Ave St Jacques upon which he was at present standing. How like the Gallic French, to have two names for everything!

Undismayed, he consulted a public clock, and found it was still early enough to adopt a heuristic approach to the problem. Over the next hour, his errant shoe-leather took him through several circuitous and frustrating iterations of the narrow Quarter. At every junction, he found himself in the unenviable position of Buridan's ass, pulled equally this way and that until at last he hit upon the rough expedient of always favouring the left over the right (as he approached), unless the junction was in the form of a cross rather than a T, in which case the right was to be favoured over the left, so that he'd be less likely to describe a quomboid of any kind. It might have been expected, en passant, that as Hackett's left leg was from birth slightly shorter than the right, and that therefore he might naturally take more lefts than rights, he would have characteristically fought against the inclination. That would be to figure without Hackett's propensity to double bluff. They might be expecting him to do precisely that, though who precisely 'they' might be he could not have said. Superstitions, like bats and suspicions, fly better in the half-light.

Quite soon though, he was moved to modify the algorithm with a proviso that reversed the preference upon arrival at the identical junction in the identical orientation. It little availed. For a fourth time in the space of twenty minutes, he found himself passing the identical hat shop in the identical direction. Was it another German who'd said it was impossible to get lost in a city? They seemed to be getting everywhere nowadays, whereas here he was standing like a prize liúdramán outside that selfsame bloody hat shop! As the cloche blanged out eleven, Hackett ruefully addressed a gendarme, who had begun to eye him much as the pigeon, or colombe, had done. 'Monsieur,' essayed Hackett, 'pouvez-vous m'indiquer où se trouve par ici la rue des Hêtres?'

The gendarme gave a Gallic shrug. 'Monsieur trouve la...?'

'La rue des Hêtres.'

'La rue d'Aisettes. Non.'

'Pas d'Aisettes, des Hêtres.'

The cheeks puffed out, as though they were about to blow a tuba. 'La rue des Êtres, peut-être?'

'Non. La rue des Hêtres... hêtres, uhm, sylvestres.'

'Ah! La rue des Hêtres Sylvestres!' His face briefly lit up, then the shrug extended upwards through his cape to the dour corners of his mouth, over his expressionless eyes, and thence to his forehead's furfuraceous furrows. 'Désolé.' The cape began to waddle away, but hesitated as a happy thought struck. 'Peut-être monsieur doit demander dans cette librarie là, hein?' As if by magic, a bookshop (and not a library, bien sûr) had been conjured into being directly facing them across the cobbled street. A sign with a woodcut of a balding figure brandishing a plume, who bore more than a passing resemblance to the Bard of Avon, declared in Engelish: ***Plaiger & Co, Purveyor of Rare and Antiquarian Books since 1904***. Hackett's heart leapt like a March hare.

He could not have explained precisely why, but he was expecting the venerable establishment to be run by a female propriétaire of the spinster class. Instead, a cursory glance about the shelves and book stacks revealed an elderly, miniature but evidently male propriétaire in a brown dustcoat who was perched halfway up a ladder with his back to the premises. He'd failed to register, or had chosen to ignore, the tinkle of the bell as the Eirishman entered. Now Hackett was no stranger to second-hand and antiquarian bookshops. Indeed, prior to his breakdown, he'd been a bibliophile and hoarder of the first order. Perhaps the erstwhile state of his Bachelor pad, all about the which tottering tors and teetering towers proliferated in an eternal state of 積ん読[95] had discouraged any lasting intimacies of an amatory nature. So it was with all the delight of a rediscovered passion that he now began to peruse the bounty all about him.

One prize soon commanded all his attention. It was a complete set, morocco-bound in deckled octavo, of the public works of Puncher & Wattmann (1922), including their ground-breaking *Anglo-Hibernian Cyclopaedia* in thirteen volumes. In the Britain of Operation Babel, such copies as hadn't been consigned to the flames were securely under lock and key. He had witnessed first-hand the doleful dispatch of an entire cartload during the infamous Barrow-in-Furnace auto da fé.

95 積ん読 (tsundoku): the act of leaving a book unread after acquisition, where it is typically piled with other such unread books.

Hackett picked out at random volume IX, Per-Qua, and was amazed upon opening it to find the frontispiece bore two things: an engraving showing the ninth volume of the *Anglo-Hibernian Cyclopaedia* itself, which occasioned a momentary sense of *mise-en-abyme*; and the imprint of the Ouroboros press, with its logo of the self-consuming serpent. He looked about, to be sure the rise wasn't being taken out of him. But from atop the ladder, the proprietor's back remained turned toward the shop.

Hackett next allowed the volume to fall open on a random page, and found to his astonishment that he was looking, in miniature and in monochrome, at an etching of the very image of the Renaissance penman who'd looked down from the shop-sign. Perhaps the coincidence was not quite as serendipitous as it first appeared, since it was altogether natural that the entry for Plaiger, Robyn (1564-1616) would be among the most frequently consulted by the casual browser. Reassured by the thought, he began to read:

> Plaiger, Robyn (1564-1616), Knight of the Order of the Garter, Head Chancer and Philosopher Royale. Eldest son of Sir Godfrey Plaiger, Groom of the Stool to King Henry VIII and Honorary Member of Chancery (q.v.); and of Margaret O'Malley, younger sister to the infamous pirate queen, Gráinne Mhaol O'Malley. Margaret had been kidnapped as a child and raised at Hampton Palace as a ward of court. A precocious reader from his earliest childhood, Robyn was schooled at St Botolph's, and went on to read Classics at Maudlin, Camsbridge, where he became a lifelong Fellow.

> In his own lifetime, Plaiger was credited with more published monographs in the fields of natural philosophy, literature, philologie, historie and historiographie than are now considered to be exclusively his own work. Of the seven dramas that were once attributed to him, only *Cardenio* (q.v.) and several inferior passages from *Two Gentlemen of Verona* and *Henry VIII* are definitively Plaiger's. Perhaps it is for the hard Latinate line he adopted during the Inkhorn Controversy (q.v.) while acting as Head Chancer and Philosopher Royale that his influence has been most enduring.
>
> Posteritie has not been altogether kind to Sir Robyn. Together with Walter Shandy, Thomas Bowdler, Jeremiah Gibber, Sir Gerry Mander MP, Charles Boycott, Dr Franz Anton Mesmer, Cpt Wilberforce Crony and William Archibald Spooner (qqv), he remains to date one of the most maligned of all Engelish men of letters. But time will tell.

The entry immediately above this one, which was illustrated by an etching of the shop and sign as viewed from across the street, now caught Hackett's attention:

> Plaiger & Co (founded 1904). Purveyor of Rare and Antiquarian Books. 13 rue de la Tour Noire. Famous Parisian bookshop in which one can find…

He slammed the book shut. For a second time in as many minutes, he'd been seized with the disabling vertigo of mise-en-abyme (q.v.).

He shook his head. With another furtive glance at the proprietor's back, Hackett replaced volume IX and selected in its place volume X. A misprint on the binding read Qua-Qua, in place presumably of Qua-Rum, since volume XI ran from Rum-Tlö. He decided to have a shufti inside to see if there was an entry for the Royal Academy of Letters. On the QT. With one final fleeting look at the unmoving ladder figure, he began to flick through the tome and noticed, en passant, there was no entry for (q.v.). If the Cyclopaedia had been a perfect closed system presumably there would have had to have been, as that other German, Gödel was keen to demonstrate if he ever completed his famous Incompleteness Theorem. His hand beginning to tremble, though he couldn't have said why, he thumbed page after octavo page until he found himself amongst the Royal Academies. Royal Academy of Agronomie… Royal Academy of Anthropometrie… Royal Academy of Architecture… Royal Academy of the Arts… Royal Academy of Astronomie… (he flicked a few pages)… Royal Academy of Music… (he flipped back a page)… Royal Academy of Law… Royal Academy of Li… (a sudden thought whimzoned so vividly into his ear that he almost tore the page as his thumb flittered backwards)… Royal Acacademy of…

'Monsieur cherche quelque chose en particulier?' This voice, desiccated but penetrating, seemed to be issuing directly from his left clavicle (scapula, was it?). At any rate, from behind his back, at the level of his left shoulder blade. He slammed the tome shut and pivorted about. The ladder was vacant. A gnome in brown coat stood before him.

'Je cherchais, uhm… c'est rien, c'est vraiment rien, monsieur.' Hastily, blindly, his fingers replaced volume X into the gap in the shelf.

'You are not French, I sink.'

'No. Are you?'

'*Au contraire.*'

'?'

'*Canadien, monsieur.*'

'Ah.'

'You were looking some sing in particular?'

'No. That is to say, yes. In fact, I was.' Hackett was flustered, though he could not have put his finger on quite what it was that had him flustered. 'That is to say,' he continued, not really certain what it was that it was to say, 'I'm looking for some-*one* in particular.'

'Ah! Who might zat be?'

Who indeed? A panoply of first names, nicknames, surnames and pen names filled the bookshop, fluttered by like butterflies and alighted all about the shelves. He might be any one of these. He might be every one of these. 'Would you… have you… did you… I don't suppose you've ever heard of a man by the name of Jim Kinch? Or…'

'Jeem Keench?'

'Writes under the name of Juisse, perhaps, or Juif…'

'*Jouisse, monsieur?*'

'Or possibly you know him as O'Reilly. Pierce O'Reilly?'

'But of course! Jouisse! Monsieur means Piers O'Riley!'

'Piers O'Riley! The very man!'

'But 'ee is not ear.'

'No. That is to say, I wasn't expecting to find him here. As such. What I mean is, I was hoping to find some information here which might lead me to him. An address, for instance.'

'Ah! An address.' The man shuffled about behind a great cairn of books which Hackett now saw concealed a desk beneath it. He rifled, he fumbled, he delved, he rummaged, he rattled and he poked and, at great length, his fingers prestidigitated a business card. 'Monsieur should try ze Lapin Agile.' The card, which Hackett gratefully accepted, showed a teetering rabbit balancing on its paw a wine bottle and on its head a captain's hat. Au Lapin Agile, Ave St-Vincent, Montmartre. Bienvenu à tous le monde.

'And if not ear, zen perhaps, le Café du Cavelier Blanc.'

'Also in Montmartre?'

'Also in Montmartre.'

'I expect there'd be little point in heading up before…?' The ellipsis invited the dusty old propriétaire to suggest an o'clock.

'Just so. Of course, monsieur is very well come to stay ear and look ze shop.'

'That's… très gentil! You're sure it'd be no trouble?' Though it was finished, out of politesse, with a question mark, this last was rhetorical, the journalist already folding up his garmungling legs beneath him and reaching for another volume of the Cyclopaedia. Here was quite simply too good an opportunity to miss. A shrug of the brown coat acquiesced, and the feet shundled back towards the ladder. Hackett found his fingers had chosen the indispensable volume that ran from Mis-Out. Running a finger down the index, he hesitated over an entry for Ouroboros. For the merest second another sensation of dizziness ran through him. But it passed. He flitted through the great octavo pages until his eyes fell upon the serpent in the form of the figure eight recumbent, ∞. He read:

> Ouroboros. Franco-Hibernian Secret Society, founded in St Malo in Bretagne in the late seventeenth or early eighteenth century, combining the political radicalism of the Wild Geese (q.v.), the cabbalism of the Rosicrucians (q.v.) and the gnostic writings of the Angevin and the Hibernian Heresiarchs (qqv), in particular as these last relate to the Ur-Sprache (q.v.), which they supposed to be proto-Celtic. Also, a trilingual Printing Press dedicated to the propagation of the beliefs of the Ouroboros Brotherhood. Their predictions as to the founding of an Ideal Republic governing the sundry lands of the Celts and based upon the revival of Brehon Law (q.v.) and the ancient language seem premature in the extreme. But time will tell.

Hackett looked up. By a loose calculation after the manner of Tristram Shandy, if every (q.v.) he looked up led to another several (q.v.) or even (qqv), he might be here not just all day, but as a result of that day all week, and thence a fortnight and so forth in Malthusian progression.[96] He would have to be selective. The propriétaire canadien seemed indulgent. But one didn't want to try his patience.

He was about to return to the index when his eye fell once more upon the logo. A self-consuming snake, in the shape of a figure eight, but lateral. Mathematically, that would make it infinity. But in what dark dream had he come across that strange beast? It was not the recurring nightmare of the chess-

96 A reference to Charles Dickens' fabled Rev. Malthus, in whose parsonage the offspring proliferated at an alarming rate.

game, the castle in the castle in the castle. And yet it gave a comparable sense of giddiness. If Teddy Mulcahy could be credited, his crazy scheme of reviving the Gaelic language in Eirland based upon the cló gaedhealach and Dinneen's abridged dictionary was not a million miles away from the lofty goals of the Ouroboros Brotherhood. Of course there were no snakes in Eirland. On the other hand, if there were four felons at large, four mad evangelists who were intent upon... he never got to complete the aposiopesis... all at once Hackett knucked his fingers. The horse doctor! The military tattoo! Was he correct in thinking that Flanders, or Fleming (wasn't that the man's name?) had a tattoo — Hackett's fingers moved to the place beneath which the heart is said to beat and tapped — just about here? And hadn't Quibble himself described a tattoo that was precisely in the shape of a snake caught in the act of eating itself?

It was already afternoon when Hackett stepped back out onto the rue de la Tour Noire.[97] It was far too late for lunch, apparently — four hours had somehow elapsed since he'd entered the librarie — but it was too early to continue his quest. His heart going pitter-pat, he decided to retire to his pension for the afternoon. This was as much to calm his agitated nerves as to consider what to do next. Passion recalled in tranquillity. Who was it had said that?

---

97 There is no evidence that a black tower ever stood next or near this street. The designation in fact appears to be a corruption of the pre-revolutionary *rue de la Tournure* (literally, 'Turn of Phrase Street'), so called because Diderot's cyclopaedists frequented a café there, though fascinatingly, in his semi-autobiographical *Rêve d'Alembert* (1769), the café itself is fictionalised as the *Café de la Tour Noire.*

Nighttown. The cobbles of Montmartre are plated in moonlight. A figure stands, gazing up at a sign upon which a rabbit in the livery of a waiter is balancing a precarious wine-bottle. From inside the café there emanates the animated warmth of French conversation, of French glasses tinkling, of ochre lighting, of musique and bavardage and chansons. As this is interbellum Paris, there may even be (pourquoi pas?) accordion music.

Hackett considered, for the thousandth time, what he was going to say to Jim Kinch, the old artificer, the builder of labyrinths, if and when he at last encountered him. Smyllie had suggested the chief interest might lie in the latter's outlandish boast, made a quarter of a century since, that he was going 'into ex-isle and punning' in order to... what was it again? Something that smacked of forgery, one way or another. And conscience. Or consciousness. And nets. He was going to fly the nets of language, the reticulae linguarum, that much he had stated as a bald fact. Hackett was lost inside the labyrinth of his imagination when his toes were met by a shadow stretching from the doorway. He looked up, and saw, silhouetted in the ochre glow, a garmungling figure in a duffle-coat with hair that was erect as the crest of a bird of prey. There was something of the heraldic bestiary in the taciturn character who now stepped out onto the cobbles carrying over his shoulder a schoolboy's satchel. Hackett was on the point of returning to his thoughts when he heard what must have been a comrade call out after the receding individual. 'Meurphy! Meurphy, weight! Attends, veux-te!'

A compatriot? Animated, Hackett skipped forwards and tugged at the man's sleeve. 'You're Eirish?' he tried, latching onto the surname as he had the sleeve. The guillemot eyes scarcely lighted upon him. For a second Hackett thought he recognised the man. 'Did you by any chance,' he asked, 'take a degree in French and Italian in University College, Dubilin?'

Without being in the least offended or offensive, the character slipped Hackett's grip. '*Au contraire*...'

Trinity College, then. 'And would you know, monsieur, of *another* Eirishman lives here, or hereabouts. A fellow by the name of O'Riley? Or O'Reilly? A patch over one eye.' Hackett covered one of his sockets with one of his palms, an aide de comprehension. Nothing. He tried the other eye, with the other palm. Not a squeak. Perhaps this Murphy (if he was Murphy) wasn't Eirish after all. Perhaps he wasn't even called Murphy, and '*au contraire*' was hardly conclusive about his alma mater. Reluctantly letting the figure, who was smiling weakly, recede down the cobbled street, Hackett pivorted about, and returned to the threshold of the *Lapin Agile*. Though he couldn't have put his finger on how, the brief encounter had dampened all expectations. Even if Pierce O'Reilly existed, which was by no means proven beyond reasonable dubit, and even if said O'Reilly were here, which was in no wise certain, was it likely he'd be any more talkative than the unnameable character in the duffle? In fact, to deal plainly and to call a spade a spade, didn't the whole bloody adventure have something of the wild goose chase about it from start to finish? All very well for Smyllie, the Eirish RM, to dispatch on a whim a minion to Paris. From within his paper realm, no journey abroad was too outlandish. But the plain fact remained, Hackett had never been an investigative journalist. His forte consisted in the composition of wry commentary, column and correspondence that gave an impression of authority, but which if you looked into it, was all so much smoke and mirrors.

But there was nothing for it. With greatly diminished expectations, Ignatius Hackett stepped into the bustling interior, and a bare three minutes later, with these expectations met in full, he was again outside. And the intrepid Ж might well have called it a night there and then if a *clochard*, who was even then advancing over the cobbles, hadn't borne an uncanny resemblance to a jarvey driver Hackett had once hailed down in the Sally Gap in Wickenlow, a cute hoor who'd somehow diddled him out of the change that was due to him. What's this the other establishment was called? It came to him. '*Mon ami, est-que vous savez où se trouve le Café du Chevallier Blanc?*'

'*Pas de lieu Rhône que nous...*' Hackett was uncertain whether he'd comprehended the low gruntle. Was this man also Eirish? Or was he a *faux amis*? Before he had an opportunity to put either hypothesis to the test, the scurril had scuttled past him and into the *Lapin Agile*. Hackett was left ribbling the back of his head. Curiouser and curiouser! He was again on the point of giving up when he heard the clop, clop of an approaching club-foot coming from the other end of the Ave St-Vincent. A figure in jacket and beret shortly appeared, one foot heightened on the platform of an orthopaedic shoe. As the *boiteux* tacked towards him in a series of corrective right-angles, Hackett reformulated the question in his head so as to iron out any *faux pas*. He then stepped forwards, unconsciously exaggerating his own slight limp to bring the orthogonal rapprochement to a halt. '*Bonsoir monsieur. Je m'excuse. Pouvez-vous m'indiquer où se trouve le Café du Chevallier Blanc, s'il vous plait?*'

'*C'est bien le Café du Chevallier Blanc ce que monsieur cherche, et pas le Café du Cavalier Blanc?*'

Here we go again! Hackett shrugged. '*Peut-être. Peut-être pas.*'

'*Hein. Si c'est bien ça c'est simple comme bonjour! Il ya a deux façons d'y arriver. Ou bien on va d'ici tous droit et puis on prend le deuxième à droite, ou on va d'ici à droite et puis on prend le premier à gauche jusqu'au deuxième à droite. C'est bonnet blanc et blanc bonnet. D'accord?*'

'*Bonnet blanc*. Right. Got it. *Merci*.'

'*Pas du tout*,' said the Frenchman, hobbling on and putting an end to their brief *pas de deux*.

Hackett took several minutes to translate the instructions into passable Engelish and then to translate the passable Engelish into the coordinates of a passable mental map of the narrow streets rising up before him. He then took a further minute to square the first set of directions the man had furnished with the second, so that at last they converged upon a putative coordinate two streets up and one across from where he was standing, or one across and two up. It remained to be seen whether the coordinates coincided with any premises by the name of the *Café du Cavalier*, or even *du Chevallier Blanc*.

They did. And Hackett entered the second calumptious café, not for the first time bothered by an uncanny feeling of *déjà vu*.

CHAPTER THE TWELFTH

in which an intimation is given of the nefarious machine being developed by the IBM Corporation, *with disastrous consequences for the Engelish language*

Chief Inspector Quibble of Semantics nodded to the delator who had been slouched behind the desk, but who stood up smartly upon his entry. Over the latter's head, a varicose map of the great metropolis dominated the office, so to sprake. Or speak. Was it not 'so to speak'? Or was that another one of their damned interpolations. 'Sprake or speak?' he queried.

'I'm, I'm, I'm sorry?' The man's discomfort was pa-palpable. Quibble's effect on his subordinates in general, and on this new batch in particular, idlers and bumblers to a man, was a source of wry gratification to the career detective. Dismissing the conundrum with a wave of his hand, he peered at the map. Red thumbtacks clustered to the North and Northeast of the serpentine Thames; yellow thumbtacks, rarer these, populated the south bank. 'Any more incidents?' he growled.

'No. Er, that is to say, one. One incident, sir.'

'Contervoc, or skaz?'

'We're unsure. That is… uhm…'

'Very well.' He pivorted about and made to go into the debriefing room. 'Sit! Sit! Sit!' And although strictly spraking he did not have eyes in the back of his head, as he left the antechamber he saw with pinpoint accuracy the man run a thumb between collar and neck before resuming his seat.

Fraiser was awaiting him in the debriefing room, as was Heat. CID, like his father before him. Dull-witted, just like his old man. Saw the whole business of upholding the law as a great game. Now Quibble had inherited from his own father, who'd been an Anabaptist Minister who'd preached an extremely literal species of creationism, a deep distrust of all things hereditary. The directorship of the Academy of Letters was a case in point. Filling one's father's shoes might be all very well for a clown, it was hardly so for a policeman. 'Well?'

'Nothing,' said Heat.

'What do you mean, nothing?'

'He still hasn't broken.'

A puzzled look met the Chief Inspector's routine question. 'It is him?'

'Oh it's him all right.'

Quibble's hand moved towards his heart. 'Any distinguishing marks?'

'He has. There,' nodded the other, he, too, playing his cards close to his chest.

'Well then?'

'He's standing upon his right to remain silent.'

'Is he?' Quibble looked displeased. The right to remain silent was not a right to which the Chief Inspector subscribed, not at a time when the Engelish language itself was facing an existential threat. Long and hard he'd argued the case with Hoare's predecessor in the weeks during which they were putting the final touches to section 31 of the Linguistic Integrity Act (1937). But for all his bluff and bluster, the old Home Secretary had turned out to be the wrong kind of Conservative, which is to say he was small c conservative, and as for the Chief Constable, his instincts erred so far on the side of liberality that he was a large L Liberal in all but name. That was the whole bloody grodlum of trying to do anything under a national government. A government with no shadow was a government with no substance. That was an axiom. An axiom that demonstrated the Chief Inspector's democratic credentials, in spite of all the recent lampoons to the contrary.

'If I might be allude tae make a wee suggestion,' offered Fraiser, who was a past master at making wee suggestions that were as obvious as they were long-winded, 'would it no' be an idea to hae a worud with the mon yoursel, seein as it was you and no' See Aye Dee that nacked him in the furst place all those years ago in Kant, when the mon was trying tae pass off old gammon as cant? I mean tae say…'

'Yes, I think we know what you mean to say,' interrupted Quibble, through bared teeth. Time and again, he'd asked Fraiser not to use the word 'nicked'. If the guardians of linguistic probity were careless in their usage, what hope the general populace? So that if the Scotsman was trying to vex him, he could hardly have chosen a more apt term with which to needle his superior, particularly when the entire shambles rested precisely upon the fact that it was CID and not Semantics who had apprehended Aloysius Fleming this time round. 'Where are you holding him, Heat?'

'Bridewell.' This Heat was damned taciturn when he had

a mind to be. Half of CID had turned taciturn, ever since the Linguistic Integrity Act (1937) had granted his own branch such sweeping powers. If Chief Inspector Quibble of Semantics didn't know better, he might imagine he was being downright obtuse. 'Your people got their court order, did they?'

'Done and dusted. We've got another seventy-two hours. Then we'll need to charge him, one way or another.'

'Hmmph.' There was an audible edge of disdain to this syllable. It was occasioned by the thought that if it had been any of his own officers, or even one of the delators, who'd arraigned this Fleming, the sanction of quarantine might have been applied. Even the most hardened criminal had been known to crack under forty days' close interrogation. But the press, with its capital L liberal instincts, had latterly begun to kick up a fuss over any and every such detention, let alone one which might involve the subterfuge of juggling a prisoner between branches. Besides, Heat wasn't a man who was prepared to play ball. Everything by the book, just like his father before him in the first Sir Æthelred's day.

It was with one hand tied figuratively behind his back then, and with a sense that he alone had taken arms against a sea of fardles, that Quibble took his slow leave of Heat and Fraiser. Hoare could not be counted upon to give him his undivided support, either. He was too much the politician. True, Operation Babel was hardly a vote-winner. Random vocabulary tests were unpopular, particularly among the immigrant communities; internment without trial was held to be counterproductive; restrictions on movement and assembly, uneconomical; his officers were distrusted; the delators, detested. But what radical medicine had ever been palatable? The body politic was diseased. Insist too insistently upon habeas corpus, and you might find one day that you are shackled to a corpse. There was one maverick politician alone who was prepared to grasp the nettle, but he'd been out of favour for decades, and had been reduced to writing a history of his ancestor the Duke of Marlboro ever since the Gallipoli debacle.[98]

The woman was waiting for him in his office, her steely gaze on the street outside. Portrait of a lady with iron hair. This one at least was not for turning. 'Good trip, ma'am?'

'Very.'

'Meant to say, that list you passed me at Froschmann's parting do. That trio of Embassy cryptologists for us to monitor. Kent, Gatewood, Tyler?'

'Well?'

'Turns out they're all for one and one for all.' Quibble noted, but did not comment on, the frundle that winced across the other's face. 'You were right to flag him. Mr Tyler Gatewood Kent has been hob-nobbing with some pretty unsavoury characters, everyone from Mosley to the Milferds to William Joyce. Think we should put their new Ambassador in the know?'

'Kennedy is Eirish,' replied the iron lady, settling that issue. The Chief Inspector squeezed the bridge of his nose, as though he were adjusting the separation of his eyes. 'All hell

98 He means of course Winston Churchill, whose disastrous Dardanelles gamble was in the process of being forgotten. After all, he was hardly the first Briton to have underestimated the Turk. During his tour of Constantinople in 1860, General Gordon 'Pasha' (late of Khartoum) found their military so indolent, sedentary and given to luxury that he nicknamed them 'the Ottoman Turks'.

has broken loose here,' he yawned. 'While you were over there.'

'*Plus ça change...*'

'I expect you've heard the latest from CID.'

'Is it him?'

'They seem to think so.'

'You haven't dropped by?'

Quibble idled with the dossier on his desk. 'He's standing upon his right to silence.'

'Ah!'

'Seventy-two hours. Then he walks Scot free.'

'Why not simply re-arrest him?'

'Ha!' This was as close to a laugh as Quibble was prepared to go. 'Here's the thing,' his finger began to tap out an idle tattoo on the dossier, 'the latest whisper from Whitehall is, there's talk of repeal. A general curtailment of the emergency powers.'

'A suspension of the suspension of habeas corpus?'

'Quite so. We have to walk on eggshells.'

'Hmmmp,' she said, a vocabulary they shared. 'What did they get him for? Passing off?'

'If only! Passing off we could work with. The passing off of false or dubitous terms, we could take a chance on. Possession, pure and simple. And even that was... not quite clear-cut.' A silence descended between them. But it was a productive silence. A comfortable silence. Nothing about the clumsiness of CID and their dubitous methodology needed to be stated.

'Any word from Germany?' asked the iron lady suddenly.

Quibble gave an involuntary start. His eyes narrowed. 'Germany?'

'You know as well as I do, Cecil. Ever since Johannes Guttenberg first put movable type into a wooden screw-press, the Bosch has been obsessed with the idea of the mechanical reproduction of language. In particular, they've been trying to crack what Leibniz dubbed the Entscheidungsproblem.' Pause. 'The decision-making problem.'

'Leibniz?' He shook his head blandly, his eyes as narrow as his mouth.

'You have heard of the Königsberg eccentric who posed the problem of the seven bridges. Yes?' Nothing in Quibble's expression suggested either that he had or that he'd been present at the Oxenford Council when his colleague Fraiser had alluded to the Prussian tyro. 'What's less known is that he filed a patent for a steam-powered press to manufacture synthetic *a priori* statements. Of course it failed. But the dream never died. Word from the Polish Cyphers Bureau is that they've now come pretty close to cracking the problem of the category errors that bedevilled it. And I needn't tell you all what that would imply.'

Quibble frundled, or he grimlied. *Had* there been any word from Germany? If there had, he wasn't ready to share it. Far better change the subject. 'Tell me,' he said, in imitation of banter, 'what's new on the other side of the pond? Find out anything interesting?'

A twitch that was the approximation of a smirk played across her thin lips. 'They're streets ahead. They're taking the matter very seriously indeed, already working on a system of verbal decontamination that'll leave us in the ha'penny place.' The vibration at the corners of the steel lady's lips was echoed in those of the redoubtable detective.

'Who's driving it? The Feds?'[99]

'Not the Feds.' She tapped her nose. 'IBM.'

'Remind me,' invited Quibble, though whether he was being ingenuous or disingenuous was unclear.

'International Business Machines. For decades they've been developing automated card-feed machinery based upon the principle of the pianola. Their acquisition, for a song, of the German tabulating firm **Deutsche Hollerith Maschinen Gesellschaft** when their losses could no longer be gainsaid helped them steal a march on their rivals.'

'Might have known the Bosch would have a hand in it.'

'There was a delegation from IBM at Kermit Froschmann's do.'

Hackett's eyes, or more accurately, the interval between them, narrowed. 'I know the brand. That old advertising jingle, '*The business of International Business Machines is business machines*', which was shamelessly purloined by Coolidge for his 1924 electoral campaign.'

'Indeed. In any case, IBM has a process in development with the Webster Institute which not only highlights every false and dubitous term in a given text, but which actively corrects it.'[100]

---

99 The Federal Bureau of Investigation, who, under the directorship of J. Edgar Hoover® were tasked with cleaning up the country. Under Hoover ® the 'Feds' went after the gangsters' molls and fences, following his maxim 'no criminal works in a vacuum'.

100 The IBM Mark 2, an electro-mechanical device which due to the inordinate size of its initial 1:6 scale blueprint, become known affectionately as 'the big blue'. It should not be confused with the British Tabulating Machine (BTM) 'bronze goddess', which though of comparable size, was so named for its bronze finish and ample curves. In his wartime memoir, Churchill distinguished between the calculating machines with characteristic jingoism: 'if the IBM could be counted upon, the BTM was to be reckoned with.'

'Do you tell me so!'

'It's still at the experimental stage.'

'Even so.'

'Plays fast and loose with syntax.'

'That we could live with.'

'Would also imply abrogating the power of decommissioning.'

'From the Decommissioner? A damned Academy man?'

'Precisely.'

'Needs must,' sang Quibble, lips finally yielding to a smirk.

'But, Cecil, I'm afraid it's entirely based upon American orthography.'

'Ah!' He tapped the dossier. American spelling could prove more ticklish.

'Not a word,' she said, 'to the Home Secretary.'

'That,' he replied, 'goes without saying.'

The soon-to-be Director of the Fifth Office of the Ministry of Information nodded and made to leave, but hesitated briefly at the door. 'What's the latest with our friend Hackett?'

The Chief Inspector gave an involuntary start. 'He's out of the country.' This much was true.

'Oh?'

'Took the boat to Boulogne two weeks ago. Not a solitary word from him since, much less a pinesse. HM Customs believe he's over there still.'

Well,' she said, opening the door and stepping out into the corridor, 'that's one less bloody Eirishman to worry about.'

CHAPTER THE THIRTEENTH

an account of the continuing adventures that befell Hackett during his Paris sojourn, leading to an encounter with a manxome gendarme

A changed and chastened Ignatius Hackett stood at the scuttle by the bowsprit of the bobbling coal-barge, watching the chalk cliffs of Dover loom over, large as aircraft hangars. There is an adage in journalism, 'sometimes nothing happens for a decade, and then a decade happens in a day'. To his troubled mind, the several weeks he'd spent on the continent had borne that one out, and in spades. Not that anyone would dream of saying that nothing had happened in the wider world over the previous decade. From Chile to Chattanooga, the coffers of every bank on earth had gone through a somersault, disgorging their riches down the proverbial toilet. Where money goes, politics is sure to follow, and entire nations were now on the march in shirts of a single colour. Advertising jingles, talking pictures and the wireless radio were the apostles of a brand new Pentecost, bringing their many tongued message into every hearth and home. Democratic roguery had given way to demagoguery; and the tectonic drift towards another European cataclysm seemed inevitable. Even the Eirish had managed a new constitution, and much to Mr Churchill's chagrin, the Treaty ports — Portlaoise, Portumna and Portarlington — were finally to be restored to the Free State's Department of Fisheries. And on their neighbouring isle, a degree of linguistic mayhem had been unleashed that had brought about an uncharacteristically draconian response.

No. The sea-change which had taken place after a decade's remission had occurred deep within Hackett himself. A number of things had conspired to bring it about. In the first place, there were his various visits to *Plaiger & Co*, a mathematical series diminishing according to the rules of geometric progression, and whose term might well have proved as infinite as the proverbial frog's crossing the room if an arithmetic depletion of funds hadn't curtailed it. In the second place there was the unfortunate interview with the feared Language Police of the 7th Arrondissement. And to cap it all, there was the ineffable encounter with the man who had a plethora of names to rival the shape-changers of Celtic lore.

Almost alone of the standing army of journalists, reporters and radio hacks that were covering the phenomenon of contervoc as it gripped the Engelish countryside in the lead up to the Emergency, Hackett appeared to be immune to the perils consequent upon exposure to the parlous terms. Of late, he'd been giving the matter considerable thought, and had come to the conclusion that, like Pasteur's dairymaid[101] whose exposure to cowpox had rendered her immune to the more common pox, his previous incarceration in Swift's Lunatic Asylum ten years before had in some ways rendered him inoculated against the

101 There is no evidence that the celebrated chemist ever kept cows, a misapprehension that may have arisen due to the homophone 'Pasteur' / 'Pasture'.

present hazard. It had to be so! Look at poor Chapman, whose every thought was becoming more and more fraught. Look at Harry Hastings, who'd been packed off to a house in the country 'on medical grounds', when everyone knew it was because he could no longer tell the day of the week nor the number of pence in a shilling. And the attrition rate among Quibble's legion of delators and monitors, not to mention the many small-time crooks and graffiti artists who were a part of the distribution network, was the talk of the town.

But if there had been any room for complacency, if there had been the slightest feeling that Hackett alone of all his colleagues was standing squarely upon a linguistic terra firma, the encounter with Jim Kinch had blown that out of the water. Some months previously, Hackett had been moved to recall a German saw that ran 'whereof we cannot sprake, thereof we should not sprake'. It is a worthy principle. The exagmination (stet) that Hackett enjoyed with Jouisse O'Riley in the course of his brief sojourn in Paris must surely belong to this category. This is not because, as the wag said, "the unfacts, did we possess them, are too imprecisely few to warrant our certitude". It was variously witnessed and attested to. A man by the biblical name of Jonas attended, while another named McGrievous or McGravy[102] has provided a précis of incidentals pertaining to the encounter. There is also a fictionalised account in the occasional writings of the quixotic Pierre Meynard. So, temporarily setting aside the worthy principle, Meynard's

102 Probably Eirish modernist poet Thomas MacGreevey (1893-1967), whose advice to Jouisse not to put an apostrophe in the title of his work in progress — "that way, dilettantes who haven't read a single word of it can feel duly smug when others leave in the apostrophe" — has been entirely borne out.

dubitous account, in translation, is here included:

> *Lit obliquely in the corner, Hackett saw a lugubrious man in pirate's eyepatch whose weary, concave face gave the impression of a waning moon — waning, perhaps, after a life of music-tormented thought. Hackett turned to the Jonas beside him. 'I've come to encounter the Forger.'*
> *'For the millionth time, it's Forrager.'*
> *'Is he here?'*
> *'He Comes Everynight.'*
> *A moment later, the moonfaced author squinnied up at him. 'You're the journeylist?*
> *'Is it so obvious?*
> *'I herd rheumours.'*
> *'Hackett,' said Hackett, extending a hand. 'Ignatius.'*
> *'The ill-borne.'*
> *'So my father held.'*
> *'When he held yourself. And where,' continued the moon-faced man, 'd'you b'long?'*
> *Hackett considered. 'Ourland. I was borne there.'*

What is known with certainty is that several days later, R. M. Smyllie received an enigmatic telegram which read:

> *have seen Finnegan stop not Quinn stop acute Witzelsucht stop doesn't know when to stop*

We confine ourselves, then, to the visible results the ineffable meeting had upon our hero; to his various iterations back to the premises of *Plaiger & Co* on the rue de la Tour Noire; and, finally, to the unfortunate episode of the gendarmerie of the dreaded 7th Arrondissement. The first occasion upon which Hackett is known to have returned to the librarie occurred five mornings after his tryst in the Café du Cavelier (or Chevallier) Blanc. What he had been doing in the meantime is anybody's guess. The propriétaire of his pension scarcely saw him, except at breakfast (tarif compris). What is beyond dubit, however, is that he arrived at the librairie with a sense of purpose that had been singularly lacking on his previous visit. The complete public works of Puncher & Wattmann was a resource quite simply too rare — so valuable as to be invaluable — to pass up the opportunity; and the Eirishman entered and set the bell a-tinkle armed with an entire foolscap page upon which was drawn up a battalion of terms which he wished to look up.

The first of these, once the customary politesse that was de rigueur on such occasions had been exchanged with the propriétaire canadien, was, (how could it not be?), the enigmatic Quinn. Hackett was not for a moment put off by the erratum 'Qua-Qua' which appeared on the spine of volume X of the *Anglo-Hibernian Cyclopaedia* (1922). After all, on his previous visit, the same volume had yielded up a plethora of Royal Academies and even, if memory could be trusted, one Royal Acacademy, so that its contents clearly went beyond Qua-Qua. Hackett was momentarily distracted by that Royal Acacademy. *Could* memory be trusted? Could Quinn be persuaded to wait? With trembling hands and with more than one peek in the direction of the miniature propriétaire, who had again taken to the ladder, he leafed through the great, deckled octavo pages until he arrived at the entry for the Royal Academy of Anthropometry, paused, and then turned back a page.

It was not there!

Dizzy, but as yet undismayed, he flitted forwards. Royal Academy of Law… Royal Academy of Li… he slammed the book shut, releasing a billow of dust. He shut his eyes tight, and when they opened again, he threw them in the direction of the propriétaire. His passive, impassive brown back was hovering midway up the rungs, oblivious to the Eirishman's confusion. Which was it now that could not be trusted, his memory, which had always been reliable, or the book, which was tangibly present between his hands? 'Ok, It's ok,' he whispered to himself. He took one deep breath, inadvertently inhaling the dust that the tome had spored out, and then readdressed himself to his quest. Quinn. There was a Quin Friary, Co. Clare, ancestral burial place of the Thomond O'Briens; and there was a Quirk, Thady, the soi-disant 'honest' narrator of Maria Edgeworth's *Castle Backrent* (1800). But there was not a single entry for anyone by the name of Quinn. At one level this was hardly surprising. The Cyclopaedia had a publication date of 1922 and had been compiled, it was reasonable to suppose given its exhaustiveness and complexity, over the previous decade, so that the absence of any entry pertaining to a Quinn, real or imagined, who was now actively manipulating the strings of the Four Horsemen of the Apocryphal from some shadowy realm overseas, was easily explained. Still, it was a disappointment.

Hackett consulted his list. The next item he had marked down for perusal was (what else?) Contervoc. His finger slid along the spines and came to rest on Vol III, Büc-Cyc. Once again, he was distracted from his primary purpose. Instead he was reminded of the conundrum the Camsbridge fellow, Bertrand 'Jack' Russell, had outlined of having a catalogue that contained a list of catalogues which included themselves and another which didn't include themselves, and whether it should include itself in the former or the latter catalogue. Hackett's question was, seeing that Vol IV ran from Dab-Fly, whether Vol III, Büc-Cyc contained an entry for the Cyclopaedia itself and whether he, Hackett, would consequently experience the vertigo of mise-en-abyme. It did not and he did not. Well and good, that settled that. Contervoc… but halt! Not so fast. The correct title of the blooming thing wasn't the Cyclopaedia at all, it was the Anglo-Hibernian Cyclopaedia, and if that was to appear anywhere, it would have to appear in Vol I. As Arthur Guinness had asked, how was that for stout reasoning? He slid his finger back two spaces and selected the first volume, Aar-Aza. But there immediately surfaced a new problem, far more ticklish than the first. Strange as it may seem, the pages of this volume had not been cut! Now Vol III and Vol IX were not only deckled, they bore all the hallmarks of having been well thumbed. There were stains, there were dog-ears, there were even occasional marginalia and (criminally) underlinings in soft lead. He peeked into Vol II, and found that its neatly cut pages began with a brief entry for the Azoological Gardens, Phoenix Park, Dubilin: *After Chester (q.v.), the second purpose-built public menagerie in the known world*, before moving to Babington, William (1756-1833): *Physician at Guy's Hospital for the Incurables, amateur geologist and chemist, founder of the Royal Academy of Geometry, &c. &c.*; Babylone, Théâtre de, Montparnasse: *Left bank establishment founded by the Ouroboros Brotherhood (q.v.), known for premiering such Franco-Irish classics as Oscar Wilde's (q.v.) 'Salome'*. How came it, then, that no previous owner or casual consultant had ever deigned to look up a word beginning with A? It was passing strange…

The propriétaire canadien had begun a precarious descent of the wimbling ladder, a huge ledger tucked under one oxter — the left, as you looked at him. And it was all that Hackett could do not to ask the man whether some individual hadn't tampered with or even replaced volume IX, with its missing entry on the Royal Acacademy, since he'd last visited the shop a bare five days ago. He also had to fight the urge to know who the previous owner of the set had been, who had displayed such disdain for the letter A. But he held off. It was, as the fella said, 'un bon temps de se taire'. Other more pressing queries were bound to surface as he went through the items on his page of foolscap.

By the time Hackett readdressed the list, any thought of looking up Contervoc had long since escaped. Instead, his heart leapt as he encountered Mamalujo. He had no memory of having put it on the list, and yet there it was, and in his own handwriting. Though like de Valera he wouldn't have taken an oath on it. Curious, the tricks that the world seemed to be playing on him ever since he'd stepped into the Café du Cavelier Blanc. Vowing not to allow his imagination to be distracted by any more mice of whimsy, he selected the appropriate volume. As though preordained, it fell open at the following entry, which had been underscored (criminally) in pencil:

> Mamalujo. Acrostic, made up of the first letters of the pseudonyms of the four founding members of the Ouroboros Brotherhood (q.v.). Two of the Wild

> Geese[103] (q.v.), Matt Adams (thought to be Cpt Adam Boyd) and Johnny Naughton, aka 'the Bird', (unidentified), having fled their native country following defeat at Aughrim (q.v.), arrived in the Bretagne port of St. Malo on Good Friday, 1691. They were met there by Patrick Sarsfield's Italo-Swiss agent Lucca Bue, and by Marc Auteuil, a ship's chandler who originally hailed from Lyon, both of whom had crypto-Catholic sympathies. It was Johnny 'the Bird', a favourite of Quartermaster Quinn (qv), who was thought to have come up with the device of the self-consuming snake…

Once more the tome snapped shut. Quinn (qv)! For God's sake, Quinn (qv)! Hackett buried his face in his hands and stretched the skin to either side of his temples. He'd searched already, and in vain, for Quinn (qv)!

But nothing was certain anymore. His head already beginning to swim, Hackett readdressed the Qua-Qua volume. He opened it, and flicked again to the centre pages. Mercifully, nothing there had changed. The entry for Quinbus-flestrin (n.) a term coined by Jonathan Swift (q.v.) in answer to Thomas Hobbes' multitudinous description of the Leviathan, also the mythical Tower of Babel and thence, by extension, jargon for any skyscraper, was followed, as before, by Quin Friary, Co. Clare, ancestral burial place of the Thomond O'Briens; and then Quirk, Thady, soi-disant 'honest' narrator

103 After the siege of Limerick brought the Williamite war to an end, the so called Wild Geese fled to the continent. The many false trails they left in their wake to confound British spies and informers gave rise to a popular expression.

of Maria Edgeworth's pseudo-biographical retrospective *Castle Backrent* (1800). Reassured, disappointed, vindicated, deflated, and not a little punch-drunk, he determined on the spot to leave the consultation for another day.

Hackett's third trip to *Plaiger & Co* took place shortly after his second meeting with the man his Parisian acolytes were calling Jouisse, though there is no record extant of their exchange; his fourth trip after their third tête-à-tête (ibid.); and the fifth and final trip on the very Friday on which he was forced, by deportation order and dearth of francs, to catch the night-train to Boulogne in the hope of working his passage back to Engeland. If the intervals between each visitation were lessening according to the Law of Diminishing Returns, their duration was increasing in inverse proportion, so that their efficacy might be described by a Cartesian quadratic. But so too the exasperation that they occasioned him, complicating the mathematics. This browser was so increasingly self-absorbed and so increasingly uncommunicative that by the time he left on that final Friday morning, even the propriétaire canadien, who had seen all types down the years, shook his grey head and tut-tutted.

It was as he was crossing the Pont au Double onto the Île de la Cité, and pondering as he always did at such times the conundrum of the seven bridges of Königsburg, that Hackett was accosted by the plainclothes gendarme. Curiously, the man's plain clothes resembled nothing so much as the get-up that Quibble of the Yard had been wearing inside the COCK & BULL, although the Chief Inspector's French counterpart was mustachioed, considerably shorter and swarthier, so short indeed that his shoes barely peeped out from under the trench-coat. Also, rather than a briar, he was sucking on a Gauloise. They exchanged words, though nothing is known of what was said, nor even in what language the exchange occurred. The long and the short of it was that Hackett accompanied the undersized Gaul to an unmarked Citroën, black, that was idling on the Quai de l'Horloge. From there they drove circuitously alongside the Jardin des Tuileries, they traversed the Place de la Concorde, muttled over the Pont Alexandre III, puttled along the Boulevard des Invalides and parked outside the Quartier Général on the Rue de Babylone.

How was it that a journalist of Eirish extraction and disreputable appearance, who was not only for once minding his own business but was by all accounts increasingly laconic, not to say autistic, had come to the attention of the redoubtable Language Police of the 7th Arrondissement? It is not clear. Records record the plainclothes detective merely as *. If further records of the arraignment were kept, they were removed or destroyed or misplaced during the dark interlude when preoccupation gave way to occupation.

All that is known with any degree of certainty is that Hackett was handed ses orders de marche.

CHAPTER THE FOURTEENTH

in which Hackett encounters a policeman dressed in motley, and is led by playing cards to the entrance of a labyrinth

Everywhere was bustle and calumption as the good people of Logdon prepared for the great annual blow-out of Bowberry Jack. And nowhere was more calumptious than the kitchens of *Brigid Waddington's Boarding House for Gentlemen* where Urs'la, the cook, who had taken quite a shine to one of her lodgers, held sway. She had a wide range of pots to potter in and a wide range to put the pots on. Morning to night, amidst great billows of steam and pepper, the din could be heard of plates, pans, pots, ladles, scullery and cutlery, so that one might have been led to believe that a great feast was being prepared to rival the mythical Fleá Bhricriú rather than for the entertainment of a mere handful of lodgers.

Hackett sat listlessly by the window. Ever since his trip to the continent, a great lassitude had overtaken him. Today he was idly watching as Oedipus, the landlady's tabby, rippled up the wall, in defiance of gravity. This contrary movement, and the way the cat slowed into a stroll, gave Hackett the unpleasant sensation that, for a few moments, the frames on the world's projector had gone into reverse. From atop the wall, the cat was watching him, unimpressed. It was as though it too sensed the lassitude that had seized Hackett of late, and the half-heartedness with which his mind now trotted after imaginary mice down inconclusive corridors that proliferated rhizomatically. Was it Bishop Berkeley of Cloyne who'd declared that a cat could look at a king? But suppose it had a mind to look at the sleeping red king out of the story. And suppose, in his dream, it was His Highness who opened the box, the one in which that German physicist had locked the cat that was neither alive nor dead until such time as curiosity looked at it, what then? It was like the eternal conundrum of the chicken and the egg and which came first, the egg that grew up into the chicken or the chicken that laid him. Or her (did an egg have a gender *ab ovo*?). It'd be easier to put Humpty-Dumpty back together again than to crack that particular one. Be a different matter if it was a handicap race, like Achilles and the tortoise. After all, you could hardly expect an egg to outrun a chicken. Unless it was downhill. And it didn't roll in an arc. Of course there was the annual race between chicken and egg at the festival of Bowberry Jack... 'You'll be back in good time for the perty, won't you?' The landlady's abrupt question bustled into his thoughts, knocking them for six.

'What? Oh! What time is it set for again?'

'Six a'clock sherp. I swear to you Mr Hackett, you'd forget your head if it wasn't screwed unto you!' She squinnied up her eye. It was no harm that her white-headed guest was at last going to venture out into God's fresh air, but it'd be constitutionally against Brigid Waddington's nature to let on she was pleased about it. 'Where's this you were off to again?'

'Covenant Garden.'

'Covenant Gerden? Without any class of a costume? Ere you mad?'

Hackett was not mad. But neither could it be denied that he'd been waxing forgetful of late. Though this would be his third year living in this corner of Engeland, and in spite of the steam and calumption which was even now billowing forth from the scullery, it had quite slipped his mind that today was the annual wassail of Bowberry Jack. Outside on the street, and particularly as one approached the great free-for-all of Covenant Garden, costumes would reign. But it was too late now to concern himself with such frippery.

Since his return from Boulogne early in February, Hackett found himself wallowing in a despond which he found impossible to slough off. In the first few days out of Dover, it was different. Diametrically so. Then he was animated by a desperate energy, the sort of manic vigour which is said to precede a fall into depression. He was moved by a wild hope, and the hope was this: somewhere, in the myriad second-hand bookshops of Logdon, he was sure to come across another complete set of the public works of Puncher & Wattmann (1922). This obsession gripped him with all the fever or fervour that the pursuit of the white whale had once gripped Ishmael. Or Ahab was it? In any event, for the first few days following his return from France for lack of francs, he scoured the boroughs of Campden, of Greenwitch, of Charish Cross for every purveyor of rare and antiquated publications. And the sufficient reason for this sudden and indefatigable obsession?

At some point, as he sat on the Paris to Boulogne night-train it came to him in a flash that Quinn (qv) was not the same as Quinn (q.v.), and if memory could be trusted, Quinn (qv) had been the pertinent entry. What Quinn (qv) suggested was not the well-known abbreviation *quod vide*, which would surely have been written Quinn (q.v.). It was rather that the recondite name should be looked up using the Roman delettering of Qvinn! So blinding was this insight that for three days and as many nights it robbed our hero of all sleep, and as he stood at the prow of the coal-scuttle that chuggled under Dover's chalk cliffs, it was all he could do not to leap overboard and swim the remaining half-a-league. What held him fast was the perennial dubit, could memory be trusted?

For three days he scoured every bookshop, new and, in particular, second-hand and antiquarian, in which from the time of Defoe the great metropolis glories. He leafed through shelves and entire libraries of books, hardback and paperback; volumes, editions and tomes of every age, size, colour, texture, condition and complexion; and when he had exhausted these he pored through catalogues, indices, fascicles, files and appendices; he delved through stacks of old journals, maps and broadsheets; he rifled reams of old reviews, broadsides, lampoons, circulars, encyclicals and periodicals; he upset music-scores by the quire; and he quizzed every owner, proprietor, shopkeeper, merchant, monger or helper so that, as the saying goes, no stone might be left unturned. It was as if the great Cyclopaedia had never existed! And on the fourth night, he slept like one of the dead.

Why was it, it might reasonably be asked, that a dubious publication dating from 1922 and whose information, as has been noted, had indubitably been gleaned over the decades previous to 1922, acquired such a hold on the Hackett imagination? What secret, pertaining to the present plague of incomprehensibility, could its arcane pages possibly contain? What clue might lie buried in its yellowing octavo pages? In answer, it is essential to grasp the nature of the questor. From the very first time he carried a schoolbag, the Christian Brother's pupil had inclined towards a cyclical view of history and her betrayals. Though there was not a misogynistic bone in his young body, he was by no means the first Eirish schoolboy to have noted that the uxorial myopia that had impelled Adam to place his trust in Eve found its echo five millennia later[104] when Dermot McMurrough named his daughter Aoife in her dubitous honour before giving her hand to that usurper de Clare; nor how the sainted Parnell's downfall was precipitated by the faithless wife of Cpt O'Shea, and how that fall was prefigured by the liaison of Claire what's-this-her-name-was and Cpt Molineux on the stage; which itself repeated the original sin of exogamy of Paris and the duplicitous Helen; not to mention of stout Cortez and Malinche, that wanton *traduttora traditora.*

Perhaps it was inevitable that a race whose foundational text was the Leabhar Gabhálaighe, the Book of Invasions penned long before the arrival of the Normans, Gallowglasses, Elizabethans, Swadlers, Parleymentarians, Williamites, Red-coats, or Black and Tans, should incline to a circular view of history. The same obsession was visible not just in the circles, spirals and gyres with which the Gaels adorned their manuscripts, torcs and reliquaries from time immemorial; it was there in the very architecture: in the Dúns and the Raths

104 To be accurate 5173 years later, according to the calculations of Bishop Ussher of Trinity College Dubilin.

and the ring-forts; in the disc the Celts stuck onto the cross to make it more palatable; in the monastic bell-towers that stood up like stone moon-rockets long before Mr Wells had dreamed up such contraptions; and in the round burial chambers of Howth and Knowth and Dowth.

But there was something deeper than a weary historical determinism at work in Hackett's water. He had, as they say, imbibed with his mother's milk a racial veneration for the written word, for nothing is more venerable to the Eirishman than the focal scríobhte. To Hackett, who had if you looked at it one way made an entire career out of the focal scríobhte, that veneration bordered upon the idolatrous. To his mind, as to his late father's, Gutenberg was the Melquiades of the modern age, and all printed matter, even the most frivolous, had about it the magical quality of the rune. Old fonts were like sanctified knucklebones, and might be persuaded to yield up a secret to any disciple who treated them with the appropriate degree of reverence, perseverance and devotion.

As to Clarke, Fleming, Mulcahy and Sangster, the fearsome foursome appeared to be in some way linked with the Ouroboros Brotherhood and its clandestine press. If memory served (the usual caveat applying), the various Wild Geese (q.v.) who'd founded the society were supplemented by at least one French or Swiss sect devoted to deciphering Gnostic and cabbalistic texts. Now from there, it was a small enough leap to imagine that the four latter-day apocryphals were modelling themselves upon the original four founders. After all, hadn't they borrowed the acronym 'Mamalujo' to designate their present brand of mayhem? So that you could argue that some of what was contained in Puncher & Wattmann's *Anglo-*

Hibernian Cyclopaedia of 1922 was likely a future history in the way that the Book of Daniel in the Bible was said to be one. Or Isaiah was it? Wasn't there an Eirish precedent for that already in the case of Kilpatrick, (or Madden?), he that was only letting on to be the traitor?

Such were the thoughts, as fantastic as they were convoluted, of Ignatius Hackett as he set out for Covenant Garden that fine morning. He was already in the vicinity of Bow Street, which is to say he was all but there, when he experienced for the umpteenth time that curious sensation that he was being watched. He looked across the crowded road into the stream of revellers, strollers, flaneurs, passers-by, pickpockets, footpads, charades, mummers, chancers and tumblers and sure enough, he caught a pair of close-set eyes just before they flitted away. They were close-set in the cap and bells of a jester who was hovering in a conspicuous manner in the vicinity of a lamp post overgrown with colourful bunting; and in no uncertain terms Hackett knew those eyes had been staring directly at him. Nodding, smirking, shaking his head, he negotiated the calumptious crowd and put his shoulder to the lamp post as though one of them were propping up the other. 'Well it's many a time,' said he, 'I've seen a fool dressed up as a policeman, but not until this day a policeman dressed up as a fool.'

Quibble's eyes, for they were none other's, flitted back to the front, the particoloured get-up lending them a comic aspect out of all character with their owner. 'You'll glow my cover,' he growled, his postbox lips not separating.

'What has you in mufti where motley is worn? You're not about to tell me it's the Lords of Misrule you're after? Only

I thought the whole point of carnival, besides driving up the price of eggs, was it was meant to be a time of lawless topsy-turveydom. Or have I it arse-ways?'

The Chief Inspector was in no humour to be jocular. 'Your griend Ж is gery quiet these days,' he gruntled through rigid lips. Oho! thought Hackett. It's like that is it? Straight onto the offensive? He allowed his eyes to be momentarily distracted by a passing Pierrot who had the distinction of having one blackened face at the back of his head and another at the front, and what was unusual was that it was the eye on the backward face that threw him a wink. 'I also hear Ж's been laying low this weather,' quoth he, temporarily disarmed.

'The question is, why has he geen laying low of late?'

'You'd have to ask him that, officer. All I've to say on the subject is **wovon man nicht sprechen kann, darüber muss man schweigen.**'

'German?'

'Austrian.'

'"**Schweigen**"?'

'Mum's the word.'

Quibble was not impressed. 'Maybe what I should ask Ж is, has he fallen out of favour with his paymasters.'

'His *pay*-masters? And who might they be, pray?'

'It wasn't yesterday I was born, Hackett. I have a nose for this sort of thing.'

'That's news to me. I mean about paymasters. That you have a nose is as plain as... well, you see what I mean.' He squinnied at him, screwing up his face to suppress the unseasonal smirk that the wimbling coxcomb was occasioning. 'Still, Quibble, you're about the last character I was expecting to see dressed up like Feste the Fool. Can I ask you something?' Quibble's expression neither invited nor refused the query. 'Who *is* Bowberry Jack? In all the time I'm here I've never got a straight answer. The landlady was saying to me it's a tradition dates back centuries, only no-one remembers exactly how it began except of course it has something to do with a Catholic plot.'

'Is that what she told you?'

'The Eirish wars, says she, though that hardly nails it down. Something to do with the big-enders and little-enders, that lost one king his head and another his kingdom. But sure she's half cracked if you ask me. I don't remember learning any of that in school.'

'I thought you Eirish were supposed to be obsessed with your history.' Quibble's eyes flitted left and right, the exclamatory furrow between them rising. 'The egg,' quoth the inspector, guardedly, 'is an allegory. I thought you Eirish were meant to be good at allegories.'

'Allegedly.' At that moment, as though it had been ordained, and who knows, perhaps it had been, a giant Bowberry Jack blundered into the lamp post and perned between them, wobbling like a dying gyroscope on legs far too thin and equivocal to support the ovine volume in its dizzy gyrations. A great trail of bunting began to ravel about the great egg and between the pair, and what with the wobbles and the revellers that were drawn like the tail of a kite behind, the calumption was so great and frenzied that journalist and jester were spun apart and lost sight of one another in centrifugal confusion.

Hackett had been disingenuous. Not insofar as Bowberry

Jack was concerned, for there are as many explanations, guesses, tales and myths to explain the origin of that Lenten tradition as there are pieces to an egg that's had a great fall. On the occasion of his antepenultimate visit but one to the Parisian bookshop on the rue de la Tour Noire, he'd consulted the invaluable Puncher & Wattmann on the very subject, and found that amongst the various explanations, the most coherent was that Bowberry Jack had been the name of a giant canon that had been used in the siege of Coalchester during the Civil War — the Engelish, that is, for Eirish wars were by long tradition civil. Fair enough, except that a footnote read: 'presumably the artillery piece was named for Bowberry Jack (q.v.).' Undaunted by a queasy sensation of *mise-en-abyme*, Hackett had, by an exhaustive process of trial and error based upon the elimination of possibilities by date and by cross-reference, narrowed this (q.v.) down to two further entries. One suggested the legendary poacher who had hidden out in Nothingham Forest at the time that King John (q.v.) was involved in his Eirish wars, and who had received the nickname either because his doublet was the colour of bowberries or because he had been born on the feast of Bowberry Jack (q.v.). Though this was the more likely of the two entries, it was the other that had gripped Hackett's imagination. This read: breed of Deise chicken, now extinct, a pair of either adult birds or eggs which was introduced to Waterfjord (q.v.) by a wine-merchant named Qvin (qv) around the same year as the Black Death (q.v.), and which was noted for its miraculous prolificality as a layer. A footnote read: its name is said to be a confused conflation of the '*nombre reversé*' cry used to ward off attacks by the manxome Jabberwock (q.v.) with the latter's fabled nemesis, the mythical beast having been beheaded by Qvin's remote ancestor, Jacques 'le Bâtard' (fils), in the eponymous ballad. So that a link had been established, buried though it might be in a footnote of dubitous validity in a dusty and possibly apocryphal volume of a publication that for the present persisted only in the picture-house of memory, between Quinn (or Qvin) and the day of wassail that was erupting all around him. Deep in his water, the journalist sensed both the imminence and the immanence of a discovery.

What was absent from any and all of the above explanations was the merest screed to connect these literary Bowberry Jacks with the anti-Catholic bias which Hackett's landlady insisted had underlain the feast day from its inception. Though on the other hand, it might be supposed that at least some of the defenders of Coalchester at the time of the Engelish Civil War may have been crypto-Catholics, always provided that it was the Roundheads who'd laid siege to the city and the Cavileers who'd defended it. But where did that leave Qvin (q.v.), and how might he be connected to the Quinn (qv) whom Hackett was desperately trying to track down? A felicitous, not to say fortuitous, thought had struck him in this regard the previous night when he'd been held awake by the maleficent mewling of Oedipus. The cyclopaedists had had an entry for Quinbus-flestrin (n.). It was Dean Swift's coinage for the Leviathan, commonwealth or man-mountain, and by extension it was slang for a skyscraper. But, suppose for a moment that 'Quinbus-' were a common prefix. Suppose it were the ablative, in the plural, of Quin or Qvin, allowing this to be a third declension Latin substantive, and the ablative covering the usual cases of 'by, with or from'. One could then gloss the prefix 'by or from Quinn', or even, if it were ablative absolute, 'after Quinn', (though why plural, unless there was more than one Quin or Qvin?).

God's teeth, if it were today and he had the Puncher & Wattmann in his hands, it'd be Qv he'd consult all right! It was this cat's or cats' cradle of thoughts which had set our hero on his journey to Covenant Garden that morning, and which entangled him once again as he gyred and gimbled through the calumptious crowd. At that very moment, a human-sized spoon made down on the Bowberry Jack and the latter, in holy terror, began to teeter and to shundle away on risible legs. At every turn, he was jostled, jabbed and gyrated by the madding throng. 'Crabble the Jack! Crabble the Jack!' the crowd crowed, to egg on the garmungling spoon and the spoon, his concave face contracted into grim determination, wimbled through them in pursuit.

Even if he'd had no wish to move, which was not the case, Hackett would have been swept along in the eddying river of revellers, and the last he saw before he was debouched into the plaza of Covenant Garden was the coxcomb of the secret policeman wimbling past in contraflow. He found himself standing abruptly amidst children. Before him was a striped tent with an opening in which Mr Punch, a cudgel in his arms, was in a dubitous parley with a constable and, of all things, a crocodile in a bonnet. The curious thing was that although the argument was little more than the vibrations of comb and paper, the miniature audience understood its every modulation, and squealed with delight at every blow it occasioned. Hackett stood for some minutes, bedazzled at the spectacle of the puppet policeman belabouring the puppet crocodile in a bonnet, and the puppet Mr Punch the puppet Judy whose baby resembled a banbh. He was so absorbed in the play that he failed entirely to notice the two playing-cards approach, and so was surprised when either elbow was gently taken and he was ushered away by a three of clubs and a knave of hearts.

He put up no resistance, and was led by three and knave to the gate of a great top, inside of which there was a funfair. The three arrived just in time to see a rabbit disappear into the doorway. Before the opening stood a man whose head was naturally as hairless as an egg, and who'd had the head painted all in white, but for several cracks sketched in charcoal black. These emanated, as it were, from a wooden spoon that was by some contrivance attached obliquely at an angle of 45° to the crown, and the arrangement was set upon a great white ruff that ran around the man's neck and sustained a bowl shaped collar, so that the whole was a perfect representation of an egg set upon an egg cup in the act of being topped. It could not but bring a smile to whomever saw it. And looking into the large eyes, Hackett found that he had been expecting the very man. 'You, here?' he said.

'You, here,' echoed the egg. Teddy Mulcahy. The likeness was inescapable.

'You brought me here. Or your cards did.' Hackett drew back his shoulders and squinnied impressively. 'Why?'

'To enter the labyrinth.'

'And what will I find there?'

'The answer.'

'The answer to what?'

'That's the question.'

And there we will momentarily leave the journalist, and

will go in pursuit of the hapless Quibble, caught up as we left him in a contrary impulse of the crowd.

The Chief Inspector had not been dissimulating when he'd brought up the subject of Ж's recent reticence. It had not escaped his attention, for he had a Cartesian nose adept at spotting correlations, that the journalist had scarcely put pen to paper from the moment that Fleming had been arraigned. That Hackett was fully aware of the detention within hours of its occurring Quibble had cleverly elicited from him in the **COCK & BULL** without in any way disclosing his own hand. He was a dab hand at that sort of play. If he had a Cartesian nose for spotting correlations, it was complemented by another Cartesian propensity: *dubito, ergo sum.* What's more, he'd discovered two further facts, again at the cost of revealing nothing of consequence: Hackett was going on, or was letting on to be going on, a wild goose chase to the continent; Hackett believed, or was letting on to believe, that he was being followed.

What had transpired on the continent was anyone's guess. You just couldn't rely on the French to cooperate, even (and especially!) when it was demonstrably in their own interests to coöperate. (And still, des Cartes was a Frenchman.) There was a rumour that Hackett had been carousing with Eirish undesirables, expats who hung out up around Montmarte and fired occasional literary sallies at the old enemy. There were rumours that he'd been arraigned by the Language Police and deported, though how like the French neither to corroborate nor deny the rumour. One way or another, he'd been a deal less troublesome since his return, and that was a development to be welcomed. Might it be concluded that it had been Aloysius Fleming all along who'd been feeding the journalist with titbits?

Nor had Quibble given anything away just now. The frustrating thing was that just as he was preparing a particularly clever play to elicit what precisely Hackett was doing here, and how much he knew about why he, Quibble, was here, the stupid bally egg had spun in between them and the pressure of the mob had swept them away and apart. The play would have to wait. For the moment, he had more pressing concerns.

That very morning, there'd been an anonymous tip-off. Now, normally Chief Inspector Quibble was not a man who put much stock in anonymous tip-offs. But this one was the sort of tip-off which the Chief Inspector was not prepared to dismiss outright. The possible pay-off was too tempting. He might be dressed as a fool, but he'd have been a greater fool to have ignored it, even though the provenance of the anonymous message was Ealing Broadleaf. And the word was, on that very feast of Bowberry Jack, in this very fair at Covenant Garden, the most dangerous man in the realm was slated to put in an appearance.

A mystery man.

A man known only by a cypher, ***Q?***

CHAPTER THE FIFTEENTH

in which is revealed who it was Hackett encountered at the heart of the Hall of Mirrors

Whether deported or not, having departed the continent, Hackett's humour had swung wildly from elation to melancholy, from frenzy to lassitude. No more were Ж's pinesses the talk of the intelligentsia, no more did the scurril articles of Myles Gloriosus Philpott scandalise Dubilin's gentile society. But he was still active. He was still in full command of all the resources of logic and language. He was still seen from time to time around Logdon Town.

Then came the feast of Bowberry Jack. We have accompanied this stalwart into the frenzy of Covenant Garden, where he was met by the risible Quibble in the coxcomb of a Fool. We have seen him whisked away by a train of fillamumbling schoolboys, and we've watched him drawn like a trump by *force majeure* to the very entrance of the Funfair. There, he was met by a character in the guise of a boiled egg set upon a plate, who promised him that at the heart of the labyrinth he would meet his destiny. Long and hard had Hackett stared into the eyes of Teddy Mulcahy. What lay inside? That was the question.

He paid his 10/6 entrance fee to a buck-toothed character in a top hat, and stepped with trepidation inside the Funfair. Just as he did, the egg-and-spoon whispered 'hall of mirrors' into his ear, and disappeared. Not for the first time, a horrible sense of déjà vu seized the hero. Without even looking up, he knew that that particular hall was through the farthest left of the three doors facing him; in heraldic terms, the most sinister. He entered. As Hackett advanced through the maze of wimbling mirrors and watched his myriad reflections stretch and squash like India-rubber, distort and distend in the manner of a melodeon, multiply and divide like a test in arithmetic, he began to replay in his mind the various possible answers to that great conundrum, *Who is Quinn*? One by one, he eliminated the suspects. It was not Teddy Mulcahy. It was not little Willy Clarke. It was not Fleming, Aloysius. It was not Agatha Sangster. It was not the Forger Finnegan. In the Operations Room of Semantics, it was bluntly stated that Quinn the puppet master must be abroad. And yet, that answer did not satisfy, either. True, there was a Noo Yawk lawyer by name of Quinn who had been hoarding every class of funny manuscript. But the lawyer had been given the once over by Edgar Hoover® himself, and had been found to be clean. So where did that leave him? What Minotaur, half Eirishman and half Eirish bull, might be awaiting him now at the centre of this crazed, minatory labyrinth?

Hackett hesitated momentarily, caught between two facing mirrors whose receding corridors multiplied to infinity, consistent with the law of diminishing returns, their twin perspectives. Was it de Selby said that, since light travels at a finite speed, to look into such an arrangement is to look back in time, so that if one's sight were good enough, and the resolution strong enough, one might discern the child that was the father to the man? Gripped by a momentary sensation of mise-en-abyme he clamped shut his eyes, and groped his way around the corner. Thus, blindly, did Ignatius Hackett come face to face with the face that had been, from the very beginning, awaiting the encounter. It took the journalist a moment to decode the opaque glasses that flashed above the mirthless grin. The epiphany came like a blow to the solar plexus. 'You!' he calloohed, when reason, like a murmuration of startled starlings came back to roost. Hackett looked from Cheshire grin to glasses, from glasses to Cheshire grin, and thence into the geometry of looking-glasses in which grin and glasses reflected and diffracted, refracted and divided, till it seemed that all the world was nothing but glasses and grins. 'How is it possible?' he cried, aghast.

'Hoy is it *not*?' a myriad mouths retorted. This, thought Hackett, must be how a fly feels, trapped in a web, seeing its reflection in the thousand eyes of the spider. 'But… *you*!' For surely the figure standing before him — the silhouette that had been concealed behind the bedazzling lights of Room 404 — was none other than the great R. M. Smyllie himself! All he lacked was poncho and floppy hat. 'Who were yoy expecting?' The man — bizarrely, it was as though the figure were surrounded by dancing afterimages — advanced the few steps sufficient to touch Hackett's forearm, as though the contact might, Thomas-like, dispel any remaining dubit. In the kaleidoscope of mirrors a thousand Smyllies, or O'Briens, advanced or receded, depending on whether it was the obverse or the reverse of the figure that was trapped in the reflected prism. A thousand Hacketts shrank from the touch. 'Yoy luke like yav seen a ghost so you doy.'

A dubit was bothering Hackett, persistent as a gnat. The trick of the man's accent was in no wise Sligo-Scots. 'You're not Smyllie?'

'Smeyly?' the cat's grin beamed. 'Smeyly's the real neem, aye. O'Brain is hereditary. It goos with the Diractorship so it does.'

'Not... *Bertie* Smyllie?'

'George is may neem. Bartie Smeyly's the furst cousin so he is.'

But... how is it *possible*?'

'Hoy is it passible.' This was not a question, rhetorical or otherwise. It was a restatement, the verbal equivalent of the reflections that on all sides surrounded them. 'I teek it what you mean bay that is, hoy is it passible that the Diractor of an Academy whose sole raison d'être is to presarve and toy act as the guardian of the Kang's Angelish can come toy halp spread a coynterfit langage. Is that what you're aboyt, sir?' Hackett's open palms made one of those gestures, repeated to infinity about the chamber, which even reversed in a mirror is universal language for assent. 'Give me leave to ask yoy, Masther Hackett. Have ye heard tal of a mon be the neme of Adward Janner as furst pleed aroynd with coy pox.'

'Jenner!' calleyed Hackett, knucking his fingers, though he'd've sworn it was Louis Pasteur had first played around with the cow pox. 'Janner, aye. What that mon discovered was a vary important pranciple. And the pranciple that mon discovered was the pranciple of vaccineetion. Give me leave, Masther Hackett, to ask yoy another quastion.' Hackett repeated the open gesture, and all about him reflected Hacketts repeated the repeated gesture. 'Whey were yoy… choosen?'

'Chosen.' Pause. 'You mean, why was I chosen by the Eirish Consular Service? Or why was I chosen by Bertie Smyllie.'

'Hoy came it that the Diractor of the Academy of Langage asked his Ayrish furst cousin to halp him oyt in luring you over hare? Ay'll tell ye. Twas cousin Bartie had the notion to tackle your vanity so it was. Twas Bartie Smeyly took scissors and peyste to old editions of the *Ayrish Tames* and concocted those wee articles that entaced yoy over here.'

'Bertie Smyllie was the bogus Ж?'

'Bartie Smeyly was the boogus Ж. Who alse had such antimate knowledge of your steyle?'

Helplessly, haplessly, a thousand appalled journalists looked on. 'But I'm still not following.'

'Not follying whey were yoy alloyed to anther into the Academy in the first pleece? Would another journalist not have done just as gude?' All about the labyrinth, the thousand Hacketts scrummelled their heads. None of them hit upon an answer. 'Did it naver occur to yoy that another journalist mayt have succumbed to any number of those wee problems, apheesia, athambia, parataxis, that beset the practationers of your treed at the bast of taymes? And noy he'd be in contact wath contervoc and what have ye on a deely beesis! Look at your freynd Chopman for God's seek! But yoy, sir, had already been throy that particular mill, whenever yoy were commatted to Swaft's Mad Hice. Yoy were layk the malkmeed of Masther Janner that had alraddy had the coy pox. Are ye with me, sir?'

A thousand Hacketts nodded, in unison. A thousand

O'Briens removed their spectacles and wiped their two thousand lenses in a thousand pocket handkerchiefs. It was an invitation to pose a question. 'Then you at least never believed I was Rooney?' None of the myriad O'Briens deemed the question worthy of a glance up from the spectacles. 'I'm not the only journalist that fell into dysphasia. Far from it.'

'Truy. But alloy me to put this to yoy, Masther Hackett. Three quastions.' He raised three strubbly fingers and counted them off singly. 'Namber One. High many other journalists can commond column-anches in the Ayrish *ond* the Angelish Tames? For it was important that Masther Davaleera mate not be yoysed as a back door for any varbal contamineetion. Namber Toy. High many other journalists still yoyse an antique tape-wrater that has neither mechonical rotary spellcheck nor rudimenthary boogus word detactor? And namber Three. High many journalists have navcr learned short-hond?'

This was the second blow to Hackett's solar-plexus. A number of fragments of knowledge began to fall into place, like so many pieces of a fallen egg. It was long known that printers and typesetters were immune to the panoply of verbal pathogens which so plagued the writing professions. Setting out their backwards type and reading it right to left as though it were in a looking-glass rendered the most parlous effects harmless. Thus too the complacency of the Germans at the height of the Phoneme War when it came to the possibility of semantic contamination. Where the French shared a twenty-six letter alphabet with their Engelish cousins, the Germans could hide behind their precious scharfes ß. Wasn't the eighteen letter tree alphabet the very reason why Dinneen's Gaedhilic would emerge pristine? And had it not been shown that the terms of contervoc lost much of their vigency when moved between media? 'So then,' he concluded, horrified, 'in the hands of other journalists...' A thousand nodding O'Briens invited him to pursue the thought. 'The fact that they jot in short-hand... amounts to a form of *translation*?'

'It robs the tarms of the holf of their vagency.' A thousand O'Briens replaced their polished lenses and nodded. 'On average, each and avery transleetion halves the half-lafe.'

Hackett closed his eyes. There was something goading him. It was a dark demon. The fork with which it began to prod was pointy indeed. 'But then,' he gasped, beginning to grasp the point, 'you wanted me to... *spread* the pandemonium!'

'Ay thought ye knyoy.'

'But that makes no sense!'

'Go back,' sprake O'Brien, almost kindly, 'to Adward Janner.'

The balls of Hackett's palms covered the orbitals of his eyes and began to push slow circles until the pressure generated entire constellations of sparks. In fits and snatches, his eyes still bedazzled with their own internal pyrotechnics, he heard the Hereditary Director of the Royal Acacademy of Letters declare how he had from the first anticipated, then incorporated, and finally exacerbated the inimical efforts of the four Lords of Misrule. 'It's obvious to a blaind man,' he declared, 'that another Yurpean war is ammanant, for all their talk of a-peacement! And ay tell yoy, all the bombs and all the insanduries will have nathin on the linguastic meeyhem that's aboyt to be released. It was may seecred dyuty to put averyone on their toes. The Home Sacretary, and Semontics, and Special Bronch, and Em Ay Fayve...'

'And me…?' squeaked Hackett, who felt as a mouse must when pounced upon by pangúr bán. He was at last beginning to understand the trap that had been laid for him from the very first step he'd taken outside Needles Nugent's dive on Lower Dorset St.

'Yoy pleed your part.'

The black demon was by this juncture having a field-day with his pitchfork. So all along he'd been a patsy, a dupe actively spreading the false terms of contervoc throughout the realm at the behest of this nefarious Ulsterman! A dubit scarpered across the labyrinth of Hackett's mind, and he pounced on it. 'If what you say is true, why did Bertie Smyllie send me off on a Wild Goose chase to Paris?'

'Ay asked him toy, is whey. Af you ever want the Franch to come to your halp, it's no gude asking them diractly. No, sir. It's no gude traying to convance them it's in their anterests toy. With the Franch, yoy have to go aboyt it claver. We've no idea what hugger-mugger Jam Kanch is up toy, but it bodes no gude. Pointless asking our Franch coynterparts diractly to keep an eye on him. But send yoy over, incognito? That worked a treat, so it did!'

Hackett considered. 'So then,' he sprake, pulling his palms away from his eyes and allowing the constellation of sparks to clear. 'You're Quinn?' The words carried only the barest suspicion of an interrogation mark. There was a hiss, which approximated to a mirthless laugh. A thousand O'Briens, or George Smyllies, shook their slow heads. Two thousand lenses flashed opaquely. 'No, Masther Hackett. You've not understood me.'

'I don't think I have.' The journalist glanced tiredly about the prison of reflecting prisms. 'So who *is* Quinn?'

A thousand grins all but grew mirthful.

'The mon in the marror.'

VOLUME THREE

THE DARK[105] CONTINENT

105 'The usage is metaphoric rather than photometric.' — Gleason op cit.

CHAPTER THE FIRST

in which an overview is given of the IBM Mark-4 'Speakeasy' programme which so brutally and efficiently decontaminated the Engelish language

That year, as Europe hurtled inexorably toward another war to end all wars, the feast of Bowberry Jack had fallen on the Ides of March. From this date on, not a single article appeared under the sign of Ж; from the pen of Myles Gloriosus Philpott there flowed not a single pinesse. A solitary telegram survives from this period. Addressed to R. M. Smyllie c/o The **PALACE BAR**, Dubilin 2, its contents are hopelessly garbled: 'raphael mai amech izabi almi stop Ж stop.' Was it an apology? An admonition? It may never be known. Stepping from the Hall of Mirrors into the wan daylight, Hackett disappeared so entirely from literary Logdon that it was as if the ground under Covenant Garden had opened up and swallowed him.

The great wassail of Bowberry Jack of '39 in fact marks the high watermark of the existential threat to the Engelish language that had been unleashed on it so many months before. A number of factors come together to explain this decline, not least the fact adduced that from this date, not a single article appeared under the sign of Ж. Whether or not one takes at face value the revelations offered by the hereditary director of the Royal Acacademy of Letters, the point remains that no more did his pinesses bear the bogus terms like spores throughout the realm. Quinn, if he ever existed, had vanished into thin air. Then there was this to consider. At the time that Hackett had been hauled into Semantics just prior to his jaunt over to the City of Light, it was apparent that the redoubtable Quibble was closing in on all four Lords of Misrule. One was already detained, albeit by CID, and if he was subsequently released without charge, much to Quibble's chagrin, it remained the case that the faces of all four felons were widely published in Wanted posters throughout the great metropolis. There was an immediate and proportionate diminution in their nefarious activity, so much so that Quibble anticipated they would take advantage of the great wassail, during which the world went abroad in disguise, to go abroad in disguise. It was a forgone conclusion.

Last but by no means least, it is worth pausing our story to gain an overview of the steps undertaken by HM Government to come to terms with the verbal contamination. During that first long, hot summer, the Phoneme War had given way to a more general panic, and Operation Babel was soon in full swing. If one considered the dreaded delators who lurked at every corner, the blacked out words in the newspapers, the close monitoring of radio transmissions and telephone exchanges, the quarantined villages, the denuded shelves in the public libraries, the travel restrictions, the random vocabulary checks, the suspicion levelled at every foreigner, turnpike-traveller, chav, spiv and itinerant salesman, the occasional hysteria of book burnings in which the classic Eirish texts featured prominently, and to compound matters, the emergence of two distinct dialects of the counterfeit cant, one to either side of Watling St, one might have been forgiven for thinking that the disarticulation of the United Kingdom was at hand.

Yet Seymour Doolittle had been correct when he adduced the instability of the SUI numbers of the falsely coined terms. Their consequent diminution according to the Law of Diminishing Returns, with half-lives measurable in weeks or fortnights rather than months or years, meant that the ravages consequent upon their propagation were inherently temporary, more akin to those of a summer cold than to a pandemic such as the Spanish Influenza. If, to begin with, the Phoneme War had yielded to a more general panic, as the Old Man of '38 surrendered his sickle to the mewling infant of '39, when the short-lived nature of the semantic disruptions and the restoration of the status quo in accordance with Le Châtelier's Principle became apparent, this panic was displaced first by acceptance, then by insouciance, then by complacence, then by irreverence, and thence by this declension by a general mirth. There were carpal carnivals, parties of tarsals, and masquerades in which maidens ran shrieking from bemasked delators. Doolittle was lampooned by Hugh Lofting as the eponymous doctor who could talk to the animals. It was a time of ribald bravery and unbridled revelry such as frequently follows upon a disaster averted.

In Whitehall it was a time of topsy-turveydom in which cabinet reshuffles were the order of the day. In Foreign Affairs a Halifax displaced a Hoare, the very Hoare who had displaced Æthelred Lord Bletchley, who then retired to the ancestral home at Bletchley Park. All about the ungrateful nation, children poked fun at effigies of Bletchley and Bracken and Chief Inspector Quibble, and the gutter press had a field day.

Not everyone joined in the general merriment, however. And it is just as well they didn't. Like the proverbial bad penny, pathogens have a nasty habit of turning up, sometimes by virtue of Mr Darwin's strategy of random mutation, sometimes by stubborn persistence, occasionally through the agency of a Typhoid Mary. In the revolutionary cells comprising the four horsemen of the apocryphal, *contervoc* and *skaz* had four pathologically dedicated Typhoid Marys, and there were periodic if short-lived outbreaks all through the spring of '39. Semantics never once took the foot off the pedal. The draconian restrictions set down by Chief Inspector Quibble may have been mitigated, the man's vigilance was not. Neither, to its great credit, was that of the Foreign Office which, foreseeing another European war, kept lines of communication open to Foggy Bottom,[106] and through Foggy Bottom to the board of International Business Machines being fine-tuned at West Hartford's Noah Webster Institute.

Great advances had been made in the latter's development of electro-mechanical decryption and decontamination devices. Toward the close of 1938, as we have seen, the Mark-2 'big blue' had succeeded in decontaminating both contervoc and standard Engelish texts, fed into it by an automated punched-card feed system, into the American vernacular. It was a laborious process, limited in its application, carried out by a

106 The quadrilateral office which stood at the intersection of 21st and C at Foggy Bottom, Washington, was the predecessor of the more famous Pentagon, renamed after the US took a side during the war. The name 'Foggy Bottom' is here being used metonymically rather than metaphorically.

room-sized machine eminently unsuitable for transportation, for exportation, or for mass production. Attempts to refine the machine, increase its range of application and decrease its size led to the Mark-3, the so-called 'little blue' — though casings in fact came in a variety of colours. Although more portable than its progenitor, the 'little blue' never really caught on. In particular, input by the punched-card method limited the system to a speed of about 25 bits per second, and problems with the interface in an increasingly multiplex world persisted. The machine did provide one useful spinoff, however. Output from the 'little blue' was read from lettered tiles which had been shuffled in a process dubbed 'scrabbling'. Before long, two entrepreneurial projectors with the unlikely names of Brunot and Butts found a way to market the process in what became for a spell an extremely popular board-game.

For verbal decontamination in an age of electro-mechanical reproduction, though, what was required was a light, portable machine which could be adapted to interface with any of the multitudinous modes of mass-media transmission, whether the wireless broadcast, the telephone exchange, the telegraph, the printing-press, the Tannoy, the Newsreel, the loud-hailer, the Chinese whisper or the moving picture. That September, a bare fortnight after Chamberlain's infamous declaration of war on Germany, the Mark-4 was put through its paces at the Noah Webster Institute. The so-called 'Speakeasy' was born, so named because it allowed the user to 'speak easy', and not because, much as the emporia that sold illicit alcohol during the era of prohibition, its very existence was hushed up.

And not a minute too soon. Whitehall was quick to see the value of the machine. If four eccentric Eirish had been able to visit chaos on the realm throughout the long, hot summer of '38, think what ravages might be wrought by a foe as manxome as Herr Dr Goebells. As O'Brien, or Smyllie, had hoped, the summer that followed the Phoneme War had acted as a wake-up call. But in any case, there were still occasional outbreaks which, annoying as they were in peacetime, might prove positively fromulous in a time of open hostilities. As well to clean up in advance any residual pockets of contervoc and skaz.

The war itself was not two months old when a delegation led by Halifax and Hoare arrived in Washington to beg FDR[107] for aid. Ostensibly, they came to solicit the pacifist to release his old and obsolete destroyers and escorts in a policy that came to be known as Lend-Lease, a rare example of the lexical doublet in International Affairs. However loudly von Bernstorff might object to such favouritism on the part of the Whitehouse,[108] how much more loudly would he have shouted if he had known that the policy included a provision for the provision of many thousands of 'Speakeasies'.

By late Autumn of 1940, there were in excess of three thousand IBM-4 '*Speakeasies*' installed throughout Engeland. (It is a curiosity that few were ever deemed necessary to the north of Hadrian's wall or west of the Severn). An entire suite

107 Roosevelt, Franklyn. American president, who thanks to his policy of direct government subvention during the Great Depression, became known as Federal Deficit Roosevelt, or FDR.

108 A figure of speech known as metonymy, the presidential home standing for the entire executive branch of government. A later president, Richard Nixon, would use it in both a metaphoric and metonymic sense to usher in a period of austerity with the homely comment: "There will be no whitewash at the Whitehouse".

of ingenious 'modulator-demodulator' interfaces meant that they could be installed to purify the input/output of every sort of transmission device, and a *Speakeasy* was the *sine qua non* of every telephone exchange, telegraph office, newspaper, printing press, recording and film studio, and broadcasting house in the land. The very fact that they were known as speak- rather than sprake-easies is indication enough of the very few nods the Americans gave to specifically Engelish sensibilities. True, there was a certain lassitude allowed, so that in deference to the absurd preferences of their Old World cousins the machines were modified to retain the quaint '-our' ending in stirring wartime words like 'honour', 'vigour', 'valour', 'ardour', 'armour', and though the prime minister might grumble, 'labour'. Also, the '-re' ending was not automatically reversed into the more logical '-er'.[109] Certain nonce words, too, the like of 'nonce' and 'zed' and 'fortnight' and 'footpath' were included in an appendix file. Nevertheless, entire swaths of vocabulary, from fardles to farthingales, from poltroons to popinjays were irremediably lost, 'got' was replaced by 'gotten', and there were even instances of the grammatical horror of 'would' following directly on 'if' in conditional clauses. Nor were the machines free from gremlins. Confronted with the preterit of 'to say', the newer models asininely defaulted to *'wazlaik'* despite every intervention to right the glitch.

It was a price that the public, in so fromulous a time, was

109 It is notoriously difficult to order letters by fiat. Infamously, the decree "i before e except after c", already challenged by science, was mocked by Bernard Pshaw's: "weirdly, the heinous couple knew neither their money-seizing heir's height nor his weight."

prepared to pay, although when *Speakeasies* were installed in libraries so as to retrospectively 'clean up' the archives, there were not a few who raised their voices in protest and petition. Among these was Professor Seymour Doolittle, whose open letter to the *Times,* both the Eirish and Engelish variety, famously concluded: 'Senator Yeats did not live to see it, but if his shade could sprake, he would surely lament with me that where, in the space of a generation, the puritan strain in Engelish Protestantism altered the country's visual heritage forever, smashing her stained-glass and statuary, white-washing her frescoes, erasing all gorgeous trace that the country had once been unreformed, how much more tragic that, in the space of a bare twelve-month, so much of her linguistic heritage should be changed, changed utterly.' In this he found a curious ally in wartime exile Charles de Gaulle, who called for the immediate 'dégringolade' of the new 'Atlantic' Engelish.

But once again we are getting far ahead of ourselves. As Hackett stumbled from the Hall of Mirrors into the wan March sunlight of '39, he was engulfed in a madding crowd of mummers and revellers and was soon lost to any who may have had the task of trailing him. Dazed, he made his way by by-paths and indirect crook'd ways as far as the *Widow Waddington's Boarding-House for Gentlemen*, where he took to his bed. For three days and nights nothing was heard from that twilit room. What thoughts assailed him, what doubts or dubits, what recriminations or self-reproaches, may never come to light. But if it was a slough of despond into which he had sunk, it was in no wise comparable to the dismal fen in which his inarticulate spirit had wallowed for months on end a decade before.

How much of what the other Smyllie at the heart of the labyrinth had revealed could he take at face value, and how much with a grain of salt? That was the crux of the matter. Was it really possible that the great RM, that champion of the free press, had been suborned by Logdon to lure him, Hackett, into so infamous a scheme, the patsy to end all patsies? He'd read the scurril articles passed off under his own bogus glyph. Could Bertie Smyllie really have been the author or, to borrow a readymade phrase, the 'scissors-and-paste man" who cobbled them together out of old Hackett articles, so that in fact he himself had been the author of his own bogus articles all along? And was it really this tickling of his vanity which had tempted him to take up Smyllie's challenge in the first place?

Hackett started. There, purling at the end of the bed, squatted Oedipus the landlady's tabby, scrutinising him as though those smug feline eyes had known all along that he, Hackett, had been unwittingly complicit in the very scandal he'd been trying to expose. But if he'd been the dupe to end all dupes, he hadn't been the only one. Chapman hardly counted, he was the perennial chump. But what about Quibble? Had he been in cahoots? Hackett couldn't believe it. Too earnest by half. Too humourless a stick. And if not Quibble, then none in Semantics. Had George Smyllie, that smiling lier, been an outlier? Or were the remainder of the Academy in on the jape? Not Harold Hastings, no, not he; and if not, not Turlough McTurcaill, either. One didn't let Tweedledee in on what was withheld from Tweedledum. Nor could he believe that Teddy Mulcahy had been in on the ploy, for all that he'd been there outside the Funfair. His plan to revive the Dinneen variety of Eirish was too outlandish, too much the coinage of that domed featherbrain.

Of course it meant that his own meteoric rise back to the apex of his profession had been nothing but smoke and mirrors all along. Every tip-off he'd been passed, every sniff of a scoop, had been a part of an infamous scheme to use the printed media, that beacon of free speech and impartial judgement, to spread the bogus terms like a pox. Even that wasn't the worst of it. To act as agent provocateur was infamous enough. But was it really possible that from the get-go, he, Hackett, was his own quarry, was *Q?*, was Quinn? Had he been chasing his own shadow all along? He'd been a pawn in a game, and the black king's bishop's pawn, at that.

It's an indication of the degree to which his reasoning had been discombobulated that Hackett's drowning self-respect now clung to one flimsy and ephemeral straw. That straw took the form of the Complete Works of Puncher & Wattmann, (1922). In particular, their *Hibernian Cyclopaedia*. In particular, Volume X of said cyclopaedia, with its Qua-Qua misprint. This volume contained his last best hope. If its compiler had inserted in it the biography of Quinn, or Quin, or Qvin (qv), then he could demonstrate one way or another whether he, Hackett, was or was not Quinn. Failing that he wished only to disappear as entirely as the legendary self-consuming snake. On foot of his return from Paris, he'd scoured in vain the bookshops, libraries, archives and second-hand emporia of the greater Logdon area. All resolution, Hackett climbed from the bed, discomfiting Oedipus. Nothing for it. To Eirland!

CHAPTER THE SECOND

in which an account is given of the circuitous circumstances which led to Hackett's secret, black and midnight journey into the heart of the Third Reich

'Dresden — they say it's the Florence of the North.'

'I think you'll find St Petersburg is the Florence of the North.'

'No. St Petersburg is the Venice of the North.'

'I believe that's Amsterdam.'

'What is?'

'Amsterdam. *Amsterdam* is the Venice of the North.'

'Well if it is itself, don't they say Dresden is the Amsterdam of the East?'

'Who does?'

'Everyone.'

'I never heard that.'

'Oh yes, that's well known.'

'Maybe over here it is. I never heard it.'

'Must be pretty, all the same.' The two men loitering in the vicinity of Quai no.3 of the Gare de l'Est, the one tall, angular and hatted, the other stocky, hirsute and hatless, each staring horizontally and at an obtuse angle with respect to the other, returned each to their own thoughts. The lower man's were fixed upon matters practical: timetables, trains, tickets; Hackett's, as was their wont, weren't. Gare de l'Est, they meandered. Est-ce la Gare de l'Est? and then, Est-ce la Gare de l'Est ou est-ce la Gare d'Ouest? and from there, Où est la Gare d'Ouest? to light finally upon Gare à qui confond les gares! His brow frundled quizzically. Gare a quai le trois? Now, what was it you called a quay in the German, that was a good one… what was he saying, quay? Platform! A quay you found beside a lock; at least, on a canal you did. Question: In what city does the Rialto Bridge span the Grand Canal? Answer: Dubilin Town. Your man Kinch would enjoy that one.

A sound shot down the track and reverberated. A shuffle followed. At once, as though jolted into action, the Tannoy cleared its metal throat and garbled garbled French into the vast echo-chamber. Hackett's night-train was approaching. As it dragged itself into view, an entire phrase learned years before came abruptly back to him: **Ist das der richtige Bahnsteig für den Zug nach Wien? Bahnsteig** then. From **Bahn**: a railway. And **Zug**: a train, from **ziehen, zog, zug**. How had he pulled that one out of his hat? A train pulled a Pullman. So the compulsion to move a train you might call **Zugzwang**…

The unexpected move to catch the overnight from Paris into the heart of **das tausendjährige Reich** as the continent lurched inexorably toward the next conflagration had come about in the following manner. Hackett returned on the boat-train from Logdon Eusless to Kingstown — heretofore, as if in anticipation of Mulcahy's crackpot scheme, rebranded **Dún Laoghaire** — and thence to Needle Nugent's doss-house off Dorset St Lr. One vague hope, one dogged obsession, drove the erstwhile journalist. He was determined to discover all that might be discovered between the dusty covers of Volume X of Puncher & Wattmann's *Cyclopaedia Hibernica*, pertaining to the mysterious Quinn, or Quin, or Qvin (qv). It was not unnatural that his first port of call should be the vaulted reading room of the National Library on Kildare St, where Second Best's ten year tenure as Chief Librarian was coming to an end. He was pleased to confirm that such restrictions as had placed vast tracts of publications on the prescribed lists throughout the United Kingdom held no sway on this side of the Eirish Sea. What was less pleasing was that the deckled pages of Volume X of the *Cyclopaedia Hibernica* ran Qua-Rum, and not Qua-Qua. It was to this anomaly, or whatever is an anomaly's antithesis, that Hackett put down the absence of any edifying entry, even as he put down the volume. He did not panic. Neither did he fret. Years ago, an apprenticeship as journalistic journeyman had furnished him with a formidable list of contacts in the book trade, and even as his shoe-leather took him shambling bootless through the antiquarian shops and second-hand bookstalls of Dubilin Town, discrete letters of enquiry were despatched to the four corners of the Free State. One by one throughout the following month, the replies returned like melancholy doves. None bore the longed-for twig — the desideratum with the desired erratum.

As the sun moved from the House of the Twins into the House of the Crab and his funds dwindled asymptotically, Hackett came to the resolute decision that, like Ulysses of old, it was time to set out on one final voyage. He had been deported from France, and it was a good bet that he remained persona non grata within l'Hexagone. Nothing dismayed, in the journalist's view the French were constitutionally possessed of a Maginot mentality — one that would redouble vigilance only on the Channel ports while neglecting the roundabout path. In short, he set sail for the Norman port of Cherbourg and thence took the overnight back to the City of Light, arriving there on the eve of Bastille Day. Two days later his last, most cherished hope of locating the Holy Grail was extinguished when the propriétaire canadien of *Plaiger & Co* informed him that the complete set of the 1922 *Cyclopaedia Hibernica* had been purchased not five days since by a Frankfurter named Funfter.

A week later, in a dive in the vicinity of Pigale, Hackett woke to a frantic kakanucking. He opened the door onto a bald pate. The caller, who from his accent might have been Needles Nugent's cousin, was short of hair, shorter of stature, shorter yet of breath, and shortest of all of patience. His domed head, which resembled a bald rock to whose flanks great fronds of seaweed clung, was bobbling at a level with Hackett's chin. Only the bare summit, so to sprake, was hairless. As if to make up for its nudity, everything from eyebrow down to big toe was luxuriously hirsute. The combined difference in height and hairiness gave the curious impression that a tide separated the two heads. Before he had a chance to sprake, a low growl resounded against Hackett's open collar. 'You're wanted.' Monaghan rather than Cavan. A more sophisticated trick to the accent. He was summoned forthwith to a meeting at the Consular Offices of the Eirish Free State. A bare twenty minutes later, a Citroën with diplomatique number-plates bearing two ill-sorted passengers muttled onto the *Ave Gral Foch* before puttling to a halt outside a stately edifice in the inimitable style of Baron Haussmann — a rare example of a

Gallic aptronym. Unnoticed by either passenger, a bicyclette turned onto the Avenue some thirty yards behind it, and glided to a stop.

The attendant at the desk nodded curtly to the short man, who was already taking the interior stairs two at a time. Two steps behind, Hackett's head nevertheless bobbled at an equal altitude as they gained the upper floor. Shortly, the Monaghan man led him into an elegant interior dominated by a great, mahogulous table whose legs were curved in the style of Louis Quinze, and whose walls were decorated by portraits of Theobald Wolfe Tone, the Napper Tandy and General Humbert Humbert. Hackett had barely time to take any of it in before his hand was grasped by, of all people, his handler of old. The bould Chandler. More than a year had passed since Hackett had set eyes on the man. For the handler, it was as though the many months had been instantaneously short circuited by the handshake. 'We need you to go back into Germany,' he nodded, frowning.

'How can I go back, if I've never…'

'That's the stuff,' Chandler winked, squeezing the hand as much as to say '*that's the stuff, you never know who might be listening*'. Clearly, he did not intend by this either the baldy specimen who'd conducted him hither nor the hedgehog-headed individual (the Ambassador himself?) who was seated authoritatively at the head of the table. A hat sat on the placemat before him. 'It's becoming grave,' gravelled the latter, as though picking up on a conversation they'd previously left off. 'The only breach our friends have in mind is with our American friends.'

'I see,' said Hackett. Nothing, as the saying goes, could

have been further from the truth.

'As if that'd be any great use to our side!' interjected the dwarf with a dark laugh, a laugh that at once located him down the labyrinth of Hackett's memory. He was the lesser of the two evils who'd conducted him from the **PUNCH & JUDY** to meet Teddy Mulcahy, the other having been little Willy Clarke. 'Hardly,' agreed Hackett.

'*You,*' interpolated the handler, 'need to set them straight.'

'Oh,' said Hackett, 'no better man!'

The seated man looked across at the short man. 'What time is his nibs due?' He was not the Ambassador, then. The short man looked up to the handler. Chandler shrugged. 'You know what he's like,' he answered the seated man. All three guffawed. A silence followed. Then the man who was not the Ambassador picked up the hat that was not Hackett's and pressed a crease into its crown. 'Wear this, so they'll know it's you.'

'You'll find it's a different country,' advised Chandler, 'to the country you knew before.' Before *what,* wondered Hackett. 'Oh, a different Gesamtkunstwerk entirely,' trumped the hedgehog-headed man with what approximated a humorous inflection.

'Where is it exactly I'm to…?'

The man who wasn't the Ambassador tapped his nose, 'ah now'.

'Once you're at the station,' gruffed the gnomic dwarf, '*they'll* approach *you.*'

Chandler gripped his forearm. 'Aithnionn ciaróg ciaróg eile,' he winked.[110]

110 A literal translation of the proverb would run 'one beetle recognises another.' There is no entomological evidence to support the contention.

'Got it,' said Hackett, reaching toward the fedora, a quail feather stuck jauntily in its band. The man with the hedgehog for hair gave him a nod. The handler handed him the hat. At that signal, for signal it surely was, the dwarf flung open the doors. Hackett made to imitate his exit. 'And whatever you say,' said the man who wasn't the Ambassador, 'say nothing.'

'Goes without saying.'

Once they were outside, and still without entrusting Hackett with his destination, the Monaghan man muttered, '*Gare de l'Est*. Nine o'clock. *Bureau de Tabac*.' With that, he pivorted about and scurried back inside. Abandoned, Hackett squinnied up and down the elegant thoroughfare, so French in the dappled sunlight. He shrugged, scrummeled, and set off in the contrary direction to that of their arrival by motorcar. Whether the maneen had meant nine o'clock that night or nine the following morning was anyone's guess. Unnoticed, a bicyclette detached itself from the far railings and, at a distance of about thirty yards, began again to tail the behatted figure.

Hackett's mind was a mind that worked by association. No sooner did he now hear the screech and shuntle of the great steam locomotive decelerating into *Gare de l'Est* than the train of his own thoughts jumped track back to Victriola Station and the trip to Chat'em; and thence to Kingsbridge and his more recent jaunt down the Waterfjord line. But it was not the geographical aspect that engaged, or rather, it did so only insofar as space had been intimately and interminably tied by Mr Einstein to time. For Hackett could never think of a train without he thought of the infamous conundrum of the speed at which a light beam left the lantern at the front of a moving engine. Moving in four dimensions. It was an Eirishman had come up with the maths. Lines, written on a canal-bank seat.[111]

Of course long before Einstein had set that cat amongst the temporal pigeons, the expanding network of railways had posed its own particular conundrum of how to tell the time on a moving train. Important, that, if you were trying to make a connection. Or if ever you were to have timetables. Standardising these had led to the introduction of standardised time itself. The fall of the ball on the Ballast Office. And it was the confusion inherent in the German insistence on calling half past three **halb vier** and half past four **halb fünf** that led to the adaptation of Central European Time once a body got over the channel; a situation exacerbated on their Eastern borders by the even more extreme Russian view of the clock.

Thus were Hackett's thoughts returned to matters linguistic. It had been donkey's, if not donkeys', since he'd exercised his German, and even in its heyday his German had been stiff-jointed. Now he was about to pass through a looking-glass where *wer* isn't *where* but *who* and *wo* isn't *who* but *where*. A thought jumped from one region of his brain (viz. memory) to another (viz. speculation). He recalled the German teacher at Newman House, a desiccated Sudeten by the name of **Herr** Schlecht insisting in his creaking voice that "**im kausalen Klauseln**" once you substituted the conjunction **weil** for **den**, the effect was to throw the verb to the end of the clause. Does it not follow, Hackett mused, that your

111 In fact a canal bridge. On his way to the Royal Eirish Academy in 1843, William Rowan Hamilton, who was forever misplacing his pocketbook, carved the equation $i^2=j^2=k^2=ijk=-1$ into a bridge along the Royal Canal. He subsequently forgot which bridge he'd carved it into, with the result that it was many years before the so called quaternions found an application.

Deutschsprachigbevölkerung was syntactically predisposed to uncover the step-logic of the new physics, the one that said that a particle might be found either here or there but not in between, which was neither here nor there? Discrete steps. The better part of valour. In Heidelberg, but was it Heidegger or Heisenberg who'd stated it? Or Böhr, was it, the great Dane who, during the Royal Institution's Christmas Lectures,[112] had overturned J. J. Thomson's plum-pudding model? Now what was the word… 'Quantum!' he calloohed abruptly, and then more quietly, 'quantum.' A low growl hopped against his collar. 'You what?' Hackett had no chance to respond. With a great billow of steam and an ear-rending screech, the great engine shuntled past them and shuddered haltingly to a halt, reversing an inch in the aftermath as though directed to do so by a law of classical physics. There were letters in Gothic script, refuting any lingering dubits that they were on the wrong quai.

A week before, he'd reached lowest ebb, having returned empty-handed from *Plaiger & Co* to the dive in Pigale, frankly franc-less. Now here he stood, he mused, amused if somewhat bemused, standing on **der richtige Bahnsteig für den Zug nach Dresden**. It might have been supposed that questions as to the nature and purpose of his clandestine trip would have been foremost in his mind. This was not Hackett's modus operandi. Plenty of time to go over the ins and outs of it once on the train. One thing was obvious, whoever these chaps had taken him to be three year ago in Dubilin, his activities in Engeland and the dupe he'd been played for hadn't changed their opinion

112 The series of annual scientific lectures were instituted in 1825 by Michael Faraday, who insisted they should be free of charge.

one jot. Half-heeded, his diminutive escort, who turned out to be from neither Cavan nor Monaghan but from the marches of Fermanagh, had been filling him in in fits and starts as to what to expect once he was delivered to whatever Agency was operating in the heart of Saxony. Time enough, thought Hackett, particularly when you take into account the motion of the train. That meant time slowed. Relatively speaking. Though hold your horses a minute! If time *slowed,* he'd have *less* time to think…

'Do you follow?' Evidently, the Ulsterman had been addressing him. He felt a bundle of papers thrust into his hand. 'Passport. Permits. Put them away.' Hackett did so. 'Currency.' A wallet, fat with Reichmarks, followed, and followed the papers into his pocket. 'Now, this letter,' a blue rectangle was pressed into his palm, 'you give only to the man who meets you off the train, and to no-one else. Do you mind me now?'

'To no-one else,' echoed Hackett, and he made to slip the letter into the same pocket as the travel documents.

'Are you mad!' gasped the dwarf.

'Oh!' said Hackett, holding the letter aloft: 'Hide it. Is that it?' Instead of answering the dwarf sputtered and stamped his foot in the manner of Rumpelstiltskin. 'I'll find a good place for it, so. Once I'm on the train.' And to soothe the immediate concerns of his minute companion he raised his hat, dispatched the letter into its interior, and replaced it on his crown. 'Will we find my carriage?' They did so. Hackett at once sprang onto the step, leaving his escort a good two feet below him. 'Anything else?'

'Your ticket,' croaked the dwarf, ill-naturedly. He held the item in such a way that Hackett was forced to bend to retrieve it. But it was a price Hackett was willing to pay to be shot of the other's company. As he again mounted the carriage, a 'Gute Fahrt' escaped from below.

He found he was sharing the compartment with one other passenger only, a man with a genial, spherical head with close-cropped hair who smiled a non-committal smile at the erstwhile journalist. No sooner had the Pullman begun to lurch forwards than the associative mechanism operating in Hackett's head began to kick in and he found his thoughts turning on Harry Hastings' great railway discourse upon cleavage. Now it was clear that a rail journey from Paris to Dresden must perforce bring him across the very tectonic fault-line which so bothered the Warden of the Academy. He was about to enact a passage across the two etymological strata of the mother tongue. What was more, he was travelling to the dark heart of Saxony. Dark, because from an Eirish point of view, that's where all the high jinks began. When they weren't being obtuse the Angles were a cute lot, and the Jutes were no pushover, but it was the Saxon who was the source of all the major grief. Three things to fear: the horn of a bull; the kick of a horse; the smile of a Saxon. Sure half the world could bear witness to that maxim. And it was *his* language that had prevailed in Britain after the Roman exodus when everything was still up for grabs, that was the point. Because it was the Saxon genitive had made the SASSNACH genetically predisposed to acquisition, that much was well known.

Nowadays the preferred term was Anglophone, though in the development of the tongue the Saxophonists had been instrumental. But whence the smile? From perfidious Sachsen?

"*Napoleon began the war with Russia because he could not resist going to Dresden.*" Count Tolstoy, whose grasp of geography was less than perfect, had written that. How able was he ere he saw the Elbe? In 1806, the Elector had sided with Boney in the great to-do against his Prussian cousins. How like the Saxon to cozen them. Was it any wonder the same Tolstoy had come to the conclusion: cousinage, dangereux voisinage. And after all, when you came to think about it, hadn't the Czar, the Kaiser and the King all been cousins? But there must be more to their perfidy. Could it be the Anglo-Saxon's hyphen that made him so duplicitous?

He looked about the compartment. Should he perhaps find a location to conceal the Fermanagh man's letter, or had he been talking through his hat? If he were to do it now, the fellow with the roundy head sitting opposite him would surely notice. Time enough! he yawned to the reflected Hackett being borne alongside through the Parisian dusk. *The track, the train*, sang the wheels. Must be of Engelish manufacture…

His reflection was now yawning in tandem. Do I know that chap, it asked, of the reflected roundhead being borne along through the window. I'd swear, agreed Hackett, we know that head from somewhere. Look at the stubble on the scalp, patterned like a thumbprint. Counterclockwise, in defiance of Coriolis. Or no. That was the reflected head. The real pattern of stubble would be clockwise. Would that correspond to the other thumbprint? He yawned, for the reflected yawn had been contagious. *The track, the train*, sang the wheels. *The track, the train*. Time enough, he thought again, and in no time at all, his mouth was open, his eyes closed, and his head thrown back. He was fast asleep, and snoring to the rhythm of the carriage.

A hand woke him. 'Fahrkarte.'

Hackett raised his eyebrows.

'Billete.'

'Ah.' After a fumble he produced the ticket. The hand took it, punched it, returned it. The man opposite him smiled. *The track, the train*, rhythmed the wheels' iambics, *the track, the train*.

'Try to stay awake,' muttered Hackett to his reflection, one of whose eyes was already closing. 'Count up to a hundred.' 'Auf deutsche?' 'No harm.' Eins, zwei and drei he began. Fine. They appeared to be in order. Vier and fünf behaved themselves. But soon after the cardinals (or ordinals?) began to sport and caper about the carriage. Elf and zwölf were positively mischievous, hiding beneath the seat and peeking out…

Hackett's head tilted back and his mouth fell open. Some time later again there was a jolt, a screech, a shudder, a jostle, and a shuntle. In obedience to Newton's laws of motion, he was bundled forwards, then backwards. The train was being shunted onto a sidetrack. The compartment was empty. He ribbled his eyes and peered into the slowing exterior. Already there was a thinning of the darkness to the east. The effect was fleeting, however, because the night sky was abruptly blanched out by intense electric lighting. The compartment lurched to a stop and, after a moment of silence, a Tannoy cackled in unintelligible metal gutturals. A dog was barking frumiously, as though translating. They were at the frontier.

The door to the compartment slid open and, along with an icy draft, two uniformed men, who between them took up all the spare room, bundled inside. Their contrasting hats were like a demonstration of geometrical prisms, the one simple, the other complex. The slighter of the two intruders, looking very *comme il faut* in the get-up of a *Gendarme or Douanier*, and with the impeccably clipped moustache that was *de rigueur* in the service, glanced from Hackett to his companion with an insouciant Gallic twinkle, as though he wished the latter to concede the whole rigmarole was *de trop*. His companion, a heavy-set Bavarian with a **Sturm und Drang** expression that flickered over a complexion ruddy as an open oven, the collar of whose **Zollbeamte** uniform pressed mercilessly into his expansive double-chin, waggled his jowls disagreeably. '**Ausweis**,' he sputtered, and when Hackett made to rise to go outside, the ironical gendarme half-closed his eyes. '*Vos papiers monsieur*,' he yawned.

'Ah!' The formalities proceeded as formalities normally do, the **Zollbeamte** frundling and giving Hackett to understand that he, the **Zollbeamte**, was a clever fellow and that he knew well what rascality he, Hackett, was up to; the other twiddling his moustache ends with racial nonchalance. Then the fat red palm of the Bavarian slapped Hackett's briefcase; and it was noteworthy that, once this had been sprung open, the ferocious, piggy eyes remained fixed upon Hackett's while five strubbly fingers registered its contents as though by Braille. He stood, nodded, and made to go, but evidently the facetiousness of his neighbour, who was nonchalantly humming *Marlboro s'en-va-t'en guerre*, vexed him. '**Hut**,' he barked.

'**Hut**?'

One fat finger extended slowly to a point above Hackett's forehead. '**Hut**! **Hut**!' Hackett's stomach somersaulted. There could be no dubit what was intended by '**Hut**.' He wanted his hat. His bulk blocked the doorway, and with it, any hope of skedaddling. Nothing for it then. Slowly, reluctantly, complaisantly, he raised the article an inch above his head, tendered it to the outstretched hand, and, to lighten the situation, he tried a quip; to wit: **Wer die Hast hat, hat den Hut...**[113] The tiny eyes, beneath eyebrows that twitched like a cockroach's antennae, remained riveted on Hackett's as a quartet of strubbling fingers registered the contents of the upturned hat. 'Hmmmmmph,' he harumphed, returning the hat, and bouncing out the *gentile Gendarme* with his girth.

Flabbergasted, Hackett collapsed. Twice he removed the hat, to examine its interior. Twice, he found that it was as empty as the compartment. Perhaps the letter had fallen while he slept? Two frantic searches suggested not. 'Well doesn't that take the proverbial biscuit?' he inquired of his reflection, which the searchlights had made all but invisible. Above the barking of dogs and of orders, the faint ghost in the window shrugged uncomprehendingly.

---

113 A liberal translation might run 'Here's your hat, what's your hurry?'

CHAPTER THE THIRD

in which further particulars are given of the night-journey into darkest Saxony; and of a most peculiar Pole who regaled Hackett during the same journey

At length the door slid open, another blast of cold air ran about his legs and the passenger with the spherical head re-entered. He resumed his seat, looked with irony at Hackett and nodded. 'Przybyszewski.'

Hackett thought for a moment. '**Gesundheit**,' he tried.

The man, however, extended his hand. 'Jakob Przybyszewski.'

'Ah!' Hackett was still in too much of a flap about the recent occurrence to trust this stranger with his own name. Besides, he'd never got around to checking the travel documents, to see under what name he was travelling. 'Delighted, I'm sure.'

'I think you have been sleeping.'

Hackett examined him, warily. 'I think you might be right.'

'While you were sleeping,' the man went on, surreptitiously sliding something blue and rectangular along the fold of his trouser towards Hackett's knee, 'I took the liberty of removing this.' Hackett glanced downwards. The man's hand was edging the small blue rectangle ever closer to his kneecap. A shock of recognition jolted him upright. 'Re-*moving*?' Hackett took the envelope. 'Surely you mean… it fell out, no?' There was a pause. 'You found it on the floor.'

'Re-*moving*,' repeated the man, his head meaningfully bobbling but discombobulating Hackett. As if on cue, the compartment lurched and the siding began to recede rearwards, which was very untoward. Hackett's eyes narrowed. The round head, over which the close-cropped hair eddied centrifugally like one of the Earl of Rosse's galaxies, seemed altogether familiar. Funny, the Earl was a Parsons and Lemaître, who'd discovered Hubble's Law, a Jesuit. Hackett's centrifugal thoughts were in danger of reeling off tangentially into ever expanding space, and he made a determined effort to reel them in. 'Do I know you?'

The round head bobbled, the eyes twinkled, but it was unclear if it was a yes, aye or no. 'The Zollbeamter have a way of asking uncomfortable questions,' he supplied.

'It was good of you to keep it under your hat.'

'Under my…?'

Hackett shook his head. 'What did you say your name was?'

'Przybyszewski.'

Hackett's brow frundled. A plentiful lack of vowels. 'Polish?'

'That would depend,' said Przybyszewski, 'upon your point of view.'

'And do I know you, Mr Pvrszmnvszmski?'

'I know you, Mr Rooney.'

Hackett started. A tanner to a make that was the name

on his travel documents! A tanner to a make your man had had a sneaky look while he'd been dozing. Just as well the Zollbeamte hadn't asked him for his name. And yet there was something awfully familiar about that bobbling, close-cropped head…

'It's not your first visit to Germany,' commented the Pole.

'That would depend,' said Hackett, 'upon your point of view.'

'You must be aware that it's no longer the same country.'

'The same as what?' The man made no answer. 'You're not a fan of the latest model?'

'Our great-great-grandfathers had to deal with an upstart Corsican corporal. We have an upstart Austrian corporal. Herr Hitler is not a man who has respect for international law. The Treaty of Versailles stipulates the number of the Wehrmacht's armaments must remain fewer than their neighbours'. Nevertheless Herr Hitler outnumbers them in panzers, and moreover planes. You too should be wary. Can she still be considered your gallant ally, this is the question.'

'Well,' sprake Hackett, still smarting from the manner he'd been notoriously abused by the servants of perfidious Albion, 'don't they say my enemy's enemy is my friend?'

'You still hold Engeland to be your enemy?'

'So long as Engeland *is* the enemy, we won't ever be lacking for friends,' he smiled, as though closing a syllogism. 'I'm sure you Polish must feel the same way. Talk about drawing the short straw when it comes to neighbours.' You Poles, he thought, not you Polish. But was he a north Pole or a south Pole? And in that instant, he had it! The fellow on the train to Waterfjord that had the noggin the like of a sphere with iron filings sprinkled over it! He knucked his fingers. 'You were following me last year around Eirland.' The man made an expansive gesture which might be interpreted as an affirmation, and might further be refined with the tag: 'and if I was, what then?' Hackett decided to try a different tack. 'What if I was to tell you I'm not the man you think I am.'

'Not Rooney?'

'Not Rooney.'

'In the land of your old enemy,' smiled the Pole, 'you wrote articles under the cypher Ж.'

'If I did, that doesn't make me Rooney.'

'Nor does it make you not Rooney.'

'Why would I lie about my name?'

'You think I can be Jakob Przybyszewski in the new Germany?'

'Another thing you have wrong,' continued Hackett, unperturbed, 'this is my first visit to this country.' He looked at the man's supercilious eyelids, which were hooding his eyes in the manner of a Kerry jarvey assessing a fare. 'I don't even have the lingo,' he shrugged.

'Wirklich? Während Sie schlafen waren, wurden Sie auf deutsche zählen.'

'I what?'

'While you were sleeping you were counting in German.'

'Was I?' Oddly, Hackett was more pleased than startled by the revelation. 'Well, if I was itself, I've only a rudimentary grasp. A hangover from my college days.'

'You are something of a linguist, Herr Rooney?'

'Herr Hackett is,' winked Herr Hackett. 'Of the amateur variety. Why do you ask?'

'In Dresden you will visit the **Goethe Institut** I think.'

This did not appear to be a question. Hackett shrugged non-committally.

'You will learn some interesting things there. German is… how do you say? Her words have a habit of assembly. Goethe himself helped to bring this about. The intention was to foster a state of mind in which the many tiny principalities would at last begin to cohere and to form a **Grossdeutschland**, even as drops cleave together on a windscreen.'

'It would appear he had some success.'

'Naturally, the strategy of **Zugehörigkeitsgefühl** wasn't without its risks.'

Hackett peered at the Pole. 'From the point of view of the neighbours?'

'From the point of view of the neighbours, yes. But not just that. May I test your German?' The man scribbled a childish sum on a scrap of paper and passed it to Hackett.

'A million take away one?'

'**Auf deutsche, bitte.**'

Hackett took up the pen, his brow frundling and tongue protruding to one side.

Neunhundertneunundneunzigtausandneunhundertneu-nundneunzig, he scribbled.

'**Ganz gut**! Now you understand the risk? Such a propensity for numerals to snowball carried a propensity to inflation over into the **Reichsmark**.'

'Well I'll be…' Hackett ribbled his chin. 'And did nobody see it coming?'

'The linguists, yes. But not the **Finanzbeamter**. Although the danger of unrestricted cohesion was well known to Goethe.

This is why he instituted the **trennbare Verben**. The, how you say? "Separable verbs". But you will see all this when you are in Dresden.'

'I daresay I will.' Hackett, finding that the blue envelope still lay on his lap, replaced it under his hat. 'Why are you telling me all this?'

'Because I'm afraid that you have a misunderstanding about the intentions of your ally. You wish to engage his help in the disarticulation of the Engelish, Mr Rooney. Is this not so?'

Play along, thought Hackett, play along. He tried, with moderate success, to imitate the cute hoor squint of the Kerry jarvey.

'What you misunderstand is the priority of the new Germany. You are aware, perhaps, of what Bismarck once said?'

Hackett ribbled his chin. That was a good one. Bismarck, bedad. Then he had it! 'There's two things you don't want to see being made,' he waggled a triumphant finger. 'Laws and sausages.'

'No, I don't mean this. **Der eiserne Kanzler** was once asked, what is the most important historical fact of your lifetime? Do you know what he replied? I will tell you. **Dass die Nordamerikaner Englisch sprechen**.'

'That the American sprakes Engelish?'

'*So*.'

'So what?'

'Precisely. The purpose of **das deutsch Außenministerium** is to engineer a breach between the two great Engelish-spraking empires. *Also*, this is why they watched with interest the efforts of Mr Mulcahy and his accomplices. Unfortunately for them, that rigmarole is likely to produce precisely the opposite effect.'

Hackett sat back. His own role as unwitting accomplice in spreading contervoc, albeit as agent provocateur, was still raw. Time to shift the fulcrum of the dialogue. 'Who exactly are you when you're at home?'

'Here, Herr Rooney, I am simply a businessman. A dealer in antique books. But, as you so wittily put it, when I am at *home*, I am with the *Biuro Szyfrów.'*

Hackett sat forwards. 'The Cyphers Bureau is it?' The title rang a bell. Quibble's office. That mystery disc he'd glanced. 'Then there's something you might be able to help me with. A disc or a rotor, about so big.' Hackett's two hands formed a disc or rotor. 'You've the letters of the German alphabet placed around the circumference. Indented on the inside the letters GS-2.' His index finger spelt out the two letters. 'Any ideas?'

'Of course. This is from the Geheimschreiber.'

'The...?'

'The *Lorenz* machine.'

Hackett ribbled his stubble.

'To you people it is an Enigma.'

'You can say that again.'

'*So.* With the failure of the counterfeit language programme, it seems they are now attempting to modify this type of device so as to *alter* as well as to transmit encrypted codes.'

'Could you be up to them?'

'There is a designation. The U-schreiber. We don't know for certain what this U- stands for.'

Hackett, whose mind as we have seen worked by association, began to swim latterly. 'Unterschlüpfenschreiber,' he tried, and then, thinking of the unrestricted submarine warfare that had led to the loss of the Lusitania, 'Unterscheidsloßschreiber?'

A shrug dismissed the suggestions. 'This is not the time for guesswork. It is imperative we find out what the U-schreiber stands for, and is intended for.'

Hackett grimlied. Was he about to be played as another pawn in another game by another player?' 'You mean,' he nodded, glumly, 'you want yours truly to find out for you.'

'Genau.' The Pole's eyes narrowed. 'That is precisely what I mean.'

'Well I'll be,' said Hackett. What he would be remained a mystery, because at this juncture the door juddered open, and a busty, tight-lipped Frau upholstered in fur reversed her sashaying backside into the compartment. In its wake, a tilted, saucer-shaped hat emerged, which was tendering a flippant ostrich feather whose tip teetered over a fox-stole which appeared to Hackett to be winking at him. The lady's slow progress, or ingress, was greatly encumbered by innumerable hatboxes, cases and bags, all bustled breathlessly inside, and she drew after her a dour Dienstmädchen who was every bit as encumbered as her mistress, and who drew after her the door.

Jakob Przybyszewski was at once all gallantry and etiquette, helping to disencumber the great dame who for her part, taking such deference as no more than her due, plonked down beside Hackett who, in obedience to the principle of Archimedes, was immediately hoisted by several inches so that the crown of his hat was crushed against the luggage rack, the net of which had dipped, by an application of Newton's Law of Universal Gravitation and of Hooke's Law of Extension, in proportion to the loads added to it. All through the remainder of the undulating journey, the woman's elbows, haunches, hatboxes and handbags showed an alarming tendency to expand, as though illustrating the principle of **Herr** Hitler's **Lebensraum**.

One way or another, her asthmatic descent into a grumbling seat put an end to the conversation.

CHAPTER THE FOURTH

in which Hackett finally arrives in the fabled city of Dresden, where he has an unexpected encounter with an old friend

Many hours later, Hackett woke to the slowing of the carriage. The train was sashaying into a vast, echoic interior the acoustics of which favoured all things metallic. His eyes were at once drawn to the impressive legend: **Dresden Hauptbahnhof**, spelt out like something out of the **Faustbuch** in imperturbable **Schwabacher** lettering. To Hackett, the **D** and **H** resembled nothing so much as a Baroque harp and lute marshalling lines of crotchets. Small wonder their mother-tongue had given birth to so many note-worthies: Orff and Bach and Offenbach; Bruch, and Bruckner; Berg, and Berger; and these times, who could forget Wagner?

Somewhere beyond it, a more modest sign suggested they were gliding into '**Gleis** 4'. Not **Bahnsteig** then. Belike **Herr** Schlecht's term had become as arcane as Vienna. He was about to pose the question to the affable Pole when he saw that the seat opposite was occupied by the latter's absence. Almost at the same moment, a head round as a bowling ball bobbled past the all-but-stationary window. At once, Hackett was on his feet. Unfortunately, the formidable Frau in furs chose this precise moment to assemble bag and baggage. Her ample backside, against which all polite requests broke like impotent waves, blocked any chance of egress, and Hackett was pinned inside the compartment until she had done with the interminable zusammenbringen. There was more than one bear, thought Hackett, perished to furnish that fur coat. By the time she had bustled out and sashayed down the carriage as far as the exit, all hopes of catching up with Pan Przybyszewski had vanished.

Hackett cast his eyes about the great chamber. All railway stations had a family resemblance, in the way all cathedrals had, and for that matter, bank foyers. The Russians had gone so far as to name all their stations вокзалы so closely did they resemble Vauxhall Station. And all of humanity, dwarfed by the overarching architecture, assumed the same entomological imperatives once inside. In no time at all a couple brushed by him, separating and reuniting without breaking their stride; a dashing figure with a violin rushed past; a train of skittering children wrapped and unwrapped about his legs; his feet became entangled in the leash of a Dachshund; and a back-tracking Gepäckträger bundled him unceremoniously to one side. Hackett alone remained static amongst all this formic activity. What was it the wee hop o' my thumb said? Wait here, wasn't that it? *They'll* know *you*. But did he mean wait on Gleis 4 or in the main foyer? It was for them to figure out, whoever they might be. By thy hat shall they know thee. Of its own accord his hand went to the brim of the fedora and satisfied itself it was in fact there and what his scalp was experiencing was not residual pressure.

Hackett had been standing for more than an hour and had

been the recipient of no insignificant number of growls, buffets and '𝔈𝔫𝔰𝔠𝔥𝔲𝔩𝔡𝔦𝔤𝔲𝔫𝔤𝔰' before he was approached, finally, by a tall gent in fur-collared coat with monacle and meticulously parted hair — the trappings of the 𝔍𝔲𝔫𝔨𝔢𝔯, the Prussian professional aristocrat — who introduced himself as 𝔊𝔯𝔞𝔣 von Beruf. Formalities were exchanged, the sort of formalities which are exchanged when two unknown characters of different nationality and social class meet clandestinely in a public forum. Then Hackett followed the aristocratic figure out of the ℌ𝔞𝔲𝔭𝔟𝔞𝔥𝔫𝔥𝔬𝔣 and across the 𝔓𝔞𝔯𝔨𝔭𝔩𝔞𝔱𝔷 to a statelig 𝔇𝔞𝔦𝔪𝔩𝔢𝔯 𝔅𝔢𝔫𝔷 the roof of which had been folded back.

As they approached it, a suspicious character in double-breasted suit and homburg loitering by a news-kiosk nodded to 𝔊𝔯𝔞𝔣 von Beruf. Now where the Devil had Hackett seen this character before? As von Beruf stepped away from him toward the very kiosk he mentally knucked, an aid to cogitation. He couldn't make out what was said, but by the nasal volubility of the man's imperfect German it was patent he was an American. At once it came to him. The goon with the triple-barrelled name who'd been earwigging all through Kermit Froschmann's going-away party at their new Embassy. What's this his name was? Kent something? Or Taylor, maybe? But what was he doing here? Before he had time to consider further von Beruf returned and they resumed their walk. A chauffeur in livery materialised and, with a Teutonic click of heels, opened the rear door. Hackett sat in. Overhead, twenty starlings, a musical score, had arranged themselves along a stave of telephone wires. A motorcycle backfired, startling the starlings, scattering them like so many minims from a Bach fugue. By the time the murmuration had reformed, staff-car and motorbike were muttling down a teeming St-Petersburgerstraße in the direction of the Albertinum.

The panorama as they were crossing the Carolabrücke quite literally took Hackett's breath away. Though he was now in Germany, as every Gothic street-sign attested, it gave him a sudden and unexpected jolt of déjà vu. And yet, he, Hackett, had never been here before! Rooney may well have been, before the ill-fated U-boat brought that other Ж to Sneem. And the Eirish Consulate may well have mistaken him for Rooney; may indeed have altered his documents to corroborate their error. But that couldn't explain the strength of the sense of… there was no other word for it, déjà vu. This was a conundrum, and a disturbing one.

Then he had it! The vista was familiar from the two views of the Augustus Bridge that hung in the National Gallery back in dear, dirty Dubilin. By the fellow that wasn't Canaletto.[114] Now, as to whether these comprised a view of the Venice of the North or of the Florence of the East, or of the Elbe for that matter, he was not in a position to say. For the cold fact of the matter was Hackett had never been to Italy either. As to whether this was a changed country, once again he couldn't say. Naturally the city had changed since your man that wasn't Canaletto had painted it, but not so much as you might imagine. He looked about him, smiling intransitively. A pair of clockwork sentries were goose-stepping to and fro, a

114 In fact Canaletto's nephew, Boletto. Hackett visualised the great artists in terms of colours. Thus Gaugin was red; Turner orange; Van Gogh, yellow Cezanne green; Renoir blue, Monet mauve and Caravaggio black. Many of these he may have encountered not at the National Gallery but rather the Municipal Hugh Lane Gallery, which is confusingly not located on Hugh Lane but on nearby Parnell Square.

gabble of fur-lined street-merchants were passionately horse-trading, whilst a rotund Polizist was frogmarching a bug-eyed ruffian past a buxom Frau upon whose head a feathered hat had come to roost, who in turn was henpecking her hapless Herr. A tram hummed past, its dong clearing a space before it in the manner of a cowbell or the clapper of a leper. Electricity apart, had anything fundamentally changed since those elegant cityscapes? It was hard to believe it ever would now. He was on the point of asking von Beruf when the latter pivorted to face him. 'You have something for me, Herr Rühnig?'

To begin with Hackett was at a loss. But then a realisation passed by electrical discharge from his hand, which in the open car was securing the hat to his head, by the long circuit of elbow, shoulder and neck, to arrive back up to his head. At once, he felt the letter tingle against his scalp. 'I have!' he calleyed, and all but lost the missal to the breeze in his eagerness to furnish it. Ernst von Beruf's monacle perused the contents without his giving away by the tiniest alteration to his features what he thought of them. It was as he watched him, trying to gauge the reaction that Hackett was seized by the queasy dubit as to whether it was the right letter at all. Suppose your man Pvrszmnvszmski had done a Rosencrantz and substituted one letter for another while he, Hamlet-like, had been throwing zeds. It wasn't beyond the realms of the possible, or even the probable. After all, wouldn't it be in his interest, as a Pole, to scuttle whatever collaboration he suspected was taking place between this Rooney character and one of the hereditary enemies of the Polish nation?

Another dubit seized him. What if von Beruf himself turned out to be ein falsche Freund? Suppose he wasn't who he purported to be but was a plain-clothes brown-shirt, working for what's this you call him, the fellow to whom they'd given the long knife? Or worse, a plain-clothes black-shirt, working for the fellow with the roundy head and glasses? It wasn't so far-fetched, hadn't a plain-clothes blue-shirt tailed him back in Dubilin? An egg-sized lump formed in his throat at the unpleasant thought of what a debriefing might entail. He swallowed it painfully. 'Everything in order?' he piped.

The **Graf** nodded, curtly. The letter he folded efficiently into its envelope and slid the latter deftly into his inside pocket. None of these adverbs did anything to calm Hackett's dubits. To make matters worse, von Beruf now leaned forwards and whispered something in the chauffeur's ear. The latter nodded, changing gear and lane. Immediately it came to Hackett's attention that they had just muttled past a neo-classical façade bearing the legend **Goethe Institüt**, outside of which the motorcycle outrider was idling. He sat forward, perplexed. 'We're not calling in at the **Goethe Institüt**?'

'**Nein, natürlich**. Why do you ask?'

Had Pvrszmnvszmski been mistaken? What instruction had just been whispered into the driver's shell-like ear? 'Only, I'd heard they'd been pretty busy of late…'

'This depends on the **Zweigniederlassung**. The **Bayerische Zweigstelle** has been particularly busy. But here in **Sachsen**, not so much.'

'What's Bayern been up to?'

'*Down* there,' sprake von Beruf, with what approximated to a grimace of distaste for what they were up to down there, 'they are most keen, with Goebbels, to raise standards all over Germany.' Had he smirked or winced? 'They wish to enact in full **Herr Doktor's Nürnberger Sprachegesetze** — the, how do you say, the Language Purity Laws. Where the choice exists, only those words which have a demonstrable Germanic pedigree are to be used. **Zum beispiel**, the **Jugendtugendbund** are enjoined to oversee that their parents and teachers treat with circumspection all verbs which have the ending "*–ieren*". *Also*, this applies to the coining of new words. You are aware for instance that in **Großdeutschland**, we have for your invention of Logy Baird the name **Fernsehen** given? *Also*, in Nürnberg they wish to apply this process retrospectively. For **Teleskop und Telefon**, they are insisting we must return to **Fernrohr und Fernsprecher**. *Also* for **Telegraf**, they are of course proposing **Fernschreiben**, and for a telephone exchange, **der Fernhof**.'

'Sounds fair enough. You heard of course there's three ways to spread news?' wittered Hackett, flopping back as he tried to prop his flagging morale. 'Telephone, telegram, tell a woman. Over here, I suppose you could also tell a **Graf**.' No smile rewarded the quip. Evidently, Ernst von Beruf was a man who took his job earnestly. 'So would the same apply to micros?'

'What means micros?'

'You misunderstand me. I mean words the like of microscope and microphone. Are they to be,' Hackett stared into the middle distance as he tried to summon up his long-lost German, '**Kleinrohr und Kleinsprecher**?'

'**Kleinrohr und Kleinsprecher**!' The idea was too preposterous to merit a reply. So they continued for **eine irische Meile** in silence until the **Daimler Benz** puttled to a dusty halt inside the court of a thoroughly modern mansion. A scarlet banner, with a crooked device that put Hackett instantly in mind of the laundry van that had put paid to his father, was frabbling to either side of the rectilinear portal, upon whose cornice was engraved, in faultless **Haettenschweiler** script, the word **Schlüsselbüro**. The palace had been built in the Bauhaus[115] style.

Just as they were about to go in, another monocled figure, this one with a scar, was exiting. He was introduced as William Joyce, Eirish by all accounts, though his monocle could scarcely have been more Etonian, and his accent about as Eirish as Viscount Bracken's. Before he had time to assimilate either the presence of the renowned Lord Haw Haw, whose faultless 'received pronunciation' they'd apparently been recording, or the fantastic architecture of the place, Hackett's attention was drawn to the undulating figure of a redhead in field grey jacket and skirt who was sashaying down a corridor leaving in her wake the unmistakable spoor of *Lily of the Valley*. Hair more henna-coloured, but still unmistakable — the mole on her cheek was a give-away. Phony Maloney, here? Or should he say, Agatha Sangster? Had they a comparable need of faultless stenography?

Before he had time to process her presence or even to choose which name to call out after her, he was ushered upstairs and into a large, well-lit room which smelt of the soldering iron. To the left as you looked stood a lathe, to the right a worktop with a veritable spaghetti of wiring in a variety of colours. The centre of the space was dominated by

115 A German modernist style of architecture based on simple shapes: the square, the circle, the triangle. In fact the term derives from a scurril article in the **Berliner Architekturblatt** in which the critic ridiculed the new style as '**einem Bauhaus ähneln**' – 'resembling a kennel'. Despite its pejorative intent, the term stuck.

a table upon which stood an outsized dactylograph of a type which Hackett had never seen in any of the numerous editorial offices and printing rooms in which he'd spent so much of his professional life. It bore the characteristic blue logo of **DGM** — the **Deutsche Geschäfte Maschinen Gesellschaft**, which replaced the **Deutsche Hollerith Maschinen Gesellschaft** after it was acquired by IBM in 1923 and which became known affectionately as '**die große blaue**.'

Upon von Beruf's entry, the mechanicals, who had been working by turns on the lathe, drew themselves to attention. The **Graf** turned to face his guest. 'You are familiar of course, **Herr Rühnig**, with the **Geheimschreiber**.' As this appeared to be rhetorical, Hackett drew back his head and allowed his eyes to half-close, an internationally acceptable gesture for the equally rhetorical 'what do you think?' 'The **Geheimschreiber** is merely an encoding machine. But the **Übersetzungschreiber**,' a hand invited him to feast his eyes on the dactylograph, 'takes the whole encoding process one logical step farther. **Bitte**.' His open hand now urged Hackett to take a step nearer the outsized contraption with the oversized name.

'*So*. The key to the whole process,' explicated von Beruf, as if resuming a talk they'd been having earlier, 'is **die Lorenze Wertwantlung**, — the Lorenz Transformation.[116] Here you can see, just as in the **Geheimschreiber**, one types in the letter into the **Steckerbrett**, *so*, and it is transformed by the rotation of these rotors *here* into what lights up *here*, *so*. But with this

116 Named for the mathematician Karl Lorenz, who went mad trying to build an electro-mechanical device to achieve what the 17th century German philosopher Gottfried Leibniz had dubbed, after attending a pirated version of Shakespeare's *Hamlet*, the **Entscheidungsproblem** — the decision-making problem.

difference. The transformation is held *ap*.' A hand hovered over a blue chamber marked with the letters ***LW***, in Sütterlin script. 'It remains in-*side*. You now enter the second letter. Then the third, **und so**, fourth. It is not until you press the **Leertaste** — the spacebar — that the transformation is complete. Then the letters for the new word show ap here, lit *ap*. It is ap to you to zen arrange zem.'

'They're an anagram?'

'**Genau**.'

'Maybe a demonstration?'

'**Ja natürlich**. *So*. I type in the German word, let us say, **wunderbar**, for example,' letter by letter, key by key, von Beruf typed in the term, 'and then I depress the **Leertaste**. *So*.' He did so. The rotors whirred. After a moment, the dashboard above them lit up, as follows: D,E,F,L,N,O,R,U,W.

'That's wonderful!' calloohed Hackett.

'**Genau**.'

Hackett's mind was now working nineteen to the dozen. 'Suppose,' he proposed, knucking his knuckles several times in rapid succession, 'suppose the word you wanted has a double letter in it. Or any two of the one letter.'

'Then the lit letter vinks,' von Beruf winked his un-monacled eye, 'tvice per second.'

'And a triple?'

'Thrice per second.'

'Clever. And this machine,' sprake Hackett, whose amazement was waxing by the minute, 'I take it it's only good for translating one way… and into *Engelish*?'

'Oh **nein**. If we replace the set of rotors, in theory we can have it translate into any language that we choose.'

'Or *from* any language?'

'Of course.'

'Aha!' calloohed Hackett, waggling a forefinger. 'It may work for words. But not every language has the same *reticulum linguae*, nor the same syntax!'

'Even so,' Von Beruf exhaled an approximation of disappointment. The set of mechanicals' heads were set nodding, as if by resonance. 'This is why we are even now vorking on a second series of Lorenz Transformations, which vill also the syntax transform.'

'Well I'll be…' Hackett was momentarily dumbfounded. 'Still, I daresay you'd have problems with the Eirish. *Unruly Gaedhilic, that was ne'er teased out…*'

'*…on the six tynes of Latin syntax.*' Hackett started. A mere mechanical had completed the couplet. Accent, unmistakably Jackeen. It would be no exaggeration to say that his flabber was gasted. The mechanical advanced, clicked heels, bowed and raised his goggles. Hackett stared. Then, his eyes all but starting from his head at the uncanny apparition, he calleyed: 'Jesus, Mary and Joseph!'

CHAPTER THE FIFTH

in which Hackett and his erstwhile colleague Malachi McCann have a most instructive dialogue in a **Dresdener Kaffeehaus**

It had been donkey's, nay donkeys', since Hackett had set eyes on the man. In college, Malachi McCann was one of the few to whom Hackett had to tip his hat when it came to languages. True, he'd gone a bit off the rails in his quixotic attempt to translate, in time for the tercentenary, *El Ingenuoso Hidalgo Don Quijote de la Mancha* back into the original Arabic. But for all that, his instinct for what Seymour Doolittle would klep the deep structures of a language had always been without par. If anyone had the wherewithal to bring off their Lorenz Transformations for them, then that man was sitting opposite him. He was whistling through the familiar gap in his front teeth ♪♫♪, ♪♫♪, a tune the reader will recognise as the incomparable *Lilliburlero*.

In those dear departed days, McCann had been of the opinion there was something clumsy in the Germanic tongues. Something inherently barbaric. He was Francophile, Hispanophile, Lusophile. They'd lost touch at the time of Hackett's verbal collapse, and the last he'd heard of him, hadn't the bould McCann enlisted in the International Brigades who earlier that year had given up on their struggle to end the bosses' reign in Spain, fighting the planes in Spain. So how could this old romantic, whose politics had always been, with Hackett's, left-leaning, be here, in the Saxon heart of the Third Reich? 'What brings you…' Hackett's hand indicated their surroundings as he searched for the adverb adequate to his puzzlement, '…*here*?' The two Eirishmen had been left to their own vices, to catch up as it were, and were sitting in a Kaffeehaus directly opposite the Bauhaus palace. 'You're not about to tell me that you, of all people, are helping design a communications system for the Wehrmacht?'

'Ach,' said McCann, scrummeling furiously at his right temple. Bodily restraint had never been his wont. 'I am and I amn't.'

'Oh?'

'The Übersetzungschreiber® isn't exactly what you'd class as a communications system. And then, **das Schlüsselbüro** isn't exactly a part of the Wehrmacht.'

'That may be so,' conceded Hackett. 'But I have to tell you I'm not convinced.'

'About which proposition?'

'How would you describe your Übersetzungschreiber®? Because it has Whitehall having kittens so it does.'

McCann sat forwards, for the first time leaving off scrummeling his temple. 'They know about the *Übersetzungschreiber®*?' he italicized the noun, though whether to indicate incredulousness or emphasis was unclear.

'They do and they don't. They know the Germans are up to something and that it's bound to be dastardly.' Hackett too sat forwards. Like Chief Inspector Quibble, he calculated that it was worth chancing a bait of falsehood to land a carp of truth. 'They know all about Dinneen's foclóir and all that goes with it.' Hackett edged so close that had he, McCann, wanted to, he could have scrummeled his, Hackett's, temple. 'They've a bloody good idea who's behind it.' Hackett allowed four fingers to rise by turn. 'Ma-Ma-Lu-Jo.' McCann sat back. Taking his cue from him, Hackett sat back. For a minute the two eyeballed one another. McCann sat forwards. Not to be outdone, so did Hackett. Then the canny mechanical's mouth leered open and let out a guffaw.

'Have I said something funny?'

'Yerra, Dinneen's foclóir. Are you for real, Ignatius?' Mirth had wetted his eyes and hatched his crow's feet to crows' feet. 'Mamalujo, mumbo-jumbo! You haven't travelled all the way out here to sprake of Teddy Mulcahy and them other three liúdramáns, I hope.'

'Then you weren't behind the plot?'

'That would depend on whom you intend by the pronoun.'

Hackett was about to say 'you, the Wehrmacht' when a thought scurried across the corridor of his mind. He pounced on it. 'Ouroboros,' he pronounced, surprising himself as much as his interlocutor. A hand touched his breast. 'One of the four had a ∞ tattoo over the heart.'

'And do you imagine,' snickered McCann, his eyes dancing merrily, 'that the members of the Ouroboros Brotherhood gad about with a ∞ tattoo over the heart?'

'Search me,' said Hackett, removing his hand invitingly while mentally running through what little he'd gleaned from Puncher & Wattmann about the arcane society. 'I always meant to ask, you being a card-carrying member since first I knew you. What exactly does Ouroboros stand for? I don't mean the etymology. Οὐρά βόρος, the fabled tail-devourer. I mean what's your rationale, your modus operandi?'

'What does Ouroboros stand for?' McCann arched his elegant fingers in the manner of the Dürer print and rested his chin on their delicate apex. Pair by pair the fingertips came apart and came together, an aid to contemplation. 'What can you tell me about the Battle of Ulm?'

'Ulm, is it? Arragh, Mc, you know I was never any use at history.'

'Forever disappearing down the footnotes and bye-roads, distracted by the first bauble you glanced at, that was ever your trouble. Let me set the scene for you. 1805. Napoleon is master of Europe. The disaster of Trafalgar hasn't happened just yet. The Austrians want to put a stop to his gallop, and they enlist the Russians to help. All is set for a grand showdown, at Ulm, on October 20th. There's only one problem. In 1805 there's twelve days difference between the Gregorian calendar and the Julian calendar. The Rooskies show up on their Julian October 20th (which translates as November 1st Gregorian) only to find their gallous allies have long since surrendered.'

Hackett shrugged. 'It was an honest mistake, anyone could've made it.'

'It was neither of the above. It was, as you put it, an example of our rationale and our modus operandi. The Brotherhood favoured the French, with their Republican ideals. That's the rationale. A whisper in the ear, a nudge-and-wink, a nugget of disinformation, that's our modus operandi. You'd be surprised how readily an ear latches onto a rumour; how readily chaos follows. Not chaos. Ataxia, the breakdown of order. When the South Sea Bubble popped in 1720, who was it touched the bauble with the little pin of doubt?'

'You spread rumours. Misgivings.' McCann's waggling eyebrows suggested they did. A dubit seized the former journalist. 'Is it disinformation or misinformation?'

'Six of one, a half dozen of the other. Once in a blue moon, a more active intervention is called for. You penned an article once on Bourdin's attempt to take out the First Meridian?'

Hackett nodded, he had. A thought came to him. 'If the breakdown of order is your goal, then it sounds to me like Project Mamalujo would be right up your alley.'

A snort dismissed the suggestion. 'Four amateurs gallivanting about the old enemy's backyard spreading dubitous vocabulary with a vigency you could estimate in weeks. Please! Goebbels gobbled it up. Any chance to throw a linguistic spanner into the,' he executed inverted commas with his fingers, '"Special Relationship". But what came of this misguided **Totale Krieg**? The Aristotelian term would be περιπέτεια.'

'My Greek's a tad rusty.'

'The achievement of the precise opposite of what one sets out to achieve. By the time the IBM-4 *Speakeasy* programme has run its course, you'll have the Windsors themselves jabbering like Appalachian backwoodsmen out of Mark Twain.' In that instant, the triple-barrelled name of the suspicious character who'd whispered in von Beruf's shell-like ear at the news-kiosk came to Hackett. Tyler Gatewood Kent. At the Ambassador's going-away do, Quibble had been observing him observing all around him. If he was here, it was small wonder the Wehrmacht was up to speed on the IBM Mark-4.

A waggish finger wagged at Hackett. 'You played your part, a chara.'

After a moment's incomprehension, indignation rouged Hackett's visage. 'I was duped!'

'Into being a pawn in the Royal Academy's game?' suggested McCann, sucking air through the gap in his incisors. 'That must've stung your pride.' Hackett grimlied. The accompanying frundle suggested that it had stung his pride mightily. 'Would it soothe the smart to learn that, even as he contrived with cousin Bertie for you to head over and spread the bogus word, that O'Brien was himself a pawn in a greater game?'

Incomprehension blanched Hackett's visage. He was teetering on the edge of *mise-en-abyme*. For a queasy minute he was recessively trapped in a dream of a rook inside a rook inside a rook. 'I don't follow,' he croaked.

'O'Brien played you. Fine. But all along we were playing him. What could be simpler?'

'But you just said, he achieved the precise opposite of a linguistic rift…'

'Sometimes, like the great Alekhine, you sacrifice a piece for an unexpected attack. There are now pockets throughout the Septic Isle where skaz and contervoc persist, and will continue to do so through the Engelishman's constitutional obstinacy. That's key. And these days, thanks to their American cousins, the adversary has never felt so complacent.'

'So I was a pawn of a pawn. A patsy of a patsy.' Hackett deflated. 'That scarcely fills a fellow with confidence.'

'Then become a knight, a rook.'

'How?'

'Join us.'

'?'

M^c^Cann's fingers separated and converged, but this time they marked time as an aid to his, Hackett's, cogitation. 'Ok. I'll bite. So I apply to be a… Brother, is it?'

'You don't "apply to be a Brother",' gruntled M^c^Cann. 'You're chosen. And once you're in, you're in for life."

'You're chosen. Then what? Some ghastly masonic initiation ritual?'

'A simple baptism, is all. Look at your own case.'

'Mine?' Hackett's cheeks partly blanched, partly rouged until they were particoloured. 'I was never baptised. Unless you have in mind in eighteen hundred and ninety-six in St Joseph's Church of the Discalced Carmelites on the Berkeley Rd. But I have to tell you, I've no abiding memory of that ritual.'

'That was when Ignatius Hackett was baptised,' grinned M^c^Cann, amused in direct proportion as his companion was bemused. 'What I have in mind is the day a certain Ciarán óg Rooney was baptised.'

'Oh? And when was that, pray?'

'That, pray, was the day your body washed up near Sneem.'

'You're an exasperating bloody man, M^c^Cann.'

'I've been reliably informed.'

'So Hackett was drowned, and I'm Rooney, is that what you're telling me?'

'The body that washed up on the shores of Bohemia had

the papers to prove it. And the game leg.'

'You're delirious.' Hackett, if it was Hackett, vainly examined the other's physiognomy for signs of delirium. 'You're pulling my leg,' he tried, but neither were there signs of jocularity. 'Rooney is a fiction.'

'If you say so. All through the Great War, the German High Command not only believed in his existence, but paid his salary. They still do. And when, in 1916, a corpse showed up on Melville's very doorstep purporting to be one Hackett, Ignatius, the intrepid **M** swallowed the bait hook, line and sinker. His Majesty's Secret Service spent the next several years chasing their tail in a state of divine ataxia. There's rationale and modus operandi for you, rolled into one. Half their spies and informers tied up keeping tabs on every move and article made by a rooky journalist who went under the moniker Ж.'

'You're telling me the Ouroboros Brotherhood was behind that…' Hackett searched for the substantive that was adequate to the sham, '…sham?'

'Can you doubt it?'

The more Hackett's mind ran over the details of his meteoric blaze across the journalistic firmament, the less he could doubt it. 'And now?' he sighed.

'And now?' echoed McCann.

'You suggested I become a knight, a rook.'

'I did.' Incisively, McCann sucked air through the gap in his incisors. 'You tell me Whitehall is having kittens about the **Übersetzungschreiber®**. I'll go bail they've not heard of the **Unsinnschreiber®**.'

'The *Unseen*-**schreiber** did you say?'

'Unsinn.' Hackett trawled the recesses of memory for long-lost vocabulary. 'A *nonsense*-writer?' His eyes widened till they resembled gobstoppers.

'We prefer to gloss it a *nonce*-writer.' Both men sat back, one like the cat that got the cream, the other like the cream the cat got. Then McCann scrummeled his, McCann's, temple. 'Tell me, Ignatius. If it does come to a foubt, whose side will you be on?'

Hackett's retort came out as by reflex. 'Journalists don't take sides.'

'That's as maybe. But sometimes a man ends up taking a side, will he nill he. I've followed your articles. I've read your pinesses. They show up regular enough in the Frankfurter Allemagne and Die Glückliche Zeitung, to say nothing of the Völkischer Beobachter. I recall a young student in college who wasn't backward in standing up and spraking with more than a spark of passion for a United Eirland. Putting the strangers out of the house, once for all.'

'Well, what then?'

'What then? You ask me what then! What we have is a once in a lifetime *chance*, my friend. Not since the great O'Neill has that United Eirland been so close.' The mechanical's hands made as if to seize a grail. 'In his day the Spanish were our gallous allies. In the time of the Napper Tandy, the French. Today it's the Germans. That's how it is. Mine enemy's enemy. Everything now depends on whether we can harness our Celtic powers to their Teutonic prowess. It's all vey well to sow discord. It takes a special kind of genius to reap it. That, in answer to your earlier question, is what we're doing over here.'

'I'm still not with you.'

'Man alive, have you wax in your ears? Have you not just seen with your own eyes the **Übersetzungschreiber**®? Now imagine the next move in the game. Ladies and Gentlemen, I give you the **Unsinnschreiber**®! If Fritz can just get the second round of Lorenz Transformations worked out… that's check!' He beamed, triumphant. 'Mate to follow in three.' Hackett considered, scrummeled his shaggy locks. 'It's not entirely clear to me,' he conceded, 'how Lorenz Transformations are going to drive the stranger from the house.' Then he shot bolt upright. 'Unless you're going to use that, that, that **Über-alles-schreiber**…'

'***Unsinn***-**schreiber**. Go on.'

'…to generate gibberish?'

McCann sat back, smug as the fat cat that got the double-cream. 'The preferred term is **Kant**. What you've seen to date is **Unternehmen Jabberwoche**. Now I give you Operation **Bandersnatch**. It's the old dream, **mein Freund**. Synthetic *a priori* statements, continuously generated by mechanical reproduction. Coupled with the **Übersetzungschreiber**® the issue of language or dialect not only disappears. One can select which population group gets which set of statements. Which set of facts. To each dialect its bespoke set of truths. At the push of a button, any target populace would be flooded with what Dr Goebbels terms **alternative Fakten und gefälschte Nachrichten**.'

Hackett was gobsmacked. Perhaps appalled. He recalled with a spin of vertigo the conundrum of the corrupted dictionary — how one could never afterwards ascertain meaning. 'It'll produce… *chaos*!'

'The preferred term is ataxia.'

'But hold. Wait one moment.' His eyes narrowed. 'What about the problem of vigency?'

'Ah, but what matters vigency when you have a willing populace? The lads from **Krupps** and **Siemens** with their interface based on the wire-recorder will guarantee the supply end. Then, to quote the Bard, "which of you will stop the vent of hearing when loud Rumour speaks?"'

Hackett nodded. He hadn't been appalled so much as flummoxed. 'Where do I come in?'

'Where do you come in? The Teutonic genius is second to none when it comes to the **Hardwareproblem**. An eminently practical people. Within a year, two at the outside, they'll have solved the issue of the Lorenz Transformation and the mechanics of the hardware. But the content? The software? Who better than a journalist, and an Eirish one for preference! That's where you come in. You advance to the eighth rank. You become **ein Beeinflusser** — an 'influencer'. That, **mein freund**, is how you come to be a knight, or a rook, there.'

'It seems to me there's no shortage of journeymen journalists who'd fit the bill.'

'Not so,' said McCann. 'Cometh the hour, cometh the man.'

'Meaning?' inquired Hackett, wary, aware he'd heard that phrase once before.

'It's precisely *because* you spend your time chasing down the bye-ways and footnotes, with no eye to the big picture. Footnotes are subtext, that's an axiom. Any fool can tackle the truth head on. That's what propagandists have done since the Holy See first propagated the very gerund. It's predictable.

Expected. Marx turns Hegel on his head, like some fulfilment of Newton's Third Law. But to cast doubt on the addenda, on the marginalia, on the minutiae, the by-the-by! To undermine by fiddling under the bonnet with the nuts and bolts…' McCann allowed a waggish index finger to complete the aposiopesis.

Hackett's blank countenance invited him to be more precise.

'When the time is propitious, you join us here. On the eighth rank, a pawn no longer. That's when we cry havoc and let slip the Hackett imagination in pursuit of whatever bauble takes its fancy. The machines will look after the rest.'

'And in the meantime…?' Hackett allowed the ellipsis complete the query.

'You return home. You lie low. When the time comes, as the fella says, don't call us, we'll call you.'

CHAPTER THE SIXTH

in which an account is given of Hackett's perambulations about Dubilin Town; and of the vigilance of the few to whom so much would soon be owed by so many

Dubilin, October 1940

All day, and it had been a blusterly one, Hackett had had the curious sensation that he was being followed by an electric humming. Or hovering. It was the kind of sound you might associate with a milk-float. But he hadn't managed to entrap the imaginary milk-float that was supposedly pursuing him in any backwards glance, as Bishop Berkeley of Cloyne would have required, so that its existence was to be dubited. True, he had twice spied a van in the livery of Brittain's Swastika Laundry disappearing around a corner. That had induced an unpleasant sensation, in the first place because their laundry-vans were associated in his mind with the unfortunate death of Walter Hackett; and secondly in that its logo recalled the Bauhaus factory in Dresden. Had he known that with the introduction of diesel-rationing that was part and parcel of the Emergency, the entire fleet of Swastika laundry-vans had become every bit as electrified as the milk-floats of the Premier Dairies, he might not have put the hum down to the tinnitus that had been afflicting him pretty much since his return to the old country.

Hackett was no stranger to being followed about the streets, though these days it was likely to be by a train of mocking school-children. He was in danger of becoming what Dubiliners dub 'a character'; an eccentric in the manner of Cashel Boyle O'Connor Fitzmaurice Tisdall Farrell, who had won everlasting fame for always walking outside of a lamp post.[117] Although he mightn't sprake to a solitary sinner in a coherent fashion for weeks on end, he was in the habit of mumbling to himself in some private language as his yawning shoes, tied with string, took him shambling around the haunts of the inner city.

One of those haunts was the reading room of the National Library on Kildare St. Here, the 'character' was treated with a certain amount of indulgence by the new Chief Librarian, a Quaker named Oates who had replaced Second Best. Indeed the Chief Librarian was one of the few sinners to whom Hackett was in the habit of addressing in the King's Engelish. Since his return, Hackett had become a creature of unshakeable habits, and one of these habits was to peruse the national and Engelish newspapers and journals, old and new, between the hours of ten and twelve, for news of the European war. Had his old pal Best been there, he might have discussed with the redoubtable autodidact the progress of the various campaigns. Alone, he wondered what Walter Hackett would have made of Hitler's

---

117 Unidentified. In his reminiscence *As I was walking down Sackville Street* Senator Oliver St. John Gogarty does mention a James Boyle Tisdell Burke Stewart Fitzsimons Farrell who 'carried two swords, a fishing rod, and an umbrella, who wore a red rose in his buttonhole, and had upon his head a small bowler hat with large holes for ventilation'. Gogarty doesn't specify any preference either way when it came to negotiating lamp posts.

European *tour de force,* running as it did counter-clockwise, and thus contrary to the logic of Coriolis, viz., from the Austrian border to the south-east through Bohemia and Poland up to Denmark, the cockade on the Teutonic helmet, through Norway thence downwards through the Low Countries and, finally, France. But there was no Second Best to argue the case. Instead, Hackett took an avid interest in anything that related to codes and to transmissions; everything from the efforts to decipher messages that were thought to be encrypted in crosswords and personal ads to the broadcasts that came from that scurril Haw Haw.[118]

What made these visits memorable for the Quaker was that, once he had perused the newspapers, the character would invariably request one or another volume of the public works of Puncher & Wattmann (1922), with a penchant for volume X of their Cyclopaedia — the National Library being a legal repository institution, publishers the world over were required to submit copies of anything '*Hiberniae Hiberniaque*'. He would ask, too, for one or another recherché text published by the elusive Ouroboros Press. But these were past masters at ignoring the legal requirement to submit a bound copy. It was the former fad that had first caught the Chief Librarian's attention. In his years before taking the helm of the venerable institute, only one other supplicant had ever requested a volume of the Anglo-Irish Cyclopaedia. This had been a Trinity alumnus by the name of Murphy, or Molloy, or

118 An allusion to honorary Eirishman William Joyce, whose show 'Germany Calling' enjoyed at its height a radio audience, in Engeland, of some seventeen millions. It is this early success which led to the BBC's ongoing love-affair with Eirish radio and television hosts.

Malone, a garmungling figure as taciturn and odd in his ways as the present character in his. Now Trinity students were rare enough birds at the best of times, rare since the college was itself home to a legal repository library, and rare too since they tended to be of the Protestant persuasion. But to put the proverbial tin hat on it, the only volume this Trinity bird was interested in was the Cyclopaedia's Volume X, which he'd insist against the evidence of his eyes should have Qua-Qua on the binding.

Little is known of what precisely the former journalist deciphered in the great domed reading room. But this much the Chief Librarian gathered. Whether through perspicacity or paranoia, Mr Hackett was convinced that a plot was about to be set in motion which would make the Phoneme War look like child's play. There was a phrase he repeated under his breath which sounded to Quaker's ear suspiciously like Dr Goebbels' alternative Fakten und gefälschte Nachrichten. Most singularly, this oddball had become persuaded that at the heart of the plot was a fishing vessel painted pea-green and klept, if memory served, the GIBBERISH.

Like any good citizen, like any self-respecting delusional, Hackett was not content to keep his paranoia private. However paltry his means, with Oates help he sent letter after letter to those in a position to do something about the imaginary plot: to the Eirish Foreign Office; to the Garda Síochána; to the Department of Fisheries. A cruciverbalist of long standing, he now became adept at composing cryptic crosswords and these he dispatched overseas to the puzzle-setters of the *Telepath,* the *Absorber* and the *Munchester Warden*. They were sprinkled with strange and recherché terms, ingenious solutions to clues that included: *mamalujo; new-variant; Bandersnatch; nonce-writer; Penzaunce; overlord.* He engaged in correspondence chess with a certain Jakob Przybyszewski c/o the Polish Government in Exile, Logdon and with the oddly named C.H.O'D Alexander, Bletchley Park, Milton Keynes; and with an obscure inmate of the Parolles' Mental Asylum in Ealing Broadleaf whose name Oates couldn't swear to but may have been Chumpman. Whether any of these letters and missals ever got past the eyes of the censors, let alone the world-weary secretaries, was anyone's guess.

But there was another side to the character during these months about which Oates was blissfully unaware. There are hints of murkier activities, intimations that all this time he may have been playing a double game. Now the Emergency was a fromulous time for all involved, a dark period during which the Eirish Free State, led by the same de Valera who'd both sworn and abjured the Oath of Allegiance, pursued a parallel policy of creative ambivalence. Those who were too frank about their loyalties and who wore their allegiance too openly on their sleeves ran the risk of internment in ollscoil na réabhlóide, the army camp of the Curragh, a cautionary fate which quickly befell the likes of Teddy Mulcahy and Chandler the handler. It was a time for restraint, for hugger-mugger.

Records from this interlude are partial in both senses of the word. Hackett was rarely seen in these straightened times without a battered hat with quail-feather. Several anonymous and redacted witness statements have Hackett's hat with quail-feather mounting the steps of the German Embassy at 58 Northumberland Rd, Ballsbridge, supposedly to have a parley with Eduard Hempel himself. Others attest to his frequent visits to the Dubilin branch of the Goethe Institut. Then there were regular sightings of the fedora-wearing ne'er-do-well on Tuesday afternoons seated on a bench in St Stephen's Green, openly playing chess with a beret-wearing veteran of the Great War whose sunglasses and stick suggested he was visually impaired. This veteran, or perhaps it was his brother, would in turn be spotted entering the Dubilin branch of the Goethe Institut or mounting the steps to 58 Northumberland Rd.

One other curiosity. Upon his return to the old country, Hackett found his paltry belongings had been moved to a more palatable bedroom upstairs in Needles Nugent's doss-house, his rent from this time on being paid fortnightly in advance by an anonymous benefactor. On foot of this beneficence, the one-time scape-grace was given pride of place at the Marconi wireless, where he was afforded the singular honour of choosing between *Radio Éireann*, the BBC World Service and the popular 'Germany Calling' broadcast for the evening bulletin. Does any of this circumstantial evidence amount to proof that Hackett had remained in contact, if not sympathy, with Malachi M[c]Cann and his Dresden confederates? The reader must decide for herself.

All day, then, Hackett had been aware of an electric hum that gained on him or fell away; but despite his street-cunning, he could not 'surprise into being' the milk-float that gave rise to it. Then, at about six o'clock in the evening, just as the bells of St George's on Temple St were ringing out the angelus, a motorised van in the livery of the Swastika Laundry pulled up across the road from Berkeley Rd, into the far end of which Hackett had just turned. Two men stepped out of the van, and began to pull bolsters from a huge sack. One, the shorter, had his back to Hackett. The other was a garmungling figure with protruding ears. Hackett stepped past them, but as he did, he heard one of them begin to whistle '♪♫♪, ♪♫♪'. It was the unmistakable trill of *Lilliburlero.* He stopped. He turned. And the last thing he saw was the gaping mouth of the laundry bag as it was thrust over his head.

Logdon, October 1940

Chief Inspector Quibble's disapproving eye followed the eruption of pigeons that swelled wavelike from the flags of Trafalgar and swilled counter-clockwise about the mighty column before subsiding. The gaze followed a page of newspaper lifted on the blusterly breeze and lofted beyond Nelson's half-moon hat toward the fat blimps that were tethered over the public buildings of the metropolis like so many walruses. If Reichsmarshall Göring imagined for a minute he could cow a stubborn people by raining down bombs on their heads like something out of Dean Swift's Laputa, he had another thing coming. Curious, he thought, his mind yielding to a rare pansúr bán impulse. After Quisling capitulated Norway, gifting so much coastline to Göring, the defence of the realm had fallen to Dowding. A rare conjugation of three gerunds.

But the last laugh was on Gerry. Even now, especially now, as Quibble exchanged a censorious glance with a delator idling rather too conspicuously against a pillar of the vacated National Gallery, in the ultra-secret Hut 14B of Bletchley Park, they would be firing up their BTM 'bronze goddess', ready to attempt a turing. Or Turing. One of the finest deceptions of the war to date was surely the invention of a mathematician of that name to disguise what was in fact a gerund. Rather than allow McTurchaill & Co coin a definition suitable for the OED, giving the whole blooming game away, a coterie of experts collaborated in the construction of a fictional biography of "A Turing" which was inserted into the eleventh edition of the *Encyclopaedia Britannica* in addition to Black's *Who's Who* (1940).[119] Damned clever. What galled was that Quibble was only in the know because of his unofficial friendship with a certain iron lady who'd grandly declared she 'was not for Turing". But for her, the goings on of that bally Eirishman, Bracken, and his precious Ministry of Information were a closed book, even to so crucial an organ of surveillance as the Semantics branch of CID.

And the point was, they'd taken their eye off the ball. All very well to fortuitously use their radio-jamming towers to foresee and forestall the waves of **Luftwaffe** raiders; all very well to intercept and attempt to decode the private messages sent by Dönitz to his underhand undersea fleet. These measures might give the populace at large the reassurance they were coming to terms with the threat of being battered and starved into submission. But for the MoD to suppose for a minute, as they seemed to have done, that the IBM-4 *Speakeasy* programme was the last word in the Phoneme War, to suppose that **Herr Doktor** Goebbels was done with his attempts to undermine the language of King, Bard and Bible — that wasn't merely naïve. It was a dereliction of duty. And he was damned if he was going to be any part of it. If an armada of new verbal shenanigans was mustering to the east, Cecil Quibble would

119 By war's end, the deception was outed. Any entity which can be passed off as a living human is said to have passed the Turing Test.

remain a very Walsingham in vigilance.

Another thing they'd fallen asleep on was the little matter of the threat from a fifth column. Crass stupidity, to imagine that His Majesty's Empire would rally to a man to the flag at a time of national peril. Just look at what those damned Eirish had done in the second city of Empire at a time when the army was caught up in the trenches of Flanders. No doubt about it, **M** and his Secret Service had been caught with their pants down on that one. William Melville, another bally Eirishman. And now that Devil in Eire who'd been part and parcel of that sneaky insurrection was refusing to row in behind Whitehall in its hour of need.

But never mind the Eirish. Who knew what mischief was afoot amongst the followers of Baronet Oswald Mosley, Cpt Archibald Ramsay, the Duke of Wellington, Arnold Leese, Lord William Joyce, Norah Briscoe, those Mitford girls and Edward Windsor himself? In the run up to hostilities, they'd been openly in cahoots with the enemy. All members of the infamous Right Club which used to meet in the Russian Tea Rooms in South Kensington under the auspices of Russian émigrée Anna Walkoff, who upon their exposure promptly did so. It was Quibble's men who'd kept the close eye on that particular coterie and given the heads up to Maxwell Knight, who'd inherited Melville's **M** moniker. And what about what's-his-name, something something Kent, who'd been seen hobnobbing with Graf von Beruf. What devil's work had he been up to, that time he'd taken a secret, black and midnight jaunt to Dresden?

No, this was not the time to let the guard down. He crossed Lesser Square, exchanging a reproving glance with a delàtor masquerading as a newspaper vendor. These were his eyes and ears, yet if Whitehall was to be believed, there was no longer any call for them. His critical eye ran down the mastheads and headlines. He lifted the *Daily Telepath*, thought again of the bizarre clues to the cryptic crossword that had taunted and eluded him the previous evening at the club. Without purchasing, he perused the solutions, and as he did so, a queasy somersault in the gut unaccountably brought to mind that jackanapes, Hackett. The one that got away. Chief Inspector Quibble sensed it deep in his water: the man had been as guilty as a poisoner in the days of the plague, spreading skaz and contervoc to the four corners of the kingdom. Gone to ground, scarpered back to their so-called Free State. Not a squeak out of him in eighteen months beyond an unceasing stream of correspondence chess he himself had cast a wary eye over. Opponent up in Bletchley Park what's more — another bloody Eirishman, C.H.O'D A, but bedamned if he could find anything encoded in the notation. KN-KB3. QBxN+. Which wasn't to say one could let one's guard down, not by a long chalk. A bumbler. A chancer. But who'd been puppet master, pulling the strings?

He continued on into So-Ho. Chinese characters with their Chinese characters. How could you police a metropolis of a hundred tongues? Surveying the bomb damage old and recent, it came to him again that if Mr Hitler imagined for a minute the island people would be battered into submission, he had sorely miscalculated. Too obdurate by half. If thirty years walking the lexical beat had taught Quibble anything, it was that your native Britain was as jealous as a dog with a bone when it came to giving up a quirk, never mind how quaint. How else explain the persistence of pecks and roods and hundred-weight; of Brummie, and Geordie, and Scouse? How else, the brisk trade on the black market in prohibited weights and words?

Quibble found to his surprise that he'd been trumpeting bars from Elgar's Nimrod. Because there was something fine, too, in this national obduracy. Something uplifting. Then, as he turned into Greek St, momentarily, something like dismay fluttered in the Quibble stomach. But no, the new gap in the terrace didn't correspond. Flanked by rubble, a sign declared defiantly 'Business as Usual'. Reassured, vindicated, Quibble negotiated a wimbling plank across a newly opened trench and entered the dusky interior of the COCK & BULL. The place was empty but for the predictable scattering of artless dodgers, none of whom appeared at all put out by arrival of the custodial eye. A surreptitious hand touched his elbow, and he permitted himself to be ushered into a backroom, the very snug in which, several years since, he'd exchanged unpleasantries with the Eirish hack Ж.

Quibble squinted down at the arm that had taken his and thence to the close-cropped, spherical head. 'Mr Pvrszmnvszmski,' he invited.

'Przybyszewski.'

'You have some information for me.'

'I have.' Wary eyes surveyed the empty room. On one wall was a poster featuring a sinking ship foundering on the caption *Careless Talk Costs Lives.* 'The wheels are in motion.'

'Indeed?'

'A night-train was observed leaving Warszawa Główna on Sondag. Destination Brest. Our source reports canisters of the newest variants.'

There was a narrowing of the Quibble eye. 'How could your source tell the destination?'

Przybyszewski moved a finger adjacent to a nostril and tapped. 'A signalman at the French border later confirmed it. Which means, they'll already have been whisked down to the U-boat pens.'

'They can hardly fire them as torpedoes.' If Quibble was being facetious, his features gave no indication of it. If Quibble was being facetious, the Pole's reply gave no indication of it. 'They'll be landed here as contraband.'

'Tell me, how the deuce do you defend eight thousand miles of coastline against contraband? Besides, how bad can the newest variants be?'

'They've begun to designate them with letters of the Greek alphabet.' A silence suggested the seriousness of this development. 'Last month a canister was accidentally opened in Danzig,' the Pole went on. 'The result was pandemonium.'

'I daresay,' Quibble winced, 'the *Speakeasy* programme will cope.' It was evident he was no fan of the brand of mid-Atlantic Engelish the IBM-4s had been spewing out.

'Little doubt about that,' Przybyszewski concurred. 'But before they do…' Quibble wasn't the man to fill an anacoluthon, so at length the Pole resumed. 'Do you remember the Battle of Cable Street?'

'1936,' Quibble's eyebrows conceded surprise. 'Your tribe.' Then, with something resembling satisfaction, he nodded, 'Mosley's Union of Fascists took quite the hiding that day.'

'There was a little trick to deal with the mounted police. Kids with bags of marbles. You let those spill over the cobbles, the mightiest carthorse comes crashing down.'

At this image Quibble grimlied. 'I fail to see your point.'

'Sprinkle enough false and dubitous terms and the pillars of authority come crashing down.'

'That was their theory before. Look how far it got them.'

'Agreed… if that was the endgame.'

The parentheses to either side of Quibble's mouth contracted, and the furrow between his eyebrows rose in proportion. 'So what is "the endgame"?'

'We're not sure. You throw the new variants with their Greek prefixes like dust into the opponent's eye, it gives you a brief window to do what you like.' Jakob Przybyszewski's furtive eyes again scoured the empty room. 'The preparatory stage they've designated Operation **Jabberwoche**. The Operation to follow on its heels, **Bandersnatch**, which appears to be a corruption of the old Bavaraian festival of **Bänders Nacht**, a night when caterwauling minstrels were suffered to wander about and compete in rival gangs. Word from the *Biuro Szyfrów* is that the **U**- in their secret programme is definitely **Unsinn**. Nonsense. Trumpery. Also, our Dresden source tells us the roll out of the **Unsinnschreiber**® is imminent.' He edged nearer Quibble's ear. '**Bandersnatch** — bespoke synthetic statements generated at will, tailored to each particular dialect. As many rabbit holes as there are Alices to fall down them.'

The parentheses contracted further, the furrow became an exclamation mark. 'If they've pulled that off…'

The Pole was not the man to leave another's anacoluthon hanging. 'Before you know it, the entire island would be disarticulated along faultlines of **alternative Fakten und gefälschte Nachrichten**. Once that cat's out of the bag…'

CHAPTER THE SEVENTH

in which the JABBERWOCK *finally sets out upon her final voyage*

Twenty-four hours after his abduction, if abduction it was and not the fulfilment of McCann's 'don't call us, we'll call you', Hackett lay stretched out on the stern of a trawler, staring wordlessly down to where the engine's reverberant flatulence burbled brown bubbles through the dark harbour water. It might have been a lesson in aquatic acoustics: the indefatigable drool rolled endlessly between hull and pier as a vocalist exercises vowels and vocables, purling their single note, the echo setting the boards ajudder. They were still tethered to their mooring, a thick hawser fixing either end of the boat, though what precisely they were now awaiting was beyond Hackett's ken. For although there was nothing unusual in a fishing trawler setting out long before dawn, even in these fromulous times, the longer they waited, the more likely it was that some cranky Customs Officious, or a nose from the Department of Fisheries, unable to slumber, might stumble across them.

Through the circular porthole, the little cabin was lit by an oil-lamp which threw the three faces into shadowy relief so that they looked like nothing so much as gargoyles hidden in the eaves of a dusk-filled cloister. They were clustered about a table-top upon which was unfrabbled a nautical chart extending from Fastnet, so named because of the plentiful fish, to Lundy, so named because of its treacherous undercurrents. The radio-set behind them gave out now nothing but low static. But the area forecast from Carnsore Point to Hook Head to Roche's Point had been favourable, with moderate easterlies not exceeding three on the Beaufort scale[120] and a pressure of nine hundred and ninety five millibars[121] falling slowly; the tide, already past the full, was likewise falling slowly, while contrariwise, to the east, a crescent moon bright as a Cheshire grin was rising slowly; so that it wasn't at all clear what it was precisely that the men were waiting for. The pair of callipers executed once more a stiff-legged saunter from Land's End to St. Martin's in the Scilly Isles, so named because of their indigenous population. It then swung drunkenly through sixty degrees, and ambled stiffly northwards as far as the Tuscar rock. There followed a protracted calculation. 'So that's it then.' Willy Clarke nodded up to his two dark shipmates. 'Where's you-know-who?' he gruffed.

'Still stretched out aft.'

'What are we bringing him along for, that's what I'd like

---

120 During the Napoleonic Wars an old French measure of the weather based on wind strength which ranged from 'beau' (1) to 'fort' (8) was refined and modified by Eirish cartographer Sir Francis Beaufort.

121 Unhappy that the unit of atmospheric pressure should be named for a Frenchman (the mathematician and gambler Blaise Pascal) and one moreover whose tendency towards depression was legendary, in 1909 the 'bar' was coined by British meteorologist William Napier with a nominal value of 100,000 Pa to the bar.

to know?' gruntled the third man, a hare-eyed ex-army horse-doctor who was in point of fact the only one of the three in any way familiar with the ins and outs of cabotage,[122] and so had been made first-mate.

'All I've been told is, when the you-know-what comes *from* Germany, you-know-who goes *to* Germany. Seems he'll be useful there once the you-know-what gets to you-know-where.'

'Yerra you know yourself.' The dark laughter of the second figure, who bore an uncanny resemblance to the garmungling carpenter who four years before had been measuring wimbling planks outside the Long Room of Trinity College, indicated a dark intent. 'I'll say this, that's one won't break radio-silence if he's turned coat.'

Perhaps they were fooled by how supine the erstwhile journalist appeared. A peculiar incident had occurred several hours before. As they were somnambulating the drowsy figure to the fishing-boat, the party had been accosted by a nun. The nun, dressed head-to-foot in puffin-like garb but with a cheeky smirk under her wimple, pushed a collection-bucket toward them. 'Could any of you fine gentlemen spare a few coppers to fix the gutters up in the Abbey?' Scent of... what was that? Oddly alluring. Alluring, too, the little mole on her cheek. They shooed her away, guffawing like louts. Perhaps it was the round of guffaws that had them fail to register the puzzled look their captive was directing rearward toward the Sister.

---

122 This term, which is defined by the OED as *(Naut.) coastal navigation and trade*, is thought to derive from the Italian navigator Giovanni 'John' Cabot (1450-1498), whose voyage from Bristol in search of Asia in 1497 at the behest of Henry Tudor was very nearly scuttled by his compatriot Giacomo 'Jim' Sabot.

Now, supine on the boat, Hackett replayed in his mind the curious encounter. For there was something altogether familiar about that nun's chirpy smirk. They were famously creatures of habit, but the habit had been out of place on this cheeky Sister. And then there was the spoor of, what was it? Eau de toilette? Hackett propped himself up, mentally knucked his fingers. *Lily of the Valley*. His mother's scent. What was doubly strange, the scent had somehow followed him onto the boat! Curiouser and curiouser. Fighting the pang of spurious nostalgia the aroma inevitably evoked, he began to sniff the air; to sniff his hands; to sniff his coat. And there it was, about the right-hand pocket, stronger than ever. His fingers burrowed in, and there they encountered a laced handkerchief. A laced lace handkerchief. A *ladies'* handkerchief! He pulled it out — it released its delicious spoor — and examined it by the fickle moonlight. In cursive eye-liner was written:

'*Imperative get coordinates to me. A. S.*'

A.S. It took barely a moment. Agatha Sangster. Phony Maloney herself! So was it a triple-game she'd been playing all along? Like the celebrated Eirish crossdresser Matt O'Hara during the last war. But could he trust her? Or was it a double double-cross?

All evidence points to his momentous decision to put his trust in the double-agent. It is conjectured that the motley crew had been so careless as to mark the rendezvous on their nautical map. From the porthole, Hackett must have glimpsed it. But then? To communicate tentative intelligence to a false nun who was no longer there was no laughing matter. Yet evidently he succeeded. As much as why he did so, how Hackett did so has been a matter of conjecture ever since. Did he, as some hold, somehow Morse the intelligence with the heel of his shoe unnoticed from the hold? Did he, as the more romantic believe, inscribe the coordinates unto the laced lace handkerchief and place it on the pier, weighted down with his father's fob-watch? It may never be known. For having completed her secret mission, Agatha Sangster was to return to Dresden, but was never to return *from* Dresden.

Some twenty minutes later, with the grinning moon hoisted a further five degrees of azimuth into the night sky and drawing after it, as it were, the morning star, the **JABBERWOCK** at long last left the embrace of the neutral harbour and set out for the open sea. Hackett was at once aware of the change in pitch of the deck and of the low burble the vessel's engine was fartling backwards into the receding harbour mouth. Still lying down, not so much because he was dog-tired as because he had no great wish to try either his stomach or his sea-legs, he looked at the silhouette hunkering to one side of the cabin. He wondered, for he was no sea-dog, whether this might not be the fabled dog-watch, so-named because in order to shorten it, it had had to be cur-tailed. His next thought as he looked back down into the moon-spangled waves was to try to fathom how in the name of all that was holy they were meant to effect a rendezvous with, of all things, a submarine. Though it was still black night, they at least could take their bearings from the star which, as in biblical times, was twinkling to the East. But it shivered him to think of the great iron whale in whose belly a crew of sweating submariners were even now stealing blindly through the inky deep. Then it came to him with a deeper shiver that, even were it daylight, the windowless

U-boat would be advancing as blind as fortune beneath the freijous waves. It was not a comforting thought.

They held their course due east for sufficient time for the pearl of the morning star to fade into an oyster sky. As he contemplated the vast ovoid flecked with feathers of pink and mauve, the patent risibility of the adage that the darkest hour is just before dawn dawned on Hackett. But he was in no condition to share the observation with the watch, for no sooner had their course heaved to onto a southward bearing than the lateral motion of the water under the bow caused the JABBERWOCK to assume a drunken trundle, and it was all he could do not to heave, too.

For several long hours they muttled southward. A brash sun had already risen above the brassy waves when the Scillies came into view off the starboard bow. Hackett's grasp of the geography of Cornwall was slight, yet he knew well enough that they had to pass between these storied isles to starboard (as you looked at them) and Land's End to larboard (*ibid.*) if they were to make the rendezvous, which was slated to take place some score of nautical miles at seven degrees South-Southeast of Penzaunce. St. Ives, from which the polygamist had set out, and to which the motley crew were to carry their nefarious cargo once the sun had set, was some seven statute miles to the north side of the peninsula. That part should be a doddle. After all, the Cornish coast had a venerable tradition of smuggling. But how were they to meet with a single submarine, the nautilus which was to spirit him to High Germany, that eighth rank where the pawn would at last be transformed to knight or rook? During the entire journey, so far as he was aware, they had maintained the strictest radio silence. Looking over the vasty deep upon which the trawler, now that its engine was idling, had begun to bobble like the most paltry of corks, Hackett was filled with bilious gobbets and gabbling dubits. The sight of two-thirds of the crew kneeling low and unsteadily over the trawler's rolling flanks and discharging according to the Law of Diminishing Returns the residue of their guts did nothing to settle either of the above.

Noon came and went, and there was still no sign of a sub. The third crew member, who alone among them could boast sea-legs and a constitution to match, had unfrabbled from the great capstan a long green net. After all it had to look to any curious coastguard that they were a bonafide fishing vessel, and whether or not any fish were fooled by the device, it had gulled a quantity of squabbling guillemots who gyred and gimballed about the JABBERWOCK like gadflies about a goat. Quark, quark, quark, they cried. Once he'd made certain of their bearings by a process of dead reckoning, the first-mate set a flippant Jolly Roger frabbling above the cabin, to act as a signal to any periscope that might draw close enough to make out its grinning death's head.

Another hour went by.

'Are you sure it was noon?'

'Noon.'

'But is German noon the same as our noon. What I mean, is their GMT the same as our GMT?' This was the second crew-member, he whose lips and ears protruded like something out of a Popeye cartoon. His sputtered inquiry from the side of the deck was dismissed by a ribald wince that flashed from the third, viz., the first-mate, to the first, who was Willy Clarke. Even Hackett, who was himself not feeling at all in the pink, was moved to guffaw.

Now, Hackett's eyes had been fixed for some time upon what he at first took to be a cormorant; but if it was a cormorant itself, its sinuous neck was moving with inordinate speed through the undulating brine. In fact, now he looked twice, it was moving so fast relative to the waves that it was drawing behind it a feathery spume. They'd seen many a strange thing in their time, father and son, on their field trips down the Wickenlow coastline, but never had they witnessed so prodigious a bird. With a jolt, he realised it could only be the periscope of U-110. What was more curious was that it slipped straight by the larboard at a distance of not more than several cables. It then continued half-a-league half-a-league half-a-league onward as though it had failed entirely to notice the fishing-boat.

Some minutes later, by a crafty manipulation of the Principles of Archimedes and Bernoulli and at a league and two cables' remove, the great iron fish surfaced. It was high time. With one eye as it were to his nautical chronometer and the other to the great vault of the sky for fear of spotter aircraft, little Willy Clarke had been growing increasingly restless. A pint-sized trawler marked on its flanks with the flag of a neutral power bobbling about on the open sea might not be particularly conspicuous or suspicious, but neither had they a permit to fish within British territorial waters. That was a detail they'd overlooked. And if they'd overlooked that detail, who was to say what other detail might have been overlooked. The crates of regular counterfeit goods, and the empty barrels of Jameson's Whiskey that had been scoured out in readiness for the irregular counterfeit goods, had been stowed openly on the deck, so that at the first sign of trouble they could be readily tipped into the brine. But that was not a recourse to which Willy Clarke would have wished to turn. It came as a great relief, therefore, to see the prow of the U-boat break the surface, dragging up the dribbling cannon and conning-tower,[123] before the whole craft lurched to the horizontal. Clarke's binoculars scanned its beam. 'Get out the lamp,' he calloohed, though Fleming, the first-mate, had anticipated the command.

Despite the league and a half that now separated them, once the flashlight on the German vessel began to flicker, the distance was as if abolished. Yet something was troubling Hackett, who was at last upright on unsteady feet. In the first place, in what base language was the message being tapped out? Secondly, was it certain that German semaphore was the same as Engelish semaphore, or Hiberno-Engelish for that matter? And thirdly, most troubling of all, was it possible that the semantics of semaphore might be contaminated by the same antics as contervoc? Or worse, contaminated with the radical solutions that the IBM model-4s were universally imposing? In fine, his mind perhaps drawn back to the 1 inch to the yard scale model of the Bray Head rail disaster, could he be witnessing another signal signal failure?

After some minutes footling and foostering, the engine once again fartled into life and the fishing-boat, trailing a lengthy dragnet and a cloud of guillemots, made a frolicsome approach until it lay within a couple of cables of the fearsome predator. A rubber dinghy, meanwhile, had set off from the

123 So named because of the duplicitous manner that a submarine sneaks up on its quarry.

latter and was making its way precariously over the mounting sea towards them. There were three men in the boat. To the fore was a smart looking naval officer; to the aft a stern looking von Beruf; and teetering in between, a green looking McCann. As the officer paddled, von Beruf fed out a thick cable, one end of which was secured to the conning-tower of the U-boat. This task had initially been assigned to McCann until he began to feel too ropey. Now it was all he could do, gripping either side for dear life, not to abandon the dinghy. Dignity had long since been abandoned.

Just as it was about to draw alongside, the dinghy disappeared momentarily beneath the rolling back of the whelming ocean. When the boat again came into view, it so fell out that McCann fell out. After a minute a head appeared, sputtering, spluttering, struggling, eyes huge and hair matted to the scalp. McCann was no swimmer, that much was obvious, and the attempt at a doggy-paddle would have been laughable if it wasn't for the sense of danger that dogged the ludicrous.

The first-mate was the match of the situation. He reached down into the waves with a boathook, and at the third attempt he succeeded in snagging the seat of McCann's pants, and hauling the distressed figure alongside. In no time at all, a draggled man was dragged on board, heavy as the proverbial drowned rat.

All through the remaining operation McCann sat bedraggled, a pool of salt-water slowly growing around him. He was feeling exquisitely sorry for himself. If he recognised Hackett, or anyone else for that matter, he gave little indication of it. Fortunately the remaining crew were up to the task of running a guy between the two vessels, and before long the first wooden crate juddered across the cable-length that now separated them. Even before it was secured on board, Hackett descried the rectilinear eagle of the Reich, and in elaborate stencil the legend: GS-5 Unsinnschreiber®. Then it *was* the dreaded nonce-writer! A second box of the manxome hardware juddered across, then a third. Then there was a pause after which a second procession of smaller, cylindrical canisters began to dance their way along the wimbling guy from U-boat to fishing vessel. On the foremost of these, scrawled crudely in faded chalk, Hackett descried a symbol he hadn't anticipated. A Greek character pranced jerkily, an *epsilon* or an *upsilon*, he couldn't be sure at the distance. The second was marked similarly. *Epsilon* or *upsilon*. The third was marked with a *phi* or *psi*. The fourth and fifth with *zeta* or *theta,* unless it was *beta* or *eta*. The sixth, seventh and eighth with *mu* or *nu.* Finally, three more containers of the redoubtable Unsinnscreiber® winced their way across.

The second crewman, meanwhile, he with the lips and ears out of Mutt and Jeff, had begun to secrete the secret cargo in the contraband Jameson's Whiskey barrels. At one point he lost his footing, and a barrel all but toppled. 'For God's sake be careful!' gruffed Willy Clarke. Unseen, a single canister rolled across the see-sawing deck, *epsilon upsilon, epsilon upsilon,* before coming to rest against the bedraggled figure in the puddle. Hackett looked on in silence. All the while the Jolly Roger's Cheshire grin frabbled above the cabin. The U-boat too had a skull and crossbones stencilled onto its conning-tower, as though it might contain something toxic, and who knew, perhaps it did. But that death's head had a fat grin, a mirthless grin, a diabolical grin, a grin that put one in mind of Reichsmarshall Göring. And if it did itself, that was in its own way apt. For from some lair deep inside the Reichsluftfahrtministerium in distant Berlin, Reichsmarshall Göring had a diabolical part to play in the goings-on of that fateful date in October.

CHAPTER THE EIGHTH

in which Hackett finally becomes a knight, or a rook;
or
how a notorious national disaster was averted

Occupied Europe had provided **Reichsmarshall** Göring with a vast panoply of airfields upon which to assemble the aerial armada which would bring the Sceptic Isle to its knees without need of invasion. But many long weeks had passed since that idle boast, and the **Führer** was growing more than a little weary of the idle boaster's pretentions. For two months the enemy's airfields had been pounded; for two more, their capital. But St Paul's was still standing, and with it, the resolve of an obstinate island race. It was time to unleash a new kind of warfare: unrestricted **Gesamtsprachekrieg**. Dresden assured the **Führer** that their **Unsinnschreiber**® was more than a match for anything the Americans might dream up; the **Bayerische Zweigstelle** of the **Goethe Institüt** assured that the Eirish cell working there had actually delivered on their Greek-prefixed gibberish which would prepare the way for **Unternehmen Bandersnatch**. Admiral Dönitz had promised he could furnish the means of delivery.

Now, from the time of the Great War, in an ingenious

policy designed by Count Zimmerman that was intended to confuse those using umlautless typewriters not of German manufacture, the **Kriegsmarine** was divided between the Ü-flotte (**Überseeflotte**), whose vessels remained above the waves, and the U-flotte (**Unterseeflotte**), whose vessels dove below. It was the kind of underhand policy that appealed to the **Führer**, and for the duration of his war the Ü-flotte (**Überseeflotte**) was under the direction of **Großadmiral** Erich 'Surface' Raeder while the U-flotte (**Unterseeflotte**), was commanded by Karl 'Dunking' Dönitz. It was Dönitz who assured the **Führer** that, while the eyes of Britain were fixed upon the skies above Logdon, a nefarious shipment might easily be landed along a coast infamous for its pirates and smugglers, particularly if the **Luftwaffe** might mount a particularly fromulous raid on the capital to divert attention. It was a dastardly plan which Winston Churchill, in the second of his monumental six volume history of the period characterised in chilling terms: '*They aimed to transport the 'new-variant' in sealed containers like a plague bacillus*.' The **Kriegsmarine** might be afforded the chief glory, but the fat airman, who until this time had been overly fond of Dönitz, was to be given one last chance.

For several days, repair crews worked round-the-clock on every make and model of Dornier and Junker, of Heinkel and Henschel, of Fieseler and Focke-Wulf, anything at all, in short, that could be coaxed to carry a bomb across the channel and to drop it once it was above a certain square-mile of Landon that, up until this time, had been relatively untouched. That square-mile was, of course, Ealing Broadleaf. If unrestricted linguistic mayhem was about to be unleashed from the counterfeit cargo even now being landed above the town of Penzaunce, what better than a simultaneous blow to the very nerve-centre which had coordinated that country's defences throughout the Phoneme War?

At fourteen thirty-five GMT, deep in a basement in Whitehall, all the telephones began to hop at once as if animated by electrical contagion. Even to the veteran ladies of Fighter Command, who were well used to bossing bundles of miniature squadrons about the great mahogulous table with their croupier sticks, it was as if the radar defence system had gone berserk. By all accounts, entire flotillas of dots were appearing by the second in the skies above Wight, and Dover, and Thames, and Humber, and German Bight. They were materialising in great waves, like so many migratory birds when the day of departure has at long last dawned. If the new-fangled electronics could be trusted, every last one of the Luftwaffe's remaining bombers were about to test the Dowding system to the very hilt. And this in broad daylight!

Unbeknownst to Fighter Defence, though evidently not to the Admiralty, some several hundreds of nautical miles West-Southwest of the Thames, in a quiet corner of the ocean somewhere between Lundy and Plymouth, a rendezvous had been effected between a neutral fishing boat and a vessel of the Unterseeflotte. What happened next has been the matter of considerable debate ever since, not least because the JABBERWOCK went down so rapidly that she left no survivors. However, in May of the following year, U-110 was forced to the surface by the tenacious attentions of HMS Bulldog and, before she too sank beneath the grey Atlantic, her crew was taken into custody, along with a fully working Enigma machine and a complete score of the Enigma variations to which it was daily set. But that is another story. As far as ours is concerned, from the accounts gleaned from the prisoners of war, the following sketchy sequence of events may be reasonably conjectured.

Just as the last of the crates containing the Unsinnscreiber® was being winched across the wimbling gap between the two vessels, the alarum was raised. Two tell-tale trails of smoke, one to North-Northeast (as you looked at it), the other East-Southeast (ibid.), could be descried staining the horizon. Now, it is well known that if one ignores the effects of atmospheric refraction, the distance to the horizon from an observer close to the Earth's surface is $d \approx 1.06\sqrt{h}$, where d is given in nautical miles and h in feet. Supposing the lookout to be of average height for the Kriegsmarine, say 5'11", and the effect of the conning-tower be allowed to add a further dozen feet to this elevation, and calculating the maximum speed of a Royal Navy Flower-class corvette to be in the region of 16 knots (relative to the water, which for simplicity we will assume to be acting uniformly on all three vessels), it is demonstrable that the U-boat did not have in excess of a quarter of an hour before the enemy would be quite literally upon it. Of course, no acting-commander could countenance awaiting that eventuality, even should his Kapitän fail to return forthwith.

Two members of the crew who were on the conning-tower have independently stated that, just before the claxon began to rasp and the fearsome cry of '*Al-arm!*' to be calleyed,[124]

124 A corruption of the French cry: 'à l'arme!'. Other notable French corruptions include 'Mayday!' ('m'aidez!'), 'all aboard' ('tout d'abord') and 'mind you' ('mon dieu').

the bedraggled figure on board the Eirish fishing-boat lurched to his feet with something resembling a canister clutched to his breast. A garmungling figure wearing a battered hat '**wie Bogarts Fedora, aber mit einer Feder**' (Witness B) who was thereby identified as **Herr Rühnig** (Witness A) approached and tried to relieve the bedraggled figure of said canister. A scuffle immediately ensued. In spite of the cable-length that separated the two vessels, the witnesses could make out cries, **auf Englisch**, of 'don't open it!', 'careful!' and 'put that down for God's sake!' As the remainder of the crew rushed to join the melee, the witnesses saw their **Kapitän**'s cap knocked from his head and, unnoticed by the brawlers, something resembling a dustbin-lid fall from the contested canister and roll across the deck. The scrum lasted '**eine Zählung von zwanzig**' (witness A, who didn't specify what imaginary item was being counted), '**eine halbe Minute**' (witness B), before the bedraggled figure was wrestled to the ground, the beleaguered canister wrested from his grasp.

Together with caps to **Kapitän**, who was standing by the capstan, and onto the canister, which had been entrusted to his keeping, some semblance of order was restored. Alone on the fishing vessel, the garmungling figure in the feathered fedora seemed aware of the dustbin-lid, which winked in the sunlight as though it were thinking up some devilment. It is unclear what precisely this disc may have been, though commentators have suggested a magnetic spool of some kind. Whatever it was, the garmungling Bogart retrieved it and slipped surreptitiously into the cabin where, it is conjectured, there must have been some class of wire-recorder linked to a Tannoy system. Both witnesses report a metallic cacophony of static preceding a cascade of garbled **kant**.

At this point, behind them on the conning-tower '**Rauch**!' cried the third watch, gesticulating to North-Northeast. Turning, the first witness saw a second column of smoke rising over the horizon above his, the third watch's, shoulder, which would have placed it on a bearing of East-Southeast. '**Rauch**!' he too callooed. '*Al-arm!*' calleyed the second witness, who had taken in in that instant that there were two columns of smoke visible on the horizon, which were likely converging on them at a rate of 16 kn.

Instantly, the claxon rasped out its urgent appeal. Witness B, who was the acting **Kommandant**, relayed the frightful news by semaphore to the fishing-boat. Over there, his **Kapitän** lost little time in commandeering the signal-lamp from the first-mate in order to tap out a reply. But now all becomes veiled in confusion. Was the wiring faulty? Was the electric circuitry shorting out? One way or another, the series of dots and dashes that stuttered across from the JABBERWOCK made no sense at all in any of the naval codes known to any of the German mariners. Behind the **Kapitän**, the other crew members raced about the Eirish trawler '**wie kopflose Hühner**', fists pushed to their ears. Undaunted, the acting **Kommandant** repeated his urgent recall, all the while the claxon flatulating as though water were shorting out its circuits. The **Kapitän**'s lamp reiterated its previous gibberish with such exactitude that a mechanical or electrical fault in the equipment could be ruled out. It made not the blindest bit of sense!

There was a long droning sound, as of an insect. At a distance of half-a-cable, there followed a desultory plop. One of His Majesty's corvettes, both of which had by now risen above the line of the horizon, the one at three o'clock, the other at half past seven, had opened fire.[125] This was not a development to be welcomed. On board the **JABBERWOCK** there was a desperate slapstick unfolding; in the words of witness A, '**Wie eine wahnsinnige Sequenz aus einem Film von Mack Sennett.**' Worse yet, any word or phrase that carried over the cable-length separating the two vessels seemed to be the veriest gibberish. Once more the **Kapitän**'s cap was knocked off his head; once more, the canister was tugged hither and tither, disgorging more of its contents. '**Müssen wir tauchen!**' yelled the third-in-command. A second shell plopped nearby, throwing up a column of water high as a Lombardy poplar. Reluctantly, the acting **Kommandant** concurred. '**Müssen wir tauchen,**' he nodded.

The account now becomes even more confused. What final mishap was it that put paid to the **JABBERWOCK**, consigning her to a watery grave with all hands on deck? Was it the case, as Cpt Griffin of HMS Walrus attested, that as the U-boat, by a clever manipulation of the principles of Archimedes and Bernoulli[126] slipped beneath the waves, there was no time to disentangle the guy that connected the two vessels? Was it not more likely, as Cpt Carpenter of HMS Tortoise suggested, that the submerging monster got somehow entangled in the

---

125 The substitution of hours for points of the compass as a nautical referent was made possible by the invention of the Harrison clock. Time on board all ships was thereafter fixed at GMT in order to avoid any directional confusion that putting back or forward the clock would entail.

126 The latter refers to the lateral flow of sea-water over the pectoral fins, the former to the blowing of air from the buoyancy tanks. It is a matter of considerable wonder that the whale pulls off the same feat in apparent ignorance of these laws.

dragnet which the fishing-boat, to allay the suspicions of any passing coastguard, had left trailing? Or were His Majesty's corvettes, as the Germans always insisted, complicit in the sinking of a neutral vessel? One way or another, by the time the first of the warships had closed in on the dreadful scene, nothing remained above the whelming waters but a solitary fedora with clipped quail feather circling counter-clockwise in violation of the Coriolis effect, that subsided by slow degrees.

At fifteen oh five GMT, the first of the dark squadrons entered the Thames Estuary between Bigfleet and Allshallows. They followed the river's course for some two-score nautical miles, took a hard right (or 'veered to starboard') once Richmond Bridge came into view and, as they swept over the red-bricked Parolles' Mental Asylum (by which each Bombenschütze had been instructed to take his bearings), they began to disgorge their cargo, like so many deadly eggs. One bomb in every three, by the estimates of the ARP wardens, was an incendiary. They seemed to be oblivious to the losses that the Spitfires and Hurricanoes, the flak, the ac-ac and the pom-poms were wreaking on their serried ranks.

By sixteen hundred hours it was all over. The last of the planes had departed, had crashed, or had limped home, and the all-clear was sounded. All of Ealing, as it seemed, was ablaze, or lay in dismal ruins. As in the worst days of the Blitz, the fire service seemed to be overwhelmed at the scale of the disaster. Marshall Sir Arthur Harris, his eye fixed stonily on a map of Dresden, declared it 'an incendiary incident'. A number of stray explosives, released early by the enthusiasm of younger crews, had struck the Parolles Mental Home; and now, a corresponding number of stray inmates wandering gormlessly amongst the rubble in open dressing-gowns added a soupçon of merriment to the general air of pandemonium. It was, in the words of an American correspondent, 'a date which would live in infamy'. But it didn't. And the fact that it didn't has been the subject of these pages.

From documents recovered from German archives in the aftermath of her capitulation, it is evident that from this time priority was no longer given to the manufacture of the **Unsinnschreiber®**. Perhaps **Herr** Hitler's eyes were already beginning to look to the East. With the loss of the **JABBERWOCK**, the programme's chief architect, **Graf** Ernst von Beruf, along with the Eirish moles Rooney and McCann, without whom the **Unsinnschreiber®** was only so much hardware, were **verloren und verlaufen**. So too, the existing stock of 'new-variants' with their formidable Greek prefixes. Over the next several years, occasional canisters of contraband Jameson's Whiskey were known to wash up along the coast of Cornwall, unleashing localised bouts of linguistic mayhem, a circumstance thought to be the origin of the myth that the Cornish kingdom had once had its own entirely unintelligible language. In any event, much as had happened when **Herr** Göring had switched focus from attacking the airfields to attacking the city, the moment had been irretrievably lost.

It had been a close-run thing. But the Empire had been saved; and her language, though irremediably Americanized, remained intact. So how is it, it might reasonably be asked, that the crouchback politician never made a laudatory speech to those few to whom so much was owed by so many? Firstly, and perhaps key to the general forgetfulness which overtook a war-weary country which, after all, had no more time for their bulldog prime minister, the fact that it had been a close-run thing is all important. Why celebrate an episode which, in the context of a schizophrenically divided Europe, could only act to highlight the parlous nature of the mother tongue? Far better sweep the whole affair under the carpet.

In the second place, who was there who could relate the story? Sir Æthelred, who in his time as Secretary of State for the Home Office had been one of the four pillars of British Democracy, had never been privy to anything more than a partial view. In keeping with the great tradition of the civil service, his own private secretaries had seen to that. Besides, the rugged figure who to this day may be seen being wheedled about his hereditary home of Bletchley Park in bath-chair and rug is no longer what is termed *compos mentis*. If Seymour Doolittle, that venerable Don, remained lucid to the very end, it is with sadness that we must relate that he died, peaceably in his bed, some time towards the end of the third year of the Emergency. Eighteen months later, Harold Hastings, late of the Acacademy, became the late Harold Hastings when he was flattened by a stray Doodlebug that failed to explode.

The discretion of Chief Inspector Quibble, on this as on most matters, is proverbial, so that little but procedural detail may be expected to be gleaned from his laconic lips. Nor from the Pole who'd clandestinely met the Chief Inspector in the wartime **COCK & BULL** — once his native country was liberated he returned behind the Iron Curtain, where he remains liberated to this day. Nor from those chess prodigies and cruciverbalists who daily carried out A Turing in Hut 14B of Bletchley Park, and who are sworn to secrecy for a period of not less than fifty years. Of the four horsemen of the apocryphal, two as we have seen were drowned, one sprakes uniquely in a private concoction of Dinneen's **Gaedhilge**, while a double-agent, a cheeky mole with a cheeky mole, absconded to Dresden, but never *from* Dresden. Who Quinn may have been, if indeed there ever was a Quinn, is anyone's guess.

Nothing more was heard of a Royal Academy of Letters, which had in any event been housed, if reports are to be believed, in a Berkeley building. Nor of the dozens of Projectors and Mechanicals who supposedly spent their lives therein. Nor, after that date that singularly failed to go down in infamy, of its Hereditary Director, O'Brien or Smyllie, nor of Turlough McTurchaill, the Tweedledee of dictionaries. It is presumed that, like the stalwart officers of RMS Titanic, they went down with their vessel. As for Ж, the inimitable Ж, we have been witness to his second, and definitive, watery end.

Many months later, with the Emergency all but over, Air Marshal 'Butcher' Harris's tactless policy of **Vergeltungs-bombardierung**[127] ensured that in Dresden, no two pieces of delft were left intact. The conflagration of the Florence of the Elbe, the date of which *has*, ironically, gone down in infamy, has meant that any record extant of what the **Schlüsselbüro** had been up to went up in smoke. All that survives anywhere are fragments; papers; briefs; orts; partial accounts from partial witnesses. To try to reconstruct the entire affair

127 A policy of bombing with a vengeance advocated by Sir Arthur Harris, who remarked 'I prefer the German term; it has a Wagnerian ring!' By war's end even Churchill was beginning to find his Air Marshall rather too bombastic. There is no evidence he ever worked as a butcher.

from these would be like trying to reconstruct a lost civilisation from the pottery fragments which Walter Hackett so disdained.

One man alone appears to know the whole story, from start to finish. He was there, by his own testimony, *in situ* and *in medias res,* right from the get-go. He accompanied Ignatius Hackett on that historical journey into the very boardroom of the Royal Academy of Letters, one blusterly Sunday in the year of the Abdication Crisis. He was privy to any number of high-level meetings; he was the confidant of the man called Ж; he was even, latterly, the recipient of that stream of coded correspondence which led, in his candid and considered opinion, to the interception of the JABBERWOCK. He was, finally, a witness to the Götterdämmerung visited upon Ealing Broadleaf and, collaterally, on the Parolles Mental Home, from which he emerged unscathed in open dressing-gown and slippers. The problem is, this invaluable testimony, such as it is, is invariably related in one of those private languages which are the bane of Ludwig Wittselsucht.

Besides which, the man is as mad as a hatter.

APPENDIX

[Note: The Appendix is a reduced and redacted summation of the various reports on the workings of the Royal Academy of Letters, as delivered by Hackett to Miss Maloney.]

1.1 The oldest surviving charter for the establishment of a Royal Academy of Letters predates the reign of Queen Anne by several decades. Whether or not the young Jonathan Swift was involved in framing this charter, the document sets out the primary purpose of the Academy as: *'the Correcting, Improving and Ascertaining of the Engelish Tongue,'* the very words used by Swift in his letter to the Earl of Oxenford and Mortimer two years prior to the actual founding of an Academy. As such, the terms of reference envisaged, provisionally, four pillars, *viz.*: (a) a provision for the standardisation of orthography, meaning and usage, based principally upon the science of etymology; (b) a provision for the coining, testing, regulation and licensing of neologisms and, as a corollary, for the decommissioning of arcane, archaic and obsolete terms; (c) a provision for the sampling, testing, ascertaining and re-stamping of terms with a debased semantic value and, in order to best effect this, the power to grant and/or revoke poetic license;[128] (d) a provision for the regulation of, the licensing of, and the trade in loanwords.

128 With the Atlee government, the poetic licence became generally available. As this goes to press one can be obtained for 10/6 through any Post Office.

1.2 Throughout the century that followed its founding, an incomparable contribution to the first of these pillars was made by the scrofulous Dr Johnson, an amateur lexicographer whose monumental *Dictionary of the Engelish Language* (1746-55) was compiled on the governing principle: 'nothing odd will do long'. It was an unforgiving policy, which led to the exclusion of many terms championed by Shakespeare himself: *cadent, twangling, tortive* and *ungenitured.* Though it, too, retained an ethic based upon the primacy of etymology, this left the Royal Academy free to concentrate on the remaining three pillars, each of which was to be placed under the wardenship of a hereditary expert '*with none taking primacy over any other*'. In fact, so great was the trade in loanwords that from its inception, the fourth pillar (or, following Dr Johnson's *magnum opus*, the third) was always the most powerful, a situation which was formalised during the crisis of the American secession when Turlogh O'Brien assumed the title Hereditary Director…

1.2.1 From its inception the Academy had been very much a Tory initiative, and it is a fine irony that it had only been opened a matter of weeks before its royal patron, Queen Anne, died 'without issue', prompting the issue of who would succeed her. When finally 'German' George, Elector of Handover, who was fiftieth in line but reassuringly Protestant, was imported by the Whigs, those who had been instrumental in establishing the Royal Academy took the decision to keep the institution's very existence a secret from the crown, a policy made easy by the sovereign's perfect ignorance of the "King's Engelish". The boorishness of the second George, the madness of the third and obesity of the fourth did little to hinder this policy of secrecy,

so that by the time of the Napoleonic wars, the very existence of a Royal Academy of Letters was generally pooh-poohed.
1.3.1 The need to regulate the illicit trade in loanwords, which had long been recognised, became patent during the late Tudor and early Stuart period, when '*from Ipswich to Harwich to Norwich to Dulwich those damn Dutchie buggers in low-bottomed yawls smuggle Low Countrie words in by the knaep-sack.*' (Philip Sydney). One early commentator on Ealing Broadleaf gives the following: *'In the days before the great Academies, colossal sums were paid for particularly prestigious words. It is difficult now to imagine what a term like "bourgeois" or "ransom" or "métier" was worth in its day; Richard II was reputed to have paid the Duke of Anjou three hundred crowns in gold for the term "lèse-majesté".'* It should be added that the evidence for the actual payment of such 'king's ransoms' is frequently anecdotal, many terms having been assimilated by force majeure.
The Royal Academy was a latecomer to the so-called 'Toledo System' of free semantic exchange. This modus operandi had been formally enshrined in the Treaties of Utrecht (1713) and Rastatt (1714), which is to say just as the Academy was undergoing its difficult and secretive birth. This datum, coupled with a hereditary suspicion of all things continental, meant that Britain was rarely more than 'a carping observer playing perpetual catch-up' (Diderot[129]) at subsequent language conventions. For more than two centuries, the Toledo System would act along the principles of quid pro quo and cui bono,

129 French Encyclopaedist, who once observed that if the Law of Universal Gravitation had been discovered by any but an Engelishman, you may rest assured that that nation would have objected to its promulgation.

taking up the enlightened precedent of Alfonso el Sabio when, in 1260 (?), he set up the first *Intercambio Libre de Palabras Prestadas* in Toledo. Far from demanding exorbitant sums and punitive royalties, it soon became a matter of national prestige to put into general circulation, gratis, such words, terms and epithets as had once been the jealous preserve of linguistic and cultural elites...

1.3.2 According to the Bonham Report of 1901, the most frequent channel by which an approach is made to this department is through Neologistics ('Neolog', see **1.4** below). Once the requirement for a new term has been identified and the specifications set out, Neolog is required, by the Law of Precedent, to forward the complete 'word-spec' to the Loan Commissioner. His brief may be described as lexicography in reverse: where the traditional lexicographer begins with a word and arrives at a definition, the Loan Commissioner begins with a definition, or more accurately a series of definitions suggested by the word-spec, so as to arrive at that word or phrase, in free circulation elsewhere, which best approximates the tonal and connotational values contained in the specifications. A lifetime's accumulated experience, coupled with a sound knowledge of national character, culture, custom and climate, all guide this search. Where but among the Germanics would one look for the quality of *schadenfreude* or *weltschmerz*; where but among the Iberians, *saudade* or the perpetual procrastination of *mañana*? The great advantages of importing a loanword rather than coining an untried neologism need hardly be enumerated.

1.3.3 Once a loanword has been identified, Bonham's Report outlines a procedure remarkable principally for its simplicity:

"An approach is made directly to the relevant Academy, Society, or Council of the host language.[130] A loan request docket is filled out in triplicate, and sometimes by return of post, permission is afforded to try out that foreign word or phrase. It remains *de jure* under loan, of course. The absolute value of the word or phrase remains with the mother tongue from which it has been borrowed." No reference is made by the euphuistic Bonham as to what language is employed in said loan request docket.

2.1.1 [This Section Blacked Out]

2.1.2 The difficulties facing Neologistics are frequently underestimated. Even at the level of denotation, which is ostensibly the easiest level to predict, it is not always obvious how a new word will behave. A prefix or a suffix of known semantic value will not necessarily retain that value when added to a stem; and the stem may become supine. A well-known example, dating from the days of Chancery, occurred when John Dee, the Queen's alchemist, put in a request for a new noun which might reinforce the phenomenon of fusion or synthesis which he had observed in his alembics. Now, the obvious prefix to add to the stem —*fusion* was, of course, *con-* derived from the Latin preposition for 'with', so that alcohol, for instance, might be expected to be: 'a *confusion* of sugar and water brought on by the agency of yeast'. Whereas, as Dee noted dryly, 'the new word better describes the state brought on by the agency of alcohol.'

130 The absence of any Hibernian Academy of Letters may account for the almost complete absence of loanwords of Celtic origin in the Engelish vernacular, beyond bog, gob, trousers, whiskey, Tory, hooligan, shenanigans, kibosh, and, ironically, galore.

2.1.3 A more technical difficulty involves the durability of the compound term. Simply put, the affinitive bond by which a stem retains a particular prefix or suffix is, once again, difficult to predict. A celebrated example, from the arcane field of etymological topography, involves the stem *-chester*, which has a high specific affinity. Examples throughout the realm abound, from Doorchester and Winchester through Barchester and Munchester to Rockhester and Chichester. Other prefixes have a higher selectivity, however, and trial and error has demonstrated that such glyphs as *Lan-*, *Don-*, *Tad-* form happier conjugations with the Latin cognate *-caster*. It is interesting to speculate that, when the Vikings of Yorvik plundered Cheshire and hacked from its county-town the unidentified glyph which prefixed the city, leaving a bare *-chester* behind them, this notorious theft might have been prevented had *-caster* been adopted by the citizens in the first place.
3.1.1 [This Section Blacked Out]
3.1.2 [This Section Blacked Out]
3.2 A critical function in the health of any somatic, semantic or monetary system (the horticultural analogy has also long been noted) is the retirement from circulation of out-moded, debased, recherché, outré, otiose, obsolete and/or archaic items. This is the remit of the Academy's Decommissioner. During the time that Lord Bonham was making his circuitous report, the Decommissioner was assessing the vigency of the noun 'desuetude". This is not merely a matter of its SUI index (see 5.2 below), since vigency must also allow for the anachronistic resuscitation of terms 'of outstanding cultural, sentimental or historical import' in, for instance, theatrical

performance.[131] Ironically, while the noun under consideration was allowed a new lease of life, the term vigency has itself fallen into desuetude.

4.1.1 [This Section Blacked Out]
4.1.2 [This Section Blacked Out]
4.2.1 [This Section Blacked Out]
4.2.2 [This Section Blacked Out]
5.1.1 [This Section Blacked Out]
5.1.2 [This Section Blacked Out]

5.2.1 The effort to quantify the expected durability of any given counterfeit term, (the so-called 'natural term of an unnatural term'), predates the founding of the Academy of Letters by exactly a century, and is to be found in an appendix to John Napier's *Mirifici Logarithmorum Canonis Descriptio* (1614), in which the celebrated Scottish astrologer first proposed the natural logarithm.[132] It was Napier himself who suggested that the natural term of decay should be calculated with reference to a table not of temporal values *per se*, but values which incorporated the notion of 'iterative usage'. The French philosopher Rene des Cartes developed the paradigm along the horizontal or x-axis of his new Cartesian geometry, for which he coined the acronym 'IUS' or '*itération de l'usage standard*' (naturally, the Engelish reversed the lettering), and posited a 'decay variable', μ (too short to be reversed), to account for the characteristic decay curve of the y-values.

5.2.2 The SUI (Standard Usage Iterate) index is thus best understood by analogy to the radioactive decay constant, λ,

131 This provision has allowed terms such as 'wassail' to be periodically fêted, much as it has afforded 'threnody' a stay of execution.

132 Napier's bones are on permanent display in Edinburgh's Museum of Mathematics and Science.

as postulated by Ernest Rutherford to model the exponential decline over time of radioactivity in a given sample. The so-called 'half-life' is related to the decay constant λ by Napier's natural logarithms, as given in the equation: $\mathbf{t_{1/2}=ln(2)/\lambda}$ (the relation of SUI to half-life is of course more complex, since the quality and medium of each utterance needs to be taken into account, so that it is more correctly termed a 'decay variable', **µ.**) If, however, Rutherford's simplified model is used as a loose approximation, then if **No** is the original frequency of an item of vocabulary, clearly $\mathbf{N(t) = No\ (1/2)^{t/t_{1/2}}}$, giving precisely the same curve as the **Law of Diminishing Returns** reflected through the axis x=y. It scarcely needs to be said, however, that the x-axis on this graph is not simply temporal (see 5.2.1 above).